Praise for Darry Fraser

'You don't have to be a lover of historical fiction to enjoy *The Milliner of Bendigo.* Well written, full of intrigue, gossip, heartache and some violence, it never stops being exciting. It is very hard to put down!'

—*Glam Adelaide*

'With all the hallmarks of a great read—fabulous, endearing characters, a gripping and compelling plot in a historic setting—Fraser has established herself as one of Australia's most loved historical fiction authors.'

—*The Cairns Post* on *The Milliner of Bendigo*

'Fraser has well and truly established herself as one of Australia's leading historical fiction writers … In *The Milliner of Bendigo*, Fraser delivers another enthralling adventure …'

—*Better Reading*

'Combines a galloping plot with well-developed and layered characters.'

—*The Daily Telegraph*

'Outstanding prose that flows and ripples through every page.'

—*Starts at 60*

'Darry Fraser is at the top of her game with her latest Australian historical … *The Milliner of Bendigo* is another wonderful tale to immerse yourself in … an absolute delight for readers of historical fiction.'

—*Great Reads & Tea Leaves*

'Whenever I pick up a Darry Fraser novel, I know a great read is in store. … Richly imagined, meticulously researched and utterly engrossing, *The Prodigal Sister* is an exhilarating historical fiction adventure with an unforgettable heroine at its heart.'

—*Better Reading*

'Darry Fraser has proven yet again that she is a master at writing Australian historical fiction … *The Last Truehart* is an enjoyable and well written tale—a great yarn, a dashing hero and a real sense of place in the evolution of Australian society of the time.'

—*Great Reads & Tea Leaves*

'Darry Fraser effortlessly weaves historical events throughout … a must read for historical fiction fans.'

—*The Burgeoning Bookshelf* on *The Last Trueheart*

'Darry Fraser has steadily built a reputation for herself as one of Australia's leading historical novelists. She's carved out a niche for herself in the adventure romance subgenre, with strong female protagonists, complex love interests, and sizzling chemistry … *The Last Truehart* is her best novel yet, and outstanding storytelling.'

—*Better Reading*

About Darry Fraser

Darry Fraser fell in love with the River Murray when her family moved to her childhood town of Swan Hill in Victoria. Stories of the river have been with her ever since and it's where a number of her novels are set. Her stories are of ordinary people in nineteenth century Australia who are drawn into difficult circumstances—adventure, mystery and mayhem, love and life, and against the backdrop of historical events. She lives very close to the mighty River Murray on the beautiful Fleurieu Peninsula, South Australia. To find out more, visit her website www.darryfraser.com

You can also follow Darry on Facebook and Instagram.

Also by Darry Fraser

Daughter of the Murray
Where the Murray River Runs
The Widow of Ballarat
The Good Woman of Renmark
Elsa Goody, Bushranger
The Last Truehart
The Prodigal Sister
The Forthright Woman
The Night on the Darling River

THE *Milliner* OF BENDIGO

DARRY FRASER

FICTION
HQ

First Published 2023
Third Australian Paperback Edition 2026
ISBN 978 1 038 97954 4

THE MILLINER OF BENDIGO

MIX
Paper | Supporting responsible forestry
FSC www.fsc.org FSC® C001695

Published by
HQ Fiction
An imprint of Harlequin Enterprises (Australia) Pty Limited
(ABN 47 001 180 918), a subsidiary of HarperCollins
Publishers Australia Pty Limited (ABN 36 009 913 517)
Level 19, 201 Elizabeth Street
SYDNEY NSW 2000
AUSTRALIA

Printed and bound in Australia by McPherson's Printing Group

John and Coral McCormack, now gone,
great mates of my parents, the late Don and Gilda Fraser.
Now that the gang is back together again,
let the laughter and the Penfolds flow once more

Chapter One

Bendigo
Saturday 10 September 1898

What on earth is it going to take with this man?

'The answer is still no, Edwin.' In the parlour, her hand restless on the mantelpiece, Evie took a deep steadying breath and met his imperious gaze. 'I do not wish to marry you.'

She'd only agreed to consider Edwin Cooper's proposal, and now that she'd considered it, all of two days, her answer was no.

Yet he continued wheedling while in *her* parlour, in *her* house. Hardly gentlemanly.

'Come along, my dear. You've given me no reason why not.' He tweaked that silly pale waxed moustache of his again.

She scoffed at that. 'Not a requirement.'

His ginger eyebrows arched. 'I doubt you'll find another man with prospects such as mine who'll put up with your—let's face it—many odd behaviours.'

Evie challenged him this time. 'I *beg* your pardon? What odd behaviours?' She was quite sure she didn't have *odd behaviours,* but just lately he'd begun to slip into their conversation the idea that there was something amiss about her. This was one of the reasons she no longer wished to have anything to do with Edwin.

Tired of it, and refusing to trade insults, she stood her ground. She'd already waited too long. This matter would be dealt with simply and with dignity, and that would be that. It was her right to refuse his offer of marriage.

Although perhaps you've been wrong on that subject before. Evie faltered a second. That'd had nothing to do with Edwin, though.

He pounced on her hesitation. 'Ah, I see that has given you pause,' he said. 'We wouldn't want to call your little *eccentricities* anything else, would we? A strong husband will ensure they don't escalate and a solid marriage will keep you on an even keel.'

The benign smile was not fooling her. *Little eccentricities!* It was a threat, she knew it, and hardly covert at that. How many husbands, how many fathers, had she read about who had put their wives and daughters away in asylums for not much more than *little eccentricities*? Why hadn't she noticed this side of Edwin before? Had he flattered her so much she'd been blind to his true character? Anyway, they were empty threats. He couldn't touch her, couldn't even attempt to have her 'seen to' for madness. He was not her husband and never would be.

Nevertheless, a chill jangled her spine. She was shocked to hear him intimate his perceived power over her and, worse, that he appeared to believe she'd somehow swoon and be swept away by these words.

'What on earth makes you think you can speak to me of that? You have absolutely no reason, and no right.' She straightened to her full height, which admittedly was not much past five foot three. Formidable though—to any intelligent person, that was. 'You don't know me at all. Three months or thereabouts since I met you, and only odd occasions stepping out, is hardly enough time to suggest anything like it, much less warrant a marriage proposal.'

He waved her off. 'Neither does a man like to be left dangling,' he said. 'Teased, some might say. You'll reconsider, I'm sure. You don't want to be wrong about this.'

Oh, spit, Edwin. You're plain awful. How did I last this long in your company? I must have been desperate or something.

Her jaw set. 'You're not left dangling, Edwin.' *You've been dropped.* 'Like most people at times,' she said as coolly as possible, 'I have been wrong about certain things in the past.' *Oh, finally admitting it, Evie Emerson.* Her internal voice again, the nagging one, and it was cutting. She cleared her throat. 'However, I'm not wrong about this.'

Could she—*should* she—have married her much-loved friend, that gorgeous man Fitzmorgan O'Shea, and traipsed around the countryside with him? They'd talked about marrying, but no proposal was ever forthcoming. Nor was one sought; it had only been … discussion. At least he was a friend, not like this individual. Although, to be honest, at the time it hadn't felt right to pursue it—and it had to feel right when marrying, didn't it? How else to put up with what she knew a wife had to endure for the privilege? She'd have to give up her job. Take up all that cooking. Bear all those babies …

Oh Lord no, I can never *imagine babies with Edwin.* Her lip curled and she had to wiggle it with a finger to loosen it.

'Let's not change things, darling Evie,' Edwin said. 'You seemed in such a hurry for us to get to know one another, especially after you were left'—his brows rose—'in scandalous haste by that last fella.'

God save me. She had not been in a hurry, and certainly hadn't been seeking someone like Edwin—at any pace—to replace Fitz. It was just that after Fitz left (in a tearing great hurry, true) she'd thought she'd be able to easily fill the gaping hole his departure had opened. But she hadn't, and she missed the banter, the laughter,

Fitz's easy-going, light-hearted nature. So when her two married friends, Ann and Posie, had introduced her to Edwin and encouraged her to spend some time with him, or at least somebody, she had agreed to placate them and perhaps to entertain herself. And then Edwin had pursued *her*, which had been flattering at first. Annoying now.

'What a cad,' he added, inspecting his fingernails.

'Don't talk rubbish,' she said, the stubborn curl on her lip returning. Fitz had not left *her*. They were friends, the three of them, she, Fitz and Raff—Rafferty Dolan, his best friend since they were boys. They'd both left, going their separate ways, off to do what it was they needed to. They had left Bendigo, but not her.

'Perhaps he thought you too old.'

Evie's teeth clenched. 'If I'm in my dotage and as yet unmarried, Edwin, it's because I'm still waiting for a good man.'

'Ha,' he burst, surprised, amused. Then shaking his head, he tut-tutted. 'Now, now, Evie dear,' he chided, a slim finger in the air.

'And don't patronise me either.'

He gave her that smirk of his, no doubt conjuring more of his platitudes. Oily things came to mind. He was certainly no substitute for either of her male friends. 'I think—'

'You heard me and I mean it,' she said. 'I don't wish to marry you. That should be the end of the discussion.' Her chin wobbled; fury had surfaced. Blast it, she wasn't calm at all. Faced with the exaggerated disbelief now on Edwin's usually bland face, she closed her eyes a moment and Rafferty Dolan inexplicably appeared in her mind. *For goodness' sake, Raff hardly looked twice at me.*

But she missed Raff, she admitted it. He was a sturdy, reliable, still-water-runs-deep man with a warm, green-eyed gaze. Perhaps she'd even venture to say, enigmatic. Mrs Downing, her employer, a local milliner, had remarked the same of him, approval lighting her features.

Raff had left for his home in Ballarat when Fitz left. *Of course.* She should— *Oh, should, should, should.*

'You look perturbed, Evie. Don't further upset yourself. Come along and take a seat with me. I'll help you settle your nerves.' Edwin opened his arm to indicate the settee by the window.

Oh Lord, he was no panacea for what ailed her. Curling her fingers, she tapped a fist lightly on the mantel. The heat and cheer from the crackling little flames in the fireplace bolstered her resolve. 'For the last time, my answer is no, Edwin. Now, please leave.'

'Oh now, now, dear. We won't have such nonsense,' Edwin said. 'Our alliance will be a wonderful thing, so what's the reason, if indeed there is *reason*, for your reticence? The problem might be easily rectified. You ladies can be so flighty, on edge. Unstable.'

Now it was a barely disguised, definite, threat. The urge to stamp on his foot and clock him in the nose with the handy candelabra was gaining momentum, whether it made her look mad or not. Instead, she tucked in her chin. 'This alliance is not for me,' she said. 'That's very clear.'

'Take your time to review. I have a few minutes.' Edwin poured himself a glass of port wine from her decanter, took a sip. Savoured, smacked his lips. 'If it's about your inheritance—I know managing money can be such a chore for ladies, my mother for one—I can assure you that when we're married, you won't have to worry about a thing.'

So, there it is. Her blood boiled. 'Edwin, I am certainly not worried about managing my inheritance. I wouldn't hand it over to you even if we did marry. I can administer what I own by law, and I will.'

Glancing at her mother's photograph on the mantel, she took strength from it. *Dear Mama.* Cora Emerson gazed serenely. Evie had her mother's azure eyes, with the same intensity, she'd been told, and the wide cheekbones they'd both inherited from a Mediterranean influence long ago. Her hair was much darker than her mother's and wasn't drawn back in the same severe-looking bun, but piled on her head in soft waves held up with combs and pins. The small cleft in Cora's chin had been handed down to Evie, too. Her mouth was set as firmly now as her mother's was in her regal pose for the photographer, hiding a wide and generous smile.

'You're huffing and puffing, my dear,' Edwin said, tugging at his jacket cuffs.

'I don't care.'

He took a breath, oh-so patient. As usual, his sandy-coloured hair was immaculately plastered to his head, and the waxed and prolific gingery moustache joined long sideburns that were tinged with auburn.

'So that's your reason,' he said and then his smile slipped. 'You want to administer your inheritance for you and your sister.' He spread his hands, a not-so-benign smile now dimpling his cheeks. 'You won't be any good at it. It's a known fact that women have no propensity for figures.' *What rot. Didn't the fool realise everyone knew his mother handled the family's purse strings?* 'But here's a thought—how about a trial period? What if I say I'll allow you to administer your money to begin with, and monitor your progress?'

Evie bit down her rage and her nose wrinkled. 'What if I repeat what I just told you? I'm aware I have the right to administer my own finances. That's not the point; my refusal of you has nothing to do with managing money.'

'My dear, in a marriage,' he went on, 'it's only fitting that the husband is responsible for all the finances. I will gladly direct you in that regard. Let's not make a to-do about it.'

Whatever he thought, it certainly wasn't a fortune to make a to-do about; only the little house they were standing in, and a thousand pounds. Evie would be sharing everything with her sibling—if she could find her sister to tell her. She couldn't do a thing until she had Meryl's concurrence, but Meryl hadn't answered any correspondence since she'd married and gone to live somewhere near Cobram, on the Murray river.

After her mother's will had finally been read, Evie pre-empted a journey to Cobram to find Meryl, and had gone to the railway station to enquire of the fare to Echuca, at the end of the railway line. Edwin had suggested he'd meet her there, to take tea afterwards. She'd been waiting in the queue at the ticket office when something she witnessed had made her decision about Edwin Cooper absolute.

'Edwin,' Evie said, now shrill and exasperated. '*Do* I have your full attention? I am not accepting your proposal. I don't need to marry you, I don't wish to marry you. I don't want to see you ever again.' Debating the sense of it only for the blink of an eye, she burst out with, 'And I'll give you a reason why not. You are not an honourable person. You were canoodling with that woman at the railway station. And that's only one reason.'

Not that it was the crux of the matter, just a very timely incident. A Miss Thompson, he'd admitted, before later denying he knew her at all. *Then* he'd said that there had been no woman, that it had all been in Evie's imagination.

Ludicrous. She had eyes in her head.

Edwin reached for his glass and sipped, resting an elbow on the mantel. 'You know very well you misunderstood the situation at the station the other day.'

Oh, so there had been a situation at the station.

His charm, once beguiling, had become something slithery. His smile wasn't working now.

'Perhaps you're just getting the shakes before the big day,' he said. 'Take up your little glass of wine and have a seat.' He nodded towards the glass on a table by her chair. 'We'll get over this hiccup.' He prepared to take a seat.

Evie drew herself up once again. 'Leave my house,' she snapped. 'I've made myself abundantly clear.' *What is* wrong *with him?*

Edwin straightened, brow furrowed. 'If you insist on this,' he said, his nostrils flaring, 'I will deem it to be a breach of contract of marriage.' His eyes gleamed as he watched for the effect of his threat.

Taken aback, she faltered a moment. 'Except there wasn't an engagement, no one knows of it,' she retorted, 'no ring has been presented, nor announcements made.'

'Ahh,' he said wagging a finger, advancing on her. 'You are only partly correct. A notice was placed in the paper. Haven't you seen today's yet?'

Shock pulsed through her. 'What?'

'Oh yes. I'm surprised you haven't already been inundated with hearty congratulations.'

'I did not give consent to that,' she cried.

'But you consented to marry.'

'I consented to consider—'

'Tantamount to consent.'

'It is *not*,' she exploded.

'My dear, how could I possibly have misunderstood your intention?'

A tight band gripped her chest. 'There is no ring.'

'Minor consideration.' His muddy stare was like a hawk over prey.

'We are not engaged, Edwin. No matter what underhanded means you have employed to meet your end, and no matter what you say to me or to anyone else, we are not engaged and never were.' Tapping the mantel with her forefinger, she said, 'I've nothing further to add. Go away and make no attempt to see me again.'

He gave a sigh and sat. 'Not until we have a proper conversation—'

'Do I have to throw something?' She snatched up the crystal decanter, one of the only things left that had belonged to her father, and his father before him.

'What?' Edwin leaped back, wine spilling onto the carpet in front of the hearth.

'You are ill-mannered, Edwin, and boorish. For one thing, you, with that woman, so blatant, especially when you agreed to meet me there—' Then like a curtain parting, the truth of it opened before her. 'Oh, you *meant* for me to see you with her.' The decanter shook. 'So you could deny it, and make me out to be mad.'

'Put that thing down and stop prattling. Your mind's befuddled.'

He said it: befuddled. A whoosh of heat hit her chest. '*Do* I have to call into the street to have someone come and physically throw you out?' She made to move past him.

He blocked her. 'Of course not,' he said, as if he were placating a recalcitrant child. 'Now look, I'd rather we—'

'*Out.*' The decanter came up, gripped at its neck by her hand.

'Evie, you're really being quite irrational.' However, not so sure of himself now, he backed up and, his hand shaking a little, placed his glass on the mantelpiece. 'I'll return when I'm assured you are feeling more circumspect.'

She gave a ragged cry, hefted the decanter again. Edwin scurried out the parlour door. She watched him snatch his hat and coat from the hallstand and rush outside without another word, leaving the door ajar.

Breath left her in a rush. *Good riddance.*

She checked the decanter. Not a drop spilled.

Chapter Two

Evie locked the front door, the key confounding her until she steadied her hand. Thank all the gods that Edwin had gone—although she could see he was slinking around in the street aiming glares at her house. What a nuisance he was becoming. At least the port wine stain at the hearth should come up if she was quick about spreading salt on it.

Turning and looking down the hallway, and despite the setting wine stain in the parlour, she lingered. It was lined with beautifully crafted hats—*even if I do say so myself*—that were hanging on hooks and ready for sale. Her millinery, her passion, the only real thing of her own, of herself. Trailing a hand along the last few, she came to a stop at her very favourite and whispered, 'How lovely you are.'

So extravagant her design, so expensive, she had purchased this one for herself from Mrs Downing. She'd crafted it on a wide-brimmed straw shell, wrapped the crown in loose layers of ivory organza, and stitched in an enormous duck-egg blue plume that trailed at the back. Then she'd added a peony-tinged bloom, a magenta silk bow, and a couple of gorgeous smaller feathers in a coral and *voilà*, a spectacular statement piece.

It would be lovingly packed later today into the large deep hat box in her room custom made for it.

She headed for the kitchen. Catching her breath, she leaned on the bench under the window. Her heart rate had climbed, and an intermittent tremble assailed her. She shouldn't have had him in her house, alone. Still, she was fine. Mostly.

Fitz O'Shea's voice rang in her head. *'Evie, at times you can be a veritable tempest.'* She had to laugh at that; she didn't feel a tempest now.

Evie and Fitz hadn't parted company in high emotion, but it had been so unlike the last half hour with Edwin. Theirs had been mutual, civilised, and with the best intent: their friendship staying intact.

'It's not a good idea for us to marry, after all, is it?' Fitz had said.

'It's not. There's no need.'

'I'm so glad we agree.'

'Yes, we're friends, after all. We'll remain friends.'

The relief had been palpable for both. In fact, Fitz had been so relieved he'd fled the town at the speed of light. It might have been mortifying if she hadn't felt the same. Off he went, pursuing life as a roving reporter, cheery as you like. Next thing, his good friend, the enigmatic, silent Raff, left town too.

Fitz and Raff.

Fitz was tallish, straight limbed, well built. Lean but solid; his clothes fit well, his gait was confident. He turned heads. His nondescript brown hair was always tousled, and his warm hazel eyes glinted with mischief.

Raff was a little taller, and broad, thanks to his mother's Nordic heritage. Those green eyes had come from somewhere ... Perhaps from his paternal Irish forebears who'd muscled in, also bestowing him hair as dark as the espresso coffee Mrs Bartoletti up the road loved.

The two men were very different in temperament, and in the way they saw the world. Fitz was a 'pen is mightier than the sword' man, someone who set off on quests to out evil wherever it was, armed only with an inkpot and nib. Brave enough, clever with words, and always after a cause, always chasing a story. Although sometimes, he was the one being chased.

Raff loved home and hearth, the fresh air, his family, his work, his friends. If there was a wrong, he'd right it, there and then. Fitz had told her that even though Raff wasted no time clobbering a threat, he was never malicious, or drunk when he acted, and Fitz had often been better off because of it. Raff was proud yet humble, solid and dependable, decisive. Honourable. He was the one always around to pick up the pieces that Fitz managed to scatter.

Honourable.

Raff had been a warm presence in their company. And once—*only once*—for a split second she thought she'd seen something else in his unguarded glance at her, a moment's cool appraisal.

Her chest clunked. *Fitz's best friend, Evie*, she scolded. *Don't keep fooling yourself on a whim.* Besides, he'd never approached her for himself. He'd only ever extended the hand of friendship, and always while in Fitz's company. And she certainly hadn't been about to come between two such friends on a flight of imagination.

Despite that, deep down, she knew that he'd reached her, touched her … *Damn it, it was a silly notion.* Yet it had kept at her all this time.

She snatched the salt, annoyed that she'd wallowed too long.

In the parlour, she sprinkled the darkening wine stain liberally with salt. It began to absorb the liquid as she watched, colour blooming in the granules. Then, stoking the little fire and taking a seat, she reached for her glass, took a sip and grimaced. Not the most pleasant she'd had. Might be nice on pudding or something, or perhaps she'd mull it come Christmas time.

An announcement in today's paper, Edwin had said. *Well.* She and Mrs Downing, her employer, had been so busy lately preparing for the hat exhibition, there'd hardly been any time for anything else, certainly not the luxury of reading the paper earlier today and gossiping over the announcements. And she hadn't heard a thing from anyone. No one had brought it to her attention with their *hearty congratulations.* Surely, the way people blathered on about such things, she would have heard by now that she was, by all accounts, engaged.

Unless Edwin had been lying. Oh, how she hoped that was so.

Crossing her ankles, she took a breath, gazing at her mother's photograph on the mantel again.

In my dotage and as yet unmarried … waiting for a good man.

She laughed at herself. Her mother would have laughed with her, telling her not to worry about her age. Cora only spoke to Evie once of Fitz after he left Bendigo. *Fitz is not for you. No need to pine.* He hadn't long been gone, perhaps three months, when Mama had died suddenly of an eruption in her brain.

Fitz hadn't replied to her letter advising him of it. Perhaps he hadn't received it.

A year later, Evie began to step out with Edwin, but now after only a few months had passed, she was finished with him too.

Until today, Edwin had never, *ever* spent any time with her at her house. Not even when they were at afternoon tea in a crowded café had Evie ever been alone with him. That should have been a glaring clue—she hadn't had any inclination to spend time alone with him. But at least no one could say there had been any immodest behaviour on her part if he did make real his threat of breach of contract. Instead, *his* open display with that Miss Thompson (or whatever her name was) would surely be enough to defend herself at court, if she had to, for 'breaking the engagement'.

She'd asked Edwin to visit her at the house so she could privately break off their relationship; it wasn't something you did strolling down the street. Goodness—she didn't know how he'd react. Once she'd made up her mind to be free of him, she couldn't wait for the right time to extricate herself. Conceding it might have been a wrong move to deliver the news at home, she could only think that he'd assumed other things—scandalous things—might have been about to occur. She snorted. *Ha. Not likely, Edwin Cooper.*

She was so pleased she'd done it before he'd produced a ring. That would have complicated matters; bad enough he said he'd announced it in the newspaper. Better still, she hadn't had to break the decanter.

She basked in the warm glow of relief. Edwin had been banished. What was next? Taking stock, she started to plan, one step at a time.

First thing tomorrow, Sunday, her only day off, she'd write to her sister, Meryl. Her last known place of abode was on the Murray near Cobram, apparently on a sheep property. Evie could only hope that her younger sister would finally answer a letter. Once she'd done that, Evie would inform their solicitor, Mr Joseph Campbell here in Bendigo, and take his advice on how to proceed.

That was the thing, though—would Meryl answer? None of Evie's letters had ever had a reply, but nor had they been returned, so that was some encouragement. Would Meryl and her husband, Roy Bayley, still be on the land? Evie hadn't heard from her sister for more than a year, despite sending frequent letters. The last time they'd seen each other, at their mother's funeral, Meryl had made it clear that she didn't want family to visit, despite family—being only Evie—willing to undertake such a journey, even though it was over a hundred miles from Bendigo to Cobram.

Meryl had turned away that same day to head back to the river. 'Too rugged up there for you, Evie,' she had said with a wry smile after Evie suggested visiting. Her face gaunt and creased, her sister looked too old for her years, and her once thick, dark golden curly hair was lank. 'No room for you to stay either,' she'd said, dropping any semblance of a smile and leaving with nary a word, much less a hug.

Not knowing why she wasn't welcome—for that seemed to be the message—Evie hadn't attempted a visit. All she'd been able to do was put pen to paper and she hadn't yet been rewarded with a reply.

Sipping again, she decided the flavour of the port wine was not growing on her.

The next step in her plan was to ask for some leave from her job at Mrs Downing's millinery. Once she'd secured the time off, she would take the train to Echuca and travel to Cobram from there. There might be a coach service, but the most likely mode of travel would be on a paddle-steamer. Either way, the next few weeks would be interesting. She'd only wait a fortnight for her sister's reply. If, after that time, she hadn't heard from Meryl, Evie would go looking for her.

On Monday morning, juggling her little purse and a hatbox, Evie dropped her letter for Meryl into the mail pillar on the way to work. She'd had plenty of time yesterday to pen a properly constructed missive to her sister. It had taken a few starts—three fresh sheets of precious paper—before she was satisfied that she'd imparted everything correctly. Afterwards she'd sat in glorious solitude and stitched the deep-blue rouleau, a twist of velvet ribbon, onto the wire frame for a toque hat. Then she'd covered the full crown in the same luxurious fabric as the ribbon, its colour the golden hue of flaxseed. With its wide, turned-back brim, the little hat would look very stylish when finished. She added a black lace bow at the front, her stitches quick and sure. A spray of tiny white flowers or a lush feather fitted at the side on the day would top it off with charm.

It was the hat she carried that morning, and on arriving at Mrs Downing's house, Evie stepped inside the tiny room at the front and set down the hatbox. 'Good morning, Mrs Downing.'

Her employer was at her workstation already, assessing scraps of fabric against an assortment of hats and bonnets on their blocks. Mrs Downing was perhaps in her late fifties, maybe her early sixties, and dressed as usual in black, she emulated good Queen Victoria, who had extended the wearing of her mourning attire for forever, it seemed. Mrs Downing's husband, bless his heart, had been gone for fifteen years. She was a mentor for Evie, a fine model of an independent businesswoman from whom to learn, and to aspire to be.

She could also talk the leg off a chair. Lately, the conversation had ventured into all manner of unmentionable things that some of Mrs Downey's older clients faced. Poor Mrs Sugden's mother-in-law had had an ovariotomy—whatever it was, it was a horrible thing—and she'd died. Shock waves swept through the clientele, and conversations were quite subdued for some time afterwards, certainly around the younger clients. 'And then there's Pennyroyal—a veritable poison,' Mrs Downey had once said, wagging her finger at Evie, who had no clue what it was, or what it purported to do. *Pills and potions and tonics.*

Evie hoped all would be calm in the studio today. All she wanted to do was make her hats, and not have to think about anything else.

Right now Mrs D had put down her fabric scraps and was distractedly flapping at a light sheen of perspiration on her neck. Her eyes lit up when she saw Evie, then they clouded a little as she mopped her brow and blew out a short breath. When she stood, her pale blonde, nearly white hair bobbed in a loose bun. 'Good morning, my dear Miss Emerson.' She hooked a finger in her collar a moment, then pointed. 'Is that the creation I think it is?'

'It is.' Evie reached into the hatbox for the little toque.

Mrs Downing clapped her hands together. 'Oh, my dear, you are an *artiste*, a true milliner. You have Bendigo at your feet, and

Mrs Mason will love it. It'll just lift the whole outfit when she wears her green. Even when she wears her gold gown, it's the right amber shade of course, it will suit so very well. Very versatile, dear.' She reached for it, studying her protégé's intricate creation. 'You've done great work.'

Evie was Mrs Downing's only employee and had been so for some time. In better economic times, Evie had often taken work home to fulfil orders for harried customers, but work had slowed considerably since the last depression began, so the sooner their excellent pieces could be sold to customers with the money to pay, the better. Despite the slower pace, she'd continued to work after hours at home; it filled her evenings, kept her busy and content.

Mrs Downing was a kind person, and the only one in whom Evie really confided since her mother had died. Oh, she had a couple of good friends. Ann and Posie were her age, but as they were married women and mixed with a different set, Evie wasn't prepared to share everything with them. They always wanted to introduce her to this gentleman, or that gentleman, suspecting that their spinster friend would eventually have to marry *someone*, and better it was someone they'd introduced her to.

Failed with Edwin Cooper, ladies. I'll share that with you.

Pushing the hatbox aside, Evie removed her hat and gloves and stored them at the base of her workstation. At Mrs Downing's extended silence—she usually talked thirteen to the dozen—Evie paid attention. There was a shadow under her employer's eyes and a pop of perspiration on her top lip. 'Everything all right?' she asked.

Mrs Downing sighed and set the toque on the bench. 'Nerves, perhaps. You wouldn't believe it, but the moment I turned the shingle around to open, Mrs Cooper was on the doorstep.'

Edwin's mother. Evie's stomach fell. Maybe he hadn't been lying about the newspaper. 'And I'll wager she had something nasty to say.'

'In a fashion. I know her type very well, Evie.' Mrs Downing gave her a sorrowful look. 'She came in to say that she was cancelling her couple of orders.'

Evie was dismayed to hear that. 'Oh dear.'

'And cancelling her daughter, Jane's, too.'

'Oh no.' Not a good sign.

'Oh yes,' Mrs Downing said, still looking so very sad.

Breaking it off with Edwin was about to impact Evie more than she'd realised. She looked at Mrs Downing, her heart sinking.

'Mrs Cooper couldn't wait to explain to me that my employee had caused her son great embarrassment, and therefore, her. That you were a blight on polite society, and that she would be taking her business elsewhere.'

Mrs Downing's delivery sent a rush of heat over Evie's face and neck. 'I'm so sorry, Mrs Downing. You see, I refused to see Edwin any longer. I just didn't like him … And that's when he tried to convince me that we had become officially engaged—'

'No, no, dear Evie.' Mrs Downing waved her off with a couple of fingers that were bent at the knuckles where arthritis had crept. 'I told Mrs Cooper that even though I had no such employee, she was welcome to take her business elsewhere should she enjoy purchasing second-rate millinery.' Her eyes sparkled.

Evie burst out laughing. 'Oh, you frightened me.'

Mrs Downing rubbed her hands together. 'I want to hear all about what you said to Edwin. I didn't know you'd accepted the man.'

'I hadn't,' Evie cried. 'I agreed to consider his proposal a few days ago, thinking that perhaps I should marry someone—*not* that I said as much to him. But I'm well of the age. Thirty is most definitely at the point of being left sitting on the shelf.'

'You would never sit on the shelf. Besides, these days quite a few girls leave marrying till later.'

'Mid- to late twenties, perhaps.' Evie huffed out a breath. 'But then I came to better sense, especially after seeing something unsavoury between Edwin and a young woman at the railway station the other day. I can't trust my judgement of character any longer. I won't be in a hurry to chance a relationship again, certainly not with someone like him.' She bit her lip. 'Apparently Edwin placed an engagement announcement in the paper. I did *not* consent to that.'

'He did what?' Mrs Downing's eyes popped a moment, then she said, 'You don't look distraught.'

'Goodness, no, Mrs Downing,' Evie said, laughing a little. 'I know I didn't consent to it.'

'It could be trouble for you, though.'

'He mentioned breach of contract,' she said quietly.

Mrs Downing sucked in a breath.

Evie nodded. 'He might have made a fool of himself, so I suppose it could end up damaging me. I just don't want a convenient *alliance* for a marriage.'

Mrs Downing patted her arm. 'Unless you're a prince or a princess, best to leave those type of marriages for people with business interests. I firmly believe that marriage should always be a love match. Ever the romantic, I am.' She squeezed Evie's arm. 'There's still time, dear.' Bending towards Evie, she whispered, 'Besides, Edwin's mother, Beryl Cooper, is an old tartar. A life with the Coopers—I'm quite sure the three of them come as a package—would be ragged.'

'I think you'd be right,' Evie said. 'But her visit means you've lost two jobs.'

'She'll be back. Especially when the invitations go out for our little exhibition, that clever idea of yours. I'll make sure she and her daughter get one each.'

Evie had suggested that they should have an exhibition of their creations in the window of the Craig, Williamson store in Elizabeth Street. The manager had agreed for the exhibition to remain for a whole week, and for Evie to change the display window every day. The hats would be displayed on blocks and on plainly dressed mannequins to make them stand out. The store would sell the items for a commission. If it was a success it would loosen some purse strings.

Mrs Downing had been more than delighted with the idea, as long as Evie organised everything, which she'd been happy to do. They'd had time to build up the stock levels and some of those gems graced Evie's hallway, awaiting the exhibition. Thankfully, the show window had been booked a couple of months ahead; plenty of time to get ready.

Evie took a deep breath. 'Speaking of the exhibition. We're so far in front with our work for the display window, I was hoping I could take some time off, Mrs Downing. You see, I've written to my sister again about Mama's will and if she doesn't answer me this time, I must try to find her. I have some savings, but if Meryl wants to sell the house, I need to be sure I can afford to live somewhere else.'

Mrs Downing surveyed the little room. 'Well, we have twelve finished pieces here, and as many at your house, haven't we?' Evie nodded. 'That's quite a few so far. Take some time off, that'll be all right. We can always do a few smaller, simpler pieces when you come back if we feel the need.'

'I'll only take two weeks. I've saved a little, so I should be fine.'

'There isn't someone you could write to and ask to check on your sister for you instead of travelling that far?'

'Short of the police, no. And that wouldn't be good, would it? Meryl would never talk to me again if I did that. I'm sure if—'

'Oh, so you *are* here.' The door had been shoved open. There stood a woman with features that were only slightly less boyish than Edwin's. Jane Cooper was a ... 'minx' was the polite word. She was the image of her waspish mother and her stuck-up brother. Her hat, an old-fashioned wide brimmed thing, was topped with a bundle of ribbons that wobbled like a bowl of not-quite-set jelly.

'*Miss* Cooper,' Mrs Downing said, getting to her feet and beaming a bright smile. 'Good morning to you. I've already had the pleasure of your mother's company today.'

'Have you? Did she cancel my order as well?' Jane Cooper's thin nose was pinched white, her nostrils flaring. Just like Edwin's.

Evie was sure Jane knew the answer perfectly well.

'She did indeed,' Mrs Downing effused. 'Explaining something about my having a dreadful employee here, which I assured her was not the case.' A little laugh and a tut-tut. 'Still, under that mistaken impression she seemed happy to take her business elsewhere.'

Evie had to admire Mrs Downing. All said with that smile, and a light tone in her voice, her eyes merry.

Jane pointed a finger at Evie. 'That employee, there.'

'Oh, goodness, and you're mistaken as well, fancy that. Never mind, can't be helped.' She started forward, which forced Miss Cooper to step back. 'Off you go, dear. Goodbye.'

Jane, who'd stumbled back, had the door shut in her face.

'Mrs Downing,' Evie admonished in a whisper. 'It'll be all over town in no time.'

'Perhaps. But two can play at that game. I'll just let it be known that they both have bills outstanding. That blinking credit idea for rich people only makes them richer and us workers poorer.' Mrs Downing took a seat at her station again. 'I've maintained all along: seven days to pay in full then the debt collector.'

'You wouldn't.'

'I most certainly would.'

'It helps, I suppose, that the debt collector thinks highly of you.'

Now it was Mrs Downing's turn to blush. 'Why, Miss Emerson, that's enough of that nonsense.' She turned to pick up a tiny fan, waving it at her neck.

Evie smiled at her. 'He's a lovely—'

The door banged open. Jane Cooper stood there in full fury, aiming a finger at Evie once more, her hat fully a-wobble. 'I'll have you know, Miss Emerson, that my brother intends to take you to court for breach of contract, and your utterly frivolous handling of his affections. I'll be a witness that you fully intended to marry him.'

Evie stared at her. 'Jane, this isn't the time or place—'

'Don't you "Jane" me, Evie Emerson. It's Miss Cooper to you, not that I want you to address me ever in future.'

'Have you come to pay your bill, Miss Cooper?' Mrs Downing asked.

Jane, startled, became haughty. 'It's … not due until Wednesday.'

'Then you *will* need to address Miss Emerson again. So, we'll see you Wednesday, with full payment for that sweet little cap in the deep royal blue with the golden feathers. If not, you may return it on the same day and it must be in pristine condition or I will charge you for it.'

'I—'

'Oh, and look, there's Mr Kingsley, the debt collector, coming up the path behind you,' Mrs Downing said. 'Do excuse me while I write him my list of collections.'

Jane Cooper turned smartly and with her nose in the air breezed past a bemused Mr Kingsley who doffed his hat at her, a slightly disapproving twist on his lips.

Doesn't he look dapper today, Evie thought. His nearly pearly-white beard had been, as usual, groomed by his practised hand. His suit coat of charcoal and the matching waistcoat, buttoned over a trim chest, would be of finest merino. Black trousers and white shirt, highly polished boots and bowler hat. Very distinguished. Professional, yet his big smile belied his trade. Some said that's how he got his good results; he was friendly but firm.

'Good morning, ladies,' he said, his warm gaze only on Mrs Downing. Just inside the door, he swept off his hat revealing a thatch of fine, dark hair, a silver thread only here and there, a complete contrast to his beard. 'I thought I'd drop by on my way to the bakery. Shall I pick up a little something for morning tea?'

'Mr Kingsley, how timely,' Mrs Downing said, a twinkle in her eye. 'If you can manage eleven o'clock, we'll be sure to have the kettle on.'

'Wonderful. Now, did I hear you say something about collections?'

'A tactic only, I'm afraid.' Mrs Downing raised her brows and smiled.

'I see. Pity. But it does give me pause.' He turned to Evie. 'Miss Emerson, I might be intruding, and please do tell me if so, but a word of warning.' He leaned towards her a little and dropped his voice. 'Be careful around that family now, my dear.' He nodded towards the retreating Miss Cooper. Startled, Evie was about to ask why when he shook his head. 'Just be aware it's now common knowledge that Mr Cooper is very upset about recent events.' He replaced his hat. 'And so, I will away for the baker and his iced buns. Good day.' Mr Kingsley smiled at Mrs Downing, gave her a little bow, nodded at Evie and left the shop.

Evie stared after him. 'Oh dear. What on earth could that mean?'

'Probably that Edwin Cooper, the fool, has put it around town already that he has been released and is unhappy.' Mrs Downing reached over and patted her hand. 'Mr Kingsley does have his ear to the ground; so be alert, not alarmed, dear Evie.'

Evie was alarmed. It was her reputation at stake. 'Do you really think Jane meant that about Edwin taking me to court?' He had mentioned similar himself and had obviously repeated it to his sister.

'It does occur, we know that, but nothing has happened so far except a show of their bad manners. Of course, he must try to save face if he made an engagement announcement that was untrue, but it mightn't go any further than a bit of bluster.' Mrs Downing picked up an empty hat block and draped a swathe of shimmering, rich plum satin around it and stood back considering it. 'Certainly think about finding your sister sooner than later.'

Evie let out the breath she'd been holding. 'Wouldn't that appear as if I'm running away?'

'Have you actually seen an announcement in the papers?'

'I haven't, and nobody's mentioned anything to me, either.'

'Perhaps we should check that first. And if you do leave to find your sister,' Mrs Downing said with that smile full of fun again, 'it will make you harder to catch.'

Chapter Three

Cobram
Wednesday 14 September

Standing dead-still in the doorway of the Cobram police station, Fitz figured it was too late to back out and ride away.

His older brother, John, a constable, glanced up from a cluttered desk and surprise flickered on his face. He gave a grunt. 'Well, if it isn't Fitzmorgan O'Shea. God-awful time to see you, first thing in the bloody morning. Ruins me day.'

Fitz shifted the saddlebags onto his other shoulder and swiped off his hat. 'Not my fault yours is the only country station for miles along the Murray.'

John leaned back in the chair and clasped his hands behind his head. 'In truth, it's not mine. I'm on a few months' secondment, if you like, while the local fella, Stillard, is away.' His dark reddish-brown hair was unkempt and scraggly, and a patchy stubble dotted his cheeks and chin. 'You gonna just gawk at me or you gonna tell me what you're doin' here?' Despite the curiosity, his gaze was flat.

Fitz had rarely been able to read John. They were as unlike as brothers could be. Dropping the bags, he pulled over a chair. On the other side of the desk, John hadn't moved to stand or to shake his hand. *No love lost there.* 'I'm doing what I always do. Tracking down a good story, selling it to the highest bidder.'

John's eyes narrowed. 'What's the good story around here?'

'Haven't found it yet.'

'And why don't I believe you? You've found something or you wouldn't be here,' John said. 'You'll grab hold of it and not let it go until you've shaken the blasted life out of it.' He straightened and pointed a finger. 'And that's what gets you into trouble time and time again. If your story's police business, leave it with me.'

Fitz held both hands in the air. 'I'm just a journalist trying to make a living.'

'You're a roaming troublemaker who writes a few yarns. You're always runnin'. I heard your last story got you chased out of Ballarat.'

The news had obviously beat him, even to an outpost like this. 'Wouldn't say "chased", exactly.'

Fitz had fled town. He'd upset a crooked trooper taking stand-over money from gold merchants, one of them his good friend, Gideon Levi. Fitz had written an article, an exposé, and had taken it to the *Ballarat Courier.* Now his name was mud with the local constabulary.

Raff, his close mate, had laughed. 'I'll make sure you get out safely, keep you out of trouble.'

Early one morning, they'd left Ballarat and had ridden hard, skirting Bendigo.

'No need to go there,' Raff stated as they edged the town.

'True,' Fitz said. 'Don't want to unduly worry anyone.'

Neither had elaborated. Raff, smitten with Evie Emerson and believing she was Fitz's, wanted to steer clear of her. Fitz, not ready to let him believe otherwise, had to avoid a possible meeting with Evie in case the truth came out. It was deceit—but he had to do it. Fitz couldn't quite let the idea of Evie go, not when he might still need her himself.

Anyway, avoiding Bendigo would stump the crook troopers, he and Raff agreed, so they'd kept east of the town, going through Kyneton. They rode via Axedale for Elmore, a little railway station on the line north, where Fitz got on the train to Echuca, his horse with him.

'Watch your back,' Fitz had said to Raff last thing before he boarded. 'They know we're friends. They might come after you.'

'Let 'em try, mate,' Raff replied, then flexed his hands, his fingers knotty. 'Can't wait.' He grinned, teeth flashing, and turned for home on horseback.

That was well over a week ago. Raff would have been a handy offsider for the story looming here in the river district. Fitz should have tried harder to convince him to stay around. But Raff had his workshop and his old pa to look after. Fitz would telegram if he needed him.

Now in Cobram, the last person Fitz wanted on his tail was his brother, a trooper, Constable John O'Shea, but here he was. *Of all people to run into, dammit.*

'Sounded like "chased" to me,' John said, interrupting Fitz's thoughts. 'You should get a real job, mate.'

'Like you?' Fitz gave the office a once-over. Two desks, papers strewn about, files piled high on the records cabinet. 'No thanks.'

John gave him a look. A muscle worked in his jaw; he wasn't happy to see Fitz, that was clear.

Can't help that. Pity Fitz hadn't thought to learn before his arrival where John was stationed. 'Last I heard you were down Beechworth way,' he said.

'Did you?' John said, his eye twitching.

'Is your good wife Edith here with you?' That would rub his brother the wrong way. Mention of Edith was out of bounds.

A fixed glare, no twitch, a beat or two then John took a breath. 'Edith decided to stay with her parents. That was two years ago.'

He'd married a woman who made him look a fool. He'd been warned about her and he couldn't escape the truth of that.

'Ah.'

'Don't start. Traipsing around the countryside wasn't what she wanted.'

'Thought a wife would want to go anywhere with her husband.' A twinge of guilt rippled through him. He'd suggested as much to Evie.

'Leave it off.' John's frown darkened. 'I doubt you've got yourself a wife, have ye?' An unfriendly glitter gleamed in his brother's stare. 'Didn't think so. What d'you want around here then?'

Fitz slapped his hands on his knees. 'I'll know it when I see it, I reckon.'

'Or you might just push on.'

Smiling, Fitz stood and shrugged. 'Or I might stay awhile.'

Papers slid to the floor as John thrust to his feet and leaned over the desk. 'Got somewhere to stay?'

'Recommend anywhere for me?'

John shook his head, knuckles on the desk. 'No.'

'I'll find a place.'

'Got a gun with you?' John asked.

Fitz saw something else in his brother's eyes, something he hadn't expected to see. Fear, maybe. 'Rifle's on the saddle,' he said, guarded. Last thing he wanted was physical danger.

'Bunk where I'm staying. There's a room.' Gruff and short.

Fitz's journalist nose twitched. He hefted the bags over his shoulder, shook his head. 'Thanks all the same.'

'Suit yourself.'

He would. Turning on his heels, outside he mounted up and took the road to Main Street, looking for a hotel. He rode about half a mile and he couldn't miss it. Cobram Hotel was the place to be. A two-storey brick building with a balcony.

Fitz hired a stall in the stable for his horse, Patto, then he headed for the bar. The hotel was busy, which surprised him, being a weekday. Seated away from the fug of tobacco smoke, he ordered a rum. Laughter and good-humoured jibes were all around him. Clusters of men stood close by, a couple of dusty, sweat- and oil-stained stockmen leaned on the bar, the few tables inside crowded with drinkers. For once, he let the noise roll. Snatching a word here or there might give him some useful leads. He didn't make eye contact with any of them, but he needed a conversation started. The story he was chasing was here; he'd come out of Ballarat with it.

Glancing around, Fitz tried to figure out who was who in the town, but they all appeared like workers from the district's runs. Then again, they'd be the best people to start with—if they'd talk to a stranger like him. Maybe someone would let go with local hearsay; Fitz would know what to do from there. He checked over his shoulder. No one interesting to look at, and no interested looks his way. No one was taking any notice of—

'Not much work around here, mate.' The bartender had wandered close to Fitz's end of the counter. He could have been a stockman. Shirt sleeves rolled up, big, brawny hands, a thatch of straw-coloured hair on his head and a moustache the same. Coin-sized pale freckles splotched his face and forearms. Only thing missing was his hat. It wouldn't be far away.

'Same everywhere,' Fitz agreed.

'Just visitin' folk then?'

'Stop-off only. Come up from'—a great guffaw from a bloke standing close by gave Fitz time to steer clear of mentioning Ballarat—'uh, Horsham way, looking for some land on something bigger than the Wimmera River.'

'Got the right river here, but not much land available. Gets snatched up pretty quick these days by folk who've got the money.'

'I heard there was a small piece, close to town.' Fitz kept his voice low, reached into his pocket and slapped down a coin for a refill.

The barman hesitated. 'Haven't heard anything's for sale.'

That hesitation right there. *For sale*. The crux of it. It wasn't for sale. Fitz knew the owner was being pressured to sell. 'That right? Well, everyone wants something on the river, I know that for a fact. Place to be.'

The barman poured him another, palmed the coin, dropped it in the till behind him. 'Sure is,' he said turning back, leaning on his fists. 'When it's not in flood.'

'True enough. I know irrigation is going ahead downriver, Mildura, Renmark,' Fitz said. 'I've heard talk that the powers-that-be want to lock the Murray and put in weirs.'

'Been the talk since ninety-three or earlier, up there in Corowa, at that Federation rally,' the barman said. 'New South Wales got free trade, and here in Vic we got protections. Most folk livin' on the river just want a fair go. They dunno if they're Arthur or Martha. Riverboat traders have been wanting better controlled flow for years.'

'Bugger South Australia though, hey?'

'That colony's got no rivers comin' off the Murray, is why. They get natural flow, that's it.'

Fitz took a swig, wanting to keep the barman talking. 'You know a bit about it.'

The big man shrugged. 'Born here, and the river's a lifeline. Gotta know what's goin' on around the place.' He nodded at a bloke who took a seat alongside Fitz. 'What'll it be, Mr Haines, the usual?'

'Usual, Big Tim.'

Haines nodded at Fitz. 'One of the boys over there said you were looking for land.'

Fitz was slipping. Someone must have heard him. 'Just on the off-chance I might be able to afford something. I don't know the area well. Might not suit, might keep going yet, maybe Yarra-wonga way.'

'Good plan, it's not bad up there.' The man held out his hand. 'Ernest Haines.' He had a mop of thick and wavy greying hair, a heavy moustache to match. Not lean, not paunchy, a man comfortable in his skin. Shrewd and confident.

Fitz, used to being sized up, took the proffered hand, leathery and callused. 'Fitz Morgan,' he said. The O'Shea part of his name needn't be aired now he knew his brother was stationed here as a trooper.

Big Tim landed a large glass in front of Haines, likely a whisky. No money exchanged hands.

'Yeah,' Haines said, nodding. 'Yarrawonga's the place to be, for sure, if you're lookin'. Not me, though.'

Fitz kept it conversational. 'You got land here, then?'

'I have. Coupla reasonable-sized runs with frontage, upriver a bit.'

Fitz tried again. 'Sheep, cattle?'

'Sheep right now, but with good water, irrigation, I might venture into orchards, maybe crops. Dunno. You?'

Haines hadn't told him anything. Fitz would extend the same.

'Not sure myself. I'll know it when I see it.' He was barely lukewarm on the idea, not genuinely interested. He'd avoided it so far: settling somewhere, attempting to eke out a living in the dirt. Chasing a good story was far more interesting. Besides, it would take careful planning to choose where to settle. Oh, for Christ's sake, he wasn't gonna do that, it was still too dangerous to stay in one spot, and for more than one reason. No, he was roving, much as he could without making a mistake, and a good thing too. If he needed to revisit the idea of settling down with a woman, he'd try again. He just didn't like the idea much, or at all.

'Pity there's no land available around here then.' Haines took a swig.

Big Tim moved away, brows slightly raised.

Fitz was being warned off. Yep, and that was fuel for a journalist's fire. 'There might be. Sometimes folk don't know they want to sell up until someone asks,' he said, 'or they might be in trouble and could do with the money, needing to move on.' He stared into his glass, the rum warming his gut, and waited.

'True enough, but I reckon most people will wanna sit tight for a while yet.' Haines took a long swallow and stood. 'I'll be on my way, Mr Morgan.' He nodded at Fitz then at the barman and wove his way through the crowded bar until he disappeared out the door.

Fitz slid another coin over the counter. That'll do; three rums was more than enough. Big Tim poured then hovered with the bottle. When Fitz shook his head, he turned for other rowdy patrons clamouring for a drink.

A man spoke low near Fitz's ear. 'If Mr Haines thought to drop you a few words of wisdom, mate, I'd be takin' notice.' He slid onto the stool Haines had vacated, his gaze on Big Tim. At a glance, his hat was oily from his hair, his grey whiskers patchy, the wrinkles deep around his eyes. Grime tracked the goosy skin over his collar. Gnarled knuckles deformed hands the size of dinner plates that rested on his knees.

Fitz looked away. 'Sounds like a threat.'

'Nah, mate. Yer new in town and he just likes to think he runs the joint, wants yer to know who's who. He's a land-hungry bastard, and Big Tim's on his books so watch what you say there, too.' He went quiet. 'Just lettin' you know.'

Big Tim approached. 'Robbo,' he said, all genial. 'Usual?' The man nodded. 'How you goin' on your place, this weather?'

'Could always use rain.'

'Same as everyone.' Big Tim glanced from one to the other, sat a glass of rum in front of Robbo, took the proffered coins and moved away again.

Robbo spoke under his breath, focused on his hands. 'Heard ye mention wantin' land. There's talk of an irrigation scheme for this place, but some are scared. If there is such a thing, no one knows how it's gonna work, how much water we'll be allowed to take outta the river, or who gets what. Haines wants to set himself up big before anyone else. If you're after buying land on the river, watch yourself.' His glance was furtive.

Fitz shifted his shoulders, moved on the seat. 'He said there's nothing for sale.'

'Only one piece he wants. He don't want no one else vyin' for it, neither. It's three mile out, sits smack bang in the middle of two of his properties on this side of the border. He owns big frontage on the opposite side too, and just this one piece is holdin' him up. Belongs to a mate o' mine.'

'So, where's your mate?'

'No one knows. He took off, his wife left on her own out there. Just yest'dy I went to check on her. No one home, but the place looked like she'd upped and took off, plates and stuff all left like she was havin' her dinner. Up and gone. Possums have been in and got the lot.'

'She's gone?'

'Nowhere to be found. Left a kid in a grave a while back, dunno why she'd just wander off.' His eyes glistened, darted around. 'Hard.'

Big Tim wandered back. 'How's the missus, Robbo?'

'Fine, fine.'

'Whaddya reckon about all this irrigation talk?' Big Tim asked, a sneaky wink at Fitz as if to say he was having some fun.

'Don't reckon nothin' about it. Got a new pump comin'.' Robbo downed his drink, and the stool scraped on the floor as he got to his feet. 'Like I was sayin',' he said to Fitz, keeping his voice as low as he had earlier. Big Tim was earwigging. 'You'll get a good pair o' boots at McFadyen's store, so get to Punt Road up Station Street.' He cocked his head to the left. 'I'm headin' there meself, I'll tell 'em to expect yer directly.' He nodded and pushed away, heading outside.

Fitz's couple of rums were taking effect. He didn't need the third one still sitting on the bar, sure that Robbo meant for him to follow.

Big Tim took his time polishing a couple of glasses. 'There's a lot of folk don't trust this idea of Federation and what's gonna happen with the river. Them politicians have to settle on somethin' about the water else they're not gonna have themselves a constitution, and so, no Federation.' He set down a glass, picked up another.

It was crucial for Victoria and South Australia, two colonies that could hold up the Federation works, that water from the Murray was accessible.

'You're in the know about all that, too,' Fitz said.

'Anyone who cares to know about it, knows. Still, a lot of people don't trust it. Robbo's one of them. Gets all skittish these days. Sees the devil on every corner. His people have got paddle-steamers out of Echuca and downriver Renmark way. Says navigation's gotta be protected, water flow an' all. If not, his family's life's work is finished.' He snorted. 'Drought don't get yer, the gov'ment will.'

Fitz had taken a ride on a steamer from Echuca to get here. There were plenty of boats still working the river, but the writing was on the wall. 'The railways have opened things up. Have to expect river trade to slow down at some point.'

'True enough, but sad to see 'em go. Riverboats have done us proud a while.' Nodding at his insight, Big Tim turned away to shelve the glasses.

Fitz poured most of his third rum onto the floor, cursing the waste of his money. Leaving a slurp in the glass, he made a show of downing it when Big Tim turned back. 'Right, thanks for the chat. Might see you again.' He stood.

'Where are you staying in town?'

'Camp by the river, I reckon,' Fitz said. He wouldn't be staying the night in the pub, and that's all Big Tim needed to know.

Outside, he swung left; Robbo had nodded in this direction. He set off on foot, didn't need to take Patto from the stable. Across the road on his right was the newspaper office. Now why hadn't he noticed that before? He'd drop in on his way back to the hotel to see if the town's reporter was in.

Robbo strode up ahead, his lopsided gait distinctive. Fitz kept a good pace behind, not wanting to catch up until the store was in sight. But the man stopped at a crossroads, and beckoned Fitz around to the right.

'Why me?' Fitz asked when he fell in step alongside. 'Why did I need to know all that?'

'Because that bastard Haines got in yer ear. He warned you off, didn't he, in not so many words.' Robbo marched along the dusty path by the road, which was hard and hot underfoot. 'Name's Cyril Robinson. Robbo.' He nodded across at Fitz, didn't offer his hand.

'Fitz Morgan.'

Robbo pointed. 'There's McFadyen's.'

The store loomed, a big timber place with large windows, a hitching rail and water trough close by.

'I don't need a store,' Fitz said. 'What I need is to get a look at the place Haines warned me off.'

Robbo rubbed his face, reached into his pocket for a tobacco pouch. 'Why that one in particular?'

Fitz didn't need to elaborate. He shrugged. 'Why not?'

'Because of Haines.' Robbo had the makings of a smoke rolling in his fingers. 'He wants the place, and me mate's not there, can't be found. Unless the rates and whatnot are paid, the gov'ment will take it back, and Haines will get his hands on it. Somethin's not right.'

'What about the police? What do they know?'

They got to the hitching rail and Robbo leaned on it. He finished making the roll-up, stuck it between his lips and struck a match to light it. 'The usual fella is away for a while and there's some new bloke there. Doesn't seem keen to investigate too much, even if someone shoved a crime up his nose.'

Fitz remembered seeing the flash of fear, or something akin to it, behind John's eyes. 'What do you think has happened out on this piece of land?'

Robbo shook his head. 'Dunno, dunno. But where's me mate, Roy, and now where's his missus?'

'You said you were out there yesterday.'

'Bloody strange feelin'.' Robbo inhaled and blew out a plume. 'Dinner table left like that an' all.' He left the smoke dangling in the side of his mouth and rubbed his hands together hard. 'I was lookin' to see if Roy's missus needed a hand. I been out there before. Sometimes took Jenny, me missus, but she wasn't with me this time.' He shook his head again. 'I had a quick look around, the possums hadn't been in for long but …' He shook out his hands, agitated, fidgety.

'I have to go by the newspaper office, but after that,' Fitz said, 'what say we meet up the road and you take me out there?' At Robbo's hesitation, he said, 'If you reckon the police aren't interested, maybe you and I can work out what's happened. Might be nothing. Maybe she's gone visiting.'

Still Robbo weighed up his options, his gaze darting over Fitz's shoulder.

'Tell you what,' Fitz said. 'Just point me in the right direction, and if you want to come with me, let's meet in an hour.'

A curt nod. 'About a mile that way,' Robbo said, 'there's a stone cairn yea high'—he tapped his hip—'on the left. You'll see the track easy enough from there.' He pushed off the rail and headed into the store.

Fitz turned back the way he'd come. His friend, Gideon Levi, the gold merchant he'd helped in Ballarat, had a brother-in-law who owned land somewhere here. *What was the fella's name?* Was it 'Roy'? Perhaps it rang a bell, but they mostly talked in surnames. Badley? Barklay? Fitz didn't want to show his hand by asking Robbo.

Gideon had told Fitz how the man was trying to keep it viable, but that there'd been vigorous pressure from another landholder to sell. Gideon and his wife Rachel were worried; when last they'd heard from her brother, he'd mentioned trouble. Was this tale of Robbo's Gideon's tale, or were there others being harassed in the district?

Intrigue and a good story—and the urgent need to get out of Ballarat—had set Fitz on his path. He might as well come to this area of the colony as any other to expose corruption. Reporting on it might take the eye of a big editor somewhere and pay good money. Keep him able to rove a little longer.

Chapter Four

Bendigo

The days following the Cooper women's visit to Mrs Downing's shop were a blur of events, the effects of which were slowly dawning on Evie. On Wednesday when she was at the post office to mail the shop's invoices, the usually friendly postal clerk was a bit leery, and didn't bother with niceties. *Everyone has bad days.* Today, Thursday, the butcher had nodded at her, a sour twist on his mouth as he deferred to his wife before handing over Mrs Downing's order of mutton. *Odd.* Then later at the bakery, Evie was barely spoken to at all, the staff not their usual sunny selves, no happy banter as she made her purchases. *Goodness, whatever's the matter with everybody?*

It all fell into place at the next stop. Waiting her turn at the counter in the drapery, an armful of the choicest fabric rolls getting heavier by the minute, she was overlooked for service time and again. Finally thumping down the rolls on the counter, she'd started to measure out what she needed, helping herself to the large cutting shears resting nearby.

'I'll do that, Miss Emerson,' the proprietor had announced, her nose slightly a-twitch and in the air.

Evie's ire was up. 'Mrs Hartwell, I wonder why you feel you must ignore such a good customer as Mrs Downing.'

'I'm not ignoring Mrs Downing,' she'd snipped. 'Two yards of each as usual?' Mrs Hartwell had pulled off a length of teal-blue satin. She wasn't looking at Evie, her gaze averted.

'Thank you.' In the ensuing silence, Evie had gazed at other shoppers, none of whom greeted her. She'd leaned across the counter. 'Whatever is the matter, Mrs Hartwell?'

The woman had continued to peel off exact measures then sliced the piece from the roll with a practised flourish of the scissors. 'Something else?'

'Mrs Downing's straw hats, her wire frames, and the packs of assorted ribbons she ordered too, please.' Stacking things into her laden basket and signing for the purchases, Evie had turned, breathless with exasperation. Startled by those who made no effort to hide their staring at her, she made her way to the front door. Pulling it open, desperate to get out of the place, she'd almost collected the two women sweeping inside. Mrs Cooper and her daughter Jane had sailed in past her.

'Baggage,' Mrs Cooper had said in an aside, without even looking at her.

'Tart,' Jane had whispered close as she passed, knowing no one else could hear.

Evie's mouth had dropped open. Propelled by necessity out the door, and with a two-handed grip on the basket she was suddenly struggling to handle, she'd stopped on the footpath. But going back inside to speak her mind would be a folly. Anger simmering, she'd marched back to Mrs Downing's and related all the incidents of the last couple of days.

'Well, it didn't take long for the gossipers to get it around,' Mrs Downing said as she unpacked the last of the ribbons from Evie's basket. 'I'd say Mr Kingsley is quite correct, my dear. The Coopers have begun an assault, shall we say.' She tut-tutted. 'You need to make an appointment with your solicitor to see what action you need to take.'

Evie sat at her station. 'I am at a loss to think why they would be so public about their opinions. After all, it's a private matter.' She'd clasped her hands so tightly her knuckles were white. 'And it's not as if Edwin lost any money.'

'Then I'd say there must be more to it than meets the eye.' Mrs Downing stood to pack away the stock.

A knock sounded, and a young blonde woman peeked around the open door. 'Good afternoon, Mrs Downing. I've just come to see if Evie is all right.'

'Come in, Posie,' Evie said and rose to greet her. 'So you've seen the paper?'

'I have.' Posie Chalmers swished inside and closed the door behind her. 'And it's spreading fast all over town and growing by the minute, depending on who you talk to.' Her wide brown eyes creased under a concerned frown. Perched on her head was a jaunty little violet-coloured boater, trimmed with woven moss-green silk and adorned by a sprig of golden wattle. It was one of Evie's creations, pinned tight on Posie's dark blonde hair, which was swept into a bun on her neck. 'It's embarrassing for you.'

'Bit of a nonsense, really,' Evie said. 'I'm more angry than embarrassed. He's being such a fool.'

Posie smiled at Mrs Downing by way of an apology and spoke to Evie. 'I had no idea you and Mr Cooper were quite so close. Ann had no idea either,' she said, a gentle censuring. 'And there's been such gossip. We were worried why you hadn't said anything. We only hoped that you might have been waiting to tell us.'

'I didn't know it was in the paper,' Evie cried. 'No one mentioned anything to me. Why didn't they?' she asked. At Posie's rueful little shrug, she said, 'Don't you think I would have told you had there been anything to report?' She sat again with a huff. 'I didn't feel close to Edwin, not at all,' Evie said. 'I mean, I made a mistake thinking after Fitz had gone—' She stopped. Mrs Downing, and Posie and Ann all knew about Fitzmorgan O'Shea. 'I made a mistake allowing Edwin, at the very least, to talk me into considering an engagement. I didn't want to sound too rude or hasty declining his offer, so I took a couple of days then told him I wouldn't accept. I had no idea he'd gone ahead and announced anything.' Exasperated she waved her hands in front of her. 'Truly, it was never meant to go public. He's being quite awful.'

Posie sat beside her and took her hand. 'I'm so sorry we introduced you to him. We had no idea he'd behave so badly.' She shook her head. 'He seemed utterly charming. When we learned that his sister had started seeing the magistrate's stepson, and then Edwin's mother introduced him to us at the tearooms, we thought … Just shows you can't trust even a good introduction. What will you do?'

'What can I do? I didn't want to make a big thing of it. I thought it would all go away when it was clear that I—'

'All go away? I thought you said you read yesterday's paper?' Posie was frowning.

An icy finger of dread feathered along Evie's spine. 'I know about the engagement notice on the weekend, not Wednesday's paper. What else is there?'

'I saw it, and Ann saw it too,' Posie said. 'He's taken a classified saying that because you broke off the engagement, he will pursue you for breach of contract.'

Evie's mouth dropped open. 'No,' she burst.

'Most certainly,' Posie affirmed. 'A low act, I said to Ann. We were worried for you and still you didn't come to find us—most unusual—so here I am.'

Evie pulled her hand out of Posie's grip, turned this way and that. 'Dear God. I'd better get to Mr Campbell and make an appointment as soon as possible.'

Mrs Downing patted her shoulder. 'Before it gets even more out of hand. This could be very damaging for you, my dear.' At Evie's despairing glance, she said, 'Mrs Chalmers, would you have time today to accompany Evie to Mr Campbell's office?'

'Of course I would. I drove myself to get here in a hurry, I couldn't let your silence go on any longer. This is awful.' She gave Evie a quick hug. 'I'm sorry I waited so long, I'm only too happy to help. Come on, we can make a quick dash across town.'

Driving back to Mrs Downing's after making an appointment at the solicitors, Posie said to Evie, 'I can pick you up tomorrow and get you to Mr Campbell's by eleven. You were lucky he had an appointment available.'

'Very lucky,' Evie said, irritated and wondering when all this rubbish would end. Making the appointment to see Mr Campbell had returned the fire in her belly, and no lingering misery was going to douse it. *What a mess*. Her sister's silence was enough to worry about, without this as well.

Posie pulled up, Evie alighted and waved her goodbye.

Mrs Downing was in the front-room studio, a worried expression on her face.

'What is it now?' Evie asked, unpinning her hat, her trepidation high.

Mrs Downing held out her hands. 'The manager at the Craig, Williamson store has sent a letter, delivered by hand, cancelling the exhibition.'

Evie's heart sank. *Oh, what a mess, indeed.*

She left Mrs Downing's at four o'clock, much earlier than her usual 6 pm. Evie remembered there were eggs and half a loaf of bread from the day before at home, so for today she could avoid the grocery store and the possibility of other people's stares. Not that she felt like eating, anyway.

Poor Mrs Downing. The reason for the display cancellation had been short and to the point: *the unsavoury character of your employee* … She had the letter with her; Mr Campbell should see it. Somehow the slander, and now libel, was spreading faster than she ever imagined.

Walking with purpose, hoping to avoid any passers-by, she kept her eyes on the footpath, glancing up only to make sure she wouldn't get run over as she crossed the road. Turning into her street, her heart plummeted. Edwin was walking away from her front door. He spotted her, and stopped at the gateway, barring her entrance, his chest out, chin forward.

Her throat tightened. Strange he was here so early in the day. 'What do you want?' she snapped.

'A change of heart from you,' he said, dispensing with niceties and any pretence that he didn't know why she was so angry. He tugged at his coat lapels, a faint smirk on his plain features.

'After what you've done?' she cried, astounded.

'And what have I done?' An arch of his brows, and a twitch of that awful moustache. 'I've only expressed my unhappiness that the woman to whom I am engaged has deeply hurt me.'

He knew perfectly well what he'd done, and what he was doing, here, in her street.

'We are not, and never were, engaged,' she seethed. 'Get out of my way.'

'I'm here hoping you'll reverse your hasty, and nervously made, decision.' He wasn't budging and was cool as a cucumber.

'As if I'm going to talk with you in the street, Edwin.'

Still he didn't move away from her gate. 'Then invite me inside where we can discuss this properly.' He began to remove his gloves.

'As if I'm going to talk with you *anywhere*,' she cried. Shakes took hold of her. 'Get out of my way,' she repeated, one hand fisted by her side, the other clutching her purse. His menace draped her, slithering over her shoulders and down her back. She might yet have to leap the fence in an unladylike fashion to escape him.

'Come along, Evie,' he said, opening his arm to guide her ahead of him through the gate. He smiled and leaned in a little closer. 'You've nothing to throw at me today.'

She didn't want to be anywhere near him, so turning smartly she marched off, back the way she'd come. If she walked fast enough, even broke into a run—

'Where are you going?' He was alongside, taking her arm.

She snatched it out of his grip. 'To the nearest police station,' she said between her teeth, keeping up her pace.

A carriage drove by, coming from the opposite direction, but the driver hardly noticed them. She forged ahead, keeping her elbows pressed close to her side, her little purse gripped tightly in her hands.

'I don't think you want to do that.' His stride was unhurried as he kept up with her.

'You are making a pest of yourself, making unwanted advances when I have clearly told you to keep away.'

'You're raising your voice, my dear.'

'Go *away*, Edwin. I can't even bear to look at you. You are doing much to ruin me with this campaign of yours.'

Steely fingers gripped her elbow again. 'And I can do *so* much more,' he said, his breath a sibilant whisper at her ear.

Air stuck in her throat. His hand, tight and hard on her arm, would bruise, but she rushed on, despite the eye-watering pain he inflicted. Gasping, her head down, she was desperate to get rid of him. *What is he doing?* He wouldn't pull her to the ground in the street, but he could drag her off somewhere. *Where is safety?* Silence roared in her head. Shying away from him, all she could think of was getting away. What did he think he was going to do? *Broad daylight. Get away from him, get away …* Her heartbeat hammered in her throat. Flee, but who could she—

'Ahoy there, Evie,' a sing-song voice called out behind her.

Horses' hooves clip-clopped nearby. It cut through the fog in her brain, and the bursting need to run dissipated a little. She faltered, and the grip on her arm slackened. Glancing over her shoulder, she could have cried. Her other friend, Ann Benton, was driving up the road towards them.

'Come along, now, Evie,' Edwin said, the menace curling his lip. 'Wave her away.'

'Ann!' Evie shrieked, gesturing madly. Thrusting away from him, she stumbled.

Edwin kept her from falling, his fingers vice-like again, her arm wrenched as he steadied her.

'Ann!' she cried.

Ann had braked and was running towards them. She slipped an arm around Evie and spun her out of Edwin's grip. 'Come along,' she said to Evie. 'Quickly.'

Her feet skimmed the pavement, keeping up with Ann. She was sobbing with relief when they got to the cart. Evie hauled herself up and kept her eyes on anything but Edwin Cooper. Ann dashed into the driver's seat and picked up the reins in one hand. In the other, she held her riding quirt high as Edwin approached her side.

'Mr Cooper, if that's what I think I saw, you had better not lay one finger on my cart to try and stop it.'

'Oh, Mrs Benton,' Edwin said smiling, his eye on the quirt and making no attempt to touch anything. 'Look at her, I was trying to help. The poor woman's distraught—'

'No doubt, you insidious creature.' Ann slashed the quirt to the side of the cart closest to him then clicked the reins for pace. 'Don't look back, Evie,' she ordered as they moved away from the curb. 'Don't let him see you look back.'

'Dear God, he's a madman,' Evie breathed, her hand over her heart. She swallowed, then wiped her mouth with the back of her shaky hand.

'We'll drive to my place, and I'll have Mr Benton fetch a constable.'

Part of Evie wanted to object, saying that she'd be fine, that there was no real harm done. But that was bravado talking, not bravery. 'I'm grateful.'

They were sitting in Ann's kitchen after they'd fetched Mr Benton, Ross, from his work, a greengrocer's shop with a very understanding proprietor. He'd set off for the police station after dropping his wife and Evie at their house.

Ann had been on her way to Mrs Downing's when she'd spied Evie marching away from her house. 'I'd read that last dreadful notice he'd placed. After speaking with Posie about your visit to the solicitor, we decided I should come and find you and then I saw him attached to your arm. That seemed shifty to me.'

'I can't understand how quickly things have deteriorated. He's frightening.'

'And I would say from what I've witnessed,' Ann said, filling their teacups, 'that perhaps he always was that way. He must have had you under a thrall.'

'A thrall?' Perhaps she had been. Bewildering. He'd certainly been dismissive of her at times, which rankled, but had she been under a thrall?

'Thank goodness you didn't get so far as to marry him.' Ann pushed the sugar bowl across the table. 'When Ross returns, you and I will go to your house and pack you a bag to come here. You're not to stay there on your own.'

'That would be such an imposition on you,' Evie said.

'Not at all, dear girl. Then we'll get you to Mrs Downing's tomorrow and both Posie and I will accompany you to Mr Campbell's. I'm so glad you're out from under Edwin Cooper's thumb.'

Evie hadn't thought of it that way at all. Under Edwin's thumb? Had she truly missed something about herself while she had been stepping out with him? *Oh dear.* Perhaps she had been … but that didn't seem like her at all. No, no. Ann must be imagining things. Surely. *Surely* …

Ann stirred sugar busily into her cup. 'To think there are such men in this day and age.' Her usually bright and cheerful face was drawn. She put her hands to her neat and tidy dark hair, which was swept up into a twirl and pinned deftly. Never a shiny lock was out of place. Still, she patted and smoothed it as if perhaps some wayward strand had escaped. Calming her nerves, perhaps. 'It's disgraceful.'

Mr Benton poked his head in the back door, snatching off his hat, revealing close-cropped grey hair. 'Constable said if you want to make a complaint, you'll have to go down there.'

Ann puffed. 'Oh, for goodness' sake.'

'He took notes, but naught he could do about it, he said, because of Mr Cooper being a good sort, an' all,' Ross Benton finished apologetically.

Evie reddened.

'Ross, if you don't have to go back to work, would you accompany us to Evie's house so we can get a small bag for her?' Ann asked.

'I do have to go back to work, me darlin', but I can do that first, see you safe back here. Come on.'

Shocked, Evie stood inside the front door of her house. 'This was why Edwin was here today.'

'Oh no,' Ann cried beside her in the doorway.

The hallway floor was strewn with her hats, and most had been trampled, a few beyond repair.

'I know it was him,' Evie seethed, but she was grateful for a small mercy—he hadn't found her most prized creation, her favourite hat, which she'd packed away in her room. He couldn't have resisted flaying her by destroying that.

Edwin had tried to get Evie to come inside—she'd have seen this damage, would have been incensed, so what had been his intention? Perhaps to do more damage in front of her, to really *punish* her. A wave of nausea hit her. Something evil, she knew it.

Ann clutched her hand and together they moved from room to room, Ross sticking behind them. In the parlour, Evie gave a cry. There on the floor, amid a pool of port wine soaking into the carpet, were the shards of the heavy crystal decanter scattered on the floor. A hammer was propped by the hearth nearby, the signature of a deliberate act. Nothing else had been destroyed in the room.

Oh, you mean, sick-spirited person, Edwin Cooper.

'Definitely Edwin,' Evie said, and closed her heart a moment to the decanter's destruction. There were other things to consider first. 'I'll need to get the locks changed. He clearly has a key, somehow.'

'Or he's broken in.' Ross Benton ducked down the hallway. 'Doesn't look like anything else has been damaged,' he called. 'Not that I can see.' He came back to the parlour, his pale-blue eyes worried, hands twisting his hat. 'What sorta bloke is this?' He nodded at his wife. 'Ann, pack Miss Evie that bag, quick. I'll be going back to that constable and giving him a piece of my mind.'

'Mr Benton, take me with you and I can make my statement. You've already missed work for me,' Evie said.

'I can make it up to the boss, I'm good for it. I'll take his early-morning shift tomorrow. Now listen, you two ladies, hurry up. I want you out of here.'

Chapter Five

Bendigo
Friday 16 September

The next morning, her solicitor Mr Campbell, a very tall and aged gentleman, sat with his large hands clasped and resting on the desk. 'Awful tale, Miss Emerson.' He had the letter from Craig, Williamson Pty Ltd open in front of him. He tapped it with a knuckly forefinger. 'This can be addressed quickly. I'll also have the police send me a copy of your statement from yesterday. Don't you worry about them, either. Then I'll send a letter to Mr Cooper.'

'Must you?'

'I am at your service, Miss Emerson, you instruct me, but my advice at this point is to send a letter using the strongest possible legal language.'

'All right.' Evie bit her lip. 'And the other matter, the advertised threat in the newspaper?'

'Oh, he can certainly make good on that, but we'll shore up an impenetrable defence.'

'Defence?' It appalled her. What on earth would a court case do to her reputation?

'We will annihilate this fellow in court, Miss Emerson, but I expect a magistrate will have done with it before it comes to that.'

Kindly eyes, and serious nonetheless, he had a wide smile. He also had a bent nose, the result of a good battering in his youth no doubt. 'Now, I happen to know an excellent investigator by the name of Bendigo Barrett. I think it's time to utilise his services. I can arrange it through my office for you.'

There was no point objecting; Evie knew this was all somewhat beyond her, and she trusted Mr Campbell. But a private detective? Goodness.

A knock on the door interrupted and a dark-haired woman in her mid twenties brought a notepad and pencil in with her. She took up a seat to the side.

Mr Campbell said, 'Miss Emerson, you remember Miss Juno? She'll take some notes for us that we will present to the magistrate if necessary.'

Evie smiled and nodded at the woman. A female secretary. How very progressive of such a gentleman.

'Miss Juno was my ledger's clerk and is now studying law, so involving her in this will be invaluable experience.' Mr Campbell nodded at Miss Juno who readied her pencil. 'So, Miss Emerson, you said you saw Mr Cooper at the railway station. What day was that?'

Miss Juno held the office door open for her. 'If indeed Mr Cooper has applied to the court, you will hear of it shortly,' she said, her expression solemn. 'Bring the correspondence to us and we will send a letter advising the next step, Miss Emerson.'

Emerging from the solicitor's office, it was clear to Evie that Edwin had contrived everything, deliberately, with no mistaken understandings whatsoever on his part. Shaken by it, she was relieved to see that Ann and Posie had waited for her in the anteroom.

'Come on, let's get back to Mrs Downing's studio,' Ann said. 'You need to get those gorgeous hats repaired and ready for that wonderful exhibition.' When Evie gave her a look she said, 'Of course there'll be an exhibition.'

Before the appointment, Evie and Ann had returned to the house to bundle up the damaged hats into boxes and bags for transporting to Mrs Downing's, then had driven by to pick up Posie. Now the three women once again squeezed into the front of the cart on their way to Evie's work.

'Goodness, this feels like we're on an adventure,' Posie said, gripping the cart rail by her side.

'One I'd rather not be on,' Evie replied from the middle seat, holding her hat on her head.

'We'll fix this nonsense,' Ann said. 'Well, Mr Campbell will. Did you know he was practising law even at the time of the Eureka battle in Ballarat? People would come from there to meet him here, to take his advice. He'd have a few stories, I bet.'

'And what about his secretary, Miss Juno?' Posie said, leaning forward. 'How wonderful, a woman in the role and she's now his apprentice or something. So advanced.'

'Maybe I'm in the wrong business, making ladies hats. I should be forging the way forward as a suffragette'—Evie raised a fist tentatively—'making my mark in a man's world.' There was a mock battle cry in her tone.

'Don't be daft, Evie,' Posie said, laughing. 'We need hats, and yours are exquisite.'

'I'm sure some suffragettes are milliners too,' Evie said.

'Quite right, and every good woman needs a hat,' Ann said. 'Do what Mrs Downing is doing and work for yourself eventually. What a marvellous woman she is, too. A paragon.' She slowed the cart to take a right turn, clicking the reins as they drove along, their pace steady. 'Have you heard from Meryl, Evie?'

'Not yet. She's on my mind more and more, and mostly unbidden. She just pops into my head, almost as if …'

'As if she's calling you?'

Evie glanced at Ann. 'Yes. Although how much of that is wanting to get out of here to avoid all this unpleasantness, I don't know.'

'Bit of both, I'd say,' Ann said.

'And I'd say, why wait a moment longer?' Posie asked Evie. 'Mrs Downing has given you leave to go to Cobram, so why not take it now? It could work in your favour—having Meryl off your mind will clear your head to tackle Mr Edwin Noodle and family.'

Ann burst out a laugh then sputtered as she waved away the flies.

'Mr Campbell said as much to me,' Evie said. 'That it would in no way harm my case. He'd see to it.'

'There you are,' Ann said, her gloved hands deftly steering the horse and cart. 'Gracious me though, how do you get to Cobram from here? We will investigate.'

'We could detour to the railway station, it's only a short drive from there to Mrs Downing's.' Posie raised her brows at Evie.

A good idea. Evie hadn't accomplished her mission the other day; Edwin's episode with Miss Thompson had distracted her. After only a moment's hesitation Evie said, 'We could. If our driver would divert?'

'We're on our way,' Ann said. 'Next turn right.'

'Wonderful,' Evie said. 'Now, would the two of you be on the lookout for a plain-looking woman dressed head to toe in pink, with light-brown hair, about my height and looking like she's fallen out of the loft over a stable.'

Posie laughed. 'Is that the other woman?'

'I want to try to find her,' Evie said. 'I want Mr Campbell to know just who she is.'

Chapter Six

Ballarat

It was good timing that Raff had set off for the post office in Ballarat when he did. The telegram had been waiting for him; Fitz was in Cobram. That's where Raff would be headed as soon as he could—now that he'd had a visit from a burly trooper with nuggety fists and a fast temper.

Raff had been bending over a wagon wheel, checking the damage on a splintered spoke. Swinging the wheel up onto his bench, he'd nearly clobbered the policeman with it.

'Jesus,' he'd hissed, dumping it on the bench. 'Mate, if you'd got in the way of this, it would've floored you. I don't want to be up for assault just because you sneak up on a bloke.'

'I didn't sneak, Dolan.' Constable Dawes had eyed him. 'But I am watchin' you, boyo. You an' that O'Shea mate o' yours better step careful like.'

Raff had given him a look. 'We will.'

'He shows his face back here, he's in big trouble.' Dawes had a moustache that twitched whether he was talking or not. Looked like a great bloody black caterpillar crawling over his top lip. When he wasn't wearing his cap, his black hair was dead straight. His missus must've used her shears to trim around a deep bowl upended on his head.

'Whatever you say, Constable. I just don't know why you think you need to strongarm the likes of me.'

That was a laugh. Nobody strongarmed Rafferty Dolan. He'd heft a wagon wheel across town on foot if he needed to. He had biceps that made buying shirts difficult, a broad back and a chest deep enough to strain the buttons on the ones that did fit. He snorted at himself, at the ripped sleeves on the shirt he was wearing. *Shirts, for Chrissakes, but bugger it, I've ruined another one.*

Dawes pointed a finger. 'He put us boys in the shit by writing that article. He shouldna done it. We look after our own business in the force.'

Raff leaned back on the bench and folded his arms. He lifted his chin. 'What do you want?'

Dawes retracted the finger and rubbed it over that crawling moustache. He glared towards the wide doorway; nobody was about. 'McCosker says he won't be goin' to gaol. That he's lookin' for Fitz.'

'Is that so?'

Bill McCosker was still in hiding. He'd been a sergeant, and the organiser of a protection gang that preyed on local gold merchants. Raff and Fitz's friend Gideon Levi had been one of them. If the poor bastards didn't pay up, their shop would be raided by 'thieves' in the night, only to have those same thieves attend to the crime scene the next day in police uniform, the smirks obvious. It was a great lark for McCosker, who'd reckoned he was untouchable until Fitz had exposed the corruption. However, for a trooper fallen from grace, going to gaol would not be conducive to a long life. Fitz had to be silenced.

'Yeah, so best warn O'Shea if you know where he is.'

Too friendly by far. 'Not me, mate. I heard he crossed the border into South Australia. Too hot there for me.' Raff kept his gaze bland.

'Where in South Australia?'

Raff was nobody's bloody fool. 'Flinders Ranges, I reckon. There's copper mining, someone said.' He'd taken a stab at a region he'd read about in the papers.

'Thought you was good mates,' Dawes said, a squint in his eye.

'Not after he got you lot looking at me as well.'

Constable Dawes tugged at his cap, nodded. Pursed his lips. 'Just thought you should know about McCosker. Only a rumour, mind.'

Rumour, my arse. It was a message sent by that bastard himself. It could've been sent in a much worse way, though. Raff dropped his arms, straightened. 'I got work to do, Constable.'

Dawes eyed Raff's flexing hands and nodded again. 'See you then.' He turned, headed for the street, and didn't look back.

Raff had resisted following Constable Dawes to peer outside; he'd already known there'd be someone watching the place. Instead he'd studied the wheel he'd been about to work on. It would have to be dismantled before a new spoke could be fitted. It was off one of the carts he loaned out, so there was no urgency on his part to start the repair today.

Now, wrapping his hand around Fitz's telegram in his pocket, he was certain he'd made the right decision. He didn't want to do nothing and stay here in Ballarat. He liked better the idea of going to find Fitz in Cobram and warn him. It would be a bit of adventure. His pa could come out of retirement, step in and take some simple jobs like the wheel spoke, leave the new builds for Raff on his return. Paddy Dolan would be only too happy, he reckoned.

Whatever he decided to do, Raff knew that because of his association with Fitz there was a risk that his shop could be torched in the dead of night as a stronger 'message' from McCosker and his cronies. Would he be putting his father in danger? At least he didn't live on the premises like Raff did. Besides, Paddy could call his other sons home if he needed to strengthen the fort. And Raff had taken good advice from Gideon Levi, who'd encouraged him to insure the property and then urged him to closely check the clauses after the racketeers had begun on the gold merchants. Some places had already been burned, the easiest way to send a message and get away with it. Not that Raff had personally been bothered by standover blokes; Gideon just advised all his friends to protect their property. Ballarat could still be as dangerous a place as it had been in the fifties, the height of the gold rush.

Flicking Fitz's telegram into the forge, he watched the edges blacken and crumble to flaky soot on the glowing coals. It would be best to disappear in the night and head out of town, maybe trek wide of Bendigo again, go up to Elmore and board a train there. It would take him days to get to Cobram if he rode, long in the saddle and slow going in this weather. From Elmore he could rail it to Echuca, ride to Cobram, or maybe get on a paddle-steamer. Good idea. He'd send Fitz a telegram later today, say he was on his way. Though it might take a day or two to organise things with Pa. Still, he had a plan.

Yep, steer clear of Bendigo, that was the plan.

Steer clear of Evie Emerson.

It would be dangerous to see Evie if Fitz still wanted to marry her.

Dangerous for Raff.

Chapter Seven

Bendigo
Friday 16 September

David Kingsley checked his reflection in the mirror on his dresser. An errant curl needed a dab of macassar oil at the point of his neat white beard. The hair on his head still had remnants of its original colour; not bad for a man on the other side of sixty.

Imminently presentable today, young David. The best dressed debt collector around. The moment his feet had hit the floor, his step had a youthful spring. The smile welled from deep inside, invigorating his mood. He'd gone to sleep thinking of Lucille Downing, and he'd woken up thinking of her.

Today is the day, dear departed Sarah. I know you approve.

He would ask Lucille to be his wife. If she accepted, it would make him the happiest man alive, for the second time in his life. He'd been happy with Sarah. She'd been taken too soon by a stroke that had instantly killed her. It had been a long five years since.

He smiled at his reflection; he was hopeful Lucille would accept. They'd been friends for years, the kind of friendship that was happy in quiet company, companionable and with a sense of promise. It allowed for open and calm conversations: Lucille with regard to her children, the struggle she'd had bringing them up by herself after her husband had died and the obvious pride in her work as a milliner that had afforded them a rudimentary education; work she continued to this day. He, with his bereavement, and sorrow at not having had children, his work earlier as a law clerk and lately as a debt collector working freelance for the bank and other trusted clients. He regaled her with stories of the undesirables with whom he often met.

His first few years after Sarah died were a fog. Just when the hollow space in his heart yawned its widest, there was Lucille at the greengrocer's. She'd been offering the grocer's wife a recipe. For just what, he couldn't recall. The only thing he remembered to this day was that he fell instantly in love. *To think, at my age.* He believed she felt the same way about him now.

Today is the day, but steady as she goes, David.

Should he get flowers? He was not so presumptuous as to purchase a ring to present her. No, no, he would rather she chose something. *If she said yes.* They would peruse jewellery together. A grand idea. She might not want a ring with a precious stone—she might only wish for a plain band like the one she already wore, now on her right hand as a widow. No matter. As with other discussions, they would come to an agreement. *If she said yes.* Then he would wine and dine her with great romance.

He left his bedroom and headed down the hallway for his coat and hat hanging on a hook. At a thought, he pushed open the door to the old parlour that hadn't been used to entertain since Sarah had died. Maybe it could be a very stylish showroom for Lucille's hats.

He closed the door, shaking his head. *Ahead of yourself, David.*

Outside and locking up, he turned to find Mr Perkins at his gate, the man who owned, among other things, the house Lucille rented.

'Good morning, Mr Kingsley. Timely, so glad I've caught you.' The man raised his hat a little and waved an envelope nervously. 'I have a job here if you will. Rather urgent.'

'Urgent, Mr Perkins? Well, we should go back indoors and—'

'Oh, not necessary. It's a quick job,' he said. The man was in a hurry. 'An eviction. Send me your usual fee for serving notice. I'll remit directly of course.' He held out the envelope, which still shook in his hand.

'I'll just take a moment to read it, then.' David wasn't obliged, like some, to take any job, and he wasn't about to undertake work that would compromise him. He took the envelope and flicked open the waxed seal.

Mr Perkins peered over the page. 'All in order, straightforward. So, you'll attend immediately?' he asked. He was a slim, small individual, clean-shaven, beady-eyed. He kept looking over his shoulder.

David followed his gaze and saw Mrs Perkins sitting in the buggy, her face set, a fixed bust of plaster of Paris immobile under her deep bonnet. He tipped his hat, then reviewed the note in his hands. The thud hit his chest with a reckoning force. *Good God, today of all days.* Heat itched at his collar, prickled his hands, but he folded the paper calmly and slipped it back in the envelope.

Mr Perkins assumed success and turned to nod heartily at his wife.

David pocketed the envelope. 'Not for me, Mr Perkins. You must find another agent to serve this notice. Good day to you.' He turned on his heels.

Mr Perkins sputtered after him. 'But—I'll have the letter back—'

David kept walking. Nothing would spoil the day he had planned, but this had certainly put a fly in the ointment. He suspected the real reason behind this sudden action of Perkins's and from where it might have originated. But dear God, he didn't want his proposal to sound as if he were a white knight in armour—*Lucille would hate that*—but neither should Mr Perkins's bloody job interfere with his and Lucille's future happiness. *Be damned to that.*

Lucille Downing tidied away loose swathes of fabric, hugging a roll of delicious cobalt blue taffeta to her chest until she found a place for it. The straw hats Evie had brought in the other day were stacked on a bench waiting for adornment, and she'd have to begin work on one of them for Mrs Carter, a lovely light-hearted and breezy client.

Peering out the window, she saw Mr Kingsley, her dear friend David, coming up the path. Her heart lifted. He was so good to look at, striding along with purpose, and such confidence. A handsome man. More importantly a kind man, with a sparkle in his eye and a crisp and dry sense of humour. What luck had been by her side when she'd met him some years ago at the greengrocer's buying his vegetables after having become a widower and deciding he could look after himself.

'Oh, what a delightful surprise,' she said swinging the door open before he could knock. 'The sun is shining, the birds are singing and my wonderful friend has come to visit me. Come in, come in.' Long past worrying about what others thought of who visited her by day, she stepped aside to let him pass.

He *was* a kind man, and one who understood her sadness on each anniversary of Milton's death. He allowed her grief. She did the same for him on his wife Sarah's anniversary. Some days there was a warm hug between them, and a kiss of friendship, and Lucille always wondered why he hesitated to ask for anything beyond that. Sometimes it was enough for her, sometimes she longed for more. Well, she just might ask it of him, and today might be that day. *The sun is shining, the birds are singing* … The sudden glow inside her made her smile.

His hat was already in his hand, and he was dressed impeccably as usual, but his lovely face was creased in a frown. 'Lucille,' he said, on familiar terms when no one else was around. 'I have some rather disturbing information.' He took a seat at Evie's workstation, reached across and took her hand. 'Come sit a moment.'

'What is it? Are you all right?' The thought of David being ill was too much. Her neck flushed. (Not the blasted surges of heat, either; this was different.) He was such a lovely man, a good friend. Well, much more than a friend, she conceded. Pulling a chair closer to him she reached over and squeezed his hand. 'Tell me.'

'I had a job come in earlier,' he said. He was clearly struggling with it. His brow was furrowed, his large brown eyes worried.

She clutched his hand tighter.

'When is Miss Emerson due in?' he asked.

'Soon, I imagine. She's gone to her appointment at Mr Campbell's and—' She stopped. 'Why do you ask?'

'I declined the job, Lucille. The client owns this house and he asked me to serve papers on you for eviction.' He gripped her hand.

'Mr Perkins?' Lucille sat still for a moment. 'Eviction? But my rent is paid up. How can he do that?'

'I haven't got to the bottom of it yet. I do know for a fact that his wife is friends with Mrs Cooper. I suspect he's acting on her wishes, or on his wife's wishes after a mouthful from Mrs Cooper.'

Lucille sat back, withdrawing her hands. 'Good Lord, how ridiculous. I should make an appointment with Mr Campbell myself. How can I be evicted if I've paid my rent? I have all my receipts.'

David spread his hands. 'I hate to say it, my dearest Lucille, but I think the Coopers mean to besmirch your character and see you out on the street because you employ Miss Emerson.'

Lucille's mouth popped open, and she closed it abruptly, incensed. 'For that reason?'

'Indeed. I don't think Perkins has any legal footing on which to evict, so I suspect this is to further unsettle the current situation regarding Miss Emerson and Edwin Cooper, who has shown himself to be quite vile.'

Lucille shook her head. 'This is just awful, so mean-spirited. First the exhibition and now my home, not to mention what they're doing to dear Evie. What on earth does that family hope to gain?' A rush of heat flew over her neck. *Oh no, no. Not now.* She reached for a fan and waved it vigorously at her throat.

'No idea, my lovely. This behaviour of the Coopers has happened so fast, my suspicious nature makes me wonder if they haven't employed the same tactics before. Seems very efficient to me; a well-oiled machine.' David's brows rose. 'Maybe similar has worked in the past to procure financial gain.'

Lucille gazed around her. The front room was very small, but the rest of the house was comfortable and well maintained. She'd enjoyed living here. Milton, her husband, a farrier by trade, had brought her here over twenty-five years ago. Before that they'd lived for some time with his mother in her two-roomed house. Their five children had all been born here. (In such quick succession, how on earth had she coped?) They'd all grown up in this house and now gone off to the city for work. Two had married and had families, all had lives of their own. Milton had died here and, luckily for Lucille, had left her in a better position than others who'd been widowed.

'I'm not sure what I should do,' she said, almost to herself.

'There's no need to do anything yet.' David reached over and pressed her hands. 'I'm going to do a bit of digging, and I know a man who could help.'

Lucille rubbed her forehead. 'I don't have enough to make Mr Perkins an offer for the house, and chances are if he's talking eviction, he's not likely to accept an offer from me anyway.' She put a hand to her throat, the internal heat subsiding. 'I can't stay here, David, that's all there is to it, not with this over my head.'

He stared, and something like indecision was etched on his face. He cleared his throat. 'Ah. Well, it's probably only an empty threat, my darling. And Perkins must find another person to serve the notice, because I doubt he has the stomach to come to your door.'

'A threat all the same. It's undermined my confidence, my security.' She squeezed his hands in return and stood. 'I need to think about this.' She didn't want to go to Melbourne to be closer to her children; she'd never have the same independence as here. Plus times were hard, and two of her married sons accommodated her other three children between them. There wouldn't be room for her anywhere with them. Besides, that would take her away from David.

She paced to the door and back, only a few feet, but she couldn't stand still. She could try to rent somewhere else …

'I'm sure we will come up with a solution, dear lady. I've been thinking—'

'David?' A sudden awful thought had struck her. 'Would Mrs Cooper have long enough arms to prevent me from renting elsewhere here?' Her heart began to hammer.

'I seriously doubt that,' David said calmly. He stood and held out his hands, pulling her into a hug as he went on. 'I'm sorry to have brought this news, but better you know in advance than not. Let's not panic. Let's work out a solid plan, together.'

Together. Oh dear, he said 'together'. Why did it have to coincide with talk of her eviction? *Lucille, what timing!* But that didn't matter, not really. Whatever the outcome of this pickle, David would always be there for her, she knew that.

They swayed a little. It was so right to be in his arms, her head on his chest. They lingered. *This was real.* Happiness with a man had come her way again. Perhaps it was time to make big changes, perhaps the talk of possible eviction was all the prompting she needed.

She closed her eyes. The strong rhythmic thud of his heart under her ear was comforting. He wasn't in any hurry to let her go. If anything, he hugged her that much tighter, and murmured something into her hair, something soothing. Love was offered to her, warm and solid.

Taking a breath, taking a risk, she said, 'I cannot give up my business, David.'

He waited a beat. 'Of course not.'

'I would always have to make my own way in the world. I've done it since Milton died. I enjoy it, you know that. I made sure that my children were well kept, and that they had a basic education.'

'Not an easy task, and much self-sacrifice, I know,' he said, softly. 'You did a fine job, Lucille, my love.'

My love. She pressed on, lifting her head to look at him. 'I've always administered my own money, paid my own bills. I always will. I must.'

'Of course. A credit to you.' He kissed the top of her head, then held her away from him. 'A man is blessed to love and admire such a woman.' He took her hands, his warm brown eyes searching hers.

Oh, my heart.

Drawing in a deep breath he brought her hands to his lips. 'And now that you've told me what I'm in for if I should ever dare propose marriage to you, I'll venture a chance. Would you do me the honour of becoming my wife, Mrs Downing?' His eyes twinkled.

A moment's hesitation herself, she gave a little laugh. 'Oh dear, I wasn't very subtle, was I?'

'No need to be. We're thinking in similar fashion, I'm happy to say. But I'm afraid, dearest lady, if I have to be traditional and get down on one knee, I might not get up again.'

'Oh, please don't, no need.' She framed his face with her hands. 'I would very much like to be your wife.'

He pressed a firm kiss on her mouth. 'I don't know why we haven't thought of it before,' he said tongue-in-cheek. 'It's a good idea and my house will suit us very well. I hope you'll forgive me for presuming, but I had already considered it.' At her look of surprise, he said, 'Asking you to marry me has been in my thoughts for a while, and this morning—even before that little man arrived—I'd made up my mind to do something about it. My house has a wonderful front room to host the town's most excellent millinery business. And I own the place, so no one can evict me.'

She gave him a smile, cupped his cheek. 'It's a *very* good idea.'

'Excited?'

She beamed at him. 'Oh yes,' and smacked a kiss on his lips.

He nodded, smiled, then taking her hands, became serious. 'But first, if you'll allow, let's be practical before high romance and excitement takes us away. I want you to get me all your rent receipts, and I want you to pack your most valuable items and give them to me for safekeeping.' At her look, he said, 'I would put nothing past this Cooper family. Then we wait to see if it goes further than a few annoying incidents.'

'I hope it doesn't.' Lucille stared at his broad neat fingernails, the smattering of dark hair near the cuffs at his wrists, the prominent veins on the backs of his hands as she gripped them. 'David, your proposal shouldn't be just because I'm under threat.'

He barked a laugh. 'It isn't, my lovely, not at all. Only a coincidence of timing,' he said. 'It's long overdue, and I love you with all my heart.' He opened his arms and drew her in.

The door swung open and three young women stood and stared at them. 'Oh, Mrs Downing. Mr Kingsley,' Evie said. 'I'm so sorry—'

'Don't be,' Mr Kingsley said, and gave Mrs Downing a brief formal bow. 'Mrs Downing and I had just wrapped up our business, and I must be on my way.'

Lucille's hand lingered in his, with no heed to it being noticed. 'Where are you going, Mr Kingsley?' she asked, and heard the worry in her voice.

'To see that man I mentioned could help. His name is Bendigo Barrett, and he specialises in investigations. I will report back directly.' He took up his hat. 'Don't forget to pack those things, will you?' He smiled at her. 'Good day to you all,' he said, and as the three women stepped aside, he left the house.

'Mrs Downing, he just gave you the most wonderful smile,' Posie commented. 'Oh, and you have one, too.'

Lucille spread her hands, lifted her gaze to the ceiling. 'Do I?'

Posie understood right away. 'Oh, Mrs Downing, how delightful,' she said, beaming at a bemused Ann.

Evie seemed to have missed things, too. She was deep in thought. 'Did Mr Kingsley just say he was going to see a Bendigo Barrett?'

'He did. Do you know him?'

'Apparently he's making a good name for himself. He owns a small sheep farm just out of town, but he's also a private detective. Mr Campbell spoke highly of him, and said he would employ him on my behalf.'

'Private detective?' Posie cried, alarm in her widening eyes.

'Ah, in that case, Posie and I should get along,' Ann said. 'There seems much for you to discuss and we'll only be in the way.' She brushed past Evie. 'I'll come back to pick you up when you've finished work. Come along, Posie, the ladies have lots of hats to repair.'

'But—a private detective ...'

'Come along, Posie, dear.' Ann herded her outside. 'Good day to you both.'

Waving off the two women, Lucille closed the door and faced Evie with a glowing smile. 'There is much to tell you, some good, some not so good, and there definitely are a lot of hats to repair, exhibition or not.'

Chapter Eight

Cobram
Wednesday 14 September

Fitz had sent a telegram to Raff a few days back. *Will be in Cobram for some time.* Raff would either reply that he was sending mail, or that he was on his way. If there was still trouble, or if he had more information for Fitz, Raff would bring it himself. The police wouldn't let up if they thought Fitz still had something to report.

On his way back to the hotel, he saw Patto still waiting patiently where he'd left him in the stables. Crossing the road, Fitz pushed on the door at the *Cobram Courier* newspaper office. Locked. Peering through the window, he couldn't see anyone inside. Maybe a good thing after all. If he was going to write a story on the strange goings-on around here, it would be better to remain anonymous. In a small town like this, he'd need to be careful getting the story into the local paper—that's if the editor wouldn't be too nervous about printing it.

His nom-de-plume, Mr Fossey, was well known in some parts for his scathing and accurate depictions of injustices, and he'd gained a following as Fitz moved from district to district. Maybe he should retire the name, let its notoriety fade. Simply signing off the next article as *Our Correspondent* would save any more so-called ill repute.

He stared across the road at the pub. Big Tim had asked him where he was staying, so had his brother. Neither man gave him a sense of security, so he'd camp out, like he'd told the barman, though the thought curled his lip a little. He'd much rather have good shelter, a bed and a bath. Heading for Patto, he reckoned if Robbo was going to accompany him to the property, it was time to meet him on the road. Fitz just hoped they weren't going to scare the daylights out of the poor wife when two fellas rode up to interrupt her day. That's if she was there.

They turned off at the cairn and the track was a good two-wheeler, well used.

'The house is a little way in off the main road,' Robbo said, a smoke dangling from his lips. He flicked away the flies, tugged his hat lower.

'Big piece of land?' Fitz asked.

'Nah. Six hundred acres. Wouldn't do no one much good on its own, 'cept for buyin' yourself a feed.'

Fitz liked the look of the country. Big old gums squatted here and there, others rose, majestic, tall and proud reaching high above. Saplings too, cheeky and strong, stood in clusters; gangly youngsters loitering by their bigger brothers. Shrubs, flowering maybe, he didn't know their names, but the area was thick with them. Powdery dust under the horses' hooves covered a country thirsty for water, and wooded plains ran for a few miles on either side of the track. Glimpses of white sand intrigued him and as they got closer to the river, he realised he was looking at a small beach.

'Plenty of those along this stretch of water, real pretty,' Robbo said. 'This way.' He steered his horse off to the right as the track split into two.

The small house appeared in a clearing dotted with the long dead trunks of trees sawn down, most likely used for the building.

No smoke curled up from the chimney. No livestock around except for a few chickens scratching and pecking over by the wood heap.

Robbo stopped. 'You around, Miz Bayley?' he called.

Silence. Not even a rustle of leaves on the breeze. A blowfly buzzed. A bird swooped on it. They nudged the horses closer.

Bayley. The name rang a bell. *Bayley … Damn.* That was the name he'd been trying to recall, Gideon's brother-in-law's name. Seems this was the place he'd been looking for. But what had happened here?

One wall of the dwelling was made of handmade bricks but the rest of it was mostly wattle and daub. Set on a small rise about a hundred yards up from the river, it had little charm despite its beautiful surrounds. Ramshackle, on a lean; there were some thick, rough-hewn planks placed in strategic positions propping it up. The roof was made of old corrugated iron, some sheets had rust chewing away at what little cover they afforded. Off to the side of the house was a decent-sized copper sitting on a stack of bricks; there'd be remnant coals underneath from when the wife had last done her laundry. Fitz wondered if there'd be any warmth still in them, but looking around thought likely not; it was clear the place had been abandoned a while. Swathes of fabric hung listlessly in two open windows that were devoid of glass. Had shutters ever been fitted to protect against the bitter winter? How the hell anyone lived like this …

They dismounted. Robbo called out again. Still no answer.

'It don't seem right, does it? Like, when you know a place is empty because folk have gone to town or whatever, it still has life, somehow. But this'—Robbo shook his head—'this place doesn't have life, you know?'

Fitz knew. 'There's no feeling.'

'That's it.'

'When was the last time you saw your mate?'

'Maybe four, five months. He weren't real happy, but never said much about what was botherin' him. Then when I come out again, weeks later, she said he'd just upped and gone one day. Left the house like usual and didn't come home.'

'On foot?'

'Yeah.'

'Drowned, maybe?'

Robbo shook his head, took the smoke from between his lips and pinched the end to make sure it was out. He poked the butt behind his ear. 'Don't reckon. Less he was chasin' somethin' an' it ran into the river, but by that time he had no sheep left. Sold 'em. And folk around here respect this river, don't take it lightly. It woulda been a bit cool then, so he wouldna been swimmin', neither.'

Fitz drew in a breath. 'Would he have …?'

Robbo lifted a shoulder. 'Who would know? I woulda said not, but life can wear a man down.' His gaze flickered away.

Fitz knew that well enough. He stared at the serene river. Any secret it had about Bayley would likely remain that way. A body might never be found if it got snagged deep below.

'So, he had sheep,' Fitz mused. 'He must have had fences then, done a bit of work.'

'I helped him do some of it, but just before he disappeared, he said he'd finish the rest himself. Wasn't too much to do. Still, even small as the place is, it's a bit of a job on your own. I was offerin' to help for nothin', a friend an' all.'

Fitz could see Robbo's concern and that he was genuinely bewildered. 'What do you think happened?'

Robbo wiped a hand under his nose then dug his hands in his pockets. 'I reckon he mighta been run off the place.' He shrugged, furtive. 'I dunno.'

'And the wife?'

Swinging his bony shoulders a little, Robbo said, 'That's the scary part. She waited a while, months, then one day, gone.' He gaped at Fitz, eyes red-rimmed. 'Where'd she go?' he asked the air, kicking at the dirt. 'Nothin's happened out here since her ol' man's been gone, no one's tried to take the place from her, far as I know. So I dunno. I dunno.' More anxious now.

'Let's look inside.'

'What for?'

'Might see something you didn't see the other day.'

Robbo trudged up to the door and hammered a fist on it. 'Miz Bayley,' he yelled. 'Open up, it's me, Cyril.' He only waited a few beats, then threw up the latch and swung open the door.

Fitz stepped inside behind him. Light poured in from the open window spaces opposite, no glass in them either, no shutters. A crude curtain, the faded fabric maybe from old flour bags, hung limp and streaked. Dust motes were suspended in the air. Sure enough, the table was set for one, the cutlery skewed, a teacup—a lady's cup—was on its side nearby, contents dried, the stain inside the cup revealing that tea had still been in it when it was pushed over.

'Possums have cleaned up the rest,' Robbo muttered and brushed dung pellets off the table. 'It's eerie. I don't like it in here.'

The table, its top scuffed, its solid legs turned, had once been a good piece, a handsome thing. Only two chairs; one was tipped over, resting on its back. By the fireplace, there was an old, stained settee, big enough for two people to sit and warm their feet at the hearth. Possum piss covered it, and droppings dotted in the sagging seat cushions. There was only one internal wall with a door in the place. Must be the bedroom, unusual in a hut of this size. Fitz gave Robbo a look.

'There was nothin' when I checked last I was here, so I just closed it again,' he said. 'Didn't want no vermin in there.'

No warning stench was obvious so Fitz crossed the earthen floor, lifted the latch, and pushed the door. There wasn't a body.

Behind him, Robbo breathed a loud sigh of relief. 'Just as I left it,' he said.

The bed was an iron frame with a thin mattress. A floral cover was on top of the quilt, and pillows in calico cases were neatly stacked. The window over the bed was shuttered, the only one in the place, and nothing had been degraded by possums that might have otherwise marched over everything, leaving their droppings and squirting urine indiscriminately. A chest of drawers and a pair of lady's slippers sat neatly underneath. A blue checked dress, its hem ragged in places, hung on a hook nearby. Above, the ceiling was intact.

The one place a woman could feel sheltered, a neat space, a sanctuary.

Fitz stood in the room, the picture before him belying the life the woman must have led.

'So where'd she go?' Robbie asked again, foot tapping.

Fitz eyed something on the dresser, a little wooden doll crafted by someone who'd chiselled delicately and scraped and smoothed the pale timber. Faded blue-checked fabric made a tiny pair of trousers. The dress on the back of the door—the woman had cut a piece from her clothes. A pullover shirt on the doll had possibly been fashioned from an old handkerchief. 'You said they buried a child here.'

'Yeah, that was a year ago, or more.'

'Where's the grave?'

'Bit of a walk, I reckon I can still find it. This way,' Robbo said, only too happy to leave the house.

They marched a fair way past the horses and into the low scrub at the back of the house then climbed a gentle rise. Over his shoulder, Fitz saw the river wind in a broad ribbon away to the west, a peaceful meandering, a quietly determined flow that took no notice of man, beast or machine. He faltered only a moment; if this place were his, he'd have built here, right on this spot, high enough up on the hill to see that sight every waking day.

A rough gouge in the bank on this side took his eye. Pointing at it, he asked, 'What's that?'

Robbo squinted. 'Start of a channel looks like, maybe Roy was tryin' to get water flowing.' A grunt of surprise. 'I never knew he started. Need more'n one man to do that.' He kept up his pace.

Fitz's gaze swept the landscape as his boots scrunched over the dry fuel load. It'd be a bastard here if the scrub caught alight. Ahead, as if to let him know fire had roared through, a narrow stand of long dead trees, burned to towers of charcoal, threaded its way down to the water.

Despite it, the piece of land was a treat; no wonder folk were vying for it. As he trudged behind Robbo, the sorrow, the stillness of the place weighed on him. Something had happened out here. He stopped, tried to hear its voice. Looking to the sky, the blazing heat of the late-afternoon sun fell on his face. A blowfly dived close, darted off. Silence enveloped him. There was nothing to—

'Oh, sweet Jesus.'

He heard a sob in Robbo's voice. When Fitz got to Robbo, the man was on the edge of a clearing, turned away, bent over and gagging onto the dust.

Wiping his mouth on his sleeve, he pointed behind him. 'That's her.'

A little wooden cross marked a mound surrounded by a low circle of rocks. Over the grave was the body of a woman, fully dressed. She'd been ravaged by nameless creatures. Ants busied about, intent with purpose. Flies rose and swooped again. Face down, she was prone over the grave, her hair straggly, scalp torn and blackened. Her right hand was flung towards the base of the cross, the fleshless fingers curled loosely around it.

It looked as if her grief had killed her.

Chapter Nine

Cobram
Thursday 15 September

The next morning, the heat hadn't yet climbed, but still sweat dripped from under Fitz's hat. He swiped it away with his forearm. The day was shaping up to be warmer than yesterday.

John sidled his horse up alongside. 'Robinson says he was showing you over the place yesterday, Mr Morgan.'

There was a tacit understanding that neither mentioned they were brothers.

'That's right, Constable,' Fitz answered.

'Why this place?'

'I wanted to know why Haines is interested in it. Easy to see now.'

John grunted. 'It's a good spot, all right, and the fact is that he owns over there far as you can see,' he said, waving an arm left and right towards the other side of the river. 'Either side of this place on this bank is his, too.'

Late the afternoon previously, Fitz and Robbo had brought a blanket from the house and pinned it over Mrs Bayley's body with rocks, then they'd headed off, agreeing to meet early back at the property. Fitz had nevertheless declined the offer of a bed at Robbo's. He'd camped by the river near town, falling asleep on his swag, wiped out with exhaustion, decay still cloying in his nostrils. He'd roused John at daybreak and together they had ridden out.

Robbo had been at the Bayley property just after dawn. 'I reckon she musta been lyin' there when I last come out,' he said, his mouth twisting. 'I shoulda searched more.'

'She'd have been well beyond help by then, Robbo,' Fitz said.

'Why did you wanna come back out here this morning?' John asked, pulling his kerchief over his nose. 'Bloody awful.'

Fitz took off his hat, scratched his head, wrinkled his nose. He'd needed a bath before now, but this reek was tangible, clinging to his clothes and permeating his skin. The body had already been out in the elements; she needed to be buried as soon as possible. 'Someone's got to do right by the poor woman.'

John lifted his chin in the direction of the grave. 'Dunno how we're gonna take her back to town. Got no steel coffin to transport a rotting body.'

Fitz lowered his voice, leaned out of his saddle a little. 'Christ, John, she died over her baby's grave. Bury her here. It's her land.' He thumbed over at Robbo. 'We'll do the digging. All you have to do is pronounce a cause of death for the coroner and the doc can write up a death certificate.'

'I know what I have to do, thanks all the same,' John grumbled. 'I've done me fair share of this before now. I have to be sure she just up and died and that no one stoved her head in.'

Still mounted, Robbo was a little distance from the grave. He'd have heard the exchange, but Fitz wasn't worried about Robbo hearing the overly familiar tone.

Horses sounded behind them. Ernest Haines and two others approached through the scrub.

'Jesus,' John muttered. 'All I need.'

'Constable,' Haines called. 'Good day.' Then he pulled up his horse, wrinkling his nose. 'Christ.'

John only nodded.

'Mr Morgan,' Haines greeted Fitz, his kerchief pressed across his face. 'Robbo,' he said as an afterthought. 'Looks like we got a tragedy,' he said, eyeing the body covered with the blanket. 'Was riding past this way to my place, thought I'd drop in to see if the missus was back home. Is that her?' He shook his head. 'Terrible thing. Reckon we could offer a hand somehow.' He waved towards the two younger men, maybe his workers, and craned another look at the gravesite.

Robbo had dismounted and didn't look happy. He walked his horse close to Fitz.

'We'll be right, Mr Haines,' John said.

Nodding towards the body, Haines said, 'Have to get a move on quick, this weather.'

'Unless there's something unusual the constable needs to report on,' Fitz said, matter-of-fact.

John snapped him a look.

Haines's saddle creaked as he shifted, the kerchief dropping a little. 'You think there's been foul play, Constable?' he asked. 'Shockin', if so.' He shook his head again at the thought.

'Just tyin' up loose ends, Mr Haines. The fellas here found her late yesterday.'

'Did they now?' Haines shifted his gaze to Fitz, then to Robbo where it lingered.

'She's been here a while,' John said. 'We'll bury her directly.'

'Surely you'll take it back to town, not bury it here.'

At the hesitation from John, and the disquieting return stare from Robbo, Haines hurried on.

'Well, the land will be—'

'*It* is Miz Bayley,' Robbo cut in, tight-lipped. 'She's already been out here a while, the constable said. Needs to be buried.'

Haines glared at him then at John, silenced and incensed.

'We'll be right,' John repeated. 'I'll do up a report.'

Haines adjusted his seat in the saddle. 'Well, if you—'

'Good day to yer, Mr Haines,' John said, his voice a little louder.

Haines shut up. 'Boys,' he said, a thumb over his shoulder. They rode off without looking back.

'How'd they know where the grave was?' Fitz mused. 'Bit out of the way from the hut.'

'He most prob'ly knows every inch of this place,' John said.

Robbo started at that. 'There wasn't any foul play, was there?' he asked, fright in his voice. 'She just died, didn't she?'

John had inspected the body when they'd arrived. 'Hard to tell. She coulda been clobbered on the back of the head.' He clamped his mouth shut as if holding back high emotion. Blinking hard, he said, 'I'd say not murder. I reckon it was dingos or dogs did this damage after she was dead. Birds and other critters maybe had a go at her.' He made fists on his hips, cast around, then slapped off his hat and kicked it. 'Fuck's sake,' he exploded, lowering his head.

Fitz dismounted but made no attempt to go to his brother.

Robbo stalked off towards the cart. 'There's two shovels and a pick in here,' he called out. 'I'll make a start with the pick beside the youngster's grave.'

'Mr Morgan.' John beckoned Fitz and headed a little further out of Robbo's earshot.

Nudging Patto, Fitz followed and dismounted with John. 'What is it?'

'Haines,' he said and checked the man was long gone. 'He came to see me yesterday afternoon, late. Said he thought the new fella by the name of Morgan looked a bit shady, that I was to watch him.'

'That so?'

'He said he didn't like the look of you.'

Fitz raised his eyebrows. 'He sending me a message through you?'

John snorted. 'I'm tellin' you to be careful. Yer still me brother, no matter what. The man's a crook, no two ways about it. He can't get past Constable Stillard, but it's clear he reckons I'm soft.'

'Thinks you'll be handy in the future, does he?'

'Don't push it, Fitz.' John tied his horse's rein to a tree branch.

'I can't abide crooked troopers,' Fitz said, scuffing the dirt.

'I know.' John began to walk then stopped, swung close. 'So in case yer wonderin', I'll tell yer straight. I'm not in his pay. Not now, not ever.' He stalked back to Robbo.

It took a couple of hours. When the hole was deep enough, they wrapped the body in the blanket as best they could and slipped her down. Robbo sniffed and snorted the whole time they cleared up the site, tossing grisly bits that had come loose from under the blanket into the hole. Then the dirt was shovelled and pushed back into the grave.

'Should get a church fella out here to say some words for her, even though I dunno which—' Robbo stopped, hat in his spade-like hands. 'Won't matter which though, will it? I'll do up a couple more of these.' He picked up the crude cross that had been on the boy's grave. 'The youngster needs a better one. I'll put his name on it, poor tyke. Maybe take up a collection, see if we can get a stone done for mother and boy. Folk need their names on the stone.' His voice jagged as he stared at the weathered little timbers.

Fitz could see the letter 'D' etched on the cross. 'What was the boy's name?' he asked as he stood beside the new mound of dirt.

'Dallas.'

Fitz raised his brows. 'Uncommon.' Something tickled his memory. *Dallas*. That had been Evie's father's name, Dallas Emerson.

'Miz Bayley named the boy after her father.'

The clunk in Fitz's chest took a moment to ease. 'And Mrs Bayley, what was her first name?' He already knew, should've figured it out before now. He'd learned years ago that Evie's sister had married a man named Bayley from Ballarat and had headed up this way. Fitz had never met either of them, and had clearly forgotten the connection.

'Meryl,' Robbo answered. 'Meryl, Roy and little Dallas Bayley.' He inhaled and blew out a big breath. 'Now none of 'em are left.'

Gideon Levi's brother-in-law was Roy Bayley. He had married Meryl Emerson.

Jesus Christ, I've just buried Evie's sister.

Robbo had headed home, peeling off at the cairn. Fitz rode Patto alongside the cart as John drove it back to town.

John was silent a while. Then, 'Need to wash up my uniform. I got a bath at my place, and plenty of carbolic soap. You an' me both need to get rid of the stink,' he said. 'Won't charge yer,' he added, a twist of sarcasm aimed at his brother.

Fitz snorted. 'Appreciate it.'

'Is that right, what you said before, that you knew the dead woman?'

'Hadn't met her. Knew of her, she's the sister of a friend.'

Fitz hadn't told any family about Evie; no need. He would have if he'd been able to go through with marrying her. It hadn't come to pass, thankfully for him. For both. Fitz knew that he'd never manage living with a woman, being married. Even now his heart rate climbed when he remembered he'd even considered it.

Fitz didn't yearn for a woman in his life; never had. He yearned for a companion, yes, a lover, but not a woman.

Augie, Augustus Pine, had been Fitz's lover years ago. But he had chosen to leave Fitz and marry a woman. He'd bowed to family pressure, the wrath and threats of his father. Self-preserving; Fitz understood it. He hadn't condemned Augie, but his heart had broken and his life had cleaved into pieces.

Fitz had hung on to Evie, he admitted that. If he changed his mind about pursuing a 'normal' life he'd need to marry. *Coward.* For good reason, he chided. If the famous, like Oscar Wilde, that genius Irish poet and playwright could be incarcerated for the way he lived, Fitz knew what form of justice would be meted out to him for living the same style of life.

He hung his head, a moment's guilt spiking. It would have been grossly unjust to Evie to fool her. He'd been selfish, petulant too, not wanting Raff to step right in. *My best mate.* He should've been honest with Raff, should've let him know that Evie was free of any promises to Fitz.

Bah. No real urgency now. Evie wasn't wasting time over Fitz, he was sure, and Raff, the great dolt, hadn't done anything about pursuing Evie either. Maybe he didn't feel strongly enough. Well, they were adults; they could work it out.

Even so, he knew he should've said something to Raff. He would.

And now this. Meryl's death. He sucked in a deep breath. *Helluva bloody reason to have to contact Evie again.* He wouldn't leave it to the police, wouldn't have John do it. It was personal.

Fitz would tell Evie himself.

John had pumped water for the boiler and, once it was hot enough, filled the tub alongside and set about having a bath in the open air.

'Better not to stink up the house.'

Afterwards, he pulled on clean clothes, tossed out the water and refreshed the tub. Dunking underwear, socks and uniform, he scrubbed up a lather. Rinsed it all in another tub of clean water and repeated until he couldn't detect the odour of decay.

'I'm done with bloody laundry. I'm headin' back to the station,' he said, flinging wet clothes over the line strung between two poles.

Fitz was carting water to the boiler for his bath. 'I'll see you there directly.'

'Don't be in a hurry,' John said. 'Haines is already suspicious of you.' Pulling on socks and boots, he said, 'You were sniffing around for land, and now he sees you and Robbo out at the Bayley place, the patch of dirt he wants. I'll never hear the end of it.' He rubbed his face tiredly. 'Just watch yourself, mate.'

'What is it about Haines?'

'Just take advice for once and leave it alone,' John said and reached for his police cap, pulled a face, then tossed it onto Fitz's filthy clothes. 'Get that scrubbed up for me, will yer?' He didn't wait for an answer.

The bath and soap were good, and Fitz could have been easily tempted to lounge in the warm water, but he wasn't going to linger. The fire underneath the boiler was roaring and by the time he'd dried off and dressed, the copper was ready. He tossed in his stinking pants and shirt. Unders went in too, John's cap, his hat, dunked with the dolly stick and a good dose of lye. When done, he scrubbed off the soles of his boots just to be sure. Wringing everything tight as possible (*Jesus, hard work*), he started pegging it alongside John's sodden, dripping clothes, when he heard a voice behind him.

'Real domesticated. Could make yourself some good money doing laundry.' Haines was on his horse in the lane behind the house, hands relaxed, the reins draped between them. 'Our Constable O'Shea must have taken a shine to you.'

'We both stank. He said I could take a bath here. Decent of

him.' Fitz hung the last of his clothes and swiped wet hair from his face. He missed wearing his hat. 'He's gone to the station.'

Haines nodded. 'So, what did you think of that piece of land?'

'Wasn't expecting to see a dead woman on it.'

'Yeah, uh, awful shame.' Haines straightened in the saddle. 'Well, reckon I better get along to the station and see the constable.' He tipped his hat and turned his horse.

'Mr Haines,' Fitz called. 'Heard you were interested in that piece of land.'

Haines stopped, twisted in the saddle. 'Might be, but we gotta find Bayley, he hasn't been seen for months.' At Fitz's silence, he said, 'Man might be dead. More likely he's abandoned it, won't be back. In which case the crown will take back the land, sell it on if the taxes can't be paid. I'll register my interest.'

'What about if there's kin?'

Haines's eyes narrowed. 'What about it?'

'Wouldn't the place go to them?'

'Nah. Doesn't work like that. Any case, his only kin is buried there.' Haines sucked in a deep breath, seemed a show of sorrow. 'Terrible thing.'

Fitz wandered closer to the fence, rested his arm on a post. 'What do you think happened to Bayley?'

Haines looked at his hands a moment, then back at Fitz. 'Just walked off the place, they say.'

'Just like that? Left a wife and walked off.'

'Happens.' Tipping his hat, Haines nudged his horse. 'Happens all the time.' He headed off down the lane.

Fitz watched as the rider turned out of sight. Where to start? If Haines owned Big Tim and had other ears in the pub, how would he get to the bottom of what was going on here? He needed information, even hearsay, to follow up. Robbo could be key. Even though he'd been on edge he agreed with Fitz; Haines was in the thick of it.

While Fitz waited for his hat to dry, he checked over the house his brother was occupying. A timber dwelling with a kitchen hut out the back, and a long-drop dunny further away. Nothing special. The rooms inside were furnished for a family. Two bedrooms, one with a double bed, a small wardrobe and a dresser with a lamp on it; the other had two single cots and a small chest of drawers. John's clothes sat in disarray in an open suitcase, the bedlinens unmade on one of the cots.

In the parlour room there were two lamps and a family photograph—two adults, two children—on a simple hutch filled with best china. A couple of low chairs and a deep settee were crammed close together facing the fireplace. A basket of ladies' sewing paraphernalia sat under the window. A table the size of a milking stool was beside one of the chairs and an empty tea mug sat in the middle of it. John's, no doubt.

He went back outside to Patto and his saddlebags. Rummaging, he pulled out a tightly wrapped packet and headed into the kitchen hut where, at the table, he unpacked an ink bottle and a nib pen, and some carefully folded paper. Now was as good a time as any to start an article for the local newspaper.

His thoughts went to the dead woman again. Meryl Emerson—Mrs Bayley—and what he should tell Evie. He had thought he should return to Bendigo and tell her face to face, but maybe he should write first and offer to bring her here, instead. *What's my place in all this?* His place was to tell Evie, he owed her that, in friendship at least.

He squeezed his eyes shut. *Dammit.* In a strange way it had hurt, leaving her. It was their friendship. That had felt right. He cared for her, loved her maybe, but not in the way a wife needed to be loved. Not that she wanted to be his wife anyhow, she certainly hadn't wanted to troop around the countryside behind him. The way he saw it, they'd saved each other from a lifetime of misery.

Thank Christ he hadn't tried to insist they marry. They were real friends and had, by all accounts, stayed that way.

So. He'd work out how to tell her about her sister after he got down a page for the paper. Taking a breath, he dipped the pen. Tapping off excess ink, he began to write.

Sir, it has come to this roving reporter's attention that there are dire shenanigans regarding the safe purchase, or acquisition, of land in this area.

It took him an hour, and many stretches of his back and fingers. He walked outside to the well, drew up a bucket and poured a fresh pitcher of water. Taking a pannikin from the kitchen bench he knocked back two cups.

He wasn't done yet. Two more to draft.

My dear Gideon and Rachel,

It is with much regret ...

The letter was short. He couldn't offer them any comfort; he knew nothing of Roy's whereabouts or what had happened to him. Worse, all he had to give them was the saddest of news about Roy's wife and son. He promised to keep searching for answers.

He dropped the pen, stood and rubbed his face vigorously. As a journalist, he could keep his emotions at bay. As a friend, he could not.

And now for the hardest one to pen. Settling at the table again, he let the words flow.

Dearest Evie,

My heart is heavy that I must be the bearer of sad tidings, however I am glad to be that person as your good friend, and not a stranger to you. Your sister, Meryl Bayley, has died here on her property in Cobram. This is what I know …

He finished up some long minutes later, ending it:

With heartfelt condolences, your old champion, Fitzmorgan.

Writing the letters had been hard. He needed to get outside again; the kitchen was closing him in. Impatient, he blotted the last of his work, and waited for it to dry. Then he folded and addressed both envelopes. He'd mail them soon.

The page for the newspaper was well dry. He folded that too, and wrote *To the Editor* on it. Then he tucked them all inside his shirt, went back to the clothesline and grabbed his dry hat. The rest of his clothes could wait until later.

Chapter Ten

Bendigo
Saturday 17 September

David had borrowed a friend's horse and cart to drive out to Mr Bendigo Barrett's property, from where the man conducted business. His two sisters, the Misses Barrett, met him at the door.

One of them, Miss Faith Barrett, was working for her brother in her capacity of secretary and in so doing, she was a testament to the man's unorthodox ways. He employed Faith, even after she'd been tainted by a terrible scandal and left an abandoned, embarrassed woman. Mr Barrett had stood by her, defying gossipers and naysayers. She was not to be hidden away. Also, David knew that Mr Barrett had won acclaim for a case in the previous year that had taken him all the way to Sydney. He'd been engaged there to investigate a family mystery—by a woman.

Mr Barrett's other sister, Joy, was in a chair with wheels attached, which would explain the wide veranda built on the ground itself—no need for steps—and a front door that opened out on to it. He was a forward-thinking man, one used to finding solutions, and had not seen fit to shelter her in an asylum. Rather, he had ensured she remained in her home under his roof, and with as much comfort as he could provide for her. Pathways around the house were wide and well maintained, allowing for her to propel herself with ease. She wheeled away after a polite introduction.

Faith indicated that they should walk a short distance across the yard to where several men were putting the final touches on another home. She explained it would be for Bendigo and his new wife once they were married.

'Don't worry that we don't seem to do things in a straight line around here, Mr Kingsley,' Miss Barrett said. 'Work has been patchy of late, so Ben will be only too happy to speak with you today, no appointment necessary.' They stopped and she called out. 'Ben? Bendigo?' From high above on the roof a face appeared over the corrugated iron. 'Ben, this is Mr Kingsley. He needs to talk to you.'

A wave of Mr Barrett's finger suggested he wouldn't be long.

They'd come in the front door, and a wide hallway had opened before them, no doubt to allow for Miss Joy's wheelchair. (Marvellous invention, and she seemed to be quite deft manoeuvring along.) All the doorways had been widened, too. (Must have cost a small fortune.) A large solid desk of some dark wood was covered with a blotter, a pen and an inkwell nearby, and a stack of well-used journals. There was a chair for Mr Barrett, one for his clerk at the side of the desk, and two chairs for clients in front, which was where David stood. A large window allowed in full sunshine, and plain-coloured heavy drapes fell to the sides. The timber floor was polished and recently installed.

Mr Barrett indicated he take a seat. 'What is it I can do for you?' He was unrolling his shirt sleeves and buttoning them at the cuffs. 'Please excuse my current state of dress,' the man said, then ran his fingers through dark hair that had a white blaze starting at his forehead.

'Not at all,' David said. 'I'm happy you suggested we get straight down to it. I was only about to make an appointment when your sister offered to call you in.'

Miss Barrett sat alongside the desk, an open journal and a pencil in her hand. David related as much of the tale as he could, while Miss Barrett took copious notes and her brother listened intently, interjecting only once or twice for clarification.

Mr Barrett leaned back in his chair. 'Are you aware, Mr Kingsley, that Mr Campbell has engaged our services on behalf of Miss Emerson?'

'Well, yes, now you mention it. I was told that yesterday.' David suddenly realised he'd just made an ethical faux pas, hadn't he? *Oh Lord.*

'In that case, while I'm happy to take any information you offer, I can't discuss any part of my investigation with you.'

'Quite. Of course not. Perhaps I'll liaise further with Mr Campbell.' David would have to confess to Evie—did it look like meddling? But surely she wouldn't mind. No, no, she wouldn't. 'It's just that we, my fiancée and I, have great affection for Miss Emerson, and would do everything in our power to protect her. To help her,' David emphasised. 'And I have to say, Mr Barrett, that if you can use legwork in your investigation, I would be only too happy to assist.' He suffered a moment's embarrassment over his lack of professionalism, then believed he needn't worry.

Mr Barrett nodded as if considering. 'You said you are a debt collector, Mr Kingsley.'

'Another occupation clawing its way up from the bottom.'

'Indeed.'

Private detective work was not thought of too highly, much the same as debt collection work. David knew each occupation had its place in an increasingly changing world.

'Someone must work for those who wish to pursue their debtors legitimately,' he said.

'Understood.' Mr Barrett tapped a finger on his desk. 'This Mr Cooper. What's his profession?'

'Not sure he has one, per se. I believe he's the son of a late property owner and that there's money in the family.'

'You said you believed he's tried this sort of thing before.'

'It seems to me that his actions are well oiled. The engagement announcement in the paper that Miss Emerson knew nothing about, and then the swift declaration of intent to sue for breach of contract, followed by the spreading of rumours in strategic stores known to supply my friend, Miss Emerson's employer. After that, the sudden approach by the landlord of my friend Mrs Downing to have her evicted has just tweaked my antennae further, as it were.' David shook his head. 'Seems far too smooth an operation to me.'

'Certainly, on the face of it. And someone named Miss Thompson is involved?'

David nodded. 'That's what Miss Emerson has told Mrs Downing. I have the woman's description, such as it is.'

'We'll take that down later. Mr Kingsley, in your opinion, to what end is Mr Cooper doing this? What's his motivation?'

'Only that he wants a court decision in his favour on breach of contract,' David said. 'If Miss Emerson is found guilty, he can expect to be awarded damages. I doubt his future interests lie in matrimony with her at all.'

'And the threat to evict your friend, Mrs Downing, how would that benefit Mr Cooper?'

Miss Barrett was scribbling furiously.

'I think he's showing Miss Emerson that he can damage her considerably, and damage those who support her. I believe it points to his possible success in the past.'

Mr Barrett sat forward, clasped his hand on the desk. 'But he might lose the case in court. It's a risk.'

'He made the engagement announcement in last Saturday's paper. It makes for a strong suit against Miss Emerson.'

'Ah yes. For all intents and purposes, agreeing to marry is a contract.' Mr Barrett held up a hand to his sister. 'Faith, do we have the paper?'

'We do.'

'That's the first thing, Mr Kingsley, to check with the *Bendigo Advertiser* and find out if this Mr Cooper has taken it upon himself to place engagement announcements prior to this instance.' He chewed his lip a moment in thought. 'Hopefully they'll be cooperative, but we might have to purchase back copies.'

David beamed at him. 'Excellent idea, Mr Barrett. I'm happy to peruse the papers for you if it comes to that.'

'Leave it with Faith, she'll handle that. If we find that Mr Cooper has taken this path before, we'll track down court records, if there are any.' Mr Barrett smiled, and his brows rose. 'I think this will be a very satisfying case to bring to its end. I'm happy to be working on it, and gladly accept whatever information you can impart.'

Standing, David reached over to shake Mr Barret's hand. 'Wonderful. Anything I find I will bring to your attention.'

David gave a description of Miss Thompson to Faith Barrett, then made his way back to the township and to Lucille's house. He'd return the horse and cart to his friend later. As he stepped off the cart, and headed for the path to Lucille's door, he had a spring in his step. He would enjoy a purpose other than his own job, particularly if it was sleuthing.

Life was worthwhile once again, more so because Lucille and he would soon be married. It was a good day all round.

Chapter Eleven

Ballarat

Raff laughed in the lamplight. 'You know me so well, Pa.' He was stuffing saddlebags with tins of food, water flasks, newspapers Fitz would want to see, cartridges for his rifle, and a spare pair of boots.

His swag was already rolled and strapped to Bluey's saddle. The part Percheron was an enormous animal, black with a blaze of white on his forehead, built to take Raff's weight, built for endurance. He could pull a laden cart with ease, a boon at the wheelwright shop. He'd bought Bluey cheap years ago from a bloke who'd come down from near Sydney, and who'd gone broke trying his hand at farming hereabouts.

Not too many of Bluey's type around anymore, the riding preference lately being for the quicker, deft breeds. He gave Bluey an affectionate slap on the neck. 'You'll do me fine, boyo,' he whispered into a flickering ear.

'What am I gonna do with the place till you come back?' Paddy Dolan held the lamp aloft. His sparse grey hair tufted out from under his woollen hat. He slept in the thing to keep his head warm.

'You'll be right, just keep the doors open and things ticking over. I won't be long, just helping Fitz, see that he's in the clear from the bastards trying to string him up.' He'd sent a telegram to Fitz earlier—*On my way*—addressed to a Mr Fossey, the pseudonym they used. 'If I'm longer than I expect, two weeks, a month, send word to Uncle Skelly and get Fergal and Red back here.' His younger brothers were down Warrnambool way, dairy farming with Paddy's brother.

'Aye, I'll send for 'em anyway. Times are tough on Skelly's farm. And you keep ye head down,' his father ordered. 'I don't want to have them scallywag brothers of yours under me feet again for good.' His teeth clamped around the stem of a pipe.

'You'd like nothing better than to have all your boys back within your sight.'

Paddy narrowed his gaze, looking up at his eldest son. 'You watch yeself, boyo. There's that roarin' quick temper of yours and ye built to power it.' He tapped a fist on Raff's chest. 'So you be careful in future, ye hear me?'

Maybe shrewd and wizened Paddy knew that the trooper spy from the other night had been dealt with. In a flash of memory Raff saw his fist slamming into the fella's chest knocking the breath from his body. Raff had picked him up like a sack of grain and dumped him two streets over on the steps of the police station.

Paddy gripped his son's broad shoulder, his bent and gnarled hand still strong. 'You goin' by Bendigo?'

'Maybe.'

'Y'are, I can tell. Good. Best you get it out of your system then, one way or t'other,' Paddy said. 'Y'are ye own worst enemy, lad, keepin' ye mouth shut around this lassie. Go and have a good crack at it.'

Nothing much got past Paddy. *There's a girl in Bendigo, a friend,* Raff had told his father a long while back when he was feeling sorry for himself. *I think she belongs to my best mate.*

Ye think?

Well, I dunno. Can't tell if they're together or not.

Chrissakes, lad. Ask the question.

I don't want to lose my friend over it. Either of them.

Who's ye friend?

Fitz.

Fitz, bah. Ye'll be no fool if y'ask, if that's what ye thinkin', but sure be a fool if ye don't.

Pa had said no more at the time. But just now, even though Raff was pretty sure he wasn't going to go through Bendigo, his pa had picked him in one.

Paddy squeezed his shoulder hard again. 'If a man don't let a woman know how he feels about her, he can cause himself a big pain.'

Raff leaned on the saddle, one hand patting Bluey's dense, broad flank. 'So, Pa, you're not that tough old bird you'd have us believe.'

'Aye, and I know more about it than you, by the looks, you great git. What is it with ye and this woman?'

'Nothing. There's nothing.' There was everything, and the more Raff thought about it the harder it was to hide it. 'She's a friend.'

'Don't be tellin' me that.' Paddy stepped closer. 'You can tell yeself all you like, but I can see it as plain as the day. No point denying it's there, and it's been there a long while. Who else has seen it, eh?'

'Pa, for Chrissakes.'

'Hidin' it from her won't do y'any good.'

'Fitz hasn't said—'

'Bah, Fitz. You go sweep her off her feet, boyo. Get yer blood rushin'. A man needs to find his woman, and grab hold of her tight.'

Raff snorted as he tested Bluey's girth strap. 'Ma would love to be hearing you saying something like that to one of her boys.'

'She's hearin' it all right. No mistake.' He tugged at the woollen cap on his head, then waggled a finger at his son. 'I did well by your ma, and she by me. She was my all, lad, and then came you boys.' His voice faltered a little.

'You missing her, Pa?'

'Aye, it's heavy on me today.' Paddy sighed, ducked his chin a moment. 'She's been gone ten years right on this date.' His voice was weary, his eyes a little blurry. 'And it still only feels like yest'dy in here.' He tapped a fist on his chest.

Raff swallowed down a rising lump in his throat, his father's emotion was a wound to his own heart. His mother had slipped away to her God in the night, no warning, and Raff had woken to his father's distraught cries from their bedroom. He sniffed. 'Well, don't waste your time on me for my woes then, Pa.'

Paddy ignored that. 'Ye gotta speak up, lad. Honest is best, no matter the hurt if ye don't like the answer.' Then he poked Raff's shoulder. 'And trust me on this. Ye won't be losing yer damn friend Fitz over it, neither.' His father gave him a nod and a quirk of an eyebrow as if he knew something Raff didn't.

Raff did know, had always known, that Fitz wasn't a ladies' man. Except for friendship, he wasn't interested in women at all. Raff didn't really even remember when he'd learned it about Fitz. It wasn't something he put his mind to. It had just always been there, rarely acknowledged. It had never been an issue between them; Fitz was his friend, from when they were kids. That was that.

There was only one short, concise discussion, Raff recalled. They were youngsters, maybe twelve, thirteen, gangly, pimples the size of anthills on both, bony shoulders, and chins and upper lips darkened with fluff. Fitz had been sobbing about being different, rejected, afraid. He'd been roughed up; Raff had dragged a couple of boys off him. Afterwards, they'd shared a meat pie that Raff's mother had baked, and then, chucking stones into the creek, Fitz had wiped his nose on his sleeve, and said, 'Will you always be my friend, Raff, no matter what?'

'Yeah, I will. I can't be like you though, all right? I like girls.' Just a matter-of-fact answer. 'That's not gonna change.'

'I know, I know that. Not what I'm talkin' about. So, no matter what, you'll always be my friend?'

'Aye, Fitz.'

Nothing had changed that, nothing would.

They'd been good friends, still were, but in their early twenties, Raff had stopped taking to late-night carousing in the pubs with Fitz. More than once he'd had to haul Fitz away before he got bashed and it had worn thin on him. For that, they'd parted company.

'You want to be clobbered within an inch of your life, fine, but I'm not being clobbered with you anymore and then havin' to drag your sorry arse outta trouble,' he growled, half-carrying a slobbering and bleeding Fitz on foot over the rough road home. 'Quit the hard drinking, and stop looking in the wrong places, you fool.' He'd flung Fitz onto the stoop of his mother's house next door to where Raff lived. 'Get some sense into you, before you get killed.'

That had been ten years ago. Fitz had given away the hard liquor, but also drifted away from Raff. They never spoke of those missing years. Then six years ago or so, Fitz had come back to himself and returned to Raff's company, sober and happier. Why he was good again then, Raff didn't know. But then something had gone wrong, very wrong, something that dimmed Fitz's new zest for life. He'd been crushed, and wouldn't say why. Raff had pressed, but apparently some things couldn't be shared even between friends.

Next thing, Fitz had decided to try to make a life with a woman, with his friend, Evie.

'Why Evie?' Raff couldn't hide his sudden surprise when Fitz had told him his plans. 'Why her?' He didn't understand. He felt out of breath—shocked, he realised. He hadn't known how much Evie had come to mean to him.

'Why not? I like her. That's a good reason.' Fitz smiled almost to himself. 'Good catch, I'd say. I think she thinks the same of me.'

'Fitz—'

'Time for me to turn over a new leaf.' The smile wasn't so confident now.

Raff's rage, fear, loss was all mixed up in one. 'But you won't be— How do you think you'll be … suited?'

'Never fear, boyo,' Fitz had said, until his bravado dropped. Resigned, he shrugged. 'I've made up my mind, and I'll make it work somehow.'

'You can't just change like that, can't change who you are,' Raff said, his fists bumping together, his mouth flattening.

'I'm gonna marry her, Raff,' Fitz said, sharp and low. 'You can't talk me out of it. Don't try.'

'It's wrong, Fitz.'

'No, it's right. For me.' Fitz gave him a stricken glance. 'We've already talked about marrying.' His glance had hardened. 'What?'

Raff had kept his feelings for Evie hidden, but that look, just then … Fitz knew. And he knew Raff wouldn't attempt to take Evie from him. Fitz had found her first when he'd gone to the milliner's studio asking for a hat to be made for him; that was a rightful claim.

Raff had waited too long.

Evie had never given him reason to make a move. She'd only ever been bright and cheerful when they were all together, delightful happy company. A glance here and there from her wasn't a go-ahead for him to begin courting. And he hadn't wanted to risk the chance of her rejection and lose Fitz because of it.

Too late anyway. Fitz's marriage to Evie had apparently been already on the table.

Now, though, maybe circumstances had changed. Fitz never mentioned her much anymore and Raff was sure they rarely exchanged letters, if at all.

So what am I waiting for?

His blood came up. He was waiting for Fitz to say it was over, that's what, waiting to hear that he had right of way with Evie, that he wouldn't be risking a good friendship doing so. He pushed thoughts of it away. *Can't think of that right now.* If Fitz needed help, Raff didn't want to be distracted. *Then* he would give Evie his full attention.

He glanced at Paddy whose warm gaze was still on him. Maybe his old man was right. *Have a good crack at it.* Get it over with. Honest is best, no matter the cost. *Bah.* He was getting soft himself with all this palaver. He stuffed another pair of pants into the bag and strapped it closed. 'Go on home, Pa. I'll send you a telegram to let you know I'm all right. You can send me one back.'

'Who can afford telegrams all over the place? You must be doin' somethin' with this wheelwright business that I wasn't.'

Raff kissed the top of his father's head and took up the reins. 'See you, Pa.'

Paddy stepped away as Raff swung high into the saddle. 'Look after yeself, son.'

'You know I will.' He nudged Bluey into a walk and slipped out the back door of his workshop. Paddy would lock up behind him, then trudge away home, not to open the place until Monday.

By that time, Raff would be on his way to Fitz in Cobram.

After passing through Bendigo.

Chapter Twelve

Bendigo
Monday 19 September

Posie had left them at Mrs Downing's so she could get to an appointment. Evie and Ann then walked to Evie's home to check on things, and to collect what mail there might have been. Disappointed, Evie stood in the hallway of her house and shuffled the mail again just to be sure.

'So, nothing from Meryl?' Ann asked.

'I thought if she received my letter, there was a chance she might have replied immediately like I asked her to do.'

'Anything could delay the mail, and who's to say when it would have been delivered to her anyway?'

'I was hopeful, that's all,' Evie said. 'I have a nagging feeling I should go there.'

'If the Edwin thing has settled down, you should.'

Nothing had occurred lately. No visits from indignant Cooper women, nor from leery Edwin. They hadn't seen the mysterious Miss Thompson at the station either, but a winking railway porter had said that perhaps he knew of their *friend*. Rolling her eyes at him, Evie tucked away the snippet to give to Mr Campbell who could pass it on to the detective, Mr Barrett.

'And on that note,' Evie said, 'I'm going to check every room.'

Ann followed. As it turned out, not a thing looked out of place, no windows broken, no malicious damage to note. After the locks had been changed perhaps Edwin's anger—or whatever it was—had cooled.

'Mr Kingsley hasn't uncovered anything more, and he hasn't heard from Mr Barrett, so perhaps there's not a lot to uncover.'

'Give it time,' Ann said. 'It's good that Edwin hasn't bothered you lately.'

Evie gave Ann a look. 'And that in itself bothers me.'

'We know the train leaves every morning for Echuca, and that paddle-steamers run up- and downriver from there. Chances are good it'll be an easy journey for you.' Ann reached over and gave Evie a quick hug. 'But Posie will have a fit if you go on your own.'

They hadn't been able to determine if there was a coach service from Echuca to Cobram. The idea of a coach didn't enthuse Evie; the riverboat would be a more comfortable, less interrupted mode of travel. The alternative was to go to Melbourne, change trains and head up to Cobram from there, but that was a much longer way around.

'Lots of women travel by day by themselves,' she said to Ann.

'It's the paddle-steamer side of things we're worried about,' Ann said. 'Few other women on them would be travelling alone. All those men onboard …'

They locked up the house after Evie had packed another bag. If she was going to leave soon, she'd now have enough clothes with her for a two week visit to Cobram. If Meryl was obliging, it should be enough time to talk through their mother's will. Evie only hoped her sister would put her up, otherwise a stay in hotel accommodation on her limited funds might well be cut short.

The next day at work, Mrs Downing had been her usual happy self, and had already started to repair a few pieces of Evie's handiwork. 'We'll carry on as if that silly manager at Craig, Williamson will come to his senses. Hopefully, Mr Campbell's letter will fix that.'

Some treasures would have to be redone from scratch; luckily, there were few badly damaged ones. Evie sat at her station cleaning a boot print from one ribbon of satin but frustrated with the damage, she discarded it and clipped a fresh piece from the roll. A few extra pennies on its price would cover the replacement material. She held the hat up over one hand to check that she'd caught all the impairment.

'A fine piece, Evie,' Mrs Downing said, admiring it. 'I do love that upturned brim at the front. It'll catch on, I'm sure.' She peered out the window. 'I thought Mr Kingsley would've returned from the bakery by now.'

Evie leaned back to peer out the window. The only person she saw had just swaggered through the gate onto the pathway to Mrs Downing's front door. 'Oh no,' she cried. 'It's Edwin.' The chair scraped on the floorboards as she pushed out of it. She sidled to the window. 'Don't answer the door, Mrs D.'

Mrs Downing thrust out of her seat, a hand to her throat. 'How dare he come here?'

Striding behind Edwin was Mr Kingsley, a bakery bag under his arm. 'Oi,' they heard him call out. Edwin turned back smartly. He had a walking cane by his side that flicked with each step.

'You stay away from this place, Mr Cooper,' Mr Kingsley said, his voice raised.

'You mistake my intention, sir,' Edwin said. Even though his back was to Evie, she knew he'd have that smirk on his face.

'I don't think I do. Remove yourself from the property.'

'I'm here to see my fiancée.'

Mrs Downing had rushed to the window's other side. 'Oh dear.'

Mr Kingsley stood firm. 'You, sir, have no fiancée and after your unconscionable actions over the last days and more, are not welcome here. You are trespassing,' he thundered.

Evie drew in a quick breath as Edwin stepped closer, the cane tapping on the paved pathway. Was he about to butt his chest on Mr Kingsley? Instead he said something Evie couldn't hear, his tone low. She knew his teeth would be bared.

Mr Kingsley straightened to meet Edwin's height. 'Out,' he shouted and stormed back to the gate.

'Oh no,' Mrs Downing said. Onlookers had emerged from neighbouring houses.

'I'll go out, Mrs D. I'm so angry, I might crack Edwin over the head with his cane and give them all something else to look at.'

'No, no, dear. Mr Kingsley has it nicely in hand.'

Edwin had begun to make his exit, stalking towards the gate.

'And make no attempt to harass these ladies again,' Mr Kingsley said loudly.

Edwin seethed another few words at Mr Kingsley then marched off.

Mrs Downing wrenched open the door and flew down to meet Mr Kingsley. 'David,' she breathed. 'What nonsense was that?'

Evie had followed her outside. 'Mr Kingsley, are you all right?'

'Lord, yes. It will take more than that sap to upset me.' He brushed at his lapels as if proximity to Edwin had left a mark. There was not a stitch out of place; he was as dapper and calm as if he'd just come from his dressing room.

Mrs Downing looped her arm through his. 'What was all that about?'

'Inside, dear ladies. Bring out the teapot,' he said heartily then ducked his head towards Mrs Downing's. 'Or the whisky.'

The tea was poured, the baker's treats of macaroons popped on a plate and there was indeed a snifter of whisky for Mr Kingsley, who'd earned it, Mrs Downing told him. Although their interaction in front of Evie had always been warm, these days it was far more relaxed and familiar. She'd pat his arm often, and he'd squeeze her hand in return.

'He made threats about going to the police. Well, I know who'll go to the police if he comes here again.'

'What a menace,' Evie said. 'I'm so sorry—'

'None of that, Evie,' Mrs Downing said. 'Clearly he'd be a menace no matter what. He's a bully, but he's been bested by Mr Kingsley.'

Evie wasn't placated. 'I've put you both in harm's way. I'm really not sure what to do.'

'At least you're at Mr and Mrs Benton's and not sitting alone in your house.' Mrs Downing reached over and pressed her hand.

Was she putting Ann and Ross Benton in harm's way as well?

Mr Kingsley downed the whisky shot in one. 'Ah, that's better. I tell you what though, Miss Emerson, I do think it would be beneficial if you were to go away for a while, so maybe that visit to your sister should be soon.'

'I think you're right, Mr Kingsley,' Evie said, and reached for a macaroon. 'Absolutely right.' She sighed inwardly. Life had been so pleasant before all this.

Chapter Thirteen

Lucille watched as Evie and Ann walked swiftly out through the gate, turned and after a quick wave were gone. She wouldn't see Evie now for at least two weeks, if not longer. *Probably a good thing until all this mess is sorted.*

She turned the shingle around on the door and twisted the key in the lock. She was heartily glad that Edwin Cooper had kept away from the place, but for the first time in her life, a frisson of fear had scooted through her. She had no idea what he might do to any of them if he retaliated.

David had stayed close by after Edwin's visit and it wasn't until Evie left with Ann for the day that he seemed to let his guard down that bit more.

'Lucille, my darling, please come and sit by me before we have dinner.' He waited until she needlessly stoked the little fire in the parlour then took a seat beside him. Opening his hand, she laid hers in it. 'I don't want you to be here by yourself.' He took a breath. 'Before we can be married, I feel that you should take in a companion boarder—'

'David, I must interrupt. I want to say something,' she said. 'You're quite right once again. I need company. So, even though we cannot marry tonight, I should like *you* to stay with me.' At the look on his face, she said, 'Or that I pack a small bag and go to your place.' And still, at his stunned silence, she went on, 'Unless of course you think I'm too forward and you would not entertain such an idea.'

'I— Well, I …' He stopped.

'Have a little think while I put a pie in the oven for our meal.' She patted his hand. 'Of course, I realise I haven't yet had a formal notice of eviction, but the fact that my landlord has been prepared to do so, and probably still intends to, is reason enough for me to smartly remove myself before it's official.' She dipped her head a moment. 'So I must apologise if I appear in a hurry to make our new life together. It's just all this unpleasantness is most unsettling.' She gave him a smile, aware she was not only rushing the situation, but also rushing this very kind and *upstanding* man. 'But I fully understand if you would rather not have anything to do with the idea, and in that case, I do hope you forgive me for being so brazen.' The creep of unnatural heat had begun in her chest.

Taking both her hands in his, he smiled broadly. 'Brazen, oh goodness. Mrs Downing, nothing to forgive, and nothing would make me happier. With your permission, I will obtain our marriage licence tomorrow and request that the registrar allows us to be married straight away.'

She took a few deep breaths, hoping the smattering of perspiration on her forehead wouldn't be noticeable. Beaming at him, she planted a firm kiss on his cheek. 'Permission granted, Mr Kingsley.'

Chapter Fourteen

Bendigo
Tuesday 20 September

Raff couldn't very well just drop onto Evie's doorstep and knock. Even if she did still reside there, what the hell would he say, anyway? *How have you been? Still stepping out with Fitz?*

Besides which, he was filthy from riding hard and sleeping rough. No woman in her right mind would receive him looking and smelling like he did. For that alone, she might send him on his way, not to mention that nearly two years had passed since they'd last seen each other.

He and Fitz had often walked Evie home in those days after they'd all been to the tearooms, the chatter lively. Conversation had been more spirited some days than others. The subject invariably turned to Fitz wanting a rover's life—with a wife in tow. The side-glance at Evie would always set her off: 'A roving life is a waste of time, and no wife would want that.' Raff always thought she meant that they'd have to stay put once they married. That wouldn't have suited Fitz.

But they hadn't married. Nothing had happened, and Fitz hadn't offered any explanation. Maybe Raff's father had been right. Fitz could be fine with the idea of Raff courting Evie. The look Paddy had given him … *Canny old bugger.* Raff shook it off, didn't want to explore any niggle that gave him hope.

Dismounting, he stared at her house wishing she'd suddenly emerge. Acutely aware he might look suspicious, he dipped to Bluey's hoof and checked a shoe. *Fine.* Checked another. *Fine.* He waited a while longer, checking this, adjusting that. Fed up with himself, he was about to mount and ride away when he saw a well-dressed, pale-faced man with a lush gingery moustache and sideburns stride through Evie's gate and up to the door. He didn't knock. Instead he took a brief glance around, barely noticed Raff, then took a sideways step to peer in the front window.

Raff's gut clunked. He squinted, mouth set, hands bunched in the reins. A throb beat hard at his temples. *What the hell is he doing?*

Again, the man took a look around. This time his glance lingered a second on Raff, who'd swung onto Bluey and begun a slow walk towards the house. Ambling by on his horse, taking his time, he might just have been passing except for his lengthy, unwavering, squinty-eyed scrutiny. The man jittered and, straightening his coat and ducking his head, marched down the short path and away from the house. He didn't look back.

Raff followed at a leisurely pace, easy on Bluey's swaggering stride, and soon the man was well on his way ahead. Turning Bluey left into a road, Raff doubled back at a slow canter. He rode two streets down and turned into Evie's once again.

Bugger me, the bloke's had the same idea.

The man was ahead of Raff and hadn't seen him. He was sprinting to the house. Two women had appeared on the stoop and one of them let out a yelp. Not Evie, but she was there. His chest boomed. The other woman clutched at her. Shouting ensued and Evie snatched her arm clear of the man's grab at her.

Bastard.

Raff nudged Bluey. The horse leaped forward and in quick time hooves trod the footpath. Then the mighty horse squeezed through the gate into the little yard.

Gaping, the women flattened themselves against the door of the house.

Bluey got his bearings then sent the man staggering when his great flank bumped him. Then his hefty rump shoved the bloke into the garden bed and, indignant, Bluey snorted and then blurted spit. Annoyed, he then stomped on the shrubbery.

Raff leaned down. 'Beg pardon. My horse got away from me.'

'Get your horse out of it,' the man bellowed from under Bluey. He floundered around in the bushes and a fragrant, lemon scent wafted up, fresh and biting. Battling the shrubs, his hat had shot off and the earlier slick head of hair now resembled a clump of stable hay matted with horseshit.

'Sorry, mate, tiny garden. We're a bit stuck until you crawl out. Otherwise, he might trample on something precious if you know what I mean. Accidentally, of course.' Raff held Bluey, but the hooves danced—only a little.

Edwin squawked.

'Hurry up, Edwin.' *Evie.*

'Yes, Edwin,' Raff said. 'Hurry up.' He tipped his hat back a little, peering down at the fella still on his back under Bluey's belly. 'Out you get.'

'I can't move,' Edwin screeched. 'He's in the way, damn you.'

'Oh, here,' Raff said and tugged on the reins.

Bluey danced a little more and the man gave a gurgled shriek.

'No, no, you're right, that's no good,' Raff said, straight-faced. 'Best idea—crawl out on your hands and knees.'

As it was, the woman beside Evie couldn't hold in her mirth and it burst from behind the hand covering her mouth.

'Edwin, for God's sake, get out from there,' Evie snapped, bending down to eye the man flat on his back.

A fair bit of huffing and puffing went on before Edwin scrambled out to relative safety. Lurching to his feet, his face beet red, he wobbled as he snatched up his crushed hat. Bedraggled, he stabbed a finger at Raff. 'I'll have you for assault.'

'Don't reckon you will,' Raff said.

Bluey's head jerked, and the man jumped back.

'It seemed to me you were sneaking a peek in the window of this house, looking all the world like a peeping tom.' Then mildly, he added, 'Edwin.'

The flush on Edwin's face deepened. He got to the gate. 'I won't forget this,' he snarled.

'Me neither.' Raff nudged Bluey forward and Edwin was bumped outside the gate and onto his backside on the footpath. 'A terrible accident might occur, *mate*, unless you move on and keep your threats to yourself.' No longer in a laughing mood, Raff dismounted. He reached down and with both hands grabbed Edwin's coat, hauling him to his feet. 'There you go.'

Edwin, eyes popping, only stood to Raff's shoulders. Wrenching out of the steely grip, he took a step back, fists clenched.

Raff leaned in closer. 'Best you don't take a swing. Now get your skinny arse out of here,' he said quietly.

Edwin turned and marched away, his crumpled hat taking the brunt of his fists as he tried to get it back into shape.

Raff led Bluey onto the footpath to turn him back towards the house. He tipped his hat. 'Ladies. Apologies for the ruined garden.'

The other woman was smiling broadly at him. 'We don't mind, do we, Evie? I'd pay money to see that all over again.'

Evie had her hands on her hips. She took a step and reached out for Bluey's muzzle, giving it a rub. 'You always were a good horse,

Bluey.' When she finally met Raff's gaze, her merry smile had his heart galloping. 'Rafferty Dolan. You are a sight for sore eyes.'

Raff walked them to Mrs Benton's house. Evie must have been taking an evening meal there.

'Oh,' Evie said, flicking her hand in the air. 'Edwin's being a pest. He clearly believes he's owed something from me,' she said lightly. 'And he's not. It's nothing.'

Whatever it was, it wasn't *nothing*, Raff decided. But he kept his mouth shut. If it were to become more of his business today, he'd deal with it.

Ann spoke to Raff, who was leading Bluey on the side of the path closest to the road. 'Do you hail from Bendigo, Mr Dolan?'

'From Ballarat, Mrs Benton. I have a wheelwright's shop there.'

'Raff is a friend of Fitz O'Shea's, Ann,' Evie said, and nothing more.

'Oh,' Ann said, her gaze blank.

Talk of Fitz was not on the cards, it seemed, but he gave Evie's short explanation some context. 'The O'Shea's lived next door to my folk in Ballarat so we've been mates for years. When Fitz got his job at the Bendigo newspaper, he moved here. I'd come to visit from time to time. All his folk have gone from Ballarat now, a brother or two live further south-east.'

'Oh,' Ann said again and fell in step with Evie, glancing at her.

The walk was brisk and, for an awkward time, in silence.

Then Evie asked, 'So, Raff, what brings you to Bendigo?'

You. 'Truth to tell, I thought I'd track down an old friend. Found myself on your street, which is why I saw that Edwin fella at your window.' *Back to Edwin again.*

'Well, good thing you did,' Ann said.

Evie turned a bright face towards him. 'How long are you staying in town?'

They waited at the crossroads for a couple of laden drays to pass.

Walking again, Raff said, 'I'll be heading off tomorrow.' He took a punt, and a deep silent breath. 'I'll be happy to walk you back home, Miss Emerson, if that bloke is causing you trouble.'

'Thank you,' she said, directing her beam of a smile at him. 'But I'm not staying at home, I'm at the Bentons' for tonight.'

Because of that fella? 'Right. That's good.' He nodded towards Mrs Benton. Then to Evie, 'And your ma? What of her these days?'

'She died over a year ago, Raff.' Evie had her head down watching where she was putting her feet.

'I didn't know, I'm sorry.' Why the hell had Fitz never said? Raff remembered that there was a sister, too, but she'd moved away long before Fitz and he had met Evie.

'Where are you lodging, Mr Dolan?' Mrs Benton asked.

'Well, I've just been camping out, but I reckon tonight I'll find a good hotel with a bath and clean myself up.'

'Try the boarding house two streets over that way, the Bartletts'. It has a sign,' Mrs Benton said, pointing to the left. 'You're most welcome to take a meal with us this evening. I'm sure my Ross would enjoy the company.'

Man, he was tempted, but it wouldn't do him any good. Instead, he said, 'Appreciate it, but I'll be on my way.'

When the two women stopped outside a pleasant-looking timber home, fronted by a picket fence and a wrought-iron gate he figured they were at the Bentons'. Ann said her goodbyes and headed inside.

'Thank you, Raff,' Evie said. 'You saved me from screaming at him all the way down the street.' Her blue eyes, the colour of the sky on a clear and warm summer's day, had a spark of humour in them. 'Wouldn't have looked too good, would it?'

Everything he'd felt for her years ago was all still there, had just been locked deep inside, tucked away. Now it burst into his heart. His breath was a little short. 'Are the police no help?'

'It's no matter, it's in hand,' she said and took a swift glance at Ann's door. 'Well, I'd better go in.' She hesitated, her gaze direct. 'Raff, can I write to you at your workshop?' Another hesitation. 'Would you write back to me? It'd be just like the old days. I'd like that.'

Now we have it, the old days. She'd want to know about Fitz, all the way. No one needed to spell it out. 'Of course,' he said, amiably enough although the warmth in his chest from before had started to fizzle a bit. He tried a smile, gave a bow of sorts, as if things were formal. 'Good day to you, Evie.'

She held out her hand, sliding it into his. 'Good day, Rafferty. It was *so* good to see you,' she said, her smile tentative. She turned and walked to Mrs Benton's door.

Surprise hit him. For a moment, Raff could still feel her hand engulfed in his. *Where it should be.* He was still staring at the door as it closed. Bluey jerked the reins. Ride away. The Bartletts' boarding house. He'd go there. Get the breath back into his body.

It was so *good to see you.* So much for having a crack at it.

Chapter Fifteen

Wednesday 21 September

Bright and early, Ann had delivered Evie to the railway station. 'Yes, I'll check for your mail. I won't forget,' Ann said, 'and I'll send a telegram if there's a court summons. And, yes, I'll let Mrs Downing know about Edwin at the house. Don't worry.' A quick hug, a press of hands and Evie was on her own.

The station was bustling with people. She took her place in the ticket queue behind a mother and four children of varying ages, all very solemn and well behaved. Evie was sure that wouldn't last for long. One little girl, perhaps four or five, wore a plain neat blue dress reaching just past her knees, and sturdy boots. Her hand was on top of her straw hat as she stared up at Evie, her sombre heart-shaped face and luminescent green eyes startling. A reminder of another pair of green eyes. Jostled a little by the throng, Evie couldn't hold her gaze for long. The queue inched forward, the girl's stare remained on her.

'You have blue eyes,' the child said, a lisp softening the loud declaration. Her mother tugged her hand in reprimand and turned to give Evie an apologetic smile.

'I do,' Evie whispered conspiratorially, leaning down a little. Her backside was bumped by a man and woman trying to skirt the four children, and she straightened, impatient with the wait.

Craning her head for a look over the people in front of her, she saw the ticket master behind his mesh window facing would-be passengers whose queries were obviously bothersome.

Wonderful. A snapping, unhappy fellow when I need information, too. I might just be snapping myself when I get to him.

The stream of people in front of her moved slowly forward, and the constant noise of voices humming, or calling out, or children wailing built to a crescendo. The mother and quiet kids shuffled in front of her, the little girl still keen to keep her eye on Evie. She gave a sudden cheeky, gap-toothed grin, and Evie couldn't help but laugh. It had an immediate effect; Evie's patience returned.

Mother and family purchased their fares and went on their way. The little girl had waved, but Evie's good humour evaporated when she got to the window and Mr Grumpy was short with her. Handing over money for her ticket, she waited stonily for his response to her enquiry.

'No,' the ticket seller said, exaggerating his response. 'I got no clue how to get from Echuca to Cobram, but someone at Echuca will know, I'm sure. You should have taken the train to Melbourne first, missy.' Tetchy, dismissive, he looked past her to address the next in line with a short nod of his head.

Big help. But it was as Evie had suspected. Oh well, at least this way she'd arrive in Echuca in daylight. It wasn't going to be an issue. It only meant finding a place to stay while waiting for a boat. Echuca was a civilised place (wasn't it?) so she shouldn't have any trouble finding decent accommodation.

There had been no reply yesterday from Meryl. After another episode with Edwin there had been only one thing to do: go to Cobram, earlier than expected, and find her sister. That way, she might avoid the constant feeling that all eyes were on her and all whispers were about her. Although, while she waited for the train, she took sneaky glances to see if that Miss Thompson was nearby. What she'd do if she saw the woman, she wasn't sure, but thanking her was a distinct possibility. If Evie hadn't seen Edwin with her, she might have lacked the resolve to break it off with him when she had.

Now there was Rafferty Dolan tangling her feelings.

Ann had latched on to it pretty quickly. 'My goodness,' she'd said in the kitchen last evening while they prepared the meal. 'You never mentioned you knew such a man as that.' There was an approving tone.

Evie bent over the peas, shelling furiously. 'He was—is—Fitz's best friend.'

'Fitz's best friend? Oh, I don't think he's only that, Evie. What about to you? Nothing else to say?'

Lifting a shoulder without looking up, Evie said, 'That's all there is to it.'

Ann considered the response. 'Hmm. Did he say where Fitz is?'

'I didn't ask.'

Ann tried again. 'He seems a different sort of friend for Fitz to have. I mean, Fitz has an education, he's a journalist, he dresses rather … nicely.' She had been dicing meat and onions, and now with a dollop of lard they sizzled in a pan. 'Mr Dolan is a wheelwright. Oh, I don't mean a lesser-class person,' she added quickly at Evie's frowning glance. 'I mean, different set. You know.'

Evie didn't know. 'Raff has the same trade as his father,' she said, not minding that Ann was after more information. 'Mr Paddy Dolan is an Irishman who married a girl from Ballarat. She was a teacher, so all three Dolan boys can read and write. Raff is the eldest.' She grew hot, perhaps being under Ann's steady gaze or, most likely, she was just sitting too close to the cooker. That's all it was. Moving her chair away, she slid the bowl of peas across the table with her. 'They all have the same trade, but I think the younger boys live somewhere south.' She took a breath. 'The Dolans' business in Ballarat is known to be quite a good one.'

'Ah, a businessman,' Ann said and sat down to peel potatoes. 'Well, then.'

Studiously nonchalant with the peas thereafter, Evie hadn't said anything else. Raff was leaving town tomorrow, so that was that. No point telling Ann she'd be writing to him and fuelling her curiosity.

At times through the night, she'd woken to recall that split-second hesitation when he'd agreed to write. Obviously, she'd put him in an awkward position; she shouldn't have been so forward. He was, after all, Fitz's friend; he wouldn't want anything to do with her, all that man-to-man honour et cetera. The conversation had been stilted, each leaving out mention of the one person who loomed large. And then Raff's smile as he'd said goodbye. Had it been a little sardonic? No, no—it was lopsided, so it was perhaps … wistful.

Oh dear. Perhaps he was attached, or even married. A thump of heartbeats coursed through her. *Oh no.*

Try as she might, deep sleep eluded her. At some late hour, she chastised herself. There was a big day ahead, but thoughts of Raff Dolan were first and foremost: that easy grin, those intelligent green eyes under his battered wide-brimmed hat. The hat was much loved and well-worn in. And was that red-and-black feather tucked in its band the same one she'd given him years ago? She smiled at that, then at the picture of him at ease in the saddle on Bluey, a big man on a big horse, standing over the awful and blustering Edwin Cooper. She'd drifted off, the smile in place.

Now on the train and seated by a window, waiting to depart, Echuca and beyond was foremost in her mind. She was as equipped as she could be for the short term, had her bag packed with the necessaries: a spare dress, her smalls for a few days, and a nightgown. She carried an extra blanket that Ann had loaned her.

A peculiar excitement bubbled in her chest. She was looking forward to seeing Meryl, at least to try and make whatever was wrong between them finally right.

The train's throaty, piercing whistle shattered her thoughts, and the carriage lurched forward and away from the platform.

Cobram was not far away. Suddenly, all things ahead of her were brand new.

Chapter Sixteen

Bendigo

'My dear, I brought a cup of tea.'

A fragrant waft of something floral reached him. David opened one eye and saw Lucille hovering close by. Before he knew it, a little moan had escaped. His back creaked. Lucille's settee was comfortable to sit on, not so much to sleep on.

'Delightful,' he said. 'Thank you and good morning.' He sat up, swung his feet to the floor, the blankets still draped over him. He had a moment's horror wondering if he'd snored the place down.

'I do wish you'd taken the children's room.' Lucille sat across from him, holding a cup as well, a little frown of concern fluttering over her features.

Perhaps he had snored. *Good Lord. Poor woman. She might think twice about marrying me.* His fault, he had insisted on sleeping here. 'This is the best place for me to be in case nefarious creatures sent by who-knows-who were to attempt a break-in,' he'd said.

Staying the night at Lucille's house was a wonderful idea, but he didn't want the awful goings-on to mar the start of their new lives together. So, after skirting the idea of sleeping in her bed, he decided, with his dear lady's blessing, that they would remain virtuous until they were wed. Then they'd laughed together—at themselves, David thought—but it was a good plan. 'This mischief from Edwin Cooper will end soon and then we'll be free to enjoy ourselves properly,' he'd said.

For a few minutes, they chatted while they drank their tea. Then Lucille smiled and stood. 'Eggs for breakfast?'

'That sounds very good.'

She showed him where he could freshen up, shave if he wished. By the time he had made his way to the kitchen, breakfast awaited, hearty and hot.

'You don't want to let me get used to this treatment, Lucille,' he said and patted his stomach.

'Only for special occasions.' Lucille eyed him. 'I don't think you need worry. You're very trim.' She dished up and joined him at the table. 'What will you do today?'

The plate before him befit a king, piled high with eggs and bacon, and steam coming from thick slices of warm bread. 'I just might venture down to the railway station and see if I can clap eyes on this Miss Thompson.' He'd just taken a mouthful of egg slathered onto bread when he noticed she was staring at him.

'I think, Mr Kingsley, that might be a job for the two of us,' she said smartly.

He chewed and swallowed. 'Of course. You're absolutely right about that, Mrs Downing.'

They decided Lucille should be the one making enquiries.

The railway porter eyed them, first one then the other. 'A Miss Thompson, you say?' He was making a calculation, rocking on his heels, his broad waist straining his buttons. 'Not the first to ask after 'er.'

'Wasn't that the name our daughter mentioned, dear?' Lucille said to David.

'Yes,' he answered, taking a curious look around. 'Our Jenny has become incapacitated, but she sent us and said we were to thank a lovely lady by the name of Miss Thompson. She met her here.'

The porter's beady eyes popped. 'Lovely? I think you might have the wrong Miss Thompson.' His grin was a mouthful of cracked and missing teeth.

'Oh, about so high,' Lucille said, her hand at her head. 'Brown hair and eyes?' Fully aware she was describing more than half the population of young women in Bendigo, she kept a blank smile on her face. She noticed movement, a lithe figure in a gaudy pink outfit had darted across the platform. 'Is that her there?' *Oh dear, where* did *she get that hat?*

The porter turned for a swift look. David shrugged at Lucille while the man's back was turned.

'Aye, that's her,' the porter answered, looking at Lucille. 'Though I doubt she'd know any lady.' He frowned. 'What'd she need to be thanked for?'

David piped up, 'You know, my dear, I think this gentleman is quite right. Our Jenny wouldn't have meant this Miss Thompson.'

Miss Thompson was smiling expectantly at another man on the platform and trying to strike up a conversation. The harried man couldn't get away quick enough and didn't know where to hide.

Lucille's eyes widened. 'Goodness, I agree. We'll have to check—'

'Course if there's money involved, *this* Miss Thompson might be your girl.' There was a leer. 'Yairs, *this* Miss Thompson requires a fee for services,' he said wide-eyed. 'Does real well, I'm told.'

David took Lucille's elbow, thunder on his face. 'Thank you, but in that case, we are most definitely mistaken,' he said stoutly and made an about-turn and marched them away.

Lucille walked briskly, trying to hold in her laughter. 'Oh, Mr Kingsley, you can sound so very affronted.'

'I can, can't I?'

She tucked her arm in his and gave it a squeeze. 'At least now we're reasonably sure what she looks like. But what on earth would Edwin Cooper want with her?' After a moment's billowing silence, she tugged David's arm. 'I meant in broad daylight at the railway station, where he knew Evie would see him talking to her.'

He thought about it then said, 'Maybe he was paying her for appearances, to set up a ploy of some sort.' He smiled at Lucille, happy with his deduction. 'That might be it.' When they reached the concourse outside, David recognised a man pulling up in a buggy. No one could miss that streak of white in his hair. 'Mr Barrett,' he called.

Mr Barrett had alighted and was doffing his hat. 'Good afternoon, Mr Kingsley.'

'This is my friend, Mrs Downing. Lucille, Mr Bendigo Barrett, private investigator,' David said. 'Mrs Downing is the dear lady who employs Miss Emerson.'

Mr Barrett dipped his head towards Lucille. 'Mrs Downing. Delighted.'

'And we have news,' David said dropping his voice. 'We believe we've spotted the elusive Miss Thompson.'

'She is just the person I was here to enquire about, Mr Kingsley. You might have saved me some work.'

'Dressed in many shades of pink, Mr Barrett,' Lucille said. 'And wearing the most dreadful hat. You can't miss her.'

Mr Barrett smiled at that. 'Then if you'll excuse me—'

'And it seems she might charge a fee.' David was wide-eyed.

'Ah,' Mr Barrett said. 'I shall have to be clever then. Good day to you both.'

'Er, you won't need me, Mr Barrett?' David asked.

A few seconds ticked by while Mr Barrett considered, then he said, 'It might not work in our favour to be seen together.'

'Quite right,' David agreed. 'Of course. Makes sense.'

Bendigo Barrett tipped his hat. 'Good day.' He headed for the station platform.

'Goodness. He's a handsome man,' Lucille said, looping her arm in David's. 'But not nearly as handsome as my David.' She smiled at him.

Chuckling at that, he squeezed her arm. 'Come along, Mrs Downing,' he said. 'Let's find that registrar and give him the hurry-ups for our marriage licence.'

Chapter Seventeen

Cobram
Saturday 17 September

McFadyen's store stocked all manner of things. It wasn't the only store in town, but here he was. Fitz gazed at the crammed merchandise. Women's things were in abundance, hanging on rods dangling from the ceiling, or packed high into pigeon-hole shelves on the wall. For men, shirts, pants, belts and boots just as Robbo had told him, adorned a long bench. Grocery items to suit any budget and taste surrounded him on timber benches and hutches. Fresh vegetables were in boxes stacked side by side on tables down the middle of the store. On the far wall at the back were wine and spirits. Sweet treats and cough mixture lined the counter itself—everything a town like this could want and need.

And there was his target, a store assistant. Two in fact; a woman was behind the counter serving a lady customer, and the man, wearing a dark apron, was brushing off sawdust as he approached. He was clean-shaven, and his short, dark and neatly clipped oiled hair was parted down the middle.

His was a cheery welcome. 'Morning, sir. How do? What can I help you with?'

Fitz greeted him with a nod. He'd spied a stack of newspapers, but further than that he hadn't really given it much thought. *Food, always a good idea.* 'I'm after a few tins of bully beef, some potatoes, too. A newspaper.'

'Right over here,' the man said, his opened arm directing Fitz to the opposite end of the store where the ladies stood. 'New to town?' he asked, ducking behind the counter for a paper bag and heading for the box of potatoes.

Fitz nodded. 'Seems a good place here, but I'm not sure if I'll stay or head upriver.'

'It's a good place all right,' the man confirmed. 'The weather's good, the river's good, the people.'

'What about land here?' Fitz asked as he sauntered down the aisle, eyeing cabbages and cauliflower, carrots and peas. He wandered back, swiping up a cherry from a full basket. 'I'm looking for something to buy.'

'Not sure I'll able to help there. I'm a townie, Mister …?'

'Morgan.'

'Well, Mr Morgan, I don't know much about the land side of things. Only place I've heard of might be available is a plot not far from here. That's if you like living close to the river, mind.' The man was piling potatoes into the paper bag. 'She can get a bit wild when she rises, if you know what I mean.'

'I do.'

'Course, only once we get a good rain, that is, and break the drought. Then look out.' He shook his head as if remembering the wild days, shovelling spuds into the bag.

Fitz held up his hand to stop him at eight potatoes. 'It looks like good land around here for crops or an orchard, maybe.' He noticed the woman behind the counter glance at him.

'Norman,' she called over as her customer left. 'If you're talking about the Bayley's place, we don't know what'll happen to it now.'

'Yairs,' Norman said, still shaking his head. 'Terrible thing.

Mr Bayley's been gone a long while, left his wife out there.' He leaned towards Fitz. 'Now she's been found dead over her boy's grave just real recent.'

News flies, small towns. 'Terrible,' Fitz murmured. He wanted them to rattle on, not shut down. 'Terrible,' he repeated into the silence, and drew a breath at the memory of Meryl Bayley. 'So where has Mr Bayley gone?'

Norman moved from the vegetables to back behind the counter. He reached overhead for tins of beef on the shelf at the back. 'Well,' he started, choosing the right words. 'No one knows.'

'Sod,' the woman said under her breath and begun unfolding and folding towels from an already neat stack. 'He just left her out there on her own.'

'Now, Maud, we don't know what happened.' Norman leaned over the counter towards Fitz. 'Hard yakka up this way, truth be known, hard all over the place—if you know what I mean,' he said and dropped his voice, glancing at Maud. 'Maybe there were other problems, y'know?'

'Is that the place between parcels of land belonging to someone else?'

'That's the one. And that's the other story,' Norman said, almost a whisper. 'Some reckon Bayley was run off the place, but they couldn't budge the missus away from her boy's grave.'

Jesus, that's the story, right there.

'They say, one day she comes into town long after Bayley had gone, and she had a black eye, and bruises here,' Norman said, and tapped his neck either side with both hands.

Shit.

'Poor woman,' Fitz murmured, remembering the day they'd found her.

'Yair, but she said nothin', she didn't go to Constable Stillard, did she, Maudie?'

The woman shook her head, her mouth downturned.

'Stillard is the usual man here,' Norman explained and went on stacking tins of beef. There were already six in the bag, so Fitz held up his hand again. 'He's off on leave, prob'ly scouting for a new post,' he said, reaching across in a stretch to grab a newspaper. 'They say he'll be leavin' here soon. Town will be less for it.'

No one mentioned the stand-in policeman. So far, Fitz had learned only one new thing, and that was bad enough to know.

'So, the newspaper office,' he began as Norman slid the paper into the bag. 'There's no one there.'

'They come in to work late today. Stay until late, too. But all the up-to-date news in the district is in here.' He tapped the paper. 'After something in particular?'

'Just interested. The newspaper usually has all sorts of information a man might need.'

'Maybe, but not everything.' Norman's glance darted to Maud, who was busy folding whatever she got her hands on, her face set in disapproval. 'There's a man, a Mr Haines,' he whispered. 'Don't get on his wrong side. He wants that land you mentioned. Some say he had the boys beat up Bayley's missus.' Norman checked Maud again. 'Maybe worse.'

Maud cleared her throat just before the door opened. 'Morning, Mr Haines.'

Norman smiled broadly at Fitz. 'There you go, Mr Morgan. I'll tally up for you.' He scooted down the length of the counter for a pad and pencil, and returned.

'Mr Morgan,' Haines greeted effusively, his large moustache stretched over a smile. 'Thought I recognised your horse out there. We meet again.'

'Ah, yes, but I'm on my way. The good folk here have just helped me with my few purchases.'

Haines eyed the large bag in front of Fitz. 'Heading out of town then?'

Not subtle at all. 'No,' Fitz answered and handed Norman payment. Taking the bag in one arm, he nodded at Haines. 'I'll be around for a while.'

As he headed out the door, he heard Haines ask something of Norman who replied, 'Well, for a few shillings, he got a newspaper, eight potatoes and six tins of bully beef, with change. Pretty good value, wouldn't you say, Mr Haines?'

Good on you, Norman.

He loaded the goods into Patto's saddlebags. Now to do some rattling of his own.

Fitz hadn't bothered to look for his brother in town; had ridden to John's house, packed away his clothes that had stiffened on the line from the dry heat, and in the last light of day, had taken up a possie on the riverbank. Not the same place as the night before, just to be on the safe side.

It was quiet. His small fire attracted bugs, drawn into the irresistible flames only to sizzle to their end. He'd thrown a couple of taties in the coals and, once cooked, he'd knocked off the blackened skins, and mashed the hot and nutty flavoured flesh into a handful of bully beef.

This is the life. A good rum would have worked, but maybe he'd already had his quota for now.

He let the flames die, let the coals simmer down to almost nothing. It was a warm enough night; he didn't need a raging fire. There was no wind, but he was wary of letting sparks freshen and fly, so just before he was ready to roll onto his swag, he took the billy down to the river, filled it and poured it over the coals. Smoke billowed as the fire extinguished.

Patto was tied nearby, and his nosebag had done its job. The saddle and saddlebags were on the ground by him. Fitz had his rifle by his side. Satisfied, he hunkered down on his swag. Maybe *The Bulletin* would take the stories, or maybe the Melbourne paper, *The Age*. Either of his articles would suit them, the Bendigo story or the emerging one here. Maybe the *Cobram Courier* would telegraph copy to other mastheads.

Drifting off in a silence, it was a while before he realised he could hear familiar sounds. The pad of horse's hooves nearby, stepping carefully, quietly. Stealthy in the still night. Leaf litter crackled.

He rolled over, grabbed the rifle, and scrambled for his horse. Patto knickered, another horse shied. Leather squeaked.

Fitz's eyes adjusted and a huge shape loomed on the bank above, a rider on a horse. Grabbing Patto's reins he loosened them off, grabbed the saddlebags from the dirt. If whoever it was started down the bank, he'd bareback it into town, head for John's place, his written pages still with him in his pocket.

Horses greeted each other again, a snort, a blurt, hooves restless. Nothing else moved on the bank. Then sparks flew as something lobbed in the air and hit the dirt with a thud near where his head had been. The figure clambered off with a hard slap of reins on horseflesh, and hooves pounded over fine dirt; no stealth needed now.

A fizz of light. An odour, biting and hot. *Gunpowder?* A fuse …

Shit.

Chapter Eighteen

The train shunted and groaned as it slowed. Clambering past, the porter said they were nearing Elmore for 'a comfort and food stop if anyone requires it'.

Evie nodded her thanks then rubbed her tired and scratchy eyes. She stretched. It hadn't been a long run from Bendigo, but fatigue had hit her soon after departure and she'd slept patchily along the way. Peering out the window she couldn't see any sign of civilisation yet. Wondering about Meryl for the fiftieth time (she was sure), she couldn't help but recall how close they'd been as youngsters, how 'joined at the hip', their mother had said. Little girls with only a few pretty ribbons, a rag doll each, and joy in their lives. Colourful books with well-worn and tatty edges after sticky fingers had turned page after page trying to snatch at the magic and mystery within. Little girls digging in the muddy dirt, squealing with excitement that they might have unearthed a gold nugget (Mama always said she'd been hopeful). The castles they'd tried to build were a little haphazard, but that hardly mattered, even when they'd collapsed and made sloppy mud puddles. Little girls who'd sobbed when the other had sobbed, whose eyes sparkled when laughter had followed. Little girls whose grubby fingers had brushed away each other's tears, smearing *sticky* and dirt across plump cheeks that bloomed with the colour of happy or sad.

And when older girls, more of the sad than the happy. Meryl had one day been a laughing girl, and the next, it seemed to Evie, she was saddened by something that couldn't be named. Meryl had wanted to sleep more, to stay secluded, to talk of dark thoughts and dark things. She had lost the power to laugh and when she'd tried, there was always a shadow behind her eyes. Meryl changed again, seemed to return to that happy young woman, but Evie came to recognise her sister's awful companion, melancholy; she had no other name for it.

Meryl fought the thing with all her strength, but there were days, as Meryl approached her late twenties, that Evie knew the beast still gnawed at her sister, making its presence felt. No amount of cajoling could budge it. At times Meryl appeared to be on the other side of it but it still lurked within, smug and devious, waiting to strike once more.

Had it finally gained control, and inveigled Meryl into a terrible act, the demon exacting its end?

Evie shied away from that. The Meryl she knew was a fighter, not with fists or words, but with a stoic resistance to what ailed her, however hard it might be to resist giving in.

The train lurched, a squeal of brakes hauled it back, and it resumed at less pace. The hazy dob on the horizon was probably the township. It would be a joy to walk for a while and stretch her limbs properly.

Chapter Nineteen

Raff had a compartment to himself and hoped it would stay that way right through to Echuca. It was a long while since he'd been on a train, and he couldn't recall if Bluey had travelled by rail at all. He was in the cabin nearest the back exit, the freight car with Bluey in it was behind. He'd arrived early at Bendigo station, on advice, to make sure he could settle the horse before the noisy bustle of other passengers wanting to board. The porter told him the horse would be fine and if Raff mucked out his stall in the carriage, all would be well. Poor Bluey would most likely have to get on a paddle-steamer, too. The horse's comfort was important, but not enough of a distraction to keep Raff's mind off what he'd read in the newspaper at the Bartletts' guest house.

Last night, he'd secured Bluey in one of the stalls out the back of the place and paid for a room and a bath. Lugging hot water inside for himself, he'd only half-filled the small tub in the bathroom and then locked the door. A clean towel and a long-handled brush sat alongside a used cake of soap. On a chair nearby was a stack of the *Bendigo Advertiser,* and a sign on the wall read, 'No Smoking Cigars'.

Stripping out of his clothes, he'd kneeled then dipped his head into the water, sudsing his hair, then he'd folded his body into the shallow warm water and scrubbed. The bath had cooled fast. Stepping out, he'd towelled off, dressed in the same clothes, snatched a newspaper from the top of the stack and headed for his room.

Eyeing the bed, he'd known his feet would hang off the end of it. At home, he'd built himself a decent-sized bed in the loft above the shop, and sorely missed it if ever he was away for any reason. Even his swag was on the short side. Didn't matter, he'd rest well enough tonight.

He'd lit the tiny lamp, stretched out on the bed and propped on an elbow. Flicking through the newspaper, he'd skipped the advertisements, and turned the pages until he'd found the main news. Some poor bugger had been killed in a cart accident. A woman had suffered fatal burns when her dress had caught alight at the cooking hearth. A little kid had had his leg severely lacerated climbing a fence (fleeing someone else's yard). The council was upset about the number of signs on a public road obstructing safe travel. The police had arrested a drunk harassing customers in a barber's shop. And—

… Miss Evie Emerson …

He'd squinted.

The engagement of Miss Evie Emerson, eldest daughter of the late Mr and Mrs Dallas Emerson, to Mr Edwin Cooper Esq., son of Mrs Beryl Cooper and the late Mr Arthur Cooper.

He'd squeezed his eyes shut, blinked hard. Pulled the paper closer and read it again. Peered at the date on the paper. Only a week or so ago. He'd sunk back on the bed, the paper falling on his chest.

His Miss Evie Emerson? Sweet Jesus. Evie was engaged *to that stupid bastard.*

He'd tried to shove away the dense disappointment. What were the chances? He didn't want to believe it, but here it was—she was engaged to some idiot who looked like he wasn't worth spit. That meant she and Fitz were well and truly over, and must have been for a while. Fitz never said. *Why?* And why the *hell* hadn't Raff bothered to ask him?

He'd groaned aloud, held his head in his hands. *No, no, no.*

After that, sleep had been elusive for long hours.

The train chugged along. He stared out the window not seeing the open country, the scrubby plains that stretched under the wide cloudless sky. Part of the newspaper page was in his pocket now. He'd torn it out and read it more than once in the crisp early light this morning. He'd then folded it and shoved it in his waistcoat pocket. *Don't know why, each time I read the blasted thing, it's still the same words.*

The pace slowed, a whistle blasted; Elmore station must be close by. He'd alight, check the horse, and maybe he'd have time to buy a bite for himself before they got underway again.

When he was done finding Fitz and done learning what the hell had happened between him and Evie, when he was on his way home—whenever that would be—he'd dodge Bendigo as if it had a plague. If sighting Evie yesterday hadn't been so fresh in his mind, would he have the thud in his chest? Would his pulse be pounding? Would the ache in his head feel as if a tight band was squeezing his temples?

Best to forget her. Best to forget.

But Fitz. He hadn't said a word. Not a bloody word. Why hadn't he told his best mate that he was no longer on Evie's dance card? And Evie had asked Raff if she could write to him. What the hell was that all about? No point writing—even if it was to ask about Fitz—when she was engaged to someone else. He couldn't work it out.

So, best to leave it alone. *Best to forget her.*

The speed dropped back even further; the carriage lurched. Glimpsing the squat red-brick building of the Elmore station he knew they weren't far from stopping. His stomach growled and that was good sign.

Enough of Evie Emerson.

He left his hat on the seat so folk would know there'd be someone returning; the rest of his stuff was still with Bluey. It was safe enough to open the back carriage door, and he stood on the steps as the train slowed and jumped onto the platform. He jogged until he reached the freight car and when the train stopped, he pulled open the personnel door.

His eyes adjusted to the dim light. Bluey was fine; there was mucking out to do, and it might as well be now. He peeled open one of the sliding doors opposite the platform side, grabbed a shovel, scooped up Bluey's calling cards and hurled them out onto the dirt. That'd do until the next stop, anyway. He dragged the door closed, checked the nose bag and the water bucket. His horse was comfortable.

Right, now food and water—or something stronger—for me.

He swung onto the steps outside the car, ready to leap to the ground between the rail lines when at the far end of the platform, two men on horses caught his eye. They were watching passengers disembarking the train, each person scrutinised and the companions who met them studied. No one escaped their inspection.

Raff didn't like it. A flurry of prickles stung his hands. He pulled back up the steps out of their sight. He'd seen one of those fellas before, recognised that posture leaning over the horse's neck, the gloved hands wrapped in the reins, crossed at the wrists, hat pushed low and a kerchief high on his throat.

Bah, could be anyone from this distance, he reasoned. But it wasn't just anyone, he knew it. *Bill McCosker. Bloody hell.*

Flattening himself against the door of the freight carriage, Raff thought fast. Were they looking for him? They'd expect him to board here just like Fitz had done the last time he and Raff had got out of Bendigo in a hurry. So he might be all right; McCosker wouldn't expect him to already be on the train.

Slipping back inside the personnel door, he felt for a latch on the inside. There wasn't one. Of course not. Horses don't need to lock themselves in, nor do cages of poultry or boxes of cabbages.

The sliding doors. He secured the bolt to the floor of the one he'd opened earlier and then sidled into Bluey's stall. Wouldn't do much good; if they did come to the freight car, he was a sitting duck.

Chapter Twenty

Evie had waited her turn at the privy then washed her hands at the tap on the station wall and mopped her face. She lifted her hat a little. Pinned tight to her hair, it wouldn't be coming off her head any time yet. It was a perky little blue straw boater, with a white feather and sprigs of deep purple lavender adorning the side. An older lady, who'd introduced herself as Mrs Leane, had commented on how lovely she thought it was. Evie had told her that it was one of her creations and reached into her purse to give the lady her card: "Miss Evie Emerson, Milliner of Bendigo at Mrs Downing's studio".

'We need more such skills up our way, Miss Emerson. Perhaps you'll spend some time in Echuca?' Mrs Leane's hat was a little worn and sat precariously on an abundance of wiry red hair.

Evie demurred. 'I'm not staying there long, Mrs Leane, I'm heading to Cobram. But if I can, I'll certainly see what I can do to help provide some lovely pieces to your local shop.' Mrs Downing might now be stuck with an overabundance of hats because of the trouble Edwin had caused. Perhaps she and Evie could transport the excess to Echuca if there was a shop that might take them.

The woman beamed. 'That would be marvellous. Good day,' she said, tucking Evie's card into her dress pocket.

What a grand idea. Evie would write to Mrs D immediately she got access to paper and ink.

A thought tickled at the edges of her mind. Could she set up a small studio herself? Branch out. *Be an independent woman.* Oh, that sounded grand, too. She would think some more on that. She was certainly skilled, and thanks to Mama, she had some means to back the venture.

Before returning to the train she'd gone in search of food. Ladies with baskets were selling bites to eat, and she handed over a shilling for a small custard tart (oh, couldn't resist) and a couple of boiled eggs. Her purchases were placed in a paper bag that cost her an extra ha'penny to keep. She'd eat on the train once they were underway again.

The day was warm, and the oily steam of the train hung over the platform. She walked through the building to the town side. The dusty concourse was only wide enough for carts to drive in and out in single file. Not much to the town, either. A few buildings here and there; perhaps a little sparse to be called a town.

A couple of ladies walking past waved to her and, a little surprised, she lifted a hand to wave back. Nobody waved to strangers in Bendigo. Children danced behind the women, little girls and boys playing some game in the dirt, squealing with laughter as they skipped along.

As she turned to head back, she nearly stepped in front of two men on horses who were riding from around the end of the station building. One of them, a kerchief high on his neck, gave her a good glare as he passed. The horses kicked up dust and twigs.

Rude. Manners these days are out the window. Brushing the dirt from her dress, she was just about to continue when one of the horsemen wheeled about, the man with the kerchief.

'Excuse me, miss, were you on that train?'

As if she would answer a stranger, especially one whose manners were sadly lacking.

'McCosker, police sergeant, retired,' he said gruffly, snatching off his hat to reveal a bald head and lush fuzzes of wiry hair over his ears.

He'd finally remembered some graces. Would that change her mind? No. She began to walk for the platform.

'Miss, help us out, just some information. A very bad man is on the loose, ridin' a huge black horse. Can't miss 'em. We presume he's between here and Echuca. We want to try to stop him getting to the river and heading downstream.' Sergeant McCosker had tried a smile, which was less than encouraging. 'Big fella, black hair, green eyes.'

Evie didn't falter. 'No, Sergeant, I've seen no one of that description on the train. Good day,' she said, her tone frosty. She continued without a backward glance and heard one of them muttering about a stuck-up something-or-other, and that they should check the post office. Too dignified to drag him off his horse and give him *stuck-up*, she marched away through the terminal to the train.

Her breath was short. She knew one person who fitted the description Sergeant McCosker had given. She hadn't lied to the policeman, *retired* (whatever right that gave him to accost civilians). She hadn't seen *a big fella, black hair, green eyes* on the train at all. Was it even Raff he'd been talking about? If she hadn't seen him yesterday, would she even have thought they might be looking for him?

Passengers were embarking again for the next part of the journey so she rushed to step on board. She knew by the reports in the newspapers that Fitz had got himself in some sort of mess with the police—had Raff been involved too? She should have asked him about Fitz, about everything, but it hadn't seemed right when she last spoke to him.

Why *had* Raff been in Bendigo yesterday? *I thought I'd track down an old friend*. Surely Fitz wasn't in Bendigo. Though Evie didn't know where he was. Uneasy now, she was sure she'd done exactly the right thing not telling that McCosker person anything. In her compartment, she sat, dropped her bag of goodies beside her. Her heart took off galloping again. She wanted to scratch her head in frustration but the jaunty little hat, pinned tight, prevented that. Well, Rochester wasn't far up the line. Perhaps she'd find out then if Raff was on board. Oh, goodness, what was going to slow her racing heart?

Her elbow on the windowsill, she watched the two men on horseback. They were now sitting idly at the northern end of the platform checking every window.

Well, the custard tart was calling. After eating, she'd wait until the train had departed and the men were out of sight before taking a nonchalant wander along the corridor.

Chapter Twenty-one

Cobram
Saturday 17 September

The boom had been deafening. Patto reared, wrenching the reins as Fitz held on tight. The last thing he wanted was to be chasing a spooked horse in the dead of night—or worse, losing the horse altogether.

No more noise. He'd calmed Patto, secured him. Then he'd found his swag, dragged it to where he'd tied the horse and made a bed, the saddle under his head, the bags kept close by. When he woke at dawn, his sleep having been fractured, light, he saw that the firecracker wasn't the only thing that had been tossed. There was a small rock with a paper wrapped around it, tied with string.

His lip curled. Such sophistication. He didn't have to read it to know what it'd say. As soon as it was light, sure enough, he saw that a bold, literate hand had written, *'Get on your way.'*

He tucked the note in his pocket and decided John didn't need to see it. Not yet anyway. He lit the fire, took his time making a billy tea and ate a few bites of hot bully beef straight from the tin. Squatting by the fire, poking the glowing sticks and coals, he wondered if he was being watched now. Couldn't see anyone, but that didn't mean much. He doused the fire then packed the horse. Time to head for the *Cobram Courier*, then drop into the post office to see if Raff had made contact. Fitz was keen to write the story about Meryl Bayley, but would have to cool his heels until he could tell Evie about her sister.

He and Patto picked their way up the bank to where Fitz thought the rider had been. Nothing but hoofprints were in the dirt. It could've been any number of local fellas who'd know their way around in the dark, but it must have been someone who'd seen him find his camp.

My money's on Haines.

Patto sauntered through town, Fitz on his back, past early traders who exchanged nods in greeting as they swept the footpaths in front of their stores. He pulled up at the *Cobram Courier*, tied Patto out the front. Opening the door, he gave a silent sigh of relief. *At last.*

'Are you the editor?' he asked a young man in a dark apron, his hands and fingernails stained black.

'He's gone home for breakfast.'

'I'm Mr Fossey,' Fitz said.

'Ah, Mr Fossey.' Recognising the name, the man's eyes widened. 'The roving reporter. It's grand to meet you, Mr Fossey. I'm Ned Wilson.'

Pleasantries aside, Fitz didn't want to linger over stories of his known exploits. 'You might be aware, Mr Wilson, that I tend to keep out of the limelight, so if you wouldn't mind keeping my visit to yourself …?'

'Course. Absolutely.'

'Your editor might like to handle this himself. Would you see that only he opens it?' Fitz passed over the envelope. Now he was here, and seeing the fervent light shining from Mr Wilson's eyes, he wished he'd simply shoved his article anonymously under the door.

'I certainly will, Mr Fossey. Keep up the good work.'

Fitz turned to leave. 'Not another soul, mind,' he said and waited for the typesetter to nod. 'Good day.'

He was quick to remount Patto, and wondered if someone crooked might have seen him in the newspaper office. *Too late now.* At least his letter would get to whom it was intended.

At the post office, Raff's telegram was waiting for 'Mr Fossey'. Typical Raff, the barest shred of information: *On my way*, he'd written. He could be anywhere between Ballarat and here. They'd talked about him getting to Echuca and taking a paddle-steamer upriver the same as Fitz had done. Either way, riding or riverboating, Raff would still be at least a couple of days away. He tucked the telegram into his pocket and turned to leave.

'Mr Fossey.' The clerk had called him back. 'We have a package here for you, too.'

Fitz took the bulky package. He presumed it would be the latest Ballarat newspapers that featured his stories, and others on the police corruption debacle. The bundle was tied firmly with heavy string and by the postmark had arrived late last week. It wouldn't be completely up to date, but better than nothing.

He headed outside for Patto and jammed the package into a saddlebag, keen to find a quiet place where he could spread out the newspapers and get lost in them. He could've written one more article, damning McCosker with information so far not aired, but he'd rather someone else reported it. *Shirker.* He'd do it if no one else had but now he had other concerns. All very well to be on the side of the right, but being righteous often meant you had to duck your head. If McCosker got to him, he might lose his head altogether.

The story he'd uncovered was just that. Someone in McCosker's loose troop of followers, made up of bad police and crooks on the street, had lost his head. It was made to look as if a train had gone over him; maybe it had, but not before someone had wielded a big enough knife, something sword-like, to execute the man. The head had been sheared clean off and had rolled from the tracks into the mud and grass seeds. The rest of the body sustained no damage; it lay as a headless whole between the rail lines. It had been discovered just out of Ballarat on the Bendigo line, but no train driver had reported any incident. The violence of the act had sent shock waves through the police force.

Reporting on the grisly find had been one of Fitz's jobs. He'd seen worse, but those had been real accidents. Not premeditated decapitation.

The public were yet to learn it had been no accident. To most people, it might have been a drunk who'd misjudged his walk home from the pub, but no one in McCosker's camp would've thought that for a minute. McCosker meant it to look deliberately staged. *Don't snitch* was the message.

The police got the message all right and suddenly ranks closed. Suspects outside the force with even a smudge on their file had been pulled in for a roasting, those who showed nerves were weeded out, scrutinised, thumped around. Some of them were yanked from their beds by the scruff of the neck. Then a gold merchant had been killed defending his shop, just as the squeeze had begun, but the man's wife wouldn't testify against the offenders. McCosker had then run to ground, leaving barely a trail.

A fortnight later, Fitz had received a note written in dainty cursive, an explosive statement from an anonymous witness to the gold merchant's murder. '*I trust you, Mr O'Shea, to deliver justice.*' Strangely, as it turned out, the merchant's widow and her children had left town in a hurry at the same time. He'd kept the note with him; didn't want it left with anyone else, especially the police right now. So he hoped the merchant's death had been taken up by a city reporter, if not the city's police. Otherwise … He shook his head. *Otherwise*, he'd have to use the note sent to him and do something about it.

The newspapers safely stored in the saddlebags, Fitz loosened Patto's reins and mounted, heading for the pub. After that, he'd find his brother. Might be time to take up space at John's place so that whoever had chucked that firecracker would leave him alone.

Chapter Twenty-two

No sooner was Sergeant McCosker and company out of sight, than Evie was on her feet and in the corridor, lurching and stumbling along. She grabbed hold of door handles and rails to steady herself.

Her compartment was close to the front of the train, nearest the coal cart and the steam engine. Heading down the carriage to the back, she nodded greetings at occupants when she passed by. There was a family with three young boys in one compartment, an older couple in another, four young gentleman in shirt sleeves and braces playing cards in the next one. The train also had a few compartments empty. There was no sign of Raff. Perhaps he wasn't on the train at all. Then right at the last compartment, a thrill of triumph glided through her. There on the seat was a hat she recognised. There was no mistaking it with the red-and-black feather tucked in the band. She stood in the corridor, swaying, staring at it. Where was Raff? He'd be hard to miss along the corridor if he'd been talking to other passengers.

At the end of the carriage was a door and beyond that the cattle wagon, not always in service on every rail run, but today, here it was. If Raff was on the train, he'd have to be in there with Bluey. It could very well be that Raff had spotted the men at Elmore station and decided to take the rest of the journey in the company of his horse.

She clumped her way back to her compartment, grabbed her bag and returned to sit with Raff's hat. Why hadn't he taken it with him? In hardly any time at all they'd be at Rochester. It was only a few miles up the track. She'd have to have her wits about her, warn Raff in case he wasn't aware those men were looking for him. Although, no horse could travel faster than the train and arrive at the next town ahead of it. Even so, she'd find Raff as soon as she could. That felt … good.

Leaning across, she picked up his hat and brushed her hand along the soft barbs of the feather. Smiling, she remembered when she'd found it. It was the day she'd first met Raff. He and Fitz had agreed to meet her at the post office then would continue on to take tea in a shop nearby. Raff was visiting Bendigo on a whim, he'd said.

'At least two days' ride, to come here on a whim?' she'd asked.

Raff was sitting opposite her, Fitz alongside her, relaxed, his grin easy. Tea had arrived with a tray of little cakes that the men subsequently cleaned up. The shop had been busy with other patrons and trade was brisk and noisy.

'If Fitz hasn't told you already,' Raff had said, 'I'm here because, apparently, he can't do without my expertise in certain matters.'

'Which only sounds like you both feel like a few nights on the town, is that it?' she'd asked.

'And business to discuss, Miss Emerson,' Fitz had said, exaggerating formality and reaching for another piece of ginger cake. 'First, allow me to say that's quite the jaunty little hat you're wearing. Another creation?'

'It is.' Evie had touched the shallow rim of her straw boater. She'd sewn on a band of teal and royal-blue paisley brocade, had made a large, soft, sage floweret out of silk, and attached a sprig of teardrops to accompany it.

'Most becoming,' Fitz had said, finishing the little cake, his eyes twinkling.

Raff had only glanced at her hat, bemused.

'I'm not distracted by your smooth compliments, Fitzmorgan O'Shea. You're not the slightest bit interested in my hat. You want me to make you another, that's it, isn't it?'

After that, the conversation had changed subjects and there had been lots of stifled laughter, the joke on some character named Porky Trotter. It hadn't been terribly interesting to Evie. She did, however, remember that at that time there had been no crooked police involved, and the day had been carefree.

Once finished with tea and cake, they'd sauntered through the town gardens on their way to drop Evie at her house. A couple of pairs of red-tailed black cockatoos had flown overhead and a large black tail feather with its distinct red band had fallen out of the sky.

'That's got to be good luck,' Raff had said, and snatched it up. Smiling broadly, doffing his hat, he'd presented the feather to her.

She'd accepted, then smartly stuck it in the band of his hat. That's when she thought she'd noticed the look in Raff's eye. It had given her a jolt for a second. Fitz had noticed, had raised an eyebrow, his glance darting between the two. Raff had worn only a ghost of a smile when he'd replaced his hat and continued walking.

She sighed now. The chug of the train was rhythmic as she smoothed her fingers over Raff's hat again. How many years ago was that feather put in it? Perhaps four or more. There'd been memorable times since then, but that was the first. Dear Raff, to have kept it; he hadn't struck her as sentimental. Perhaps it reminded him of their happier, go-lucky times. These days, Fitz was off roving somewhere, Raff was being chased—she was sure—by a policeman, *retired*, and she was looking for her estranged sister.

Resting the hat on her lap, she studied it. Rough and stained, it had a hole where his fingers would pinch it when he sat it on his head. He loved this hat, that was clear. She should make him a new and different one, a dashingly handsome piece that he could wear to an art show, or a musical evening—not that he struck her to be the type. But oh, how gallant he would look. She would wear her ivory and peony to accompany him. Such a handsome couple they'd be.

Wonderful Raff. Was there ever a way to reach him?

Looking closely, she could see that the feather had been sewn onto the hat through the band. Raff, or someone, must have pierced the quill to secure it. Turning it over, she studied the band on the inside.

Her breath hitched. Where the feather had been sewn, someone had painstakingly stitched the initials: EE.

Chapter Twenty-three

Bendigo

Lucille gave a big sigh. Standing in her front room she was among masses of hats on their blocks, on hooks, in boxes and on the workstations waiting for repairs. A froth of lace and netting, feathers, and bits and bobs filled the benches and climbed up the walls.

Poor Mr Kingsley, her lovely David, might have a blue fit when all this paraphernalia got to his front room. Plus when Evie came back, there'd be another female working in his house. Not to mention the women who would arrive for appointments throughout the day.

She was certain she and David would find a way to work through it all soon, but that was enough thinking of these things for now. It was to be a wonderful day, they were to be married within the hour.

Turning side on, she checked her profile in the prized mahogany cheval. As would her clients when they first tried on their purchases, so grateful for a decent mirror. Lucille moved this way and that, checking her back, straightening her skirt, brushing down the loose folds, before adjusting her hat. It was wide-brimmed, and crammed with gorgeous organza flowers in ivory and pale pink that would have turned heads at the races. No demure veil for her; she wasn't a blushing and virginal bride. She was about to be married in a registry office and could suit herself about what she wore. Stepping confidently into marriage, she'd present herself on her wedding day as a successful, poised and stylish woman.

Her gown had no bustle, thank goodness, and no frill, nor was it overdone with lace. It was an elegant and simple design in pale-rose satin, draping to the floor. Ever pragmatic, her only concession to wedding fashion was a demi-train that could be removed if she was to wear the dress for other occasions. She'd done all the work herself, and good for her. If she had a mind and could bear the fuss, she might venture into dressmaking. *Oh, don't be silly, Lucille. What a bother that would be. There'd be more prima donnas being fitted for their gowns than there would be at the ballet.*

A knock sounded. She took one last look at herself then, with a smile to welcome her fiancé, she opened the door.

'Well,' David breathed, and stood back to admire her from head to toe. 'You do look magnificent, my dear Lucille.' Then he leaned in to press a kiss on her cheek. 'I should get you to the registrar quick smart before you change your mind.'

'Why on earth would I change my mind? You are too devilishly handsome, David.' He carried a top hat, bless him, and wore a beautiful dark morning suit and coat-tails. 'I admit, though, I had a moment of second thoughts when I looked at all this … stuff I'll be carrying to your home.'

'Not at all, dear lady.' He peered around her. 'My front room is probably twice this size. What a delight all your stuff will be to me knowing that you are in your element, safe, and right under my nose.'

'You're also very likely to have chattering women in and out of the place most days. Won't that be an intrusion?'

He touched her cheek lightly with a fingertip. 'I'll be well out of the way, so chattering women will hardly bother me at all.' He took her arm as they stepped outside. Pulling the door behind her, he locked up, and dropped the key into his pocket. 'My only worry is that your children aren't here for you today.'

'I … will miss them, the girls certainly, on a day like today, and the boys and their wives, of course.' For a moment she felt the smart of tears, the distance from the family acute. 'And Evie's not here either, but as sad at that all might be, I won't let it—' She stopped abruptly, blinking. There at her gate was a footman, of all people, waiting to hand her into a charming, closed carriage drawn by two white horses. 'Oh, David,' she said, delight in her voice.

'We will go on a small tour of the town in our finery, to announce to all and sundry that our nuptials are imminent. Then after the ceremony, we will tour to the Shamrock, only the finest hotel in Bendigo, for our wedding lunch.'

'This is beautiful.' She couldn't believe her eyes. The footman, resplendent in attire reminiscent of earlier in the century, handed her with great aplomb into the carriage then took up position in the driver's seat. As David slipped in beside her, she said, 'I have written to my children, explained we've eloped.' She leaned towards him. 'That sounds deliciously decadent.'

'Eloping is absolutely fine with me, my dear.' David took her hand in his and tapped the ceiling with his cane that had rested by the door.

The carriage lurched forward.

'So now, Mrs Kingsley,' David said to Lucille as the carriage dropped them back to her house. 'You must pack something just for the evening, and we will return to the splendour of the Shamrock for our dinner and our first night as husband and wife.'

'I'm astounded. Have I married a rich man, Mr Kingsley?'

'Unfortunately not, dear lady. But I can certainly lavish one splendid night on my new bride with the best the city has to offer.' He handed her through the door, into the chaos of her front room. 'Then tomorrow it's back to business. I've organised a couple of fellows to help us with the move. But for now, madam, your carriage awaits.'

Lucille headed for her room to pack a gown for dinner and fresh clothes for the next day when she heard a knock sound on the front door. She turned back but David had answered it.

'Mr Barrett,' David said, greeting the private detective.

'Mr Kingsley, your neighbour told me I might find you here. I must also apologise for interrupting your wedding day—and I offer heartiest congratulations—but I thought you'd like to hear the information I've acquired sooner than later.'

'Of course, of course. Come in.' He cast about, careful where he put his feet. 'Although with two of us gentlemen in Lucille's front room I'm afraid we might be a little cramped.' They were amid dozens of hats, rolls of fabric, yards and yards of feminine fluff and frippery, and barely a square inch other than dainty chairs on which to sit.

'No bother.' Mr Barrett removed his hat.

Lucille had come to stand at the studio door. 'Good afternoon, Mr Barrett.'

'Mrs Downing. *Kingsley*. My congratulations.' He dipped his head. 'I was about to tell Mr Kingsley that my sister has discovered two announcements from our Mr Cooper, one he posted in the *Bendigo Advertiser* some three years ago, and another just over two years ago. It seems he's been kept well occupied, poor fellow, being the brunt of rejection and filing for breaches of contract.'

'I bet.' David hadn't missed the sarcasm. 'Two? And were there court appearances?'

'For the earlier one. He was awarded a considerable sum against a Miss Corinne Hampstead. We've yet to find anything for the more recent breach.'

'Hampstead. We know that name,' David said and looked to Lucille for confirmation.

'A well-to-do family in Melbourne,' she said.

'Yes. Her father is in construction, doing well now that the economy has turned for the better,' Mr Barrett said. 'His company has had some contracts up this way.' He rolled the rim of his hat in his hands. 'Maybe the idea of all that new money made her an easy target.'

'Indeed. And the family paid?' David asked.

'Oh yes, thirty-five hundred pounds and damages.'

'*What?*'

'Cooper produced witness statements that attested Miss Hampstead had made it quite clear that she intended marrying him. And there were even more unpleasant implications, which I won't go into. The sum demanded was much more initially, but he finally agreed to the lesser sum the family offered. They were fortunate to be well rid of him.'

'What a business,' David said. 'And nothing on the second episode?'

'Only the lady's name so far, a Miss Horton. But if it did go to court, we will find the paperwork. We'll be able to present solid proof to Mr Campbell that, in fact, this gentleman'—again the sarcasm—'has rorted the system, and other ladies before he's had a go at Miss Emerson.'

Lucille huffed. 'Miss Emerson shouldn't need a defence against such an unsavoury character.'

'Indeed.' Mr Barrett smiled. 'It will go towards shining a light on just the sort of rat he is. With a bit of luck and good management, Mr Campbell should have him run out of town.'

'And what of Miss Thompson of the Pink?' Lucille asked.

'Needed some persuasion to tell, but finally said that she was paid to be at the railway station at a certain time on the particular day so that Miss Emerson saw her with Mr Cooper.' He spread his hands. 'That's all I have to report at this time.'

'Scandalous woman,' Lucille said, tut-tutting. 'Dreadful man.'

'Mr Barrett, please send me your invoice when convenient,' David said, beckoning Lucille.

'My services are rendered to Mr Campbell's office.'

'No, no, please let me take care of this, at least, for Evie,' David said, a glance at Lucille for her approval.

'Very well, thank you. And now I'll leave you to your happy day and bid you goodbye.' Mr Barrett headed for the door, sidling past the heavily stacked benches and tables.

'Mr Barrett, one more thing,' Lucille said following him. 'Will Miss Emerson have to defend herself in court against the charge?'

'She should be there if it comes to that, but Mr Campbell of course would front the magistrate for her.' Mr Barrett smiled again, and that intriguing white lock of hair fell onto his forehead before he donned his hat. 'And believe me, he's something to see in action. A wolf in the courtroom.'

Later that evening, with no thoughts for anything but themselves, they sprawled on a bed in the Shamrock hotel's finest room. Lucille's head was on David's chest, her fingertips running lightly over the wiry silver hair that covered it. His arms were around her.

'I have to admit,' she murmured, 'I wasn't completely sure how I'd manage that.'

'That makes two of us, Mrs Kingsley. But if I do say so myself, I think we managed rather well.'

'Splendidly, in fact,' she said and tilted her head to kiss him on the mouth.

'I had no idea your hair was so long and so soft,' he said, and picked up a lock to wind its silky waves in his fingers. 'I look forward to seeing it in all its glory every day for the rest of my life.' Then he kissed her, caressed a full breast, and hugged her closer, his hand sliding to her bottom.

Naked on the bed, her leg over his hip, with the sheets askew and two champagne coupes beside an empty bottle, Lucille Kingsley thought she'd done surprisingly well. Her body had changed considerably once she'd entered her fifties. And an enormous amount of time had passed since she was last with a man, her late husband. She'd had a moment's apprehension earlier, wondering if … things could still be … accommodated, but there'd been no need to worry. *Things* worked very well.

David's hand slid between their bodies, lightly brushing her pubic hair, back and forth, a tingle beginning under his fingers.

Lucille closed her eyes and nestled closer, believing they would do just as well again, very soon.

Chapter Twenty-four

Cobram

Robbo was in the pub, worse for wear, likely three sheets to the wind. Fitz headed over, grabbed him when the poor fella looked about to take a dive into a table. 'Robbo, what the hell are you doing?'

'I couldn't take seein' her there like that, Mr Morgan. All burned up by the sun and chewed over.' His eyes were bloodshot, bleary as if he had been crying for hours, and he was as drunk as a lord. He flung an arm over Fitz's shoulder and allowed himself to be shoved into a chair.

Big Tim at the bar shook his head, kept on polishing a glass. 'Shouldna let him in when we opened, but he was already blubberin' at the door. Good thing he's the only one in here so far.'

Fitz laid a hand on his shoulder. 'Robbo, Mrs Bayley wouldn't have suffered. She'd have been dead before the animals got her.' He didn't know that, but hoped it. 'Put it out of your mind.'

Robbo crumpled, dribble and snot running. 'But nobody cared to go check on 'er. I shoulda, I shoulda.' He held his head in his hands.

Guilt chews away at a man.

Big Tim came over with a towel, and a bowl of water. 'He can clean himself up a bit if he wants,' he said gruffly. 'He ain't the only one feels bad about Miz Bayley.' He turned away back to the bar.

'She had no one else,' Robbo croaked. 'My Jenny didn't like her much, too prickly, she reckoned, but that ain't no reason to just leave her out there on her own.'

Fitz dunked the towel. 'Robbo, hey, clean up a bit, mate, you'll feel better. Let's get some food into you.'

'Can't eat, can't eat,' Robbo said, taking the wet towel and rubbing his face hard with it. 'All them weeks, months out there, on her own.' He swung an arm around and pointed at the bar. 'An' your boss made sure of it,' he yelled.

Big Tim stopped polishing for a moment. Fitz held up a hand, indicating he'd try to calm Robbo. There was still no one else around.

'Let's get away from the pub, let's walk. C'mon, Robbo,' Fitz said, hauling the bloke to his feet. 'Come on.'

Robbo wasn't finished yelling yet. Fitz made progress, heaving and shoving him towards the door where John met them, still tucking in his shirt. Fitz stumbled out the door with Robbo under his arm.

Behind him he heard Big Tim. 'Good timin', O'Shea.'

John gave the bartender a look but addressed Fitz. 'What the hell are you doin'? I could hear the ruckus from the street. It's barely nine in the morning.'

'I'm not drunk. He is,' Fitz said, lugging a near comatose Robbo into the sunlight.

'God almighty. All right, bring him to the station, poor bastard,' John said and turned, walking away. 'Not the first time I've seen him like it.'

'Well, help me,' Fitz called out.

John tramped back and held Robbo under the arms. 'Get yer horse then.'

Fitz untied Patto and between the two men, Robbo was slung over the saddle. He'd gone quiet.

On their way to the station, Fitz spoke to his brother. 'So's you know, he's just accused Haines of deliberately keeping Meryl Bayley isolated while she was alone on the property.'

'Keep your voice down.' John marched alongside, his mouth grim, his frown deep. 'Can't prove anythin' of the sort so don't get in the middle of this, I'm warnin' you.'

Robbo started crying again, hanging uselessly over Patto's back. 'She never hurt no one, her so sick after the bairn died.' He hawked a great gob and spat. 'He was tryin' to drive Roy off, then Roy just flamin' disappeared.'

'Shut up, Robinson,' John said between his teeth.

'Haines did it,' Robbo said quietly, repeating it in time with the plodding of the horse. Then he shouted, 'Haines did it!'

John cuffed Robbo across the head. 'I said, shut up.'

'For Chrissakes, John,' Fitz said.

'Keep out of this.' John glared at him over Robbo's back. 'Have to shut him up until we get to the station.'

Robbo shouted, sobbed, snivelled. By the time they got to the police station, he'd gone quiet again.

'I'll put him in a cell, let him sleep it off,' John said. 'Wait here.' He headed into the station and came back with a set of keys. 'Bring him around the back. If I get time, I'll take him out to his wife, though she prob'ly won't want him like this.'

There were two cells, each a small room with a cot fixed to the wall and a bucket. Fitz and John manhandled Robbo inside, then John slammed the door and locked it.

'Not lookin' forward to cleanin' that up in the next few hours.' He gave a sharp nod of his head and Fitz followed him into the station. 'Haines will know about this in thirty minutes flat.'

Fitz slumped in the chair at his brother's desk. 'So don't tell me there's nothing going on.'

John took off his cap and threw it on the desk, rubbed his hands through his hair. 'Bayley didn't want to hand the place over to Haines. Haines didn't like that. Something happened, and I don't know what.'

Fitz stared at him. 'This can't be new. Haines must have been standing over people around here for a while.'

John banged his fists on his desk, his voice low. 'You don't know anything. Don't stick your bib in, this isn't one of your playtime stories.'

Fitz ignored the jibe. 'Haines is a criminal, John,' he said. 'Tantamount to a murderer if what Robbo says is true.'

'Robbo, poor bastard.' John wiped his hand over his mouth and nose. 'He'll be next if he don't watch it.'

Fitz sat there, stumped. His brother knew about this—whatever it was. Extortion at least. 'And Bayley and his wife?'

John shrugged, seemed to have lost his fire. 'No way of knowing what happened, is there?'

Fitz shoved his hands in his pockets. 'I was camped at the river last night and someone chucked a firecracker at me.'

John gave him a bleary-eyed glare. 'I should give a tuppeny toss.'

Battening down his temper, ignoring the vulgarity—his brother's tried and tested way of belittling him—Fitz continued. 'Tied to a rock following it was a message telling me to get on my way.'

'Good advice.' John dragged his chair out from the desk and sat down heavily.

'I can't leave yet, John. I know Meryl Bayley's sister. I need answers for her, at least.'

The bleary eyes squinted. 'That's not the reason you're here.'

Fitz tapped the desk with both hands. 'Now it's part of it. I came here after hearing about water rights, corruption and such, and walk into murder.'

'Dramatic.' John scoffed. 'It's not bad trouble over water. Just rumours, rumblings. No one trusts what's happening.'

Fitz leaned forward. 'And what is happening?'

John chewed his lip. 'What were you doing at the newspaper office?'

So he had seen Fitz there. 'Hoping for an interview with whoever runs the show.'

'Forget it. They report what they're told to report.'

'Don't know too many newspaper men who do that, John, but I know a few policemen who do what they're told.'

'Brother or not, watch your mouth,' John growled.

'Why aren't you looking into what Haines is doing?'

'Because as far as I can see,' John said as if talking to a child, 'he's not doing anythin' against the law.'

'He ran Bayley off his property and sicced his mongrel men onto that poor woman. Did God-only-knows-what to her.'

'Did he? Did they?' John stabbed a finger the air towards Fitz. 'Keep yer bloody voice down. Don't bust yer balls over it, mate. You of all people know we need proof, and without Bayley, or his missus, we've got nothin'. Not a thing.'

'I ask a few questions, go out to that property and a firecracker's hurled at me with a message. That's not nothing.' Fitz cocked an eyebrow. 'Or was it you threw the cracker?'

John gave him a look. 'Don't be a daft bugger.' He sat back in his chair. 'What are you gonna do?' When Fitz met him with a quizzical look, he added, 'Stay or leave?'

'Stay.'

'Then I want you where I can see you. Where I'm staying. Bunk in my room.' John's voice was tired. He was worried.

It suited Fitz. 'I'll take you up on that.'

'Good. Now for Chrissakes, let me get on with the day.'

Fitz pushed out of the chair.

'One more thing, little brother,' John said, pulling open a drawer and flipping Fitz a key. 'Lock the house whenever you leave it or if you're ever there on your own at night.'

'Lock it? You're joking.' At the mean look on John's face, Fitz said, 'All right, will do.'

'If Haines smells somethin' off, he'll be onto yer quick as look at yer.' The glare was loaded. 'He doesn't need any excuse, either. You hear me?'

It was a clear enough warning.

Outside, Fitz pocketed the key, thought about the next article for the newspaper he was carrying around in his saddlebags. Wasn't the best place to stash it, nor was the house. Maybe at the police station itself.

Maybe not. For more than one reason, John and his association with Haines had him jittery.

A firecracker message chucked at you in the dead of night will do that.

Chapter Twenty-five

Echuca

Evie peered out as the train grumbled and belched and finally stopped at the Echuca platform, wheels squealing on the tracks for the last few yards. Snatching up her bag and Raff's hat, she stepped into the corridor and waited with fellow passengers eager to get off the train. She tapped her foot, craned her neck and finally the porter opened the doors.

Raff had to be here; she hadn't spotted him at Rochester.

Disembarking, and dodging around others, she hurried out of the terminal building. It was hot and dusty; a northerly was whipping through the thin canopy of gum trees nearby.

Skirting the concourse until the end of the cattle car was in sight, she took a breath and stared at a couple of men unlocking the main door. No suspicious-looking horsemen were lurking.

And there he was, leading Bluey out of the wagon and down the ramp.

Her heart gave a little jump. 'Raff.' She waved his hat. He didn't hear her, didn't see her. 'Raff,' she called again and ran closer, dodging farmers and their handcarts as they headed to collect crates of chickens and bags of seed and whatnot.

His near-black wavy hair loose in the breeze, he scowled as he recognised her. A furtive look at the platform, then he put a finger to his lips.

Startled, she faltered, then dashed forward. 'They're not here,' she said in a furious whisper.

Bluey only wandered off the ramp, despite Raff tugging his reins. 'Who's not here?' he asked hoarsely, his frown still dark. He grabbed his hat from her and plonked it on. 'Thanks.' Peering around her, he said, 'What are you doing in Echuca?'

'I'm going on to Cobram from here. My sister's there.' She clutched her bag in both hands, trying to keep up as he strode along.

'Your sister's in Cobram? Jes—' He stopped short. Took a breath. '*Who's* not here?' He was still checking behind and ahead of them.

'There were two men at Elmore, one said he was a policeman—'

'Looking for me?' He glared at her.

'What is it?' When he didn't answer, she went on. 'He said he was retired, so I can't see why he'd—'

'Evie, please, did he give a name?' He stopped under the shade of an enormous gum. Bluey nibbled at a tuft of grass. Taking Evie's hand, Raff tugged her behind the tree trunk, out of sight.

'Um, McCluskey, I think. He described you.'

'McCosker.' He dropped her hand, as if just realising he'd had hold of it.

'That's it.' She'd never seen him agitated, ever, not even yesterday when he was bumping Edwin to the ground.

'Did you tell them anything?'

'No,' she cried. 'They were strangers, why would I answer them at all? Besides, I didn't know you were on the train.'

'And you say they're not here?'

'They didn't get on board. I tried to find you, to warn you, just in case. That's after I found your hat.' She pointed at it, nervous now. 'I knew it was yours.'

Taking it off, he rubbed his forearm over his face. 'Right,' he said, and took a deep breath. 'Let's get you where you need to be. How are you getting to Cobram?' He jammed the hat back on.

'I don't know if there's a coach service, and I don't fancy it if there is. I know there'll be a paddle-steamer from here. Far more pleasant.'

'Oh, Jesus,' he muttered.

Or that's what she thought he said. Worried now, she couldn't help her querulous tone. 'What's going on? Why are we hiding?'

He ducked out from behind the tree to check the surroundings again.

'Raff?'

When he looked back at her, the old Raff had returned. He gave her that easy smile. 'If they're not here, there's nothing to worry about. I saw them at Elmore too, it's why I ended up with Bluey in the cattle car and stayed there.' He headed for the road, leading the horse. 'Come on, let's get you to the wharf, it's only a twenty-minute walk.' He sat her bag on the saddle.

'Why are they after you?'

He took his time answering, as if he were weighing things up. 'Not me, exactly.'

That could only mean one thing. 'Fitz,' she said.

Raff waited a beat then nodded. 'He's upset some people.'

She hurried to keep up with him. 'How unusual,' she quipped, a laugh fading off. After a few brisk paces she said, 'So, what's he doing here in Echuca?'

Chapter Twenty-six

Echuca

Jesus Christ. Raff marched along the footpath, leading Bluey, Evie keeping up with him. He'd been going to get on a paddle-steamer heading for Cobram too. Would that still be the right thing to do now?

McCosker. Why the hell would he drop his name to a random woman at a railway station, and tell her he was a retired policeman? Unless he was hoping to fluke it, telling any law-abiding passer-by who he was after. Maybe McCosker wanted Raff to know he was on the lookout. And why had he been at Elmore? How—

Pa.

Shit. He'll have to telegram his father, make sure he was all right. Maybe he should go back …

'Raff?'

Nah. Pa would be fine. Any trouble and he'd call Redmond and Fergal back quick smart, if he hadn't already. Raff would telegram, then ride on to Cobram, dammit. He didn't want Evie anywhere nearby if McCosker was up here somewhere; wouldn't be safe. Besides, he didn't want to be spending any more time in Evie's company than he had to.

Wrong. He wanted to spend a helluva lot more time in her company, but that wouldn't work out for the best. For him. Now. *Dammit.*

Another three days' ride to Cobram. Then again, that's where Evie said she was going. She'd most likely see Fitz there, with Raff, then there'd be more explaining. *Bloody hell.* He had to tell her.

'Raff?' she pressed, annoyed.

'He's not in Echuca, Evie. He's in Cobram. I'm on my way there.'

Now she too was quiet. He glanced across. Her face glowed red, but that could've been because of the pace he'd set. *Nah, it was because she'd just blushed an almighty shade. Damn Fitz.*

Her head was down. She was watching where she put her feet, her mouth set. 'Well, he has a perfect right to be wherever he wants to be,' she said, with surprising gusto.

He wasn't going to comment either way; he was smarter than that. Besides, coming from an engaged woman, what she'd said was true. She shouldn't give a tinker's damn.

'How are you going to get to Cobram?' she demanded, eyes still on the ground.

'I'll ride.' Then again, with the threat of McCosker, he might just take a fancy to really upset that Edwin idiot. He could take a ride upriver with the lovely Evie on a steamer, and spend days and nights in her company. In fact, if Raff was that sort of man, he'd tear her away from the fool and make sure she wouldn't marry him.

So what's stopping you?

Raff wouldn't steal any man's woman, even if the bloke was a bloody arsefly and so wrong for Evie. She had her own mind but he'd be saving her from a fate— Jesus, he would have to marry her then. But that wouldn't be so bad … if she'd have him.

If a man don't let a woman know how he feels about her … Have a good crack at it.

Not good timing, Pa. My head's all a-spin.

'You should take a steamer, too,' Evie said, without looking at him. 'It'd be fun. Easier on your horse, as well.'

Christ, last thing I need is an invite. He grunted at that. 'Bluey is just fine.' He strode on, cursing Fitz and his crusades to right all the wrongs when there were—mostly—good troopers around to do the job. He cursed his luck at meeting Evie Emerson again only to learn that she wasn't engaged to his good mate Fitz—the bastard who hadn't bloody said a thing to the contrary—because she was engaged to some flamin' skinny imbecile who'd fallen out of an oil tin. *What the hell was she thinking?* He cursed that he wasn't exactly sure what he'd do with her on a paddle-steamer headed for Cobram. Then he just cursed for the hell of it.

Evie was alongside, puffing as she kept up with him.

The wharf came into view and he cursed aloud. 'Bloody hell.' There were two mounted troopers watching folk. 'Evie, this way.' Raff turned Bluey and headed across the road to a laneway that ran into the next street over.

'They could be here for anyone,' she called softly behind him.

'Could be,' he said over his shoulder, 'but I don't want to take any chances.' Stopping at the corner of a brick building, a pub, he checked up the street. 'I'll go this way and stay out of sight. You'll be fine,' he said and took her bag from the saddle, handing it to her. 'Go up the street here and take a right turn back to the wharf and you'll be able to buy passage on a boat.'

Dropping her bag to the ground, she patted her face with the back of a wrist and adjusted her hat. 'Raff, the men I saw at Elmore were not in uniform. It's more than likely these two know nothing about you.'

'The men after Fitz are known crooked troopers and murderers. McCosker might still have clout in ranks all over the colony, so I can't be trusting any of them right now.'

'Murderers?'

Raff checked the street, left and right, then dropped his gaze to her. 'I can't lead them to Fitz, Evie.'

Evie slapped at her skirt and dust rose from it. She blew out an impatient breath. 'What if— Would they expect you to be travelling with someone else?'

Raff gave her a look. Then startled by what she meant, he thundered, 'You're not travelling with me.'

'Don't look so astounded. What if I buy two fares and whatever it is for Bluey to get him onto a boat,' she said, 'then right at the last minute you sneak on board.'

He was thinking, but not about sneaking anywhere. In Ballarat he'd told Constable Dawes that Fitz had gone downriver into South Australia. If they were thinking around corners and reckoned it was a decoy then they could very well be waiting here.

He checked the street again. Apart from a few pedestrians, there was little movement. A cart rounded the corner and pulled up in front of a merchandise store, the driver jumping to the ground and heading inside. Further along, a shopkeeper took up a seat on his veranda and began enjoying a thick sandwich.

'I'll ride to Cobram,' he said again, still thinking.

'All right. Well, off you go then.' She was huffy. 'I've got to get a move on. I really don't want to stay in this town if I don't have to.' Evie picked up her bag. 'Perhaps I'll see you there. We could all have tea somewhere again like old times,' she said, a snip in her voice.

What was she so bloody annoyed about?

Those maddening blue eyes of hers had flashed before she ignored his earlier direction and headed back the way they'd come. 'Good day, Raff,' she said with a toss of her head, her nose in the air, only a glimpse of glossy dark hair under a jaunty hat. The dimple in her chin was pronounced and her fun-loving, generous smile was nowhere in sight. He fumed.

At that moment, the mounted troopers sauntered by the wharf end of the lane. Raff drew in a sharp breath when they stopped. They'd seen her, and they'd seen him.

Shit. If he shot out of sight now, he'd look suspicious. And there she was, his plucky little Evie, heading into the jaws of the devil as if she didn't have a care in the world.

She doesn't. I do. *What the hell is she about to walk into?*

Keeping hold of a tetchy Bluey, he waited. Nothing else he could do. He took a breath and leaned back against the wall of the pub, a foot on the brickwork. If he smoked he could be rolling the fixings, as relaxed as you like. He watched with a glance here and there, nonchalant as could be, until he didn't like what he saw.

Chapter Twenty-seven

Echuca

'Help ye, miss?' A constable doffed his cap. He was an older man with leathery and lined skin, sporting a big moustache, the long whiskers falling into the creases around his mouth. He peered over the top of her to stare down the laneway.

'Oh, thank you, just a direction. I need to buy a fare on a steamer. Where's the ticket office?'

He raised an arm and pointed to his right. 'Cross the road, and a bit further up. Can't miss it.'

She smiled, nodded her thanks.

'Which way you headed?'

Evie didn't hesitate. 'Cobram.' She had nothing to hide and the police certainly weren't looking for her.

'Only a couple of boats in this morning are goin' upriver. You might be lucky. Try the *Sweet Georgie*, miss. She takes a bit of freight, but mostly passengers these days. She has some real fine cabins.'

She nodded her thanks and kept moving, intent on finding the ticket office.

Then, 'Miss, are you on your own?' one of them called, suspicion in his voice.

Evie turned to see him pointing at Raff, leading Bluey, making his way back towards them. His face was like thunder. *Blast you, Rafferty Dolan.*

'Oh, that's my brother, Constable,' she said loudly. 'Come along, Stanley,' she added gaily, then lowered her voice for the constable's benefit. 'He's a bit slow, you see.' Evie kept walking, the smile plastered in place until she could hear Bluey's hooves clip-clopping over the sound of her pulse banging in her ears.

Stanley came alongside, his gaze on her cool, not amused. 'I'm a bit slow, am I?'

'You were clearly following me, looking like a warrior about to rampage, so no wonder the constable asked who you were. If you want to ride poor Bluey to Cobram, out of town is that way by the look of it.' She pointed. 'The police are headed in the opposite direction.' She hefted the bag into her other hand. 'I'm going to the ticket office.'

Raff set his jaw. 'The warrior was going to say a few words if they'd tried to detain you.'

'Excellent. That would have drawn attention to you whether they're crooked or not.' Evie stepped under the veranda at the ticket window. 'Good afternoon,' she said as a man fronted, his face pleasant, sweat popping on his forehead. 'I believe there's a boat by the name of the *Sweet Georgie* going upriver and it has cabins for passengers,' Evie said. 'I'd like to buy passage, if I may, to Cobram.'

'Ah yes, just a moment. I reckon the captain is on the wharf now. I'll see if he can help ye.' The man peered around her at Raff and the horse. 'All of ye?'

Evie took a breath to say—

'Yes. My sister and I, and my horse, thanks,' Raff said.

'Right y'are.' The man disappeared.

Raff wasn't looking at Evie, but said, 'Better the ticket man thinks we're siblings too in case he's asked anything by McCosker's men.'

'And don't we look like siblings,' Evie said, exasperated, and took out a handkerchief and mopped her neck and face. *So hot.* 'You changed your mind,' she said quietly.

'Stanley believes he will be safe with you. Don't disappoint him.' He was intent on the street, and on those who were coming and going. His hat, with her feather, was firmly on his head and tugged low.

The ticket fellow came back to the window. 'Cap'n MacHenry is coming up to see ye.'

He told Evie the price and she swallowed, handing over the pound notes. *Must be a luxury boat.*

Rounding the office outside, a tall, strong-looking man, dark hair, dark eyes, perhaps in his early forties, nodded at her. He tipped his hat and scrutinised Raff. 'I'm Dane MacHenry. You for Cobram?' he asked him.

'Me, Miss Emerson, and the horse.'

'I've only got one cabin available, so that'll do for Miss Emerson if you're happy to spend the few nights on the deck, Mister …?'

'Raff Dolan,' he said. 'I'll be fine on the deck with Bluey.'

'Right. Board when you're ready. Go to the gate and follow the wharf. Neat little white boat. I'll let my wife know we have passengers. Hope you like kids.' He grinned. 'We depart in an hour. Three nights, three and a half days to Cobram if we don't strike trouble. Excuse me.' He nodded and strode off.

'Why did you tell the captain your name?' Evie asked.

'I'm not spending half the week on a boat lying to him, bad enough the ticket fella. And who's the captain going to tell? When the conversation gets around to it, I'm a friend escorting you to your sister, which is the truth. Let's go,' Raff said and took Evie's bag once again. 'Sooner I'm out of sight, the better.'

Evie stood for a moment and watched as Raff and Bluey headed through the gate. She roused herself and following him down the boardwalk, hot and thirsty, she spotted the neat boat tied up to the wharf on what would have been the second level landing for the current water level. *Sweet Georgie* was emblazoned over the wheelhouse.

Captain MacHenry mentioned a wife and kids on board. So she and Raff wouldn't be on their own.

Her heart thudded a moment. Oh, that would have been too much.

Chapter Twenty-eight

Cobram

Fitz had no sooner removed the saddlebags from Patto at the back of John's place than Haines was in the laneway again.

He called over the fence. 'Got a minute, Mr Morgan?' Dismounting, he leaned on a fencepost and, not waiting for a reply, said, 'Heard ol' Robbo was a bit of a bother just before.'

John had been generous with the time it would take: Haines hadn't waited long at all.

'Don't know much about it, Mr Haines,' Fitz said, the bags still in his arms. 'Poor bloke needs a rest, I reckon,' he said, tapping his temple. 'Constable O'Shea is helping him out.'

'Got a mouth on him when he gets full, hope he didn't offend you at all.'

'Offend? Not in any way.' Fitz smiled. 'He wasn't really making much sense.' He should have been an actor on the stage.

Frowning, Haines was impatient with the pleasantries. 'Wouldn't want him sayin' anything untoward around the place.'

'I wouldn't know one way or the other,' Fitz said and shrugged the bags in his arms.

Haines lifted his chin towards them. 'You stayin' a while?'

'Might do.'

Pushing away from the fencepost, Haines said, 'Didn't realise our constable was carefree with visitors stayin' in the police house, and all that.'

'Only another night here,' Fitz said, not worrying about his lie. His congeniality slid a little. 'He's been hospitable.'

Haines nodded, his frown still drawn low, whiskers twitching as his jaw set. 'Well, Mr Morgan, let me know if I can help you in any way.' He remounted and rode off.

No thanks. Fitz juggled the saddlebags and watched him go. At the back door, he'd wondered what Haines thought Robbo might've said. Accusations made by a drunken fella, his tongue loosened, might hold some truth.

Inside the house, he unpacked the bags. He and John would enjoy reading from the bundle of newspapers. He stacked his spare clothes on the dresser; a bit of air would do them good. When he got to the damning letter from the gold merchant's wife, he scouted for a good place to stash it until he could ask John if there was a safe at the station. He hesitated, debating the wisdom of that again. If something happened to him, the letter could be destroyed. Justice would not be served. It mattered to the dead man's wife and kids. He tapped the envelope in his hand, thinking. Fire would destroy this place, a tinderbox of dry twigs; couldn't hide it here. If he kept it with him, he could be jumped, and anything on him stolen or destroyed. He'd have to take it to the police station, best of his options. It couldn't be left for someone like Haines to acquire, maybe the very person who'd tossed the firecracker.

Locking up as requested, he headed back to the town. He steered out of sight; Haines was just coming out of the police station. So it wasn't the best place for the letter, after all. And what of John, was he really trustworthy?

Haines mounted and rode away. Fitz nudged Patto along, trying to decide his next move. His eye on the station, he was ready to just ride by when Robbo staggered out the front door. John was behind him; a pat on Robbo's back, a nod and a glare to Fitz, then he returned to his office.

Jesus, not even a couple of hours to sleep it off. 'Robbo,' Fitz called and drew alongside as the man shook himself. 'You all right?'

Abashed, Robbo took his hat and slapped his thigh with it. 'Yeah. Been doin' that a lot lately. A few drinks, then cryin' like a baby. Dunno why.'

'Going home?' Fitz had slid off Patto.

'Reckon I should.' He jammed his hat back on.

'I'll walk with you.'

'It's four mile.'

'Not far. Don't want you falling asleep on the roadside in this weather. Walk it off. I got water in my bags.'

They trudged out of town, Robbo taking the flask of water and drinking steadily. 'Missus will have a few words to say.'

'I bet.'

Fitz let Patto's reins drop. The horse would walk along without needing to be led. He used his hat to swish flies, then tipped some water over his head before slapping on the hat again. Fine dust covered his boots, and in places the track gave in to holes and his feet sank. Drought, more drought, and bloody drought again. Been a long one this time. Nearly six years and no end in sight.

Robbo handed back the flask. 'Jenny, she is. As good a woman as you'll ever find,' he said. 'Puts up with me.' He gave a short laugh, eyes on the ground as he walked. 'Heart as big as a barn door. She can turn her hand to anything, loves a good laugh, gets on with folk.' He glanced at Fitz then. 'Most folk, not Miz Bayley. She found her difficult.' He shrugged. 'I already told you that.'

'Would your wife know if Mrs Bayley talked to any of the other ladies?'

Robbo sniffed and held out his hand for the flask again. Drank deeply before shaking the flask. Empty. 'Sorry.'

'No matter, I have more.' Fitz tucked the empty bottle into the saddlebags that now only held water bottles. He reefed out a full one and offered it. 'Did any other ladies visit Mrs Bayley out there?'

Robbo stared into the distance. 'She can tell you herself. I reckon that's her in the buggy comin' our way.'

Maybe a quarter mile off, Fitz saw a two-seater heading towards them, a woman driving. 'I should leave you to it, then,' he said and gathered up Patto's reins.

'Mr Morgan, stay for a meal with us. I'd be able to thank you with that, at least, and I'm powerful hungry right now.'

The buggy stopped up a few yards away and Mrs Robinson pulled on the brake. 'Cyril Robinson, you better be in a fit state to fix my garden fence like you promised.'

'I will be. This is Mr Morgan. I'd like him to have some of that mutton stew you're so good at, maybe some damper, too.'

Fitz lifted his hat. 'Morning, Mrs Robinson.'

She eyed him up and down, no doubt assessing he wasn't some swagman trying to pull the wool over their eyes. 'Good morning,' she said and gave a nod of assent. Her dark eyes were shrewd, freckles dusted her nose and cheeks and her clear features were candid. Thick brown hair was in a ribbon at the back of her neck, no fuss, and her bonnet was tied under her chin.

Robbo clambered up beside her. 'Follow us,' he said to Fitz.

Jenny turned the buggy and headed back the way she'd come. 'I hope your head is splitting, Mr Robbo,' Fitz heard her say.

'It is, Mrs Robbo.'

Their farmhouse yard was a neat set up of fenced areas, a chicken coop, a lean-to for the buggy, a stall for their horse, and a clothesline with flapping sheets and other linens hung on it. The boiler stood nearby.

Dismounting, Fitz smiled. 'Fine-looking house, Mrs Robinson.'

It was a small timber place with a sturdy veranda, its posts the trunks of the straightest trees he could imagine. A well-made door was in the centre. The two open windows on either side had shutters pegged back, and the house looked deep enough to be spacious inside. A handsome brick chimney boasted a thin plume of smoke idling high into the sky.

'All thanks to this one who needs to go and wash off his doldrums before he comes inside for his drink of tea.'

Robbo got off the buggy and headed for the boiler. He dipped a bucket, withdrew it full of water and set about dunking his head and lathering with a bar of soap.

Jenny Robinson drove the buggy to the stall, and Fitz followed to tie Patto to the rail. When she got down, she said, her voice low, 'Thank you. He told me he'd met a good man.'

Fitz wasn't sure what to say to that. 'He's seems a good man, too.'

'He is. But these days, some things seem to … bother him quite a bit, if you know what I mean.'

They both glanced at Robbo still trying to wash off the hangover.

'He doesn't like that Mr Haines much,' Fitz said.

'Nasty type if you cross him. Cyril questions him, but when the goings-on get too much …'

'What goings-on?'

'The awful things he reckons Haines has done.'

The letters burned in Fitz's pocket.

Robbo yelled that he had soap in his eyes. 'Jenny, get me a towel, wouldja?'

'Coming,' she called out, walking towards the house. Then to Fitz, 'I throw the grog out when I know he's thinking too much,' she said quietly. 'Wasn't quick enough last night. He must have walked all the way into town while I was asleep.' She gave him an apologetic look and grabbed a ragged towel hanging from a nail on one of the veranda posts. 'Here you go,' she said and slapped it into her husband's outstretched hand. 'Come in for tea, Mr Morgan.'

Fitz stood at the foot of the veranda. 'Don't want to be in the way.'

'You're not.' She shooed a fly, picked up a corner of her apron and dabbed her forehead. 'Will be good to have some decent conversation.'

Inside, dropping his hat on a hook by the door, Fitz asked, 'Has Robbo ever had any trouble from Mr Haines?'

Mrs Robinson shook her head. 'Haines knows one of us would yell blue murder if he did anything.' She flattened her mouth and gave a pointed look towards a rifle leaning against the fireplace. 'Cyril's a bit soft, but I've been a good shot in my day, so if we're ever threatened …' Her voice drifted.

'That bad?'

She checked outside to see Robbo still trying to wash off the grog. 'We're in fear of Haines and his men turning up here because he's just plain nasty when he wants to be,' she said to Fitz, 'but so far nothing has happened to us, probably because we've got nothing he wants. Robbo knows they got to Roy Bayley. Then when Roy disappeared, Cyril kept checking on Mrs Bayley. She wouldn't say anything about it to him, fear again, probably, so he wanted me to look in on her.'

A glance outside again at Robbo. 'She wouldn't say a word to me either, even when I saw the state she was in after they'd beaten her up.' She shuddered then. 'Lord knows what else they did to her, but she just told me very clearly to leave her alone and not bother returning.' Rubbing her hands on her apron, she said, 'After I first met her, I told Cyril that I didn't like her. Then I thought that perhaps she wasn't right up here.' She tapped her head. 'Especially after her little boy died.' She chewed her lip. 'His death got to Cyril real bad. We lost two boys as little ones. Pertussis.'

Fitz closed his eyes a moment. *Whooping cough.*

She took a breath. 'Anyway, I know one day Mrs Bayley told Maud at McFadyen's in no uncertain terms that Roy would come back, but he never did.'

Robbo stood in the doorway. He sighed, a long sad breath. 'I could do with some tea, Mrs Robbo,' he said.

Jenny Robinson served tea, and then they ate hot mutton stew and warm damper, spooned into deep china plates.

'Haines wants that piece of land come hell or high water,' Robbo said. 'My guess is Roy wouldn't sign it over to him, or whatever has to happen with it bein' a settler piece of land.' He pushed his plate away.

Fitz frowned. 'So no proof that Haines was doing something illegal?'

Robbo shook his head. 'And every time I start thinking about all of it, what he's done, what's happened to folk around here,' he gave Jenny a wan smile, 'I lose my …' He waved both his hands at his head. 'And I can't get my brain workin' for a while afterwards. I only got suspicions, but who'd listen to me anyway?' Shaking his head again, he said, 'We've talked of movin' on, leaving here, but the drought … now the depression. Fat lot of good Federation will do anybody.' He wiped his mouth with the palm of his hand. 'What about you, Mr Morgan? What are you doin' here?'

Fitz decided against admitting he was a journalist. He said, 'I was looking at land around here, now I'm not so sure.' He realised then that his presence on their farm might be putting the

Robinsons in more hot water. 'So, I must let you get on with fixing that garden fence, Robbo.' He stood. 'Thank you for the fine meal, Mrs Robinson.'

They both stood with him, and Robbo said, 'Thank you, Mr Morgan. If I can repay you—'

'That was offering me the good meal, remember?' Fitz headed for the door, the hot breeze drying his skin.

'If there is something we can do,' Jenny Robinson said, her hands clutching her apron. 'Please just say.'

Fitz stopped. He wanted a few more days, checking facts, if he could stand to be here. If the paper had published what he'd delivered and someone like Haines put two and two together, he might not have that time left. John's place wasn't safe from intruders, and with Haines in and out of the police station, secreting his letters there wouldn't be such a good idea.

'There is one thing. It would take a load off my mind if I could leave some letters in your safekeeping. All this travelling around …' He shrugged, spread his hands.

Bemused but happy to accommodate, Mrs Robinson said, 'Of course. I'll put them safe with the ones from my mother.'

He nodded his thanks and pulled the letters from his pocket. He'd sealed each. 'Appreciate it. I'll be back to collect them when I'm ready to leave the district.' He had faint hope he'd know more about Roy Bayley's whereabouts by then.

Mrs Robinson read one envelope. 'Should you not just post this one, Mr Morgan?' she asked, holding up the letter addressed in full to Miss E. Emerson.

'I'm not sure I should just yet,' he answered and gave her a rueful smile.

'Ah.' By the look on her face, she'd misinterpreted, happily.

That was fine with Fitz: it wasn't a love letter, not *that* sort, anyway. 'Good day to you both.' He grabbed his hat from the hook, dusted it off on his thigh and put it on. Striding out to Patto, he hauled himself into the saddle, waved and rode away. Felt better, not having the letters on him, but he laughed at himself.

Worrying for nothing, O'Shea.

Chapter Twenty-nine

On the Mighty Murray
Thursday 22 September

Raff was looking ahead upriver, leaning on the shovel after clearing the small hillock of Bluey's calling cards from the deck.

'In some places the water's down, so travel will be slow. I expect better levels upstream, closer we get to Cobram,' Captain MacHenry said. 'For how long, I don't know.'

MacHenry was a skilful navigator, but there'd been times Raff wasn't sure how he did it. He glided around huge snags or slipped past the odd barge, loaded with logs from the Barmah Forest and floating downriver waiting for a tow. Taking tight bends, the *Sweet Georgie* held her own.

Nearly three days travel already had so far tested Raff's patience, and his self-restraint. Evie crowded his thoughts, and other areas of him. He made sure to find plenty to do, and thank God there wasn't long to go now.

Joe O'Grady, an older Irish fella, was also on board. He'd been with the MacHenrys for years and ministered to the boiler and the engine and, on occasion, had charge of the wheel. He'd taken a shine to Bluey, said his love of horses ran deep, that Mr MacHenry had a fine stallion at home and had started a stable of the horse's progeny. He'd take time to converse here and there with Evie when he was on a breather from chores, Raff noticed. She seemed her happy self, and sometimes laughter ensued.

Mrs MacHenry and Evie enjoyed one another's company so there'd hardly been a chance to talk to Evie privately. The four children were enough of a distraction, filling the days with laughter and mischief. Will and Tom were twins, eight years old, full of beans, and already deft hands when required. Then Miss Layla, six and a half she'd told him, the image of her mother with coal-black hair and a cheeky grin, and Jessica the toddler, chubby, fun and into all things, especially Evie's hat, which had come off second best.

The river didn't tolerate the careless. Whenever the little girls were on deck, their mother had each on a harness, tethered to her with a lead. The boys were constantly warned about shenanigans and Mrs MacHenry—Georgina—was sharp if there were any transgressions. Raff had grabbed one of them by the seat of his pants before the lad had gone overboard, swearing not to tell his fierce mother as he swung the bawling, scared lad back to safety. Raff wasn't sure he'd enjoy being at the end of Mrs MacHenry's wrath, either.

One night at dinner, the children fed and already abed, the MacHenrys, Joe, Evie and Raff were partaking of their meal in the cramped galley.

'I love my kids, but I so look forward to the peace and quiet once they're asleep,' Mr MacHenry had said.

'Is this journey a holiday for you all?' Evie had asked Mrs MacHenry.

Mrs MacHenry had laid down her cutlery and taken up her glass of wine. 'It's probably the last trip on the river for us for some time.'

The captain had then taken up the conversation. 'We have our farm downriver of Swan Hill. The crops are struggling, so we've embarked upon the beginnings of a horse stud, and I'm hopeful of some success.' He pushed his plate away and leaned back. 'Trade on the river is in decline—drought, and the railways coming through—the writing is on the wall. It's the end of freight-carrying paddle-steamers. We'll wind down the riverboat operation. So, as this might well be the *Sweet Georgie*'s last trip, with minimal freight, we took the opportunity to have the family on board together.' He smiled at his wife then, warmth in his eyes. 'There'll be hard days ahead on the farm. Family means everything to us, so this will make some happy memories to take forward.'

Mrs MacHenry reached over and squeezed his hand. The affection between them struck Raff. How easy it was, how genuine. He let his gaze drift towards Evie. She had her eyes on their hosts as well, then caught his look and shied away, taking a sip of wine.

'Me,' Joe piped up. 'I love the bairns, rowdy, curious. Full of life.'

'You're herding them away from the rails all day,' Mr MacHenry said.

'They're not a problem now, they've worked it out over time,' Joe answered. 'It's just a pity the wee lads won't get to learn their father's riverboat trade.'

'It'll be a different trade they learn,' Mr MacHenry said and lifted his glass in salute to the man. 'From me, and from you.'

That night, after Evie had departed for her cabin, Raff had just thrown out his swag on deck when Joe wandered from his bunkroom. He carried a jug and two pannikins.

'Warm night,' he said. 'Moon's up, means I won't sleep for ages. Thought you might like to share a tot.' The light on the river glowed in a ribbon over the narrow ripple of the tide.

'Glad to,' Raff replied.

Joe poured the rum, handed a cup to Raff and then sat cross-legged on the boards of the deck, his back against the base wall of the wheelhouse. 'Bluey's takin' to river travel, I see.'

Raff lowered himself to the swag. 'He's a good horse. I can take him anywhere.' He lifted his cup at Joe then took a sip. It was good rum. 'So where's home, Joe?'

'Swan Hill now, with the family.'

'Family?'

'Ah, I meant the MacHenrys, on their run. I missed the chance for me own.' He shrugged a little. 'I adopted the MacHenrys, or t'other way around. No matter. They're me family now, and I couldna think of a better one.' He exhaled heavily. Maybe Joe had taken more than a tot or two before he'd found Raff on deck.

Silence drifted a while.

'Been with them for long?' Raff asked.

'Aye. Worked with Mr MacHenry's pa, old Tom, for years and years, on and off, when he could afford to have me. The lad, Dane here, was off making his fortune in Sydney when the old place fell on hard times. Tom got killed, so Dane came home to the farm, and with money in his pocket. He made it good again, much as he could with the drought an' all. He got himself a wife and then the bairns came.' His voice drifted. Joe was in a reflective mood, loosened up by rum no doubt, and maybe by memories from long ago.

Quiet descended again. The night was still, not even a breeze rustled the leaves on the old gums that towered over their mooring.

'She seems a nice lass, your girl,' Joe said, musing.

Raff was glad of the dim light. 'Miss Emerson's not my girl.'

'Oh.' Joe said after a beat in time. 'My mistake, is it?'

'Mmh.'

Bluey nickered, took a slurp from his water bucket, gave a derisive blurt.

Bloody horse was almost human.

Joe took a drink from his cup and poured another. He offered the jug to Raff who took a splash. 'Coulda sworn I've been seein' somethin' between ye.' Then he groaned as he stretched out his legs. 'Gettin' old.' He got comfortable. 'Shows how outta touch I am then. Sorry, lad, should be mindin' me own business. Glorious nights like this one can do a man in; a bit to drink and he's thinkin' he sees it everywhere, that thing he never claimed for himself. I miss 'er, you know, even still. Me girl, Maeve. Long before me time with the MacHenrys.' He held up his empty cup to peer at it. 'Sweet mother Mary, nothin' like a maudlin drunk Irishman.'

Raff ducked his chin, swirled the liquid in his cup and then took another swig.

'I'll say this, though, an' then I'll shut me trap,' Joe said. 'I seen what I seen between you and the lass, even if ye canna see it yeself. Don't be like me, don't let a good one get away on ye, lad. It'll haunt ye the rest of yer days.'

'Mmh,' Raff repeated. Joe sounded like his old man. 'I'm only escorting her to find her sister. We're friends, and I'll look out for her. That's all.'

'All right, lad, whatever you say,' Joe said. He poured himself another tipple and held the jug towards Raff. 'Another tot?'

One more, and Raff was done. It was getting late; the moon had risen over the trees. The night remained calm except for maybe the sound of a kangaroo bounding on the bank.

Joe slumped on his side to the deck and his snores rumbled softly, belying what he'd said earlier about not getting to sleep. Raff drained his cup, and lay down, hands behind his head. *Don't let a good one get away.*

Easier said.

By the next morning, after dawn to dusk travel so far, MacHenry said that they should make Cobram the day after around midday. Raff worked with Joe in the boiler room or loaded more firewood with him from the stacks on the bank. Had put his back to it, glad for something to do. He'd helped save some time, MacHenry told him, so the journey would be a little shorter than expected, all being well.

Late afternoon and Mrs MacHenry was teaching a few lessons for the three older children, the youngest girl was asleep. Mr MacHenry and Joe were in the wheelhouse. This was a good time to talk to Evie. At others, children would interrupt, or adults were around, conversation shared. Mealtimes were communal. Mrs MacHenry hardly enjoyed cooking, and Evie agreed with her, but the meals were hearty, and Joe, certainly, liked his feed of fresh fish that he and the boys caught. The evenings were especially rowdy until after dinner, but then Evie would disappear to her cabin. And he wouldn't follow to talk to her there; he dared not.

Now at last, she was by herself on the bench seat under the only shade on the boat, a canvas sail used for the sole purpose of protection from the weather. He could speak to her now. Outdoors. For anyone to see. All above board.

Chapter Thirty

Evie squinted up to see who had blocked the glaring sun.

'May I sit with you?' Raff asked. He doffed his hat then held it in his hands.

'Of course.' She shuffled a little on the seat and Raff sat beside her, his legs stretching out. 'I never knew quite how beautiful it could be. And to think that Mrs MacHenry can steer the boat. There are such possibilities here. Now I envy my sister living beside such a wonder as this river.'

The day before, Mrs MacHenry had taken the wheel and Evie had to remember to close her mouth at the shock: not only at Georgina in the wheelhouse and in charge of the boat but that she was dressed in *trousers*.

'I do a short stint, a very short stint these days, in the engine room too. Can't be in a dress down there.' She laughed at Evie's stupefied expression.

More, Mr MacHenry was in charge of the children that day, although he just couldn't help coming to the wheelhouse on occasion.

'For supervision—he doesn't fool me,' Georgina said and winked, 'or hoping to dodge four active children. Joe gives him a hand there though.' She adjusted the wheel incrementally. The sleek steamer obeyed instructions, with barely a ripple on the water.

Evie listened, mouth open again, to the MacHenrys' story, struck mostly by how Georgina had once owned a paddle-steamer company.

'I'd be happy to just have my own millinery business one day.'

'That's big in itself.'

'First, I have to know my sister's thoughts on our mother's will then I can perhaps plan …' She shrugged.

'All things are possible,' Georgina told her, and then nodded towards the children on the deck. 'Just not all possible at once.'

They'd chugged past wide plains, and dense forests or patchy vegetation, and now sandy beaches dotted here and there. Massive trees had fallen into the river or on the dun-coloured banks, and the roots of upright trees clawed towards the water desperate for a drink. Birdlife was in raucous abundance—parrots and ducks and robins and more, none of which Evie was able to name.

A sombre white family standing high on the riverbank outside their ragged hut stared as the boat steamed by. Further along, a black family by their cooking fire, children laughing and cavorting, waved madly and the MacHenry children waved back.

Evie saw two of the most brilliant sunsets she'd ever seen (she only saw one sunrise, she was loath to admit). And the river itself was a living, breathing entity—calm and meandering, vibrant and dangerous, moody and mysterious.

A whole different world.

'Do you ever wonder why you live in a town, Raff, when all this is out here?' Evie asked.

'It's like every holiday,' Raff said, his head bowed, his dark hair ruffled. 'Nowhere is as rosy once you arrive to live in it.' He hadn't shaved for a few days and the dark stubble on his jaw showed the odd glint of silver.

'And you've had a holiday to know, have you?' she asked with a smile.

He gave her a laugh. 'I'll tell you this, I don't know anyone anywhere living this drought who thinks life is better in the country,' Raff said.

She took in a deep breath. 'I often wonder how my sister is faring. She grew up in Bendigo, far from hardship.'

The low chug of the boat was reassuring, but the big presence of the quiet man alongside her was unsettling. She thought she knew him, but things felt different this time, weren't as easy-going as before. Was he hesitant to tell her about Fitz? No need; she realised she didn't have to know anything about Fitz at all. He was just common ground, chitchat about him might relax them. This was the first occasion on the boat she'd had time to talk to Raff alone. When his gaze settled on her, her heart didn't seem to know what to do: jump about in little leaps or thud continually. Somehow it was doing both.

'Are you all right?' he asked.

That was out of thin air. 'I'm fine. Why?'

'You worrying about your sister?' His hands clasped, he was rolling his thumbs one over the other, his forearms on his knees as he leaned forward.

'I hope I can find her. Hope she talks to me.'

'Any reason why she wouldn't?'

'None that I know of,' Evie answered. 'But last time I saw her was at Mama's funeral and she wasn't terribly forthcoming with conversation.'

'Well, now you might have happy things to talk about,' Raff said, gazing at the deck floor.

Goodness, he's a sight to look at. What would he think of her? She had to laugh at herself. Here she was, in a simple blue dress, a straw hat, chewed on by a teething child, no stockings (too hot) and light boots. Certainly not a statement of style, no fashion plate. Another snort at herself. *How silly.* He'd hardly notice a fashion plate or otherwise.

And Raff, battered hat (with *her* feather), a work shirt open to reveal a flat, dense chest, and ragged sleeves that his biceps seemed to have destroyed. His moleskins were stained with soot and oil from the boiler room, and his sturdy boots were scuffed, in need of a good polish with dubbin.

He was the most marvellous thing she'd ever seen.

Evie gave a doleful smile. 'Mama's will is not exactly a happy subject.'

'No.' He concentrated on his hands.

She faltered in the silence then said, 'I'm sure Meryl wouldn't be interested to hear about my job or anything. She never was.'

He was staring ahead into the winding expanse of the river. 'I meant your engagement. That's something happy to talk about.'

It slammed her. Evie's face flamed; she knew it had. It would be burning a deep crimson, starting at her neck and going all the way up to her hairline. 'Oh, but—'

'I read it in the paper, Evie.' Raff was back looking at his hands, fingers linked, one thumb rolling over the other.

'I'm *not* engaged,' she said, her voice sharp.

'I read it in the paper,' he repeated, this time between his teeth. 'Engaged to that Edwin fella. The peeping tom.' His hands stopped moving but he still stared ahead. 'You could have said.'

Evie's blush rushed up her neck again. *Dear God.* 'It's not true, Raff. He placed the announcement without my knowledge.'

'How does that happen? You must have agreed.'

'I never did.' Her pulse hammered, though why she felt as if she had to defend herself further, she wasn't sure. 'I—*he* wanted me to consider him for marriage.' *My God, how mortifying.* 'I wasn't interested, but he'd already made the announcement before I gave him my answer.'

She watched a muscle work in his jaw, and the stiff black whiskers seemed to ripple. He gave her a look, those cool green eyes appraising, then his gaze was back on the water.

'Raff, it's true.' Hurrying on, she said, 'Then he put in another announcement to say that the engagement was over, and that he intended to pursue me for breach of contract. He'll take me to court.' Taking a breath, she sat up straight. 'He also set out on a campaign to discredit me, and my employer Mrs Downing, her business and the suppliers and customers with whom I work.'

He nodded, non-committal.

'Days before you caught him at the window,' she said, her words rushing again, 'he met me on my front steps, expecting to be asked inside, when unbeknownst to me he'd already been inside my house and had damaged hats I'd prepared for a display.' Evie's teeth clamped down on her lip before continuing. 'It was about to become extremely unpleasant when, thank goodness, Ann came along in her buggy.' A glance at Raff wasn't helping; his mouth was tight, and his frown was deep. 'After that, he came to my place of work threatening all and sundry. And then when you were there, you saw him being a nuisance at my house, peering in the window.' She deflated then, slumping.

'Nuisance?' That's all Raff said, as if he hadn't heard correctly.

'Yes. I've already appointed a lawyer, and I believe the services of a private investigator have been secured.'

'Nuisance?' Raff said again, this time between his teeth. It appeared he'd heard nothing else.

'Well, more than that, I suppose—'

'A bloody deviant,' he ground out. 'Had I known all that, I'd have made sure Bluey stomped on more than your garden.'

Will and Tom rushed down from the wheelhouse shouting with glee, only to be roared at from above by their father: '*Get back up here.*' The boys, wide-eyed, took one look at Raff and scampered back the way they'd come, feet thumping on the steel steps.

Their conversation was being overheard. *Oh God, how embarrassing.* 'So Mrs Downing, my boss, thought it was best if I left for Cobram earlier than planned to ease things.'

Raff took off his hat and rubbed his hair. 'Do you think it will go to court, the breach of contract?'

Evie nodded. 'Mr Campbell, my lawyer, thinks so.'

'Evie.'

Is he disappointed? He was, she heard it in his voice. *No, no, no, he can't be.* She didn't want that. Clasping her hands together, she tried to order her thoughts. The short time on the boat, cruising this beautiful river, and Raff Dolan not ten feet from her the whole time, had had her believing that something good was in the air for her, something that had been under her nose for years. And now this could blow it all away.

'I can only hope that Mr Campbell clears my name. He and the private detective, Mr Barrett.'

Raff was taken aback. 'Private detective?'

'Yes, Raff,' she said, exasperated. She'd told him so, only a moment ago. 'An investigator, Mr Bendigo Barrett. Very respectable person, by all accounts. Cuts quite a distinctive figure. Hair as dark as yours, but with a white streak here—'

'I'm not interested in his damn hair colour. A private detective? Not usually a profession of good reputation.'

Evie bristled. 'Mr Campbell is working with him, so he's good enough for me. I'm to wait for a telegram sent to Cobram advising of the court appearance.' She only glanced at him. 'But I did *not* consent to marrying Edwin Cooper.'

A blowfly zoomed between them and Evie swatted at it. Bluey gave a couple of shudders and snorts and swished his tail as if he'd copped the fly. The boat took a gentle bend and chugged at a slow rate of knots, moving into the centre of the river. Nothing moved on the banks; not the leaves in the trees, and no people, no animals in sight. The landscape had been baked into a still-life painting, serene and immutable.

'Good to know that's cleared up,' Raff finally said, jaw tight. He stood. 'Man like that needs his arse kicked.'

Evie couldn't agree more, with the language and all, but Raff needn't be quite so angry. 'I don't see—'

'I don't need to hear anything else,' he growled. He jammed on his hat and strode to Bluey, reefing his water bottle from the saddlebags.

'Oh, good to know that too, Rafferty Dolan,' she called after him, irritated. 'Because you certainly don't need to be quite so … proprietorial. Perhaps it isn't only Edwin Cooper's rear end that needs kicking.'

Joe turned up at the end of the bench, wiping his hands on a rag. 'Could use a hand in the boiler room, lad,' he said across the deck to Raff. His grin was broad. 'If you're free, that is.'

Evie glared at Raff as he took a long swig, shoved the bottle back into the bags and headed for the boiler room.

Chapter Thirty-one

Bendigo

Lucille had hat boxes stacked high in her arms and could only see to the right of them. The cart carrying her household goods was at the end of the gate.

'Mrs Downing, what on earth are you doing?'

She had to make a full turn to see who'd spoken to her. It was Mr Perkins, her landlord. Her *former* landlord. Handing over the boxes to one of the two fellows David had employed to shift her furniture, she didn't bother correcting the little man with her new title.

'Well, sir, what does it look like I'm doing?'

As if put out, he stood to his full height. A weedy man, he would have blown over if Lucille had puffed. 'I think—well, it appears you're moving out.'

Oh, Mr Perkins. Such a clever deduction. Not only were there a number of boxes already outside the door waiting to be picked up, but the two men were now carrying out rolls of fabric, and the cutting benches would follow.

'Quite so. I believe you were about to evict me, so I have taken it upon myself to save you the trouble.'

'You can't do that without notice.'

Don't splutter, man. 'I am paid up until two weeks from now, and I will use the remainder of that time to clean the house to my standard after I've emptied it.' Standing with her hands on her hips, she said, 'And I will have an independent witness write a letter attesting to the same.' Lucille had no idea if he'd stoop to accuse her of leaving the place dirty, but she was taking no chances. 'So, unless you have something more to say in defence of your despicable behaviour, please get out of my way.'

'I don't know what you mean.' Indignant, his face diffused with a beet red.

'Mr Kingsley certainly knows.'

'Ah. Well, a misunderstanding.'

'Not by me or by Mr Kingsley.'

The men were now moving her sewing machine, a Singer 27, the very latest model and brand new, and so handsome on its treadle table. 'Secure that very well to the cart please, gentlemen.' She knew just where to put it in David's front room.

'I can't have you leave, Mrs Downing. You are an excellent tenant, have been for years and years.' Mr Perkins was turning his hat in his hand. 'I made the mistake of listening—'

'It's too late. I would never feel confident here again. I've already found another place, so much bigger than this one, where I am assured I will never be under threat of eviction.' Lucille gave him her best scowl.

He ducked his head. 'You'll not find a better landlord than me, Mrs Downing.'

'I doubt that, Mr Perkins. I now have a landlord who is not under Beryl Cooper's thumb. You have her to thank for my leaving. Good day to you.'

'We'll see about this,' he began.

'See about what?' David asked as he dodged the men moving more hat boxes and blocks, mannequin heads and baskets of ribbon.

'Mrs Downing is leaving,' Perkins said to him, astounded. 'She's given me no formal notice that she's vacating the premises.' He leaned closer to David. 'You said you weren't going to serve the notice, so you shouldn't have informed her of the eviction.'

'My duty is to protect the woman I married from such contemptible treatment.' David stepped out of the way as the men strode back to the house for more furniture. 'Naturally, the new Mrs Kingsley will be residing at my home from this day forward. You were about to evict her so we've saved you the trouble.'

'The new—? I need formal notice,' Perkins blustered.

'You *gave* formal notice, and I have the proof,' David thundered in return.

Mr Perkins pointed a finger then thought better of it. He spun on his heels.

'Do you have proof, David dear?' Lucille whispered.

'I kept his nasty little eviction notice after he tried to have me serve it. I told him to find someone else to do it. Clearly, he's thought twice about it and found he's come off second best.'

'Oh dear,' Lucille said. 'He can't do anything, can he? I don't want any legal trouble.'

'You are paid up, in advance, and his intent was just nasty. Proof,' he said, patting his pocket as if he had the paperwork tucked there. 'He won't find anyone as diligent a tenant as you, and that's all he's worried about now.' David took her arm. 'Forget that. Let me tell you what I've discovered.'

Before he could begin, the removal men reported that for now, the cart was full.

'We'll be right behind you,' David said. 'Mrs Kingsley will want to supervise the unloading.'

Locking up, Lucille followed David to his buggy. 'Tell me what you've learned.'

David clicked the reins and once out on the road, he leaned in so he wouldn't have to raise his voice. 'Mrs Benton, Evie's friend, told me that Edwin Cooper was seen peeping into Miss Emerson's house.'

'*Peeping?* How dreadful. Poor Evie.'

'Then right while Mrs Benton and Evie were there, a large fellow on a large horse practically trampled Cooper into the shrubs before running him off. Someone Evie knows. A Mr Dolan.'

'Ah, yes. A friend of Evie's.'

'Good thing he showed up. I'll report all this to Mr Barrett directly, but after we unload this first lot at our place, I'd like to take a drive to Miss Emerson's to check all is well. If Cooper has resorted to peeping, I wonder what else he'll do.'

'Awful man. Good idea.' Lucille reached across and squeezed his arm. 'David, I do love the sound of "our place".'

It hadn't taken long for the men to unload Lucille's goods, and David, bless his heart, had already emptied his front room of the scant furniture that had been in situ. Keen to have her sewing machine under the big window, the rest of her millinery accoutrements could wait until she'd made final decisions about where her tables and benches should go.

Oh, what a lovely, bright space.

The men were given a key and instructed to return to the old place to transfer another load.

David was beaming. 'There'll be a hive of wonderful industry in this room, I'm sure, Mrs Kingsley.'

Lucille beamed right back at him then found she had to smartly fan herself.

At Evie's house, all seemed to be in order, at least from the front. David pulled on the handbrake and helped Lucille to the pavement.

The small bushes had indeed been trampled. 'Nothing a little pruning won't fix,' Lucille said. 'Once I'm settled, I'll do it myself for the dear girl.'

A neat cottage of timber, the house sat close to the footpath behind a low picket fence. On either side of the solid door were large windows, one belonging to the parlour and the other a bedroom.

'I can imagine just which window the blackguard was peeping into,' David said. 'If he was peeping, I don't understand why he made it so obvious.'

'Perhaps the large man with the large horse got to him first.'

'Let's have a look around, just in case.'

Dense shrubbery, grown over the little pathway, secluded one side of the house from the street, but David and Lucille found their way through easily enough. Out the back there was an outhouse, a boiler and laundry tub on a stand, and a clothesline, similar to almost every other house like it anywhere. Unusually, a narrow veranda ran the width of the house, offering shade to a number of potted plants by the back door.

'Lovely idea,' Lucille said and admired what she thought were miniature roses. Colourful geraniums were everywhere. A healthy wisteria ambled over the wrought-iron lacework overhead. 'Do you know, I've never been here. It's beautiful.'

David stepped up to the back door. It banged open and clocked him hard in the face. Down he went on one knee, blood erupting as he pitched onto his side. Lucille screamed in a quick rage and kicked at the fair-haired man who tried to shove past her. Stumbling, he swung a fist that skimmed her hip. Then he leaped over David and sprinted towards the other side of the house.

'David, David,' Lucille cried as she slumped to her knees by her husband. She patted around his waistcoat and pulled a handkerchief from a pocket to stem the blood on his face.

His eyes fluttered open. 'I'm all right.' He felt his mouth and tested his nose. 'I don't think it's broken.'

'It's your eyebrow,' she said, dabbing. 'It's split.'

He tried to sit, and blood dripped freely. 'Who was it?'

'I'd say only one guess. Can you stand, my dear? We need to get you to a doctor, and see the police.'

They sat where they were until David said he was steady enough to get to the buggy. The flow of blood had eased, but his white beard was stained with it, along with his shirt and waistcoat.

'We'll try the police first. You drive, Lucille. For the moment I'm a bit wobbly.'

As they staggered together around the other side of the house, along which ran a driveway for a cart, two troopers were marching towards them.

One waved a baton. '*Oi*, you there. You've been reported trespassin'.'

Stopped in shock, Lucille's mouth fell open.

The bloodied handkerchief still pressed over his eyebrow, David muttered, 'Dear God, how far will Edwin Cooper go?'

The troopers hefted David into the buggy, his head was too woozy to attempt it by himself. They assisted Lucille in beside him then led the horse to the police station. Pulling up out the front, one of the constables handed the reins to Lucille.

'And just how do we contact the owner of the house, missus?'

'I won't know how until I hear from her, hopefully within a few days. Miss Emerson has gone to Cobram.'

The constable nodded. 'And why would Mr Cooper be sneaking around in her house and hammer your husband here with the door?'

'To create more trouble, no doubt. Last week he was seen peeping in the front window, and was chased off.'

'By who?' the constable demanded.

Still looking a little peaky, David cleared his throat. 'We don't know his name, but he's another witness once we find him, along with a Mrs Benton, Miss Emerson's friend.'

'Constable, I urge you to take your colleague here and go back to Miss Emerson's house. Anything could have happened inside.'

'Hmm. I reckon a Mr Benton came in to see us t'other day.' The man's handlebar moustache moved as he pursed his lips. 'I'll look for that notice in the paper about the breach of contract.'

'And you'll also contact Mr Campbell, the lawyer? He can verify our relationship to Miss Emerson.'

'Aye, we know Mr Campbell.'

'Good. Thank you for being so obliging. Do you think we might be allowed to go now?' Lucille asked.

''Fraid not yet. We'll need a statement.' He waggled a finger at the police station. 'In you go.'

By the time they got back to David's house, the removal men had made good and the place was full of Lucille's possessions, which spilled into the hallway. The men were nowhere to be seen, nor was the key to her house, so she assumed they were still loading.

'Tomorrow we'll make an appointment with Mr Campbell ourselves, Lucille,' David said, taking his time stepping around the boxes and bags in the hallway. 'I'm not letting Cooper get away with this.'

'You need to see a doctor.'

'I don't think there's much damage. I'll get a good shiner though.' He tried a smile. 'The bleeding's stopped. Shouldn't need stitches.' Dabbing his eyebrow with the ruined handkerchief again, he winced.

'The sooner that awful man is apprehended, the better.' Lucille took his arm and helped him through to the kitchen, thankfully free of any of her boxes, so far. Settling him into a chair, she stoked the oven and set the kettle to boil for the washbowl and a pot of tea. Then she heard the removalists at the front door and met them in the hallway.

'This is the last of it, Mrs Kingsley. We'll just squeeze it in here—' The younger man stopped short, eying David's bloodied beard and shirt.

The older man lugged in a stack of her framed pictures and said to her, 'We put the bigger stuff and the other boxes around the back. Weather's fine, so we'll leave it for now and shift it in tomorrow fer ye. We got it out in time, though, missus, we made sure o' that.' He flicked a glance at David. 'Y'all right, Mr Kingsley?'

'Yes, yes, thank you.'

'What do you mean, "in time"?' Lucille asked, bemused. There was plenty of time.

'Oh. Aye. Bailiff came along to change the locks.' He handed her a now useless key and tipped his hat. 'We'll see ye in the morning,' he said and they left.

Lucille stood a moment, taking it in. Swishing back to the kitchen, she removed the jumping kettle from the stovetop and poured steaming water into the washbowl. 'Did you hear that, David? Mr Perkins has changed the locks. We just got my belongings out in time.'

He nodded. 'Mr Campbell's office first thing in the morning, my dear.'

Chapter Thirty-two

Cobram

That morning, the bakery had drawn Fitz in. He loaded up with a meat pie, and a bag of lemon slice. The pie he'd have soon, the sweet would last a bit longer and would do for later in the day.

His brother was in the station office.

'Been a big day?'

John grunted. 'Quiet one, so far.' He shrugged out of his jacket, snatched off his cap and hung both on the wall behind his desk. 'I have to report to the coroner about Mrs Bayley, get it over and done with, so if ye're gonna eat, do it out there, would ye?' He jerked a thumb over his shoulder.

Fitz nodded, his mouth full, and headed out back. Moments later the station's front door burst open. Startled, he chanced a look through the gap between the hinge and the back doorjamb. John's bum had only just hovered over the seat at his desk when Mr Haines stormed through the door, a bunched newspaper in his hand.

'Seen this?' he demanded and threw it onto the desk.

John remained on his feet. Fitz ducked away. *Haines could have froth coming from his mouth.*

'Page three,' Haines thundered. 'Letters to the Editor.'

Fitz peeked again.

Haines jammed a finger on one section. A lock of his hair flopped onto his forehead and he flicked it off. 'Read it aloud.'

John picked up the paper and cleared his throat. He read the first line. '"Sir, it has come to this roving reporter's attention that there are dire shenanigans regarding the safe purchase, or acquisition, of land in this area …"'

John's brows arched as he read on. '"It appears to this observer that a certain dark element of society in the region has taken it upon itself to bully and harass decent people out of their home and off their property, for the sole purpose of preposterous commercial gain."'

'Well?' Haines barked.

John read more. '"Now it is discovered that the untimely death of a young mother has occurred on this same property, perhaps the result of abandonment or, more likely, from the departure of her husband in sinister circumstances some months prior, regarded to be the work of this dark element."' He stopped. 'I've read enough.' Dragging in a breath, he tapped the page. 'It's signed "Our Correspondent". Could be anyone's handiwork.'

Fitz knew his brother would have no doubt in his mind whose handiwork it was.

John looked steadily at Haines and lifted his shoulder. 'Besides, it's not true what's written, is it, only conjecture?'

Haines looked about to combust. Blustering, covering, he said, 'How would I know? I mean, it implies someone is up to no good, that's for sure.' He puffed for a bit, shying from John's scrutiny. 'It's—inferring things.' Shutting his mouth, he tried to stem some of the fury.

John rubbed his ear. 'No way of knowing who wrote it. The newspaper fellas won't tell me, I know that, and it's not breaking any laws that I'm aware of. Doesn't name anyone. There's nothin' I can do.'

Haines glared at him. 'I reckon it's that new bloke in town, poking around where he shouldn't. The one who was out with Robinson and found the dead woman.'

Fitz remained frozen in place.

John lifted his shoulder again. 'Could be.'

A finger stabbed the air. The heavy greying moustache covered the twisted mouth. 'Have a word to him.'

'About what exactly, Mr Haines?' John knew the man couldn't say anything without putting himself in it.

Haines had nothing. His face bloomed red, stark against his greying hair. 'He's on dangerous ground, that fella,' he spat. 'Tell him that.'

'You want me to warn the new fella that he could be in strife, Mr Haines, is that it?' John kept his voice even. 'Might sound like a threat.'

Haines blinked hard, thinking hard. 'Might save a life,' he said, holding his temper. 'This sort of rot—he slapped the paper—'incites trouble.'

'Well, no one sets much store by anonymous letters,' John said. 'Still, I'll let the new fella know to be careful, that there are rogues about.'

Haines's nostrils whitened. The moustache moved, and a finger pointed. 'You do that, Constable.' He marched out the door.

John waited a few beats and, still staring at the front door, let his breath out slowly. 'I'll bloody kill you, Fitz.'

Fitz headed out to the Bayley's place next morning, wanting to see if there'd been any activity out there that shouldn't have been. What he thought he'd do if he found any evidence of foul play, he wasn't sure. Reporting it to John might be next to useless. It would be grist for the mill, though. Something to keep the pressure up on Haines, something 'Our Correspondent' could wield.

Not in any hurry, he and Patto wandered out of town, the horse well fed and watered. The day was a warm one again, and about to get warmer, no doubt about that. Sweat trickled under his hat, but dried before it dropped into his eyes.

A mood descended. *Shit, I'm feelin' it today.* Solo, riding down a story, no one with whom to share it when he got home after his day. Was this the place to find that other half, someone to live his life with? He was pretty sure it wasn't.

He'd long weighed up country living compared to a city life and still hadn't come to an answer. In the country he couldn't keep to himself enough; the city was too blowsy, aggressive; he'd learned that the hard way. Still, it had to be either-or. Maybe he should reconnect with family again. John, anyway, who hadn't exactly driven him off. That was encouraging, though how to do it was beyond him. He'd have to step carefully; John was touchy. There was no solution, he knew. If he kept looking for one, he'd never find it. Instead, when you least expected, things had a way of finding you, but it was the devil itself not to think about it or wish for it.

At the turn-off to the property, the gruesome vision of Mrs Bayley lying over her baby's grave hit him. Feeling sorry for himself paled in comparison to the desperate misery that Meryl must have experienced. Evie had lost her sister in awful circumstances; what the hell would she go through when she found out? The letter he'd written, the one Jenny Robinson had in her keeping, was on his mind. Had he said enough to Evie, conveyed the depth of his sorrow at the loss of her sister? They were friends, he and Evie. Maybe he should go and find her instead of writing her a note and mailing it, keeping her at arm's length.

What would he feel if John was killed, or died suddenly? He shrugged. Loss, for sure, and he might even miss him, mourn for a bit, but they hadn't been mates, not for years. Had been once; a long time ago John was the only one at home who hadn't outright shunned him.

Fitz had lost contact with other family members. Lawrence, the eldest brother, had told Fitz never to darken his door again. His mother told him in no uncertain terms that he should change his ideas about his place in the world or God would strike the evil from his soul. (Fitz had never been too worried that God would strike anything much.) His father's reaction had been interesting. Although he'd banished Fitz because his wife had insisted, it was done with a rueful smile, and what seemed to be a saddened heart. In the dead of night, not waking Fitz's mother when saying goodbye, the old man had hugged him. 'If only we could live the life we were born to live, eh? Be careful, son.' He'd gripped Fitz's neck then and pressed their foreheads together. When he kissed Fitz warmly on both cheeks and held him hard with tears in his eyes, Fitz knew without a doubt that which he'd always suspected. He was the same type of man as his father.

Bah, water under the bridge. His parents were dead, the farm gone, and he had no idea where Lawrence was. He snorted to himself. It was only luck—good or bad—that he'd come across John. And it was only luck—all good—that he hadn't been hauled off to prison, or worse, to meet his fate for being the person he was. The thought of prison shook him to his bones.

His one significant relationship had ended when Augie had buckled under family pressure and married a girl chosen for him by his family. Marriage to a young woman who didn't know any different was deemed a suitable cover and it was reckoned would most likely 'curb his tastes'. Before that, Augie had always steered clear of his family. When he did visit home, Fitz was never in tow. Augie hadn't been good at hiding who he was, his affection for Fitz had been honest and open. When Mr Pine, his father, heard the rumours, he put his foot down. Hard. Augie resisted for a long while, but one should never tempt fate, as was the case.

A journalist too, Augie had accompanied Fitz on assignment to a town where they were set upon, strung up naked in a horse stall, and beaten. Freeing themselves in the early hours, having to steal clothes to face the world, Augie had been frightened to his core by the violence. He told Fitz that he'd resist his family no longer and would wed at the earliest convenience. Fitz couldn't convince him; crying, pleading made no difference. Augie had been too frightened. Heavy with grief, Fitz let him go. Even though a hollow opened in his heart, Fitz had no doubt that if they'd continued to run the gauntlet, both might have been lured to their deaths.

Had Augie's father orchestrated the attack? The man had made his position clear about Fitz's presence in his son's life.

Fitz never laid eyes on Augie again, and he declined an invitation from Augie to correspond, to keep their relationship alive. He also declined an invitation to the wedding and spent that week drunk until having to better care for Patto stirred his good sense. Bedraggled, thin and stinking, he found a hotel with a bath and sobered up once more. The furtive, clandestine meetings with carousing and clever slim-limbed men since hadn't shaken his fear of being caught, but temptation was harder to beat down. That discovery was frightening, too.

After Augie, his friendship with Raff had continued, strong and platonic, as always. He hadn't ever told Raff about Augie. Though his mate never knew it, he was probably the only reason Fitz hadn't done something mortally stupid. He'd then tried on the idea of marriage to Evie, and gladly found it was not the solution for either of them.

Trouble was, loneliness was beginning to bite, more than it had before. He blew out his doldrums. *Old news, Fitz.*

The Bayley hut came into view. No signs of anyone nearby. *Good.* He dismounted, and he and Patto ambled around to the side of the house. Gazing down a slope to the bank of the river a little distance away, he couldn't hear a thing, not even the birds.

Peaceful. Not a sound. He should visit the graves.

Patto shied, stomped. Fitz turned to see—

A mighty whack cracked him over his left ear. He went down with a grunt, his hand catching in the stirrup. A shot rang and Patto shrieked and jerked, then dragged Fitz down the slope. His arm wrenched and when his hand came free Fitz stumbled, then rolled down the sandy bank. On his back, a kaleidoscope of colour burst over his sight. Gazing up, he caught a dim wavering glimpse of a man watching, on foot, high above.

His head thundered. Blood streamed.

'You lot,' Haines said to a figure splitting into two. 'Throw him in the river.'

Footfalls thudded. Dirt smarted his face. Hands grappled. Two faces swam over him. A creep of black was shutting down his sight, so he closed his eyes.

Chapter Thirty-three

Cobram

John wasn't overly concerned that Fitz hadn't come back to the house last night; he was a big boy. *Hah, he'd find this town too small though.* He'd be careful, the idiot, wouldn't he?

Now that these two fellas in police uniform were standing before him in the station, he was sure Fitz would have to be real careful. Dread seeped into his gut.

Dishevelled, hot, and bleary-eyed, one of them, clutching his hat, said, 'Constable, I'm Sergeant Bill. We've been riding hard, day and night as you might be able to tell.' The man's head was polished and sweaty. A wiry dense red froth that traced the base of his skull and hung over each ear was the only hair on it.

John flicked a glance at the two men. They smelled like they hadn't seen a tub for weeks, but the uniforms were clean, creased maybe from being packed away, maybe not worn lately.

He straightened. 'Sergeant,' he said. 'What can I do for you? I wasn't aware we were expecting any troopers.'

'We're chasing down a dangerous individual by the name of Fitzmorgan O'Shea. Come across him?'

John's face tightened, he could feel it. *Christ, now what?* He'd have to introduce himself to this bloke at some point. A sergeant, for cryin' out loud—

'What's the matter with yer?' the sergeant erupted.

'Funny thing, Sergeant, my name's O'Shea. Stunned me a bit,' John said. *The truth and all.*

Sergeant Bill stared at him, grunted. 'Ah, well, are there any strangers in town? Any bloody ratbags trying to make trouble?'

Mr Haines stepped into the station. 'Plenty of ratbags, Sergeant, but no trouble,' he boomed and nodded towards John. 'I'm sure the constable here has it all sorted. I'm Ernest Haines, resident of the district. What are you here for?'

John stared at him. What the bloody hell business was it of Haines's?

Sergeant Bill gave a short laugh. 'On private police business, Mr Haines, if you don't mind.'

Haines propped for a moment, then after a look at John and throwing back a glare to the men, he acquiesced. 'Of course. Apologies. I'll wait outside.'

'Good idea.' Sergeant Bill watched Haines leave. 'One in every town,' he muttered. 'So back to the troublemakers, Constable.'

John took a breath. 'If they're in trouble here they generally run, take the punt across the river to Barooga and keep going further into New South Wales. They know we can't touch 'em there.' He grimaced. 'Do I need to post a lookout for this character? What's his description?'

Sergeant Bill nodded at his companion. 'Go ahead, Porter.'

'Lean sorta fella,' Porter said. He was a doughy-looking bastard with squinty eyes, a surly mouth and a face that might have been busted open by fists. 'Dark-haired, smart, well spoken. Reckons he's a reporter. Wanted for libel, contempt of court, tryin' to change the course of justice.' He lowered his raspy voice. 'Murder.'

Murder? John nearly swallowed his tongue. 'Well, be assured we'll get him if he shows himself around here.'

'Might be travellin' with a big fella—black hair, green eyes, type of bloke could lift a cart by hisself.'

John shook his head.

'We'll need lodgin's, Constable. Any room at the station house?' the sergeant asked.

'No, Sarge,' John said, thinking quickly. 'That's Constable Stillard's home. I'm in his spare room until he gets back. You could try the pub.' If this bloke was a real sergeant, John could number his days on the force because of the lies he was spruiking.

The sergeant hesitated. 'When's Stillard back?'

'I'm expecting him today. Soon.' *Another lie.*

Sergeant Bill, uneasy now, glanced at his offsider. 'In that case, we better press on. Barooga punt, you said?'

John nodded. 'Not far along the river from here. Punt conveys itself, you're bound to catch it soon enough. Someone's usually around to collect the fare; sixpence each with your horses.'

Bill and Porter took off. John slumped to his chair.

Shit, Fitz. Murder.

Chapter Thirty-four

Cobram
Saturday 24 September

Raff lifted his hat and squinted into the distance. The Cobram landing.

Joe called down from the wheelhouse. 'The punt is on its way back from t'other side. We'll pare back here and wait. Don't wanna snag its cables and winches.'

Across the water, the sluggish carrier had just left the New South Wales bank, heading for their side of the river. On it were two horse and buggies, two single horses and six men.

MacHenry stood alongside Raff on the deck. 'Pull in anywhere along here, Joe,' he called up. 'Not scheduled to take on freight.' He turned to Raff. 'This is your stop.' He handed Raff three pounds.

'What's this for?'

'Can't charge you passage when you worked your way from Echuca.'

'Appreciate it.' Raff pocketed the coins. Evie had paid the fares; he'd give the money to her.

'If ever you're up Swan Hill way, look us up. Our horse stud might need a wheelwright of our own by then.'

Raff watched the punt get to halfway across. 'You're optimistic of better days.'

'I am. Hoping to breed Walers. There's going to be high demand for a sturdy breed of horse for use on properties and also for the military.' MacHenry clapped him on the shoulder then shook his hand. 'I'll go back up to the wheelhouse before I see you off.'

The *Sweet Georgie* idled and Joe came down the stairs, heading for the stern and the heavy rope, waiting to tie up.

'I'll be right back to give you a hand, Joe, just grabbing the last of our stuff.' Raff ducked into the galley where Mrs MacHenry had packed bread and cheese for him and Evie to take, extra vittles to save them some money. The bundle clutched in his arms, he was about to head onto the deck when he spotted two men wearing police caps, and close by on the bank. He flattened himself on a wall inside, out of sight. His breath rushed out of him. *McCosker.*

'Hey there, who's the captain?' he heard one of the men call out.

Mr MacHenry had been on the threshold of the galley when he heard the voice. He took one look at Raff trying to make himself small in the already tiny galley, a query in his gaze. *Trouble?*

Raff nodded, then shook his head. Pulled a face.

Joe answered. 'He's in the wheelhouse. Can I help ye?'

MacHenry didn't move.

'We need to get over to the other side,' the voice replied.

'Well,' Joe said, all laconic, 'punt is on its way.'

'Too slow for us. You get the captain, he'll wanna take us across.'

Raff, eyes fierce, shook his head at MacHenry again then baulked as Evie excused herself past the captain and entered the galley. Her bag in hand, her smile dropped as Raff took a step and hooked an arm about her waist. Pulling her to his side, a finger pressed to her lips for silence, he shielded her from the galley doorway.

MacHenry did an about-face and headed out the way he'd come.

Jesus. 'Stay still, Evie,' Raff whispered. 'That fella out there is no good.'

Evie nodded, clutched his arm with both hands.

Joe called out, sounding impatient. 'Can't take ye across, no room for ye.'

'Get that bloody great horse off and there will be room. Police business, mate.'

'He's my horse, mate.' Raff could've kissed Joe. 'Listen, Constable—'

'Sergeant.'

'—the time I get me horse off,' Joe continued, 'and the boiler stoked up again, the punt will be on this side. Won't save no time us takin' ye.'

MacHenry had returned, passed the galley door on the other side. He was heading for the deck.

'I'm ordering you—'

'Sergeant, is it?' Raff heard MacHenry call out. 'As my man here said, you'd be better headed for the landing. You see the punt? Twenty yards to go and then it's on this side. It's only a six-pence each with your horses, but me, I'd have to charge you ten times that much.'

'Police business, I said,' McCosker bellowed.

'Five shillings a piece.'

Evie's nails were digging into Raff's arm, her hands hot. She was standing rigid beside him, her breath quick on his neck as she leaned closer to speak. 'That's—'

'McCosker,' he murmured. *And the bastard knows Bluey. Christ, I hope MacHenry holds out.* He clamped a hand over Evie's, a quick squeeze of reassurance. When she gripped his fingers, it gave him a jolt.

'You, man,' McCosker shouted, cantankerous and self-righteous. 'Put the gangway across.'

'Sarge, look, the punt's in,' the other trooper called.

Raff heard McCosker again. 'We'll be back for ye, mister,' he snarled. 'I don't take kindly to being disrespected.'

MacHenry waited a beat. 'Good day to you, Sergeant,' he said mildly.

Raff heard the horses move, and dared a look outside.

Evie dragged on his hand. 'Raff, don't.'

'It's all right, they've taken off.' He didn't let go of her but pushed away from the wall and peered out the doorway. The troopers were making their way along the bank to the punt.

MacHenry appeared in the doorway. 'My wife and children are on board.' Joe arrived alongside, peering around him into the galley. 'It's bad enough trying to keep four children quiet and inside a small cabin, but quite another to keep my wife contained. Tell me I did the right thing, Mr Dolan.'

'You did, Mr MacHenry. Those two are crooked troopers out of Ballarat. They've got warrants on their heads.'

'That so?'

'Aye, that's so.'

Evie stepped forward, still clutching Raff's hand and took a breath. 'A friend of ours is a journalist who reported on that man's corruption, and worse. The sergeant's come after our friend and he knows Raff by sight. They're out to do harm.' She squeezed Raff's hand, hard.

Joe lifted his brows, smiling broadly at Raff then at Evie. 'So, lad, don't get off the *Sweet Georgie* until the troopers are on the other side of the river and the punt is on its way back without 'em.'

'True enough.' MacHenry regarded Raff, his blue eyes dark. 'My wife tells me that Miss Emerson confided in her about her journey, and that you're both looking for this mutual friend.'

'That's right,' Raff said. The troopers were now out of sight. 'I had no idea McCosker was so close. I'm sorry we put your family in his way.'

'Nothing happened, Mr Dolan, and we've been through worse than talking to a belligerent trooper. Now, the moment those men are on the other side, we'll get you off my boat.'

Waiting on deck, Evie held her bag and her battered straw hat the toddler had chewed. Mrs MacHenry and the kids had come to say goodbye. Tom and Will solemnly shook hands with Raff. The family would have heard everything.

'Would he have shot you, Mr Dolan?' Tom asked.

'He might have.'

Joe came down to slide the gangway to the bank and bounded across it, a thick rope in his hands to sling around a tree trunk.

'Mr Dolan, did my husband mention,' Mrs MacHenry began, 'that we should be here again in a week? If you need passage back to Echuca by then, look out for us.'

'I will do, thank you. Good to meet you.' He tipped his hat and turned to Joe. 'Thanks for stalling that trooper, Joe.'

'I don't like police at the best o' times, not least ordering me to take 'em anywhere. Besides, they looked skint. We wouldna got paid and I bet they didn't pay for the punt neither.' He took Raff's proffered hand. 'Good luck, lad. With everything,' he said, a tilt of his head at Evie, his eyes alight. Then he headed back to the wheelhouse.

'Miss Emerson,' Raff called, tight-lipped. Evie was extricating herself from the clutches of the young girl. He hadn't forgotten how well his little chat with Evie earlier had gone. That 'proprietorial' thing.

'Coming,' she responded. 'Goodbye for now, Layla.'

Raff led Bluey off first then held out his hand for Evie. Over the gangway on dry land, she let him go, turned and waved. The family waved back.

'Just over the rise is the township, Miss Emerson. Good luck with your sister,' Mrs MacHenry said, one arm over Layla's shoulder, the other jiggling a squirming little Jessica. The two boys had already forgotten Evie; a game of chasey around the deck was far more interesting.

Evie waved again and trudged up the hill behind Raff. Her bag was tied behind Bluey's saddle.

Raff was thinking hard. The two policemen had got off on the opposite riverbank. Would they be back? Would the police here know about Fitz, or know McCosker was a rogue trooper?

The best places to look for Fitz were the newspaper office and the pub. The police station was the last place to visit. First thing, though, he'd better find somewhere for Evie to stay. He doubted they'd find her sister any time soon, and Evie had said that she wasn't sure she'd be welcome to stay there anyway.

He checked over his shoulder. Evie was watching her feet as she traipsed over the little rise. They hadn't exactly mended what amounted to a spat over her non-engagement to Edwin peeping-bloody-tom Cooper. Raff couldn't put his finger on what had happened there exactly. She wasn't saying much. But maybe she'd decided not to talk to him because of their … conversation, or maybe because she was busy looking forward to seeing her sister. Or Fitz. *Bloody Fitz, damn him.* That she'd even considered marrying another fella, meant she'd left Fitz in the past, didn't it? Or maybe she hadn't really left him behind, and this Edwin idiot had just been a distraction.

Jesus Christ. This stuff was beyond him. A man should just flat out speak his mind, just like his pa had said; it's not like he wasn't used to saying what he wanted, whenever he wanted. He just wasn't used to speaking his mind to Evie Emerson.

Nah. He'd wait until he found Fitz. If she looked like she was all moony over him, he'd forget it. He'd *try* to forget it. Did she even know that Fitz wasn't a ladies' man? Did ladies even know that sort of stuff? *How do you tell ladies that stuff?*

Well, it wasn't up to Raff to tell her. But if Evie was all for Fitz, Raff would threaten to break his mate's bloody neck if he didn't tell her himself.

At fifteen or so Fitz had said something like, 'I still don't like girls. Ma said I would but I don't.' At first Raff had joked around that Fitz didn't know what he was missing—until he realised there wasn't a joke in it. After that, Raff, who didn't understand and didn't care what Fitz liked or didn't like, simply remained a friend and that had endured. Not once had it ever been anything other than best friends, not even when they were rolling drunk as young men had there ever been anything else. It just wasn't Raff's way, and Fitz knew it. Besides, Fitz always called him a big lug, not his type.

Evie was hurrying to keep up, and finally spoke. 'Raff, where do you think we should start?' She had a hand on her hat and the other bunched in her skirt as she clambered over the sandy bank.

'Pub,' he barked, still thinking of throttling Fitz.

'Not for my sister.'

Then he softened, scratched his forehead. 'The pub is usually where Fitz gets his stories. We can find a shop for you to sit in and have a drink of tea or something, ask the ladies there about your sister.'

'What about a newspaper office if the town has one? They might know of Fitz and of Meryl. I could go there while you go to the pub.'

He waited at the top of the rise for her. As she came alongside, she was puffing. 'We'll see,' he said. 'You'd be better off talking to the ladies.'

'We will see.' She stood a moment, a firm set to her mouth, and pulled off her hat. She swished it in front of her face then plonked it back on again. 'I'm not going to sit around sipping tea while you're off at the pub.'

'I won't be whiling away my time,' he rapped. 'I'll be looking for Fitz.' He headed for the town, for the buildings he could see. 'Where else could you be asking after your sister?'

She was silent for a moment as she kept up, then said, 'The post office.'

He marched on. That was a good idea. He'd get her to the post office, wait for her, take her to a store for a cup of tea, then he'd find a pub. If he had no luck there, he'd find the newspaper office. He didn't want to go to the police station, but he might have to. The next thing would be to find lodgings. For Evie, at least.

Then he'd go in search of Fitz.

Chapter Thirty-five

Cobram

Evie pointed. 'There it is. I'm sure I won't be long, just need an address for her.' She barely waited for Raff's frown to clear and for him to nod assent, sweeping ahead of him. The post office had been difficult to locate and eventually she'd had to ask directions of a local person. Raff hadn't been happy letting her out of his sight, but she'd be careful; his surliness was most likely worry rather than him being a pain. *Goodness, it's warm here.* If her heartbeat would just stop racing, she'd have a chance to cool off after the horrible excitement on the boat.

McCosker had given her a huge fright—had he seen her, he might have recognised her from the railway station—and it had taken all her wits not to leap over the side of the boat to get away. But when Raff gripped her hand and she held her nerve, things felt different. Joe had been wonderful. Even Mr MacHenry had been calm in the face of such antagonism from those troopers. And Raff had held her tight, had kept her by his side. *Gracious, it's not just the sun making me warm.*

But then he got all prickly again. *Who could understand men?*

She finally entered the post office, its lack of signage inconvenient, ahead of another woman who'd smiled cheerily. Her bonnet, a very old-fashioned style in plain, unbecoming calico shaded an open face with freckles. The hat would have to go, but the freckles were refreshing to see. Many ladies tried to hide the spots dusted from the sun, but it gave a woman an air of happy-go-lucky, in Evie's opinion, even though a hat would protect her from acquiring them. She nodded her thanks and returned the smile, stepping towards the counter. No one else was about. The floorboards creaked underfoot, her boots making the only other sound.

'Good afternoon,' she said to the short and rotund man behind the counter. 'I'm new in town and looking for my sister. The only address I have for her is care of the post office. Can I have a residential address for her, please?'

'If I have one, madam,' the man said, his belly pressed against the counter, his sleeves held back from his wrists by bands on his thick forearms. He must have been hot in his waistcoat and cravat, but his face was without a sheen of sweat. She couldn't be sure that her own appearance wasn't shining from the effects of the weather. 'What's her name?' he asked.

'Mrs Roy Bayley,' Evie said.

She heard the gasp from behind her, at the same time the clerk's mouth dropped open.

'Er …' he began, and seemed at a loss.

'Excuse me, miss,' the woman behind her said. She indicated that Evie should step aside from the counter. 'It's all right, Mr Evans. I'll help here.'

'Righto.' The clerk smartly turned away from the counter.

'I'm Mrs Robinson,' the woman said to Evie.

'Miss Emerson. My sister is Meryl Bayley. How can you help me?'

'Mr Bayley and my husband were good friends, Miss Emerson.' Mrs Robinson was steering Evie outside. 'Let's find a seat. There's one outside. Do you have someone with you?'

That alarmed Evie. 'What is it?' she asked, glancing at Raff as she came out the door. One look at her face and he straightened, pushing off the hitching rail where he'd waited. 'Raff,' Evie said, 'there's something wrong.' When Raff reached her side, she said to the woman, 'Please just tell me. Mr Dolan here is a friend.'

Mrs Robinson nodded at Raff, her gaze evaluating. She sat, her cheery face of earlier now sombre. 'Miss Emerson, I have the most awful news, I'm afraid.'

Evie allowed Raff to help her onto Bluey's back. He gave her a leg up, trying to look anywhere but at her, adjusted a stirrup so she could fit her foot into it and waited until she'd organised herself in the saddle. Raff, on foot, then led the horse down the road to where Mrs Robinson had directed them before she'd gone off in her cart. 'My husband and I will meet you somewhere on the road and take you the rest of the way to the Bayley property,' she'd said.

Evie was numb. How could Meryl—or anyone—just wander off and die like Mrs Robinson had suggested? The kind woman had told her only the barest amount, but declared that she, and her husband, Cyril, would do what they could to help. After all, she said, Evie and Raff were strangers in town.

'How long before the turn-off she mentioned?' Evie asked from high on top of Bluey. Her throat was tight and sore from withholding sobs.

'Not long.' Raff was subdued.

'I should walk, Raff. I feel quite silly perched up here. Would you help me get down?' He hesitated and she said, 'I'm not going to have the vapours or anything.' There was still no reaction so she gathered her skirt, deciding to dismount by herself. *Goodness, Bluey is a big horse.* It would be a little difficult getting down without falling in an undignified heap on the dirt. 'Would you please help me get off?' she cried. 'It's a long way down.'

Raff reached up for her, his hands on her waist, and she slid ungracefully from the saddle, a leg trailing awkwardly over it. Finally back on her feet, he let her go as if he'd brushed a hot coal. Sweeping the creases from her dress, and modesty preserved, she sniffed. Blinked. Started to walk. Keeping up with Raff who stared ahead.

His condolences had been swift and heartfelt, and now he seemed not to know what to do with her. That made two of them. *Meryl, dead.* Her sister. It hurt to think.

Mrs Robinson had relayed only scant bits and pieces. The woman had kept glancing at Raff, and Evie thought perhaps she'd been reluctant to say too much without knowing where he fitted in the picture.

After a time, valiantly keeping up with his stride, Evie said, 'I don't know what to do, Raff.'

He nodded. 'Understandable. I think the best we can do is wait for the Robinsons and take it from there.'

'And finding Fitz?'

Another hesitation. 'Wherever he is, he'll keep,' he said, his gruff tone a surprise. 'You all right?'

'If you're kind to me I'll collapse.'

He made a noise of sorts. 'Can't have that.' He pointed at a cart in the distance, stopped up the road. 'That might be the Robinsons. Do you want to remount and we can hurry it up?'

She nodded. Foot once again in the stirrup she clambered over Bluey's back unaided, puffing, not caring that her skirt had ridden to her knees. In the saddle, adjusting as best she could and rueing her bare shins, she gave a start when Raff swung up behind her. She didn't dare move. Despite her bereavement and the discomfort sharing the saddle, the solid wall of him on her back, hot, sweaty and dusty, was real, and right. Just like on the boat when he'd shielded her from McCosker. His arms around her as his hands gripped the reins, he was loose and relaxed. Yet not for one minute did she think he'd let her slip to the ground.

Bluey lengthened his stride to a slow canter, and Evie did her best to keep a good seat, her knees tight; it had been so long since she'd ridden a horse, much less one this size.

Winding back the speed as they got closer, Raff pulled Bluey up at the cart, and touched his hat. 'Raff Dolan,' he said to the man driving. 'This is Miss Emerson.'

'Cyril Robinson. Ye've met me missus here,' he said as Mrs Robinson nodded. 'This way.'

The cart turned onto a track and drove steadily for a short period of time. Evie stiffened and took in a sharp breath. She'd be there, where Meryl had been, very soon. When Raff's big, callused hands took hers from her lap, sliding them onto the reins with his, tears plopped to her cheeks. Grateful he couldn't see them, she had no doubt he knew they were there. He squeezed her hands the once and kept them in his grip.

The track was lengthy, narrow in places where the scrub leaned over it, as if the drought had loosened roots. In other places the way ahead was wide and clear enough for her to catch glimpses of the river winding in the distance. She thought she saw a white and sandy patch of beach.

Oh, had Meryl been happy here in this dried-out country? Had she loved it? What had she done out here? How far away had she been from someone else to talk to other than Roy? She wondered about Mrs Robinson. The woman seemed about Meryl's age; Mr Robinson perhaps a bit older. Her chest ached, her throat was taut. Why oh why had she not tried harder to reach out to Meryl before now, tried to visit earlier, even if she'd have been rejected? Her acerbic sister might have relented if Evie had travelled to find her, had more robustly attempted a reconciliation. She drew in a breath and let it out in a heavy sigh, and Raff pressed a little closer. Bluey trotted along behind the cart.

The track wound around to a clearing and there stood a little house, a hut really, but sturdy and well maintained. When the cart pulled up, Raff halted Bluey and dismounted. He held out his hands for Evie.

Mr Robinson alighted the cart and his wife climbed to the ground. 'I knew your sister and her husband,' he said. 'Knew Roy better, o' course, but well, then he, er …'

'Then he what?' Evie asked.

'We dunno where he is. He's been gone maybe six months.'

Evie gaped. 'Six months?'

'More, prob'ly.' He looked to his wife for verification. She nodded. 'There's a bit of a walk to the graves. This way,' he said. He slung water bottles over his shoulder and went ahead with his wife.

Graves? More than one?

She hardly noticed the sun beating a thrum on her head. Leaves crackled underfoot. When the Robinsons stopped, the first thing Evie saw was the little cross standing at the head of a small mound lined with rocks. A second mound, more recent and alongside, was unmarked.

'I'm, um, workin' on new crosses for them,' Mr Robinson said. 'Thought it proper.'

Evie stared. Raff reached for her but she moved away. 'She had a child?' she asked. Her lips were dry, her tongue thick and the lump in her throat refused to dislodge.

'A boy,' Mrs Robinson said. 'He died a year or so ago, not even a toddler. They didn't know what of. He was in his cot, didn't wake up.'

Glassy-eyed, Evie crept closer. She peered at the cross. 'Is that his name on it?'

'Dallas.'

Evie's hands flew to her face. 'My father's name,' she cried in a whisper.

Raff was beside her. 'You know what happened here?' he asked Mr Robinson.

Standing close by, twisting his hat in his hands, the man said, 'We found her, just by accident really, lyin' over the boy's grave. Seemed it's where she died.'

'Oh.' Evie almost couldn't hold back the sobs. She swallowed, gulped air. 'You both found her?'

Mr Robinson shook his head. 'I was with a Mr Morgan. He'd come to look at the place and I showed him this part too, without knowing—' His voice cracked.

Evie glanced at him, noticed the tears forming, his chin puckering. Poor man. He seemed so nice, caring.

'Mr Morgan, you say?' Raff was gruff again.

'Yeah, we wandered in to check for signs of Mrs Bayley. He, er, helped me in town and wanted to know about Mr Bayley gone missin'.'

Mrs Robinson had come to stand beside Evie. 'I believe you might know Mr Morgan, Miss Emerson.'

Bemused, Evie shook her head, but then she couldn't make much of anything right now. 'No, I don't think so.'

Mrs Robinson withdrew an envelope from her pocket.

'What was his first name, did he say?' Raff asked.

'It's Fitz,' Mr Robinson stated.

Evie turned to Raff. 'Fitz was here.'

'He wanted me to safekeep this for you.' Mrs Robinson pressed the envelope into Evie's hand, but she was watching Raff.

Evie stared down at the envelope before showing Raff. His face was set, his frown deep, eyes glinting.

'Let's get out of the sun, maybe go back to the house,' Raff said, beckoning her. 'Mr Robinson, have you seen Fitz recently?' He was striding, Evie hurrying beside him.

'Call me Robbo. I saw him, a day or so back, not since.' Robbo was keeping up and so was his wife. 'Jenny will take you through the hut, Miss Emerson. Your sister's things and all.'

Evie nodded, numb, the letter clutched tight.

Mrs Robinson took her arm, more for companionship than for help. They fell back behind the men. 'He left another couple of letters, too,' she said. 'I think he was worried.'

'About what?' Raff called over his shoulder.

'Not sure,' Robbo answered, 'but we talked about a few things. There's a crook here, name of Haines. Caused a bit of pain hereabouts, I can tell yer. We think he tried to drive the Bayleys off this place. Then Roy was gone, but the missus wouldn't leave her little 'un's grave.'

Evie hiccupped a sob.

'You all right, Evie?' Raff asked, pausing long enough to look over his shoulder. Seeing her nod he strode off again.

'Your Mr Morgan seems a good man,' Jenny Robinson said, offering encouragement. 'He can't be far away.'

Raff said nothing, just marched on.

Evie agreed with Mrs Robinson. 'He is a good man.'

At the house, no one wanted tea; it would mean lighting a fire to boil the billy and Evie didn't need to stay for too long right now.

Raff made the same clear. 'I'll want to find Fitz, sooner than later.'

Mrs Robinson took Evie to Meryl's bedroom, pressed her hands tightly and left her sitting on the bed, closing the door as she left the room. Leaving the letter beside her on the bed, Evie's sobs came silently. They scraped her throat as she rocked with her face in her hands. *Meryl, little Dallas. And Roy. Where was he? What happened here?* No answers yet. No answers. She groped for her hanky, mopped up, blew her nose. Sat with shaky breaths as she tried to calm down.

After a time, she stood and ran her hand over the neat dresser, a little dust coming away on her fingers. She didn't open the drawers. Noticing the dress hooked on a peg on the back of the door, she walked across the room to touch it. A simple day dress, a little ragged and well worn, patched. No scent, no trace of Meryl. Her heart lurched, squeezed, when her gaze fell on a little wooden doll dressed in trousers, the fabric of which matched the poor dress hanging on the door.

There was hardly anything else in the room. A pair of men's good boots sat under a small table, a bag of some sort of implements on top. Roy's shaving gear, perhaps. The room was suddenly too hot and she rushed to the window, unlatching it with fumbling fingers. Leaning out to catch the air cooling her face, with a sigh she let her gaze drift down the gentle slope towards the river—

'Fitz,' she whispered, disbelieving her eyes. Her heart thumped. She stared hard at the prone, but unmistakable figure on the bank, the water lapping his boots. '*Fitz!*' she shrieked. Nothing moved on him, not a hair on his head. She burst out of the bedroom and raced past a startled Jenny Robinson who was cleaning away the mess in the kitchen.

Raff had led Bluey away from the house to tie him up in the shade of a gum tree.

'Fitz is down by the water,' she shouted at him as she rounded the house. Her skirt in both hands, she flew over the rough and patchy dirt to the edge of the riverbank. Slipping and sliding the rest of the way, stumbling, she fell to her knees and scrambled on all fours to the heap that was Fitzmorgan O'Shea, lying on his back, the side of his head a bloodied, matted mess.

Raff skidded to his knees beside her. 'Jesus, Fitz.' He picked up a hand, felt for a pulse. 'He's alive.' Bending to Fitz's chest, he said, 'Heartbeat's not robust.' He pressed his hands over Fitz's legs and arms. 'Nothing broken.'

Evie sobbed once. Fitz was blank, his eyes closed, his mouth slack, and he was filthy, as if he'd been in the river and had crawled out. He was badly sunburned.

Robbo had slipped in behind them. 'Let's get him up the bank.'

They pulled Fitz to his feet between them, then Raff scooped him up. Fitz hadn't made a sound. His head lolled, his eyes closed, his skin bright and angry where the sun had got him. Evie swished flies away until they got him inside the house.

'The bedroom,' Mrs Robinson said. 'You men get him out of those clothes. Miss Emerson, throw open the shutters, let's get the air in. Wet something to drape over him. I need fresh water, quick as you can.'

Evie unlatched the shutters and flung them against the walls. She pulled back the bedcovers, dragged away a sheet, ran back to the river, dunked it furiously. Once it was sodden, she clambered up again, her boots and her dress saturated.

Raff had shucked Fitz of his boots, shirt and trousers, and grabbed the dripping sheet from Evie. He threw it over Fitz who was now only clad in his worn out long johns.

'Don't die, you bugger,' Raff whispered.

Mrs Robinson trickled water from a bowl over Fitz's face and head. Dragging a chair close, she sat beside the bed, and tipped a little into his mouth, watching it dribble over his tongue. 'Was his hat anywhere?'

'I'll find it,' Robbo said.

'Find his horse. Patto won't be far away,' Raff called after him.

Evie sagged on the doorjamb. 'There's a nasty wound on his head.'

'His scalp is sunburned too,' Mrs Robinson said, still trickling water over him. 'I need a hat to fan him off.'

Raff snatched his off his head and handed it over. Backing away, he scraped something underfoot. He picked up Fitz's letter to Evie. Catching her eye, he set it on the dresser and didn't look at it again. He dropped his chin as he filed past her out of the room.

Fitz remained motionless under Mrs Robinson's ministrations. Evie stumbled back into the kitchen room. Groping for a chair, she sat and stared into the empty fireplace. Her sister's death, the death of her nephew she'd known nothing about, and now Fitz injured and … dying. Her chest was leaden, her limbs clumsy. All she could do was gaze around.

Mrs Robinson had only got so far tidying away the remnants of a long abandoned meal. Possum droppings dotted the floor and the mantel, and the discarded broom Mrs Robinson had wielded rested by the kindling basket. That was something Evie could do now. She would light a fire and get the billy boiling after all; it was clear they'd be here a while. Maybe there was another bucket somewhere she could use to carry water.

The kitchen was stuffy. Popping off the chair, she rushed to the windows, tucking aside the worn curtains. Opening the door, she used a rock nearby as a doorstop, no doubt its purpose, and stepping outside, couldn't see anything to lug water up from the river. She stood a moment, trying to corral her thoughts. They tossed about in her cloggy brain, unruly, disjointed, not landing anywhere. Paralysing.

'What do you need?' Raff asked, coming from the side of the hut. His voice was jumpy as if he was trying to catch his breath.

'A bucket for water. I'll get the fire going, find the tea leaves. Cups. I don't know, I don't know,' she said, her breath short as she gazed towards the scrub that shielded the house from the path to the gravesite. She put a hand to her head as Raff slipped past her.

Turning back inside, she found the tea in a box with a couple of pannikins, a used book of matches, candles, a small sewing kit, a thin cake of lye. No sugar anywhere, no flour or tobacco, or tins of food—

Oh, Meryl. What terrible despair you must have endured.

The last time Evie had seen her sister was when Meryl left their mother's funeral. She'd been off-colour then, perhaps in the early stages of her pregnancy. *Meryl hadn't said anything, not a thing.* Evie closed her eyes and tears squeezed out to roll down her cheeks. Her heart hurt. She didn't know how to deal with any of this. So many unanswered questions.

And here I am, just standing around like some weepy nincompoop with Fitz half dead in the next room.

Sucking in a last ragged breath, she sniffed, swiped at her face, smearing dust with the tears. She kneeled to the fireplace, grabbed twigs and leaves from the basket, packed together the makings of a fire and reached into the box for the matches.

By the time Raff had lugged a large tub inside, the fire was crackling and she'd found decent pieces of wood to load it up. He set down the water and she dunked the billy and then a pitcher and sat back on her heels.

Robbo called from outside. 'Got 'is horse, he wasn't far off.'

Evie staggered to her feet and went to the door. Dear Patto was looking happy with himself. He still had his saddle, along with Fitz's rifle and saddlebags.

Robbo studied a hat in his hand. 'No blood on it.' He handed it to Raff who shoved it into the tub and took it to the bedroom. Robbo filled a pannikin of water from the pitcher, had a long drink, and sat opposite Evie, who slumped in a chair. 'Don't you worry, we'll get the rest of this cleared up, Miss Emerson.' He lifted a hand and waved it around the room. 'She always kept a clean house, did Mrs Bayley.'

Evie nodded, unable to speak.

Jenny Robinson came out of the bedroom. 'Cyril, I'll go home, pack some things, food, bedding, some ointment and come back. Perhaps you would go into town and bring Dr Kennedy here. I don't think we should move Mr Morgan without his say-so.' She gave Evie a wan smile. 'I'll be an hour or so, all right?' she said, and Evie nodded.

Raff came out of the bedroom. 'Take Fitz's horse, Robbo,' he said. 'Leave us the rifle and saddlebags.'

Robbo loosened Fitz's rifle and belongings and handed them to Raff as his wife drove off. Then he mounted Patto. 'It's gettin' on in the day. If I find the doc, we'll be back as soon as possible.' He wheeled and galloped off.

Raff headed for Bluey and unstrapped his rifle and bags and came back inside.

'Why would you need another rifle?' Evie asked.

'Do you know how to shoot?' Raff's cool, flinty stare seemed to glide through her.

She shook her head.

'You might have to learn quick. The wound on Fitz's head is not from a fall. Someone's bashed him.' He jiggled the rifle and pouch lightly in his hands as if checking their weight. 'And they might be back.'

Chapter Thirty-six

Bendigo

Lucille and David, seated in front of Mr Campbell's desk, waited as the lawyer read the court's paper. He adjusted spectacles that perched safely on his misshapen nose with fingers that dwarfed the delicate wire frames. His brows rose as he read.

'So, we have here a summons for Miss Emerson, on the tenth of next month. Plenty of time to build a bit more of a case against this scurrilous Cooper. Your police report after his attack on you will add weight, too.' He nodded at David. 'I'm pleased to see you are recovering well.' He glanced to the back of the room where Bendigo Barrett stood. 'If you will, Mr Barrett, please have a seat here with us. I believe you've been busy.'

'Thank you, Mr Campbell.' Mr Barrett settled in a chair next to Mrs Kingsley. 'I have secured a written statement from Miss Thompson, the lady in pink at the railway station, and I've also found instances of Mr Cooper's previous attempts at what amounts to extortion. Not a charming fellow,' he said, and pushed at the errant white lock of hair that fell over his forehead. 'I've had experience with this type of man before. They're not easily dissuaded; their intent is often all-consuming to the detriment of their prey, and they're very hard to bring to justice.' His gaze drifted a moment, as if he were remembering another such incident. 'In this case, it seems it's not only the man himself who is a predator. It looks to me as if his mother and his sister are in on the scheme, too.'

'Poor Evie,' Lucille said, fanning herself. 'Terrible business. Terrible.'

'Indeed.' Mr Campbell leaned back. 'We'll certainly use what Mr Barrett has uncovered to date, and what you, Mr and Mrs Kingsley, have provided as to her good character, along with your witness statement about his attack on you. It might be enough to prevent Miss Emerson from ongoing litigation.' The lawyer lifted his chin towards the detective. 'And Mr Barrett assures me that the unfortunate ladies victimised by Mr Cooper's previous attempts have been contacted. We hope at least one of them will provide a statement, so Miss Juno will follow that up.'

Mr Barrett said, 'I'm unsure about the very first lady I found. Her family paid the agreed sum and the, er, problem went away. If she replies to my further request, I might put it to her that Mr Campbell would enjoy representing her to recoup her family's losses.'

'I would indeed enjoy that,' Mr Campbell said. 'Now, Miss Emerson must receive notification of the summons as soon as possible. You say that she is away.'

Lucille was fanning madly. *Oh my Lord, not the surges now.* She felt a light sheen of perspiration on her forehead. She inclined her head towards David.

He nodded at her, a slight twist of worry on his brow. 'Yes,' he answered Mr Campbell, 'to find her sister in Cobram. We've been asked to telegram her if this came to be, so if there's nothing else, we'll get to the post office and let her know. It's some days' travel to and from there I believe, so the earlier she's aware of the issue the better.'

'By all means. Thank you for coming in today.' Mr Campbell tabled the folded letter in its envelope, the original from the magistrate's court. 'I'll go through this with her when she returns. Mr Barrett might have something else for us by then, too.'

The private investigator stood when David drew Lucille to her feet. 'If there is anything more you can think of,' Mr Barrett said, 'drop a note to my home. Good day.'

Outside on the busy street, Lucille pulled at her collar.

'Are you quite all right, my dear?' David asked.

'Terribly stuffy in there, wasn't it?' she replied, and flapped her hands in front of her face.

'I hadn't noticed.' He peered at her. 'Are you unwell?'

'Just in need of fresh air. Goodness, it came over me quickly.' She could stamp her foot, it was such a bother. Seems she hadn't escaped the brunt of what other contemporaries had suffered. And, oh dear, the treatment for such an affliction was anything but reassuring if she were to go by the information the ladies shared.

'Let's get you home,' he said. 'Can't have the pair of us out of action if we're going to be needed. Can you manage if we go via the post office and send Evie the telegram?'

'Of course, I can. I'm not ill, nothing to worry about,' Lucille said, grateful that as quickly as the sudden feverish rush of heat had erupted, it fell away, leaving her sticky with perspiration and a little boggle-eyed. She hoped she wouldn't be headed for the madness some suffered and be dragged off to an asylum. She looked up then at David's trusted smile, let out a relieved breath and took her husband's arm. 'Nothing at all.'

Chapter Thirty-seven

Cobram
Saturday 24 September, late afternoon

Constable John O'Shea knew his face was red. The burn of anger had clawed over his neck. Haines was in the police station again, and two of his men were standing by him, their faces set, pugnacious and threatening.

Haines was caustic. 'I don't want any bastard out there on that property, you hear me?' He jabbed a finger at John.

'How the hell am I to stop people wandering around the countryside? And it's not yours to warn folk off,' John fired back. 'I've heard your cronies here get up to that sort of thing.'

The finger jabbed again. 'It'll be my property soon enough and I don't want anybody getting ideas about it. You just make sure no one goes out there.'

'If I find you and your mates here harassing anyone else—'

'Constable O'Shea.' Cyril Robinson burst through the door, his eyes squarely on John. 'You best get out to the Bayley property.'

Haines and his two men turned. O'Shea stared.

'That new fella, Fitz Morgan. Someone clobbered him, and he's near drowned at the Bayleys' place.' He stopped, breathless, then turned to find Haines was glaring at him, his two men restless. He stopped, mouth open.

John gaped.

'Near drowned?' Haines's face mottled with fury. He stood rigid, glared at his men. One of them backed up a little.

John erupted into action, grabbing a rifle from the wall rack and pocketing a handful of bullets. He snatched his hat off the peg, marching towards Haines. 'If this has your mark on it,' he seethed through clenched teeth, his face blanched, 'I'll come for you.' He shouldered Haines out of his way and stepped onto the road.

Robbo followed, throwing himself onto Patto's back. 'I'm gonna find the doc, head back out there with him,' he said.

'That's Fitz's horse,' John bristled.

Robbo's face set. 'I didn't steal it. Mr Dolan said to take him.'

'Mr Dolan?' Then John's memory tickled. 'Big fella, black hair?'

Robbo, still wary, nodded.

Dolan, the wheelwright family who lived next door in Ballarat when they were kids. Fitz's mate. Raff, that's it. Raff was his mate. *What's going on?* 'The doctor has gone to old Mr Beattie's,' he told Robbo. 'I saw him there earlier. Hurry up.'

Robbo took off. John rubbed his head hard, slapped on his hat. Dolan is out there with Fitz, and a pair of bloody troopers is lookin' for him. And just now, Haines's men looking suspicious—

'You watch yourself, Constable,' Haines said, pushing past, nudging John aside, his men following. 'I won't take your nonsense,' he puffed, all for show and loud enough for onlookers to hear.

John took no notice; he'd deal with the arrogant bastard after he found Fitz. People were staring. Two ladies had stopped on the street, mid stride, eyes wide. The shopkeeper across the road who'd been brushing down his windows, watched, leaning on his broom. Two men tying up their horses at the next rail found sudden interest in their saddlebags, hats hiding their faces. Three town kids darted in and out, one shouting in a mimic of Haines's boom, 'I won't take your nonsense,' before John took a swipe at him with his boot.

His rage boiling, he ran to the stables at the back of the station, fitted a bridle to his horse. Wrenched the saddle from the rail, threw it on, buckled the girth, and climbed up. *Jesus, what's Fitz got himself into now? Clobbered, near* drowned? *Jesus.* He shoved his hat into a pocket and kicked his horse into a gallop. *Jesus Christ, Fitz.*

Never had the run out to a place taken so bloody long. *Don't die, brother, don't die.* He flicked the reins and his mount picked up speed. Damn gelding hadn't had a run for a while, but he lengthened his stride and the road sped under his hooves. *Hang on, Fitzmorgan. Hang on.* He rode hard, pushing his horse. Emotion roared up from John's guts, clawing at his throat. He had to blink hard, and swallow. Good thing the day was too hot, the breeze they made too swift; tears—if there were any—might've dried before they landed on his cheeks.

The turn-off was ahead and he slowed up, steering the horse onto the track. Backing off a gallop, he threw the reins away once he saw the hut ahead and clambered off his horse. Stumbling, he got to the door. 'Fitz,' he yelled and pounded inside.

Chapter Thirty-eight

Raff thrust out from the bedroom, rifle aimed squarely at the trooper's chest. Evie stood, her eyes wide in shock, her dress filthy and her face bleary.

'Dolan. Where's Fitz?'

Raff's mouth dropped open and the rifle lowered a little. 'John?' He stepped back, jerked a thumb towards the door he'd just come through.

'Alive?' John's breath stuck in his throat, his feet rooted to the spot.

'Yeah.' Raff rested the rifle by the door.

John barrelled past Raff, who followed. There was Fitz, sodden, still out cold. Creeping forward, John sat on the chair beside the bed and gaped at the sunburned skin, blisters forming. He peered at his brother's scalp. Blood encrusted a gash and the lump around it. 'What the hell?' he whispered.

'Reckon a rock, or a lump of wood blindsided him,' Raff said from the doorway. 'Evie here, Miss Emerson, found him down by the river. He hasn't come round yet.'

'How long?'

'Not sure. A fair while, looking at the sunburn. Waiting for the doctor.'

'He's on his way.' John scooted the chair closer to where Fitz's head lay on the pillow. 'Who's Miss Emerson?' he asked, looking back at Raff.

'Mrs Bayley's sister.'

'Christ,' John muttered. His voice low, he said, 'Don't let her know I'm Fitz's brother.'

Raff nodded. 'All right.'

John turned back to take up Fitz's hand but he hesitated to touch it. It too was burned. He grabbed up the rag lying in the bowl and dribbled water over his brother's arm. 'Christ,' he said again, closing his eyes a moment. 'Could it get any worse?'

Raff grunted. 'Yeah. There are crooked troopers out of Ballarat after us.'

John looked at him. 'A Sergeant Bill, is it?'

'Might be,' Raff said, frowning. 'Bill McCosker, bald on top of his head with a frizzy red mane, and another bloke who looks like an old boxer.'

'Sounds like the fellas I saw this morning.' John rubbed his head hard with both hands, the damp rag smearing the dust on his forehead. 'I sent the pair of them over the river. God only knows where they'd be now.'

'We saw them take the punt.' Then Raff nodded towards the bed. 'Fitz named McCosker and his mates for corruption in a newspaper report, and McCosker's come after him. He'll be back. He's wily enough to know when he's been sent on a goose chase.'

John stood, dropped the rag back into the water bowl. 'Could use a drink,' he said, heading out of the room.

Miss Emerson's hands were clasped tight. 'Billy's boiled, Constable,' she said. 'I'm Evie Emerson, from Bendigo.'

John didn't offer his name. 'Miss Emerson, I hope you're not harmed.'

Raff came out from the bedroom. 'Fitz was chasing a story, got into some bother.'

'Clearly,' John said. 'Why are you two here, though?'

'We were all friends once Fitz got to Bendigo. He met Miss Emerson there some years back.'

'Not an answer.'

Raff watched Evie as she roused herself and headed for the bedroom. He stood aside as she glided past him, head down.

'Friends, is it?' John asked.

Raff was in no mood to explain. There'd been no love lost between Fitz and John in their later years. Yet when John had dropped into the chair and had gone to take up Fitz's hand, he couldn't deny that the man had been rocked by what he saw.

The constable was helping himself to a pannikin of tea from the billy, then he dragged a chair out from the table and slumped into it. 'I was only out here a few days or so back.'

Raff, standing at the bedroom door, heard him but took no notice. Instead he was watching Evie as she sat with Fitz. What might have been in the letter Fitz had left for her?

She bent towards Fitz, squeezing the wet rag over his neck. 'Don't die, Fitz,' she was whispering. 'Please don't die ...'

The words clenched Raff's heart so tight that for a few moments he missed what else she said. But the next words he heard nearly undid him.

'... love you, Fitz, so don't you dare die. There are two of us—'

He turned away before he heard any more, his mouth tight. A lump of rock sat on his chest, thunder beating where his heart was supposed to be.

'What?' John asked.

Raff wiped his mouth with the back of his wrist. 'Nothing. He's fine. Evie's with him.'

The policeman relaxed a little, his hands cupping the tea. 'So Fitz might have bit off more than he could chew this time?'

'Maybe.'

'This Bill McCosker. Why aren't other troopers after him? How come he's roamin' around the countryside if he's so crooked?'

Raff lifted a shoulder, eyes cold. 'Slippery fella.'

John frowned hard, and an ugly twist pulled on his mouth. His voice dropped. 'Or is he after Fitz for some … other crime?'

Raff was carefully blank. 'Not that I know of.'

John gave a grunt, out of sorts. 'Right then.' He shifted in the chair, as if uncomfortable with his thoughts. 'I might not have been in touch too often, but he's still me brother.'

Crossing the room to the open door, Raff surveyed outside. No sign of Robbo with the doctor, or of Mrs Robinson returning with her cart. Was getting late. *Just have to wait.* Wait while Evie was in with Fitz, whispering in his ear.

Leaning on the doorjamb, the warm air moving around him—

A searing whistle reached him a split second before the timber beside his head smashed with a dense *thwack*.

'Shit,' he roared and dropped back, kicking the rock free of the door and slamming it shut, dropping the latch.

John had hit the floor. 'See anything?' he rasped.

'Nothing.' Raff scrambled for the rifle resting against the bedroom door, snatched it, sat on his backside checking the chamber and barrel. 'Evie,' he called hoarsely. 'Close the shutters in there, hurry.'

Raff heard them bang shut just before a shotgun blast peppered the door. Splinters flew inside, scattering over the table.

John crawled to the fireplace, grabbed the rifle alongside it and checked it was loaded. 'Jesus, I hope Robbo and his wife take a bit longer to get here. They'll walk right into this.'

Raff crept to one of the windows and tugged the flimsy fabric across the space. Not a sound from outside. He peered out of a gap. 'McCosker and his mate, the boxer. Circling in front.'

'We just want O'Shea,' one of them yelled from outside.

'How the *hell* did they find Fitz here?' John raged in a hoarse whisper.

Then another rifle shot boomed and a squawk rent the air. The boxer's hat had flown off and he was hightailing it down the riverbank and along the water's edge, dust flying under his horse's hooves. McCosker wheeled, shock etched on his face. One more shot rang out and a tree branch, low over his head, exploded, was ripped clean off the trunk, and shards of wood showered him. Still another shot pounded into the earth behind his horse. It reared, then took off, its scream piercing the air, McCosker holding on for his life.

A horse and cart pounded into Raff's view. A stranger was driving, and two horses were tied behind. Jenny Robinson was in the passenger's side, a rifle in her hands, barrel open. She thrust it to Robbo in the back of the cart who pressed another into her hands. She took quick aim again and fired in the direction of the bolting horses.

The stranger, a lean man with grey hair stuck on his forehead below his hat, a large patrician nose and a dense moustache, hauled the cart up in front of the house. 'You in there, John, you all right?' he shouted, the gravelly voice clear. Thrusting the reins to Jenny, he alighted and grabbed a bag from the back.

John snatched open the door. 'Quick, Doc.'

'He's in here,' Evie said, beckoning the doctor from the bedroom doorway.

Raff ran to the cart, held the reins as Jenny laid the rifle at her feet and pulled on the brake. 'Told Mr Morgan I was a good shot in my day,' she said, matter-of-fact, and climbed to the ground. Then she turned to pick up the rifle. 'Lucky I am. I didn't realise they were police until they took off.'

'Police gone bad, Mrs Robinson. And they're still alive, don't worry.'

'Damn right they're still alive,' Robbo said, jumping down. 'She weren't aiming for 'em.' He went to her and squeezed her in a bear hug. 'Good practice, me darlin' wife.' He smacked a kiss on her cheek and took the rifle from her, carrying both his and hers inside.

Jenny Robinson wiped her forehead with her arm, rubbed her shoulder where the butt of the rifle had kicked.

'You all right?' Raff asked.

She straightened. 'I most definitely am.'

'You're a steady aim with a rifle.'

There was a steely gleam in her eye. 'I'm used to having to protect what's mine, and a woman, alone at times out here in the bush, well, she has to know how to look after herself. It would do every woman good to learn how to use a rifle.'

She followed her husband indoors, leaving Raff beside the cart laden with swags and provisions. He wondered if she was as steady as she looked; he knew he wasn't.

Robbo appeared again. 'We got two crooks on the loose firing rifles and shotguns all over the place, and the only proper trooper in the district is in here with us. We do have a crack shot in my missus. But what are the chances they'll be back?'

Raff took in a breath. It was Fitz they were after, and him as well, when it came down to it.

'I know what you're thinkin',' Robbo said. He kicked the dust at his feet. 'They'll be watchin' most likely. We should go now, not stay.'

Raff knew it. McCosker wouldn't leave any witnesses, that's for sure. *Evie.* The Robinsons. The doctor. 'Yeah.' He was thinking hard. He'd go after McCosker. *The only way.* His breath came short. It meant leaving Fitz and Evie with the others. 'You a good shot with a rifle, too?'

'A fair shot. Enough to be scary.'

They had five rifles between them; his, the two Robinsons', and Fitz's and John's inside. There'd be enough ammunition but still, it was too dangerous to stay. He stared across to the scrub. 'I don't like it here.'

Robbo eyed the perimeter of the yard. 'Don't like it much, meself,' he muttered.

Raff turned back inside, unease at his neck. Mrs Robinson was instructing Evie how to load a rifle. An oiled rag and a box of casings sat on the table where they were working.

Evie gave Raff a shaky smile. 'As a milliner, I don't know I'd make a good shooter.'

'You won't have to,' Mrs Robinson said, and reached over to squeeze her arm. 'But we will need you to load up for us.'

Evie's smile dropped away. 'Raff, do you think more police from Ballarat will come here?'

'I don't know.'

'Ballarat?' Mrs Robinson was surprised.

'Fitz is a journalist,' Raff said to Mrs Robinson, and leaned the last rifle against the table, placing the box of casings there too. 'He'd exposed McCosker's corruption in Ballarat. That fella had men on the force extorting the gold merchants for protection money. Once Fitz's stories got to the papers, the police had to act, but McCosker took off.' He checked John, who was loading his rifle, his head down, listening but saying nothing. He'd said he didn't want his connection to Fitz known. Raff wasn't about to say anything about that. He made up his mind and took a breath. 'Evie.'

She looked up, a light in her eye as her gaze met his.

'You'll be going back to town with the others. I'm going after McCosker and his mate.'

Her face fell, her frown swift. 'No.'

He had a sudden need to be gone, without having to explain himself further to her, or to anyone. No point staying here anyway; he was better off hunting. He stalked across the room to grab his rifle.

'Raff,' Evie said, wiping down her dress, leaving traces of black powder over it. 'Don't.' She wrung her hands. 'Fitz will be all right now the doctor is treating him. We can take him home together.' She was firm about it. 'Please don't go after those men. Leave it to the police.'

Mrs Robinson had her gaze fixed on Raff.

'It'll be dusk soon, so if I can find them, I'll keep them from following you back to town.' Raff reached for some filled casings and, pocketing them, kept his gaze steady on John. 'Fitz and I should have stopped McCosker long before now.'

'You're not a vigilante, Dolan,' John growled. 'Don't go off half-cocked.'

Raff met Evie's angry gaze briefly before he got to the bedroom door. 'Doctor, can Fitz be moved into town?'

The doctor finished up with a threaded needle at Fitz's scalp, listened to his chest, then put his ear over Fitz's mouth. He opened eyelids and peered in. Taking a breath, he sat back. 'Don't think it could do any more harm. Better chance I can keep an eye on him back there.' He unrolled a long bandage and wound it around Fitz's head. 'Have to be careful how we handle him.'

It was good enough for Raff. 'Let's move Fitz into the back of the cart.'

'Raff, don't go,' Evie said again, standing straight, her eyes fierce. 'I—we—need you with us. We—'

'Dolan, I'm giving you an express order. We *all* go to town now. Clear?'

Safety in numbers. It was a better idea to escort Evie—and Fitz—back to the town. Then Raff would do what he damned well pleased. Biting down his frustration, Raff swiped a hand over his mouth. He took a long look at Evie.

'That's what you want? All of us to go back to town?' he asked, abrupt and frowning.

Bewildered but relieved, Evie said, 'Of course it's what I want.'

And McCosker gets away. Damn it. Raff was gruff. 'Robbo,' he called outside. 'It's back to Cobram.'

Chapter Thirty-nine

The sun beat down. Evie didn't know where her hat was. Perhaps still at Meryl's house. She would've taken it off, of course, once they'd got Fitz up from the river. Couldn't remember, but she didn't have it now. *Damn, blast, bother.*

It was hot, not unbearable for her in the back of the cart, but Fitz needed something to keep the sun off his exposed head. His long johns were still in place, and he was on Meryl's bedding that had been tossed hastily into the cart. Only half his body was covered by the sheet the doctor had flung to her. She tugged it up a little. It fell short of reaching his shoulders but trying to retrieve another would disturb him.

Always a firm build, lean and able, now Fitz looked different. Perhaps because she hadn't seen him for a while. Or perhaps he was ill—other than a rock splitting his skull, that is. She stared down. His poor head rested in her lap, her legs splayed apart so he fit between them. It was unladylike, but that couldn't be helped. The doctor said he had to be kept still.

She'd never had any girlish swoons over Fitz despite the man's beautiful face, his confidence, his intelligence. He was a familiar face from the past, loved but … *different*, changed. How strange.

The smattering of his whiskers was out of place; Fitz would never have let a beard grow. His fine brows had a slight pucker as if he might have pain somewhere deep. She smoothed a finger lightly over them, afraid to irritate the sunburn underneath. She couldn't remember touching him before, except for when he'd handed her into a cab or the like. His skin was clammy, and a light sheen of sweat bubbled on his forehead.

She twisted, checking for something to grab to create some shade. It was difficult. Twisting again, she caught sight of Raff watching her. So keen was his gaze that her heart gave a jump. 'I need to cover Fitz's head and chest, Raff. Would you please pull something free?' she asked, raising her voice over the noise of the cartwheels, again perplexed by his stern frown at her. She followed his gaze. There was a good deal of her shins exposed; her dress had ridden up. The sight of her slim calves dusted with fine, light downy hair ... 'Blast it,' she whispered. Frustrated and shaky, she hurried to push her skirt over her legs, struggling with Fitz's weight.

Shunting Bluey alongside, Raff gave her another glare and threw the reins to Robbo. 'Hold him a moment.' Climbing out of the saddle and into the cart, Raff grabbed the hem of her skirt on either side of Fitz and tugged hard until Evie's shins were covered. Fitz was out to it; the doctor had given him a tincture. If he'd felt discomfort, there was no sound from him.

She was stunned to silence, her face dried of tears, her armpits fresh with perspiration, her mouth open.

Raff caught an end of Fitz's discarded shirt and yanked it from under him. He pitched it to her. 'Try that,' he said and clambered out and onto Bluey, taking back his reins.

Well.

The shirt was big enough to do the job. She slid her hands into the dirty sleeves and held it up over Fitz. Tossed a little as she was by the cart, the shirt made its own breeze. She thanked Raff, but he was concentrating, scouting the road ahead. Every so often, he swivelled to check behind them. His rifle was across the saddle, his face was closed, and he wasn't taking any notice of her at all.

Of course he's gruff, Evie decided. *Poor Fitz is his best friend, and he could've been killed by those horrible men, or burned to a crisp and left to die, drowned or sunstruck.* Her arms had started to tire holding up the shirt. The cart bobbed her about as her thighs held him still.

Not a pretty sight.

A sudden, ridiculous urge to bark a laugh struck her. She coughed instead, her throat catching. *That would not do.* Raff directed a cool glance her way, and she suppressed the manic thrill that had begun to rocket through her. She didn't think *any* of this was a laughing matter, not for one second. She clamped her mouth shut. Tears burned.

What on earth is wrong with me?

Relief, that must be it. Heady relief that Fitz was alive, that Mrs Robinson's shots had scared away the criminals, and relief especially that Raff had not ridden off all over the countryside after them. Relief that she was out of Meryl's home. Away from the awful sadness, the foreboding that had descended on her at the little house with its emptiness and despair, and its lonely, desolate graves. *Oh, Meryl, Meryl. Little Dallas. Was it only this morning I'd been happy, leaving the* Sweet Georgie *with hope in my heart?*

Grief and exhaustion hit with a heavy whack. Her arms trembled, tears burst, a sob stuck in her throat. Holding the shirt above Fitz's face, she couldn't even wipe her nose. Her face screwed up. *Oh my Lord, mortifying.* She tried to hide it, made it worse.

Raff started towards her then stopped as the constable—Raff had called him John—leaned in from the other side of the cart. 'It's all right, Miss Emerson. That's exactly how I feel. You cry for both of us.' His eyes were bleak.

What kindness to say such a thing. She hadn't expected it from him, a toughened policeman. It undid her completely. Tears flooded her cheeks. She couldn't stop them and sobbed hard, gulping soundlessly. *Good Lord. Now is not the time, Evie Emerson.* Not *the time. Get a grip.*

Mrs Robinson reached back and handed her a hanky. 'Not long before we're back in town,' she said, her voice gentle.

Evie laid the shirt over Fitz's face before mopping her eyes. *Ridiculous. Stop crying, you fool woman. Fitz is far worse off.* She dropped the handkerchief, sniffed loudly and resumed holding up the shirt, her arms aching already.

'Riders comin',' Robbo said under his breath. He kept the cart and horse at an unhurried, steady pace.

Evie froze, the tears halted. She couldn't move far enough to peer over her shoulder at what was ahead of the cart. 'What's happening, Raff?'

A short shake of his head and a cool shot from those green eyes was warning enough to keep quiet. Impassive, and in rhythm with Bluey, he cut a calm figure; easy in the saddle, confident. Staring ahead, he wrapped his big hands loosely in the reins and draped them casually over the rifle. The red-and-black feather in his hat jiggled in the breeze he made, and for an odd moment it seemed as if … as if it were a lady's favour given to a knight before a joust.

Evie, how stupid. But she couldn't take her eyes off it. Tears, sniffles. Blast, she must have had a touch of the sun herself. She dragged her gaze away when she heard the constable say, 'It's Haines and his men.'

Raff nudged Bluey until they came level with Evie. Another glare at her, then eyes ahead once again. The doctor rode up alongside him from the back of the cart. On the other side, the constable rested a rifle in the crook of his arm.

Flanked by men on horseback, the odour of sweat in the hot air sharpened in her nostrils. Her heart skipped. She dared not try to twist to stare at what approached.

The constable's face was wary, and alert. Raff squinted, gave his hat a tug to shade his eyes.

Cartwheels crunched over the baked road. Leather creaked, horses shied and nickered. Flies buzzed, dived towards Fitz. She flapped the shirt hard.

'Evie,' Raff murmured. 'Drop the shirt over Fitz's face now and cry hard. Say nothing, even if asked.' He was unreadable, stony.

The shirt sighed over Fitz as Evie's hands flew to her face. She wept. It burst from her with heart-rending, real and jagged sobs that would not be stopped. The cries tore from her, chest heaving.

Someone who passed by on horseback said, 'Sorry to see that, Constable O'Shea. Who is it gone to God, might I ask?'

Evie gulped a sob, not sure she'd heard correctly. *Constable O'Shea?*

The constable cleared his throat. 'That fella came lately to town. You saw him at the Bayleys' with Robinson and me.'

'Ah, him. Well, that's no good, is it? He seemed a decent fella.'

The policeman grunted. 'Move on, Mr Haines. We're tryin' to look after the lady here.'

'Course, Constable.'

The backs of the new riders came into her view as the cart kept going. Evie watched through her fingers, bleary-eyed, as the men took a wide berth around Raff and the doctor. One man caught her eye as he checked the cart, his grey hair tufting from under his hat, his dense moustache curved down. He tipped his hat at her before she resumed weeping in her hands.

The sun had begun to relent, dropping low in the clear sky, softening the late afternoon with an amber glow. Heat still rolled around her. The tears had dried on her cheeks, but her throat was thick and aching.

Haines and his riders faded into the mirage further along the track. Evie glanced at Raff who just kept on, his eyes front. *Raff.*

Sighing, too sad, too tired to put more thought into any of it, she lifted the shirt from Fitz and once again held it as shade for the rest of the way into town.

Chapter Forty

Haines waited until the cart carrying the dead man was well behind them and on its way to town before he sent his men back to his home property. The sight of the Robinsons had unsettled him. Why were they out and about carting the dead body?

He needed to be at the Bayley place in a hurry so he doubled back to the track. Uneasy, unnerved, he didn't like to think that there'd been anything left that needed tidying up. The stupid bastards who worked for him mightn't have done the job properly, but at least it had been Morgan shrouded in the cart. Was he alive when they found him? Had he said anything? Dammit, not like he could bloody ask.

The Bayley place had to be ready for him, with no loose ends floating about to attract the wrong sort of attention. Bad enough the woman's grave was fresh. He wondered if it could be shifted, that and her kid's grave. Get rid of them both.

At the hut door he dismounted. It surprised him to see shots had been fired at the dwelling. He hadn't noticed that before. Shards of timber had been blown off the doorjamb, and the wall was peppered with holes. He put his nose to one then peered at it. It was recent, real recent. A short tree branch lay shattered on the ground not far from his feet, white sap pebbling on its jagged edges. There'd been other trouble out here. Pulling at his collar, he thanked his lucky stars he wasn't around at the time. Things could have backfired. Before long, he'd raze this hovel to the ground and thrash any interlopers he found causing a ruckus—

Was anyone still inside? He loosened his shoulders. Swallowing the spit filling his mouth, he pushed open the door and stared into the light room. No one here, thank Christ. He let out the breath he'd been holding.

I have to defend what's mine. This is my *property.*

It's not yet, a faint voice in his head pointed out.

Bugger it.

He kicked the dirt under his feet, despising the nervous sweat that dripped under his shirt, snaking its way to his belly. When he got back to town, he'd warn off the temporary trooper with a good blast of indignant landowner fury, then he'd give that no-hoper Robinson a box around the ears, lay him out for a week. That'd put the district on notice, that he, Ernest Haines, wasn't to be tackled. Things would settle down then.

Outside, standing at the back of the hut and facing the river, he stared across the serene water to his property in the neighbouring colony. He was safe, he just needed to play it calm. *And stay calm.* No one would know it was him who—

'Mr Haines.'

He spun, saw two men mounted, and in tatty uniforms. *Jesus.* Crept up on him. He recognised them from when they'd first tramped into the police station that morning: Sergeant Bill and Constable Porter. Didn't like 'em then, didn't like 'em now.

'How do,' he said, his voice firm despite his guts taking a turn. *What are they doin' here?*

'We meet again,' the sergeant said, all congenial. 'This your place?'

'Good as.'

'We were watching from the scrub earlier. Saw you pass a cart on the main road.'

'That's right.' Sweat dripped again. That could also mean they'd seen him get rid of his men and turn back here alone.

'We're looking for a fugitive. The cart was carrying a wailin' woman, leaning over a body maybe.'

Haines sniffed. *Steady.* Wiped a hand over his mouth. 'It was a body. Some fella by the name of Morgan.'

'That all you got?'

'Fitz Morgan.'

Sergeant Bill nodded at Porter, his offsider, and muttered something about O'Shea under his breath. The local trooper, of course. Haines couldn't read the look that passed between the two men.

'Dead?' the sergeant said to Haines.

'A body, yeah.' *Thick as two planks.* 'Uh, something musta happened out here, but the constable's got it in hand, looks like.' Haines steadied his horse and mounted. Best to lead these two away from the property. 'Visit the police station if you need more information.'

Porter leaned forward. 'But the bloke in the back of the cart was dead, right?'

'What I said,' Haines snapped, then backed off. 'He was all covered over and that female was bawlin' her eyes out sittin' with *the body.* Dead enough for ye?'

Sergeant Bill straightened, his mouth working as he chewed back a grin. 'Well, well.' Seemed *dead enough* made him happy. 'Still, we'll verify with the local constable. Means our journey might have come to an end, if that's the case.' He sat for a moment. 'The woman in the back. Who was she?'

'No idea. Not from around here. That big bloke seemed to have his eye on her.'

The sergeant's brows rose. 'Ah yes, him. And the man and woman driving?'

'Local nobodies.'

'I see.' He tipped his cap and looked about to wheel his horse when he said, 'One more thing. Mind if we take a look inside?'

'Go ahead. I'll be pulling it down the moment the place is signed over to me. It's barely more'n a humpy.' Haines watched as they led their horses to the shade of a tree.

And hurry up about it. Don't want no trooper poking his nose in.

His sweat was still dripping as Bill and Porter dismounted and wandered past him to the door, a hot and musty odour in their wake. It was only when the sergeant put his fingers to the gunshot splintering the doorjamb and laughed, that the sweat chilled and rolled into Haines's pants.

He needn't be worried. He was as safe as can be. The nasty taste in his mouth slid down his throat. No one other than his men knew he'd clobbered Fitz Morgan with a rock and left him to die.

Chapter Forty-one

Bendigo

'Mr Kingsley,' Lucille cried, rushing into the kitchen room of his house—their house—the daily newspaper in her hand. 'You must look at this. The man has stooped far below decency.' She thrust the paper at him, folded at the page she wanted him to see. 'Read that, there. Oh my Lord, it's awful. He's wasted no time. A good thing the poor girl has already been gone for days.'

David reached for her hand and took the paper in his other. 'What is it?' As she sat beside him, he poured her a cup of tea. She blew into the cup then sipped. Then she pulled a small fan from her pocket and waved it in a frenzy in front of her face.

David read, his brows coming together. 'Awful is right. It's malicious innuendo and … This is character assassination.' He read aloud. '"… That I implore the unsuspecting gentlemen among us to be aware of such a beguiling creature as Miss Evie Emerson, who has destroyed my future happiness. Prior to my acquaintance with her, a certain gentleman, Mr Fitzmorgan O'Shea, who has since fled the town, was known to have escorted Miss Emerson for quite some time. He mysteriously took leave of Bendigo, and Miss Emerson, certainly of dubious character, became free to seek her next target and employ her tricks, shall we say, on the next unwary fellow. Which leads this author, who undertook investigation, pondering the very character of the absent Mr O'Shea: unsavoury, and perhaps unlawful of habits himself, being …"'

David stopped before he uttered the words aloud. 'Well, I'll not read on,' he said, slapping the paper to the table. 'I believe I finally know what the scoundrel is up to. It's preposterous and, quite frankly, stupid of him.'

'And that the editor sees fit to publish such rot,' Lucille exploded. 'I've a mind to tweak his ear hard. What sort of journalism is that? I hope Mr Campbell and Mr Barrett have seen this.' The fan was still furious at her neck and face. 'We'll have to telegram Cobram to let Evie know—'

'The moment the telegram is sent, there's a big chance someone will alert the papers to Evie's whereabouts,' David said, his hand covering the offending letter to the editor as if shielding his sight from it. 'The damage might already be done following our very first telegram.'

Lucille lowered the fan and squeezed his arm. 'Would she even be there yet?'

'Quite possibly.'

'Oh dear. Is there a chance she might see this in newspapers published elsewhere?'

'Hard to know, my dear. I know nothing about how newspapers work.' He tapped the table. 'Mr Campbell will act swiftly, and demand a retraction before Cooper's devious little plan fully spawns.'

'But too late for Evie, too late for her reputation.'

'The harm is done, dear Lucille. We can only support Evie through this time and hope that Mr Campbell will blast this crooked villain from the courtroom to the prison. We'll visit Mr Barrett this afternoon and make him fully aware of this.' She gave him a look. 'We will visit him *this morning*,' he amended smartly.

Lucille thrust to her feet, paced the kitchen. 'We must warn her. I'll cut it out of the paper and send it to her at Cobram by mail today, and hope she receives it soon. At least she will be armed with the knowledge of his absolute unscrupulous nature before she returns.' She opened the drawer of the hutch. 'I will remove the unsavoury parts, and censure what a young lady should not have to read. That scurrilous newspaper.'

He stood back as Lucille took to the newspaper with the kitchen shears, the large blades snapping deftly through the broadsheet.

She collapsed into her seat again, the little fan working hard. 'Oh, it's quite set off these inconvenient rushes of heat. My heart-beat is hammering.'

Alarmed, David rose to pour her water from the pitcher. 'Here, have this. It'll help, my dear.'

She grabbed the cup, dunked a large section of her pinny deeply into it then dabbed her forehead and neck. 'Yes, much better, thank you.'

Chapter Forty-two

Cobram

Evie's arms were leaden, and try as she might, she could barely hold them high enough to keep shade over Fitz's face. She could only blow flies away with her breath, could only lift a shoulder and press her face against it to stop the dripping sweat. As the cart rocked over the hard road, the bones in her backside complained.

More blisters rose on Fitz's cheeks and forehead, and tiny ones bloomed, growing to join bigger ones. *Oh, my good God, it looks messy.* She hoped there wouldn't be any infection.

She dropped her elbows a little to rest. Her head drooped. Late in the afternoon of her first day here, and already she'd learned she'd lost a sister, a nephew and most probably some time ago, a brother-in-law. Now Fitz; would she lose him too? A lump closed her dry throat.

A thought struck her, and her glance collided with Raff's before his stare cut back to the horizon. He was unreadable, easy-going on his horse, not hurried, not panicked. Solid. Dependable.

I won't lose him, too.

Her glance darted away. It didn't bear thinking about.

Robbo's voice distracted her. 'We take the back way in, Constable?'

'Down the laneway.'

The cart turned right off the main road, tossed into a pothole, clambered over old wheel ruts and bobbed along a track, turning left through a gate. The doctor rode ahead a little and as Evie craned to see, he was dismounting and tying up at a rail. The back of a doleful weatherboard house came into view, and the cart soon pulled up.

Mrs Robinson leaned back towards her. 'We're at the constable's house, Miss Emerson. Won't be long until the men get Mr Morgan out of the cart and inside. Can you manage a bit longer?'

Why did everyone call Fitz 'Mr Morgan'? Raff hadn't corrected them, so she wasn't about to. She only nodded, lowering her elbows again to rest. The shirt hung over Fitz's face, the sun at least not scorching any longer.

The doctor leaped into the back of the cart, swept away Evie's hands, and opened Fitz's eyes gently. Peering into the left one then the right, he grunted. 'Tonight will tell,' he said. 'Ready, gentlemen?'

Robbo and Raff eased Fitz to the edge of the cart. Evie thought she would faint with relief after his weight had gone from her legs. She found it hard to move, tried to stand, crouched instead, gripping the side of the cart.

'I'll unlock the house,' the constable called from somewhere.

'Bring the bathtub, fill it with water,' the doctor ordered. 'We'll dunk him in the yard, cool him down quickly, then get him inside. Keep his head up, though.'

Evie gasped. 'Dunk him?' She'd never heard of that before. People were only ever sponged to cool off the skin, she knew that from her school days if children became burned from the sun.

The doctor's glare pinned her. 'Ask any sunburned river man or man burned from a boiler fire, miss. A good dunking in cool water.'

Evie nodded and clambered off the end of the cart, the blood rushing back into her stiff limbs, prickling her toes. She stood a moment, dazed, watching Raff hold Fitz in the tub, trying to trickle a drip over Fitz's split mouth and swollen tongue, the blisters on his face roaming. At last, she saw his Adam's apple bob, heard a thin sputter, a slurp.

Jenny came back and touched her shoulder, handing her a cup of water. 'Come along, Miss Emerson. We have men to feed. The night might be a long one.'

Robbo had left for the grocery shop, the butcher's and the baker's, with a list in his pocket that Jenny had written. The constable told him to mark it up on his cards at the stores; he'd deal with it later.

The doctor said Fitz could be lifted onto the bed in the constable's room, leaving him to dry off naturally. 'I'll be back in the morning. Keep him cool. If he wakes, give him more water. He'll have an almighty headache. If the wound becomes red and swollen, come find me immediately. Good day to you.'

Raff followed him outside, and Evie scurried to catch up. As the doctor swung into the saddle, Raff thanked him.

'He was lucky,' the doctor said. 'The whack on the head and the sunstroke each could have killed him. Can't tell if he was in the river for long. There might still be long-term damage.' He rode off.

Evie stood alongside Raff. Her eyes felt scratchy, puffy and were squishy when she blinked. She would look a sight, she knew, the dirt and mud on her skirt, her hair all messed up. She'd wager her nose was red and not just from the sun. Dried up and worn out, she was grieving, hurting and numb at the same time, as if everything was locked down tight.

'I don't think I've ever had a day quite like this one,' she said, her voice croaky.

He didn't meet her gaze, only murmured, 'Mmh,' before ducking his head, turning to go inside.

'Raff, wait.'

He turned back, his eyes so sad. He kept his shoulders straight until for a second or two, they slumped just a little. Suddenly, she didn't know what to ask for herself, or what she needed to say. It was Raff who needed. She stepped closer, put her arms around her friend, around his waist, and rested her head on his broad chest. Her tears didn't come. Instead, comfort rolled over her as she stood there, even though he didn't hold her, didn't move. All she had from him was the strong thump of his heart under her ear. She was the one offering comfort.

A moment passed before his arms slid around her, hard, warm and solid as he pulled her close. He held her there, tight against him, holding her grief and their fears, a refuge, a safe haven each. He dropped his chin to her hair. She closed her eyes, breathed in deeply.

It felt an awful lot like home.

Chapter Forty-three

Cobram

Raff was grateful Mrs Robinson insisted on cooking. Beef, potatoes and gravy in the kitchen, and damper under a cooking fire in the yard. Tired and hungry as he was, he wouldn't have been bothered fixing a meal for himself, bugger anyone else. He'd just as soon roll out his swag under a tree and sleep. The aromas coming from John's kitchen, and from the cooking fire outside, meant that there was nothing for him to do anyway but wait.

Earlier, John had found Robbo cleaning out the cart. 'I don't want you and your wife going back to your place tonight, Robinson. I don't want any more pot shots taken and mishaps occurrin'. Whoever bailed us up at the Bayleys' is still roamin' around. Stay here.'

Robbo had checked with his wife, who nodded. 'All right, for tonight.' They put themselves to good use; the missus cooking, Robbo cutting firewood, feeding and grooming the horses.

Nearer dusk, John departed for the police station, and before he left, confided to Raff. 'I have to write a report, it can't wait. I can avoid introducing Fitz as my brother around here,' he said, his voice low as he stood by his horse, 'but I'll have to name him for my superiors, and no one except them need know right now. I'll mail it, not telegram. That should keep it from the papers.'

'What are you going to do about all this?' Raff asked, though the answer was moot. He'd do his own work on it.

'It'll be all over town soon enough, something will shake loose. They'll show their hand again, I'm sure of that.' John climbed into the saddle.

'You got an idea who hurt Fitz?'

'Don't take much thinkin' about it. Haines didn't like the look of Fitz right from the start, and then there are those two troopers who know you're here, too. So what are the chances one party or the other?' Scratching his chest, he took a deep breath. 'It's good you're here, Raff, it's good to see you. Good you're lookin' out for him.' He didn't know where to look.

'He's my mate, John.' Raff hesitated. 'I knew who he was from the beginning, knew it long ago—'

'Stop, all right,' John said, glaring at him, holding up a hand. 'It's against the flamin' law, so I don't want to hear it about me own brother. But at this point, blood is thicker than worryin' about who my brother fancies.'

Raff gave a laugh. 'I can assure you, he doesn't fancy me, never has. And vice versa, I might add, in case you're wondering.' His gaze was steady.

John tried clearing his throat. 'Don't ask me to understand it of him, of any of 'em.' His voice was still gravelly. 'Anyway, keep an eye on Fitz. He might give us a name if he wakes up. Just don't let anyone know we're related.' He remembered something. 'And you, mate,' he said, pointing a finger and with the stern glare of a righteous policeman. 'No vigilante stuff.' He wheeled about and rode off.

Raff headed inside. Fitz was still out to it and despite the reddened skin, the milky-looking blisters and the ragged line of stitches in his head, looked comfortable enough. Evie had insisted on being the one keeping him cool and it had run her ragged.

She'd lost everything in a few short weeks, today the worst of it, yet she kept on. She loved Fitz; Raff had heard her say so. *All right, fair enough: Fitz hadn't heard*, but he had.

Then in the cart at Mrs Bayley's … He'd hauled Fitz between Evie's legs, doctor's orders, snatching his hands away fast. *Even half dead, the bastard had prime* bloody *position.* And earlier, standing in the yard in broad daylight, holding the only woman he wanted—a woman who wasn't his—his damn brain wouldn't work. He'd been stupefied when she'd wrapped herself tightly around him. *Christ, but how good had that felt?*

He exhaled through taut lips. His task was to get Fitz to safety, and Evie, of course, but Fitz was paramount. Stupid bastard had got himself into a right fix this time, and Raff had no idea how to get him out of it—if he came out of it at all.

Sitting on his backside, resting against a fence post, the view coming out of the back door was no respite for his jangled thoughts. Evie was headed for the pump, a pitcher in her hands, and gave him a tired smile. Filling the pitcher, she headed back. *If I'm not careful* I'll *be a stupid bastard. I've got no idea how to get out of my own fix.*

It was still light enough to see Jenny Robinson coming to check the contents of the cast iron oven under the coals of the firepit. She scraped the embers back and forth, lifted the lid with a stout stick. Tapping the crust, satisfied with the damper and replacing the lid, she piled red hot coals high over it again. Wiping her hands on her apron, she swiped her forehead with an open palm and retreated to the house. Inside, Robbo's silhouette wandered, and lanterns and candles began to flicker. He'd already settled the horses, the cart was chocked, and he'd taken the rifles inside before returning for all the bed linens.

Be dark soon. A man should heft himself into the house and see what chores still needed to be done. Raff stood, dusted off his pants. John hadn't returned. What was taking him so long?

The kitchen was off to the side of the main house, a small room made of sturdy brickwork, hot and stuffy. Mrs Robinson was poking at a lump of sizzling beef in a deep pan, shunting spuds around in the lard. Saliva loosened; he couldn't remember last eating.

'Need anything?' he asked.

She smiled tiredly. 'Not yet. It'll be a little while before it's ready. Perhaps you could find more chairs.' She waved the roasting fork at the single chair Robbo occupied at the table. Her husband was cleaning a rifle, the bullet makings in a bag at his feet.

Unsettled, Raff headed for the house; maybe Fitz had woken. Who was he fooling—he wanted to have time to sit with Evie. He toed off his boots at the back steps, took a lantern with him from the hook just inside and padded a few feet down the hall. When he got to the open door of John's room, he saw Fitz was still on his back, his mouth slightly open, eyes closed, the ragged line of stitches clear on his scalp. His breathing was even.

Evie had fallen asleep, her head on her arms on the bed cover. A letter sitting alongside its envelope was just visible. Raff came closer, recognised Fitz's neat and tight cursive. The one from Meryl's hut. He refused to read any words past *My dearest Evie*. His chest thumped. *Get over it, Dolan.* Ignoring the letter, he rounded the end of the bed, treading softly as the floorboards creaked, to stand by the other side. He peered down at Fitz. There was no frown on his face, he seemed in no pain. Some of the blisters on his forehead had collapsed, and his sunburned skin, while still red, had lost some of its anger. He checked Evie, her shoulders rising and falling in her sleep, her breathing easy.

Glancing again at the letter, he saw that the first few lines had been about Mrs Bayley but beyond that, he couldn't see; the page was under Evie's forearm. What else would Fitz have told her? What might he have declared?

Why the hell think that? He straightened. *Idiot.* The man was informing an old friend about the death of her sister. Maybe they had communicated more in recent years—how would he know? *Christ almighty, Dolan, it's your fault you don't know. You never asked Fitz about her.* But Jesus Christ, but it wasn't something you asked a mate; it should have been volunteered. Besides, Raff didn't want to be Evie's second choice because Fitz had other—

Bah. Maybe the events of the day were getting to him, and his brains were as fried as Fitz's. He couldn't remember the last time a gunshot had narrowly missed him. He laughed at that. *Never been shot at, is why.*

Kneeling by the bed, he studied Fitz's face then his weathered forearm. The underside of it bubbled with blisters. He touched the part of Fitz's arm that was not damaged. 'Fitz,' he whispered.

Nothing, not a movement, not even his eyelids.

Raff checked over at the sleeping Evie again, sure she wouldn't wake. 'Fitz,' he said, shaking his arm a little, his voice more urgent.

Still nothing. The doctor had dosed him up. Maybe he just needed to sleep off this sunstroke. Raff knew of the affliction, but had never experienced it. He leaned over to peer at the wound in Fitz's head, the stitches clean around the matted hair. Evie must have sponged it off.

He stood, found a bowl of murky water, carried it to the open window, drew aside the flimsy curtain and aimed the contents out. Pouring clean water from the pitcher and rinsing the rag on the dresser, he lay it over Fitz's neck.

'Come on, old mate. Wake up,' he urged, but there wasn't any movement.

He and the Robinsons ate in the kitchen after Mrs Robinson had looked in on Evie.

'Let her rest there. She might be a bit stiff when she wakes, but at least she'll have slept. I'll get her to a bed if needs be,' she said, spooning potatoes onto Raff's plate.

Robbo was carving more beef. There were a dozen boiled eggs, cabbage browned off with onions from the roasting pan, and hot damper. The gravy was thick and tasty, the beef juices rich and satisfying. Raff felt his spirits lift as his stomach filled.

Robbo scraped a chunk of damper through his gravy, poked it into his mouth. 'I'm thinkin' one of us should stay on watch tonight,' he said around his mouthful.

'Agreed.' Raff glanced at the rifles resting against the back wall of the room. *Where is John?*

Mrs Robinson insisted that Evie retire to the parlour room where she'd laid out the swags and the linens from the Bayley house on the floor. Saddles, and spare blankets from the police house did as head rests. Hardly the comfort of a pillow but Evie hadn't seemed to notice. She moved as if numb, Mrs Robinson told Raff. As soon as Evie lay down and had pulled a thin sheet over her, she was asleep. Jenny took a pitcher of water and cups with her and found a chamber pot for the room. She'd bunker down beside Evie, leaving the men to keep watch outside. She had two rifles in the room with her.

Robbo took first shift in the kitchen room, sitting in a chair, facing the door, rifle over his lap. Raff settled on the floor on his swag and closed his eyes. Sleep proved elusive. Round and round in his head thoughts flew of his father, his brothers. Fitz. Evie.

Evie, Evie, Evie.

Something was shaking him. Raff's eyes popped open.

'Your turn, mate,' Robbo said. 'I can't keep awake any longer.' The candlelight flickered across his features, his bleary eyes owlish in the dim glow.

'Right,' Raff grunted, tossed off the cobwebby haze of sleep, stumbled to his feet, and stretched. He took a walk outside to piss, came back and grabbed his rifle. Settling in the chair just vacated, cradling the gun over his lap, he asked, 'John back yet?'

'No,' Robbo said, settling on the floor. Soon his soft snoring was the only noise Raff heard.

Chapter Forty-four

Cobram

Dusk had crept in. The town was quiet, shopkeepers had locked up and were walking home or were climbing wearily onto their carts for the drive.

John tied up at the front of the police station. Why the hell had he decided to come here at this time of the day? Yeah, he had to write a report, but it could have waited until tomorrow. He'd told himself it'd be fresh in his mind if he did it now. More's the reason, he couldn't stand to see his younger brother, Fitzmorgan, lying there half dead.

He was useless at the house, only hanging around under the morbid mood that had descended further since leaving the Bayley farm. Damned terrible turn of events. The Robinsons had been dragged into it, Raff Dolan had turned up with the Emerson woman looking for her sister, and his brother had been cracked over the head by persons unknown. He'd had to get away, he'd needed to do something constructive. Best was to leave the house, come here and write up a report; that made sense, and he'd do it in the quiet, in solitude, like he was used to. Order his thoughts in peace.

The keys jangled as he turned the lock in the door. Shoving it open, he stood for a moment, his eyes adjusting to the dim light.

He hadn't yet worked here at night, but he could put his hand on a lantern easily enough. He closed the door, strode to a bank of cupboards against the wall, opened the middle one and grabbed the lantern.

Settled at his desk, inkpot filled and nib dipped, he began to pen his report. By the time he re-read what he'd written, it felt odd mentioning 'Fitzmorgan O'Shea, my younger brother' in his dispatch. But his superiors had to know all the facts, and all his suspicions. Fitz's arrival in town had coincided with Haines's escalating belligerence, *after* Roy Bayley's disappearance and Mrs Bayley's bashing (he knew about it, although she hadn't reported it), then her lonely death on their property. John had experienced the menace from Haines, and then from the two troopers, Sergeant Bill (McCosker, as he now knew) and Constable Porter, in search of a fugitive: Fitz. No doubt about it. He reported that those two were travelling the colony, had been in police service in Ballarat, and were now with dubious character. Then he wrote how he'd come to find Fitz bashed, near death, and afterwards, the shots fired at them at the Bayleys' property. Could it have been Haines? Or had it been the troopers on the trail of their so-called fugitive?

John tore the anonymous article from the newspaper about the standover tactics of a certain landowner and folded it within the three pages of his report. He knew full well it was Fitz's hand; could be none other. If nothing else, it would alert the police for the need of more protection here. Unless the threat was removed in the meantime. He ended his report with the recommendation of needing more police to bring Haines before the court, to curtail his activities.

He'd only just slipped it into a drawer to revisit the next day before mailing it when the main door opened, unhurriedly.

'Constable O'Shea, you're working late,' Bill McCosker said and sauntered inside. Porter was on his heels. Beyond him, another man stood on the veranda, holding a lantern high, checking left to right down the street. Haines.

John had never seen the man nervous. His heart sank. *Trouble.*

At McCosker's nod, Porter closed the door behind them shutting Haines out. 'I got to thinkin' some more,' McCosker said.

John started to get to his feet. 'Thinkin' what, Sergeant?' It irked him to use the rank, to keep up the charade. He knew McCosker was a fraud; he'd been disgraced and dismissed.

'Stay where you are.' As a warning, McCosker nodded over at Porter who'd drawn a handgun. 'Thinkin' again about that real big coincidence, that your name is the same as the man I'm lookin' for.'

John stared at him, shrugged. 'Common enough name, even you'd say so.' They wouldn't be able to see the rapid pulse beating at the base of his throat.

McCosker considered that, then shook his head. 'Thinkin' also that the cart with the body in the back today hasn't reached the undertaker yet. It's situated at what I presume are your quarters.'

Wily bastard. He saw us coming back into town. John hadn't seen them, none of them had, and only Haines had passed them on the road. *Haines.* Was he in with them, too? Is that why he's on the doorstep now? A thought tickled him, but he couldn't grab it, his thudding heartbeat was getting in the way of any logic.

McCosker leaned forward over the desk. 'I just hope you weren't about to write a report, O'Shea.' He tapped the inkpot gently.

John thrust to his feet, the chair barrelling into the wall behind him.

Porter's gun cocked and he shouted, 'Don't move.'

Haines flung open the door.

A shot boomed.

Chapter Forty-five

Bendigo

Lucille regarded Mr Barrett keenly as the private detective silently read the letter in the paper.

Leaning back in his chair, Mr Barrett almost smiled, letting the paper drop. 'Well, well, well, Mr and Mrs Kingsley,' he said. 'Edwin Cooper is feeling very hard done by. Not only suing for breach of contract, and bad enough if he's lying, but he feels he must destroy Miss Emerson altogether, along with her friend.'

'Our thoughts exactly,' David said.

'Surely that's against the law,' Lucille said, fanning her neck.

'That is for Mr Campbell to pursue and a magistrate to ascertain, although untrained as I am, I have to agree. But all I'm doing is collecting the pieces of the puzzle and hoping they fit together to give us a picture. I think it's shaping up.' Mr Barrett's lock of stark, white hair fell over one eyebrow and he pushed it back with a flick of his hand. 'I've never understood what drives a person to do things such as this. I understand why there are murders and violent, grisly crimes, and I understand theft in the pursuit of riches not one's own,' he said, his voice drifting, thinking perhaps of something else. 'But I've never understood the need to destroy an innocent person's reputation. To what earthly benefit?' He looked at David. 'Unless in this case there is a benefit and I'm unaware of it.'

David lifted a shoulder as if he couldn't say but Lucille answered, 'We know Miss Emerson is about to come into an inheritance. I believe her mother left a small amount, very modest. That's why Evie went to Cobram, to try to find her sister in order to share the estate with her.'

Mr Barrett pursed his lips. 'Maybe it's a tactic of his then. If Cooper goes hard publicly on Miss Emerson, he might think a magistrate will settle a greater amount if he finds in favour of the plaintiff.' He was still frowning. 'Tell me, what should I know about this'—he consulted the newspaper—'Mr Fitzmorgan O'Shea? Is it true that there was a courtship with Miss Emerson?'

Both Lucille and David hesitated.

Mr Barrett understood. 'If Miss Emerson were here, instead of you, her very good friends trying to defend her reputation, what would she tell me of Mr O'Shea?' He looked at Lucille.

'Mr Barrett,' she started, 'I have known Evie for a long time as a fine employee and a very gifted milliner. She and Mr O'Shea appeared to be very close at one stage, and for quite some time. We—and all her friends—thought marriage was a possibility, a natural progression if you will, but no engagement followed.' She licked her lips and fanned some more. 'Mr O'Shea is a journalist, you see, one who wanted to move around like some travelling salesman.' She pulled a face. 'Well, of course, travelling wouldn't have worked for Evie. Nor for him either, I imagine, having a young wife in tow, perhaps a baby too, if he was pursuing a story.' Her brows twisted, the fanning stopped. 'No life for a young woman brought up the way Evie was, expecting a solid home and hearth. She didn't say too much about it when it ended, but she was clearly upset. More bewildered, even though I believe she initiated the split.' She wondered if she'd said too much. A glance at David confirmed it, and fidgeting a little, Lucille took a couple of deep breaths, and stopped speaking.

'Mmh.' Mr Barrett took a moment. 'So did Mr O'Shea not have any financial prospects?'

'Oh dear me no, not enough for anyone to get their hopes up. Nor did Miss Emerson. No, no, theirs was never an acrimonious break up, just sad, really.' She closed the fan, tucked it under her hands in her lap. 'As painful as it was for her, all Evie told me was that it just hadn't felt right to continue. I can't say she even knew quite what bothered her.' Lucille clamped her mouth shut.

'But they remained friends?'

'At a distance. I'm sure they never saw each other again.'

Mr Barrett took a deep breath. 'What does this Mr Cooper think he has over Miss Emerson?' he mused quietly. He tapped the article. 'It looks to me as if he's poking the bear with his aspersions on Mr O'Shea's character.'

Lucille opened her fan again, flapping madly, and glanced at her husband whose face had flushed. He might soon have need of her fan.

'What is it?' Mr Barrett asked both.

'It could mean something even more sinister from Mr Cooper,' David began, 'that has a propensity to drag down a number of quite innocent people, by association.' He ducked his head before continuing. 'I—we believe that Mr O'Shea is not at all a ladies' man. Not at all,' he emphasised.

Lucille saw the detective's comprehension. 'And we believe it is that to which Mr Cooper is alluding,' she said.

Mr Barrett looked over the letter then nodded. 'Oh yes, I see now.'

'If Mr O'Shea is also dragged through the mud, he could end up in gaol, at the very least hunted down, and his associates also likely tainted. The threat for Mr O'Shea is very real. Evie would be under greater pressure, and more likely to give Cooper what he wants in order to have him just *go away*. I think this is Cooper's ultimate plan, and his total pursuit,' David said.

Mr Barrett stared at them. 'Ah,' he said eventually, and a gleam entered his dark eyes. Sitting forward, linking his hands, he said, 'In that case, we had better get plenty of dirt on Mr Cooper himself.'

'A sterling idea, Mr Barrett,' Lucille said, and the little fan fluttered hard once more.

Chapter Forty-six

Cobram
Sunday 25 September

Evie woke, a dull click rousing her from sleep. It must have been early; the glow of dawn was filtering through the thin curtains of the parlour room. Parched, she groped for the cup of water she knew was by her side, grabbed it and slurped down a mouthful. Her teeth felt woolly, her head ached, her stomach growled. She sat up. Her backside ached too, a legacy of sleeping on floorboards. Despite all, she'd slept well.

For a moment, as yesterday's events rushed by in her mind, she held her face in her hands. *Meryl. Fitz.* She needed to see Fitz. And Raff. She began to stand when Jenny Robinson gripped her arm tight, a finger to her lips, eyes fierce. Tucked under her arm was a rifle.

Jenny pulled her back to the floor. 'Lay down, lay still,' she whispered furiously. She pressed herself against Evie's back, hiding the rifle between them. One of her arms was steely as it wrapped around her.

Evie froze. Ears straining, she could hear soft, tentative footfalls on the boards in the hallway. She sucked in her breath, silent and shallow. The door creaked open, and after some moments, closed again. Squeezing her eyes shut, she hoped her lungs would hold out. Her pulse pounded in her throat, thudding up through her jaw into her temple. More footfalls and then another door opened. Fitz's room.

She breathed out slowly, turned, mouthed at Jenny, *Raff?* Jenny shook her head hard. They sat up awkwardly.

Jenny handed Evie the rifle and jiggled it a little in Evie's hands. She pointed at the chamber. It was loaded. Evie lost her breath then, stared open-mouthed at Jenny, who shook her head again, wagging that finger as if saying, 'don't you dare'. Blinking, Evie nodded.

Dear God.

Silently, Jenny crawled over the tangled bedding of linens and blankets to take up the other rifle. Digging into her pocket to bring out a round, she quietly and gently loaded it in the gun, her fingers steady, but her face screwed up. The effort to silently push it into place was painstaking. She couldn't do it.

'Damn it,' she breathed. 'Here, take these,' she said and shoved two more shells into Evie's skirt pocket.

Evie swallowed the lump in her throat as Jenny slithered to the door, pressing her ear against the jamb. The footsteps were receding; whoever it was, they were heading outside. Jenny clicked in the round—the same sound that had woken Evie earlier—and breathed a sigh of relief.

Where on earth is Raff?

Jenny crawled back to her. 'It's two policemen,' she croaked. 'They came creeping around just on dawn.'

Evie knew who it must be. 'They're after Fitz.' She'd heard his door open moments ago. Her heart bumped in her throat. 'They didn't come to this room.'

A hesitation. 'No need, perhaps.'

A chill wound its way up Evie's chest. They'd found who they were looking for and their method of … disposal … was silent. A knife, or strangling, or—

Oh, Fitz.

Where is Raff?

'Come on. Pull on your boots, hitch your skirt,' Jenny said in a harsh whisper. At Evie's stricken face, she said, 'They weren't in his room long enough to do anything to Fitz. We'd have heard.' She shook Evie's arm. 'But now they know where he is, they'll come back later, so we're not staying in here like simpering ninnies. We're going to front them. We're going out that window.'

Of course we are.

Jenny took Evie's rifle. 'You saw me load it?' Evie nodded. 'Good. Remember it.' She bundled her to the window and helped her straddle the sill. Jenny whispered again. 'Lower yourself, drop quietly, then I'll hand you the two rifles. You'll learn real fast how to use yours.'

Chapter Forty-seven

'Has Constable O'Shea returned?' Robbo asked, pushing himself off the kitchen room floor and groaning. He spun around and checked the oven, lifted the hot plate and peered into the coals.

Raff shook his head. He lay his rifle on the table. 'No, and that's a worry.' Standing, he stretched, shook the life back into his hands, stiff from holding the gun. 'Gone dawn already, and no sign of him.'

Robbo stared at him. 'Trouble somewhere, maybe?'

'Maybe.'

Robbo reached into the log basket and shoved a bunch of sticks and dry leaves into the oven. He blew into it until a wisp of smoke rose. Raff heard a crackle as the flames licked over the new fuel. Robbo plonked the kettle on top.

'Time to see if the patient is awake,' Raff said. Outside he took a turn left, heading behind the privy, needing to relieve his bladder before he went into the house. He unbuttoned and took good aim at a dried tuft of weeds. Job done, he buttoned up and headed for the pump, stripping off his shirt. Grabbing a thin cake of soap from the brick mount, he worked the lever, dunked his head and scrubbed the cold-water lather through his hair and into his armpits. He rinsed, rubbing his eyes vigorously, dried off with his shirt and shrugged back into it.

'Ah good, smelling all pretty. While you were takin' a piss, we took the liberty to see what we could find.'

Raff swivelled, stared up at McCosker and Porter on horseback. McCosker's rifle was aimed at his chest. *Jesus Christ.* He hadn't heard a damn thing.

'Seems we've found the someone we're after, on his back, inside. Being so crook and all, won't be no trouble to take him, and ask him politely what else he knows. Don't need you, though.' McCosker lifted his chin. 'Get your mate out here, without his rifle.'

Robbo stepped into the kitchen doorway. He'd have heard everything.

McCosker beckoned him. 'All the way outside and put the rifle on the ground.'

A thunder beat under Raff's ribs. *Where the hell are the women?*

Chapter Forty-eight

Evie had stared wide-eyed at Raff, who thankfully hadn't seen her when she'd peeked around the back wall of the kitchen. Wasn't exactly the sort of thing she imagined ever watching Raff do, but there he was, broad back straight, standing and taking his morning's ablution, happy as a lark.

Then that horrible man loomed.

Jenny was close to Evie's ear. 'We'll slip along this wall. I'll step out first, then you, all right?'

Mortified, Evie chanced a glance over her shoulder at Jenny. 'And do what?'

'I'll fire a round, then you will. It'll give our men some time to find cover.'

Evie gaped. 'I've never fired a gun.'

'You're about to. You lift it to your shoulder, point, drop this lever to load, close it,' she said demonstrating with hand movements, 'take a breath and shoot. Just don't hit Raff. Squeeze the trigger—don't yank it. The gun will bang into you hard, so be aware.'

'What if they shoot back?' Stupid question. Of course they'd shoot back.

'They're not expecting us. We'll surprise them,' Jenny said. 'Come on.' They sidled to the corner. 'Ready?'

No. But Evie nodded.

Chapter Forty-nine

Raff heard the lever action of a rifle behind him, saw McCosker look beyond his shoulder. The man's eyes widened in amused disbelief, and a chuckle erupted. Porter straightened in the saddle, the rifle coming level with his shoulder.

'Would you look at that, Porter? A little lady—'

A round boomed. Raff's ears split.

Porter's horse stomped, reared and the rider landed heavily on the dirt, his gun flung wide. 'Chrissakes,' he yelled. 'She bloody shot at me.'

'He's not hit,' Mrs Robinson called. 'He just fell off his horse. Goodness, the loud bang must have frightened him.'

A rifle reloaded behind Raff, practised, swift. *Jesus, she is one cool-headed woman.*

McCosker had swung away from Raff to check Porter, swung back again, lifting his gun.

'Raff?' *Evie.* Shaking, by the sound of her voice.

A glance sideways and he caught her on the edge of his vision. *Christ almighty, she's got a rifle too.* The hair on the back of his neck stood on end. Stock still, his gaze went back to McCosker, who wasn't laughing now.

The disgraced policeman pointed his rifle at Evie. 'You don't look like you know how to use that thing, girlie.' He settled his shoulders, and the sight came up to his eye.

He wouldn't bloody shoot a woman. Raff sucked in a breath. Why the hell had Evie stepped out into McCosker's sight?

'But don't dare *me*, mister,' Mrs Robinson called out again.

McCosker swung towards Jenny. 'Couldn't hit me yest'dy,' he scoffed.

'Today I'm aiming at you.'

McCosker snorted, swung back, his eye over the sight, and spoke to Evie with a grin, a leer. He was toying with the women. 'How 'bout you, girlie. Game?' Theatrical, it was menace only; the bastard didn't need to line up at this range.

Raff's fists shook; one move from him and McCosker would take a shot, just for show. The rifle veered back to Raff, the sight at McCosker's eye for real this time. Blood boiled fast, sped in Raff's veins, his chest filled with it, his head—

'I'm told it's just point'—Raff heard Evie and then a lever open and close—'and shoot.' And she did.

Raff dropped to the ground, the shot clanged in his ears as it whistled past him and thunked into a wall of the house. Another shot rang out, a horse squealed, reared. Raff rolled on his side then staggered to his feet. Jenny had advanced on McCosker, the rifle back at her shoulder. Beyond her, Evie had landed flat on her back, skirt a-foof around her knees. Struggling to sit up, her elbows scraped in the dirt. Her shot had blasted past Raff and missed McCosker, whose own shot went wild when his horse pawed the air. Jenny's rifle had fired again, aimed above his head, and when the horse recovered his nerve, McCosker wasn't waiting. He dug in the spurs and they bolted into scrub beyond the lane that swallowed them up.

Another round boomed, but Robbo's shot missed the fleeing McCosker. He marched out of the kitchen, reloading. Porter scrambled for his gun. Jenny loaded again and fired, its blast peppered across him, and he fell back, yowling.

Despite shaking, Evie scrambled over and snatched the rifle she'd dropped and stood, waving it madly in Porter's direction.

Robbo fired another round into the scrub and yelled, 'Missed him again, bugger it.'

Raff had other worries. Out of nowhere, a rider had stormed up the laneway and charged through the open back gate, rifle ready. The horse charged, and hooves slashed too close to Raff. The butt of Haines's rifle came up ready to slam down on Raff's head when another round blew the air apart.

Haines howled. His rifle shattered at the barrel, the bullet exploding inside the chamber. His forearm snapped, and blood erupted. Broken pieces of the gun rained down. Raff grabbed him out of the saddle and aimed a cracking fist into his face. Haines went limp on the ground and Raff sat on him a moment, inhaling the hot stink of gunpowder and coppery blood in the air, his ears ringing in the silence.

Jenny and Robbo were agape at Evie. She was on her backside again, dress around her knees once more, her legs bare to her boots. She fumbled with the rifle, trying to figure out how to open it. Bullet casings had scattered out of her reach.

Raff got up unsteadily and reached out. 'Evie, give it here. You'll kill someone with that.'

She handed it over, shaking uncontrollably. 'I … could've killed *him*,' she said, aghast. Then, mortified, she avoided Raff's gaze and pushed at her skirt. 'I was bound to hit something, though, wasn't I?'

Raff snorted a laugh, sank to his knees by her side. 'Grateful it wasn't me,' he rasped. Thankful she was alive and unharmed, he grabbed her shaking hands, his head low over them. He was about to press his lips to her hot and grubby palms when he heard a roar.

'What in the *effing bloody hell* name of *Jesus effing Christ* is going on in my town?'

Robbo was in the kitchen doorway, rifle barrel open across his arm, staring at the mounted trooper with a handgun drawn. A grin split his gunpowder-smudged face. 'Mornin', Constable Stillard. Welcome home. Thought you said nothin' ever happens in this town.'

Stillard tucked away his gun and dismounted. 'You won't be smiling when I tell you the news.'

Chapter Fifty

Evie hung her head, sitting by Fitz in the bedroom. The shakes hadn't totally gone; she'd wielded a deadly weapon, and had fired upon not one person, but two.

Jenny had patted her shoulder earlier. 'Beginner's luck. I wouldn't have been able to pull off that shot if I'd tried. If you like, I can teach you to hit something you aim at.' She'd laughed.

For goodness' sake, I'm a milliner from Bendigo. A hat maker. A ladies' fashion stylist, not a gun-toting circus performer. Who was that woman in America—Annie Someone, a crack shot? *Good God, I'd be outlawed for murder instead of applauded for my efforts.* The thought she might have done dreadful damage had, at first, made her feel sick. It dissipated after Jenny finally got some food into her.

Her gaze drifted to Fitz. She had been the only one allowed to stay inside the house while Constable Stillard grilled Raff and Mr Robinson in the kitchen, Jenny hovering there with tea and damper. They'd tied Porter to a veranda post, ignoring his whining about his shoulder, injured when a tiny pellet from Jenny's last shot had hit him.

Once or twice, Evie heard Constable Stillard yelling. 'Dead, you hear me? The station … My effing house shot up … Lucky my family is not …' She couldn't hear who answered him, if anyone. She tried not to focus on whoever, or whatever, was 'dead'.

Footsteps sounded in the hall.

'Is he awake yet?' Raff was in the doorway. His dark hair had been scraped from his face, and the dense shadow of a beard barely disguised the set of his jaw, all hard angles.

Evie shook her head. 'I think his breathing is easier.' Raff was staring at her. At her filthy, tangled hair, her dirty dress, her blackened hands and fingernails. None of that had mattered earlier when he'd bent over her hands outside.

Constable Stillard pushed into the room behind him; Jenny and Robbo nowhere to be seen.

'This the reporter?' he asked of Raff, nodding at the bed.

Raff's eyes were still on Evie as he answered. 'Yes. Fitzmorgan O'Shea. John was his older brother.'

'Miss, out of the way if you please.'

Evie clambered to her feet and backed away from the bed. 'Brother?' she asked of Raff, who nodded. She hardly remembered if Fitz had ever mentioned a brother.

Constable Stillard took the seat and searched for a place free of sunburn to tap Fitz. His shoulder. 'Mr O'Shea, wake up.' He tapped again. 'Mr O'Shea,' he said louder.

Fitz's eyes opened. He seemed alert. Evie nearly cried out.

'Mr O'Shea, I have some terrible news for you.'

Evie glanced at Raff whose eyes were bleak. What had he just said to the constable? *John* was *his older brother.*

Oh no. Now Fitz's brother.

Fitz was trying to sit. Raff hooked an arm under his shoulder and stuffed the meagre pillows behind him. Then he stalked out of the room, without a glance at anyone. Evie heard his heavy tread as he left the house. He was going to go after McCosker, she knew it. Evie took only a moment, staring at Fitz before she turned and ran into the hall. Raff was already outside, marching into the kitchen.

'Raff.' He didn't stop. '*Raff,*' she shouted, sprinting out the back door and across the small yard. 'What are you doing?'

He came out rolling his swag and, reaching Bluey, threw it on the saddle. He tightened the girth. 'When that boat of MacHenry's comes by here, you be on it, you hear me?'

'What?'

'Get your passage back to Echuca then get on the train and go home.' He slipped a foot into the stirrup and swung up.

She grabbed Bluey's halter as Raff turned him. 'Don't, Raff. Don't go after him.'

'Go home, Evie.'

Still she held on, shaking her head.

He bent from the saddle to pry her hand from the halter and gave a frustrated growl. 'I have to chase him down. You understand that.'

'He's a madman, Raff. We need you here—Fitz, and the Robinsons.' Her eyes, intense, were on him. 'And me,' she said, fiercely.

His hand was wrapped tight around hers. He focused on her, his gaze on her mouth, her nose, then he stared into her eyes a moment. 'If you ever really do need me, Evie, I'll find you.' He dropped her hand, turned the horse and took off.

By the time Stillard left for the station, a subdued Robbo had been told to make the police house safe, and Jenny busied herself preparing food. Evie tried to help Fitz, but he floated in and out of sleep, mumbling he was woozy, pushing her away. Perhaps he just wanted to be left alone, to grieve; Constable Stillard had related that Fitz had understood his brother was dead. She couldn't even hold his hands for the sunburn. Best to leave him be.

Sometime later, Jenny came in with a lantern.

'Is Raff back yet?' Evie asked.

Jenny shook her head and squeezed Evie's shoulder. 'It'll be another long night, if not a few nights,' she said. 'But your Mr O'Shea will be fine, he's showing all good signs.'

Evie smiled, grateful for the woman's calm company and Fitz's improvement. Now it was her Mr Dolan she was worried about.

Three days later, Constable John O'Shea was buried. The Cobram townspeople had come out for it, attending the graveside ceremony. O'Shea hadn't been among them long, but it seemed fitting that shops closed for half the trading day; a good member of the constabulary in their town was being laid to rest after a violent ending.

They'd nearly all locked themselves in their homes and shops on the day he was gunned down at his desk, so none of the townspeople could tell the usually unflappable Constable Stillard they'd seen anything. One man, a retired gent who hadn't been able to move quickly enough to escape the street, said he'd seen Mr Haines on the veranda about to barge inside the station before the shot rang out. The bystander had fled into an alley. Moments later, peering out, he'd seen Haines and another two men leaving on horseback. They were troopers, for sure, the man had sworn.

Both Haines and Porter were in the lock-up, a leg iron on each—neither going anywhere until a police escort arrived from Melbourne. Both had sworn, bellowing over the other, that McCosker had shot Constable O'Shea dead.

On Fitz's request, Stillard had interrogated Haines about Roy Bayley's whereabouts, or his demise. He'd denied any knowledge of it, and only moaned about his injuries.

Porter had constantly shouted, 'McCosker's coming back for me, yer makin' a big mistake keeping me here.'

Constable Stillard mostly ignored him. Only once, he'd shouted in return, 'The coward's run off, you blasted fool, left you deep in it. Unlikely he'll return, so shut up.'

A dose of laudanum for Haines and Porter from the doctor had stopped the yelling.

No one owned up to cracking Fitz over the head.

Stillard had found Constable O'Shea's report in the desk drawer; it was damning of McCosker and Porter, and Haines, who hadn't escaped condemnation. The constable wasn't too happy about 'that big fella, Rafferty Dolan', disappearing, either.

At the cemetery, Evie had wanted Fitz to stay in the cart but when John's coffin was about to be lowered, he insisted on standing by the grave. The pall bearers waited until he was ready, head bowed. Fitz wore no hat, out of deference of course, and his scalp was too tender, besides. Someone had given Evie a large umbrella and she held it above their heads, her arm looped in his.

Her emotions stayed in check almost throughout. There'd been no funeral for Meryl, no chance to say goodbye. At one point, Fitz squeezed her arm close. 'We said a few words for your sister,' he whispered, as if he'd known her thoughts. 'And Robbo has promised to carve new markers.' Only then had she allowed tears to sneak through. Fitz squeezed her arm again, and she held on tight.

Afterwards, people had filtered back through town from the cemetery, walking or driving to their homes, and quiet had descended once more. Robbo had driven Evie and Fitz to the hotel for lodgings. They'd had to move there; repairs had begun on Constable Stillard's quarters and he was eager to bring his family back to their home.

Jenny said goodbye. Before she left, she handed Evie a thick envelope. 'These are the other letters that Mr Morgan—Mr O'Shea,' she corrected, 'left with me for safekeeping. He should have them back now.'

One was addressed to a Mr and Mrs Levi.

The other was addressed to The Editor of the *Ballarat Star* newspaper.

Chapter Fifty-one

Somewhere by the Mighty Murray

A sleepless night spent in the saddle, Raff crept through scrub, or along sandy banks that edged the silent run of water. McCosker would stay close to the river, keeping his bearings. Where the hell was he? Ahead? Or had he circled back behind, watching, maybe lining up a shot?

Moonlight shone intermittently. Each time a breeze rustled leaves, Raff thought it the whisper of a malevolent presence, furtive and skirting discovery. At times, his heartbeat was so loud in his head it muted other noises of the night. Sometimes he sat motionless, the warm dry air filling his lungs a remedy to calm his nerves. Bluey's ears served as his, and flicked or lay flat. The big horse kept a quiet countenance as if by instinct.

Raff tracked doggedly into the breaking dawn, his eyes sticky, bleary. He squinted and blinked as the sun's early glow bloomed through the trees. Light cut across the river, and far up ahead, he saw a rider saddling up.

There. The bastard had camped, managed to sleep, maybe. No fire, no swag, but he'd unsaddled at some point in the night.

Maybe it was a ripple on the air, or maybe it was the keen sixth sense of the hunted; McCosker turned on the last pull of the girth strap and saw Raff. He swung up fast, let out a yell as he hit the saddle and kicked his horse into a run, heels pounding.

Raff and Bluey hauled up to the top of the bank and, dodging sturdy trees, pushed through the scrub. Bluey drew on reserves, gained ground with long, powerful strides. Hugging his mane, Raff missed low slung branches but not the sharp sting of drooping leaves as they whipped his face, pricked his eyes.

McCosker pulled away into a clearing then headed into the scrub's cover further up and disappeared from sight. He'd be right at the river's edge again, so Raff turned for the river, dropped Bluey to a slow canter and dragged out his rifle. Light streamed onto the water in wide gauzy ribbons and he watched for puffs of fine dirt suspended in the air. Into a thicket disturbed by hooves, horse dung and musty earth spiced his nostrils.

Close.

A rifle lever clicked, unmistakable on the still air. Raff swung Bluey. A *crack*. A round whizzed past and *whacked* into a tree trunk. He caught sight of McCosker wheeling away on top of the deep bank. Raff nudged Bluey and they leaped forward. McCosker kicked wildly at his horse, veered about, aimed rein-free, his mount dancing under him close to the edge.

'I'll get you and then I'll go back for that little chit you're filling up,' he bellowed, and then he fired.

Raff flattened himself on Bluey's neck, the bullet searing past him, overhead.

But the blast had spooked McCosker's horse and, grappling for purchase on the loose soil, it tipped, screaming.

It fell hard. McCosker bounced out of the saddle, landed with a crunch and bounced again, dropping face first into the water, plunging beneath the surface. A few feet deep only, but that would do it.

The horse scrambled, squealing as it righted itself and took off uninjured, stirrups and reins flapping.

Raff stared at the unmoving body. 'Don't reckon you'll be going back anywhere, mate,' he muttered, Bluey stamping under him.

Amid the settling dust, staring down the deep drop to the water, Raff glared at the body for a long time. McCosker was either already dead, neck broken, or he was drowning, unconscious. Hushed ripples lapped the bank. No air bubbles. Time passed; he didn't know how much. He let it breeze by. A day and a night's ride from Cobram along the river had been rough, hard and hungry. He'd found McCosker, but a horse had cheated him. Raff had wanted to kill him.

Dismounting, he tied Bluey to a branch then tramped down the bank. Loose dirt filled his steps until he hit firmer ground at the water's edge. Satisfied that the last twitches of life in the body had fled, he walked a little way along the shore, pulled off his boots and stepped into the river. He snatched off his hat, tossed it and rubbed his sweaty head, the dirt gritty on his fingers. *Filthy.* Wearily, he shucked his shirt, dropped his trousers, kicking them off, and sank knee-deep in the river, scrubbing till he felt clean. Soap would have to wait.

Done, he made his way unhurriedly back to shore, well away from the inert form, then dried naked on the bank in the warm air.

Cheated by a horse, aye, but best not to have to confess to a killing.

The better part of him was relieved that he hadn't done it. He wouldn't have to tell Evie he'd killed a man. The better part of him wanted to tell her—

He took a breath. She'd be in Cobram, looking after Fitz. Maybe they were reuniting … So what good was blathering to himself about her all bloody day and night?

Donning his clothes and boots, he took up his hat, stroked the red-and-black feather stitched tight to the band. He turned it over, ran his fingers over the initials sewn on the inside.

It wouldn't be Fitz for Evie. It couldn't be.

He headed for Bluey, the dark mood unshakable.

Chapter Fifty-two

Cobram
Friday 30 September

Fitz was much better; his head still carried stitches but the wound was repairing well. He'd been walking through the day, careful of the new flesh, pink and clean, emerging under the dead flaky skin. To rest, he'd take a seat on a bench in the shade. Sometimes, he'd made it to the bar. Thankfully, he could now wield a nib pen comfortably. Evie returned his first article, the one he'd handed to Jenny Robinson for safekeeping, and helped him amend it, bringing it up to date.

Nothing had changed in Evie's situation. Meryl was dead and buried. Died of natural causes, the doctor had said, and written up a death certificate to that effect. When not with Fitz, Evie wandered the town. She considered borrowing a horse to visit her sister's grave, but her energy flagged at the thought. Meryl wasn't there; no need to revisit where her body had been laid to rest, where memories Evie didn't even own would haunt her. Raff was gone, and Fitz didn't need her. More than anything, she longed to be back in the studio in Bendigo, chatting to Mrs Downing, creating her masterpieces of millinery for the local ladies, or taking afternoon tea with Ann and Posie.

With her thoughts turned to home, and to the problem that

would still face her there, she headed for the post office. For too long, she'd put off a visit there. Goodness knows what news awaited her. It was with trepidation that she collected her mail.

Oh yes, there was the telegram: a summons awaited her at home. Evie had to accept the inevitable. There was also a letter addressed to her in Mrs Downing's handwriting, sent later than the telegram; the sender was Lucille, Mrs David Kingsley of his address, which did bring a rueful smile. Evie was happy for her mentor. She hoped Mrs D wouldn't lose too much of her independence. Mr Kingsley seemed a nice man, but husbands didn't seem to enjoy having wives who were too self-reliant.

Finding a seat near the river, under a tree and shaded from the late afternoon sun, she read the contents of the brief note, then the clipping of Edwin's vitriolic letter to the editor. Her heart sank. Not only had he made his lies about her public, but he'd dragged Fitz into it as well. In the early days in Edwin's company, being an open and honest person, she'd confided of her friendship with Fitz. Edwin had used it in a most despicable way. She sighed sadly. What an evil, nasty man. Fitz needed to know what Edwin had done, that a court case was imminent, and that she'd have to leave Cobram soon, but he'd already retired early today, pleading a headache. She'd have to catch him early tomorrow before he used all his energy.

She tucked the pages back into the envelope and faced the water, its serene flow not the distraction she'd hoped. *What day is it?* Surely the MacHenrys were due back on their paddle-steamer tomorrow.

Where is Raff?

The next morning, she shot awake. Sitting up in bed, she hugged her knees and hoped today Raff would arrive and return to Echuca on the boat with her. If he was coming back.

He *had* to. Where was he? Had that awful man McCosker caught him somewhere? *No, no, no.* She rubbed her face. Despite sleeping, she was tired, not refreshed, not rested at all.

She'd dressed, and was about to go in search of some breakfast when she found Fitz at her door, his fist raised ready to knock.

'Are you off somewhere?' she asked, glancing at the bag at his feet.

'I'm leaving,' he said, blithely. 'It's time. Patto's been well cared for by the boys at the pub, he's fit as a fiddle, and so am I. Nearly,' he conceded, flexing the fingers on his right hand. 'So there's no reason for me to stay.' Tiny bits of dried flaky skin clung to the middle of his forehead and dusted his cheeks.

'Leaving,' she echoed. 'I'm to be here by myself, am I?'

'Get on the next boat to Echuca and go back to Bendigo before this business with Edwin Cooper blows up.'

The letter from Mrs Downing, um, Kingsley, and the summons certainly meant she had to agree with him. 'I will, I have to, but about that in a minute. What of your stitches?'

He shrugged. 'Someone along the way will help, or I could just do it myself.' At her protest he cut in. 'It's best I leave sooner than later. I'll mail off my story to the papers, requesting that they telegraph it to other mastheads.' He smiled. 'There'll be plenty who don't like it, so I need to keep moving.'

'Fitz, first there's something I need to tell you, to discuss. And … there's Raff. Where could he be?' She went quiet.

'Raff? Hmm.' He inclined his head. 'I'm ordering tea and eggs for breakfast in the dining room before I leave. Join me.' At her hesitation, he said, 'Constable Stillard has given me some information.'

It was futile to demand he tell her there in the hallway. She retrieved her purse, and a hat she'd purchased locally, an unimaginative little navy blue cap-like thing with a dull-coloured feather sticking out of it (nothing she could do about it without her sewing kit) and followed Fitz downstairs. She wore a plain clean dress in tiny checks of blue and white that she'd brought from home, and although it was a little creased, it would have to do. Still, she couldn't help brushing it down every so often, hoping to banish the wrinkles …

Oh, for goodness' sake, Evie. It wasn't the dowdy hat, it wasn't the wrinkly dress, it was having to tell Fitz—somehow—what Edwin had inferred in the newspaper.

Fitz asked to be seated at a table away from others, which suited her. Better not to have ears flapping for what she had to impart. The waitress took their order for eggs, poured tea and left for the kitchen.

He eyed her. 'That thing's not one of your creations, is it?' he asked and nodded at her hat. When she shook her head, he said, 'Didn't think so. You should start up your own brand, Evie.'

'The thought has crossed my mind. It's not impossible. I'd do well, I think.'

'You would.' He smiled at her. 'I present the renowned Milliner of Bendigo.' He waved an arm, a theatrical flourish.

Evie could stand it no longer. 'What information did the constable have for you?'

He lowered his chin. 'Before we get to that, I want to say a few things. The first, how sorry I am about Meryl.'

Her throat bobbed. 'You wrote me a beautiful letter of condolence.' No tears came but she blinked anyway.

'That was in lieu of seeing you in person. I had no idea we'd meet again here.' He didn't elaborate and, clearly a little ill-at-ease, fidgeted in the chair. 'I take it you knew nothing of your sister's son.'

Evie shook her head. 'She hadn't said a thing. I don't know why. But she … There was something wrong, a melancholy that seemed to consume her and, in the end, she turned away from Mama and me. Not even a letter.' All their years growing up, had they ever really known each other? They'd grown apart, she admitted. The saddest thought was that Evie didn't believe anything would have changed even if Meryl had lived. 'You never really know someone, not even your own sibling.'

Fitz shrugged. 'Hmm.' There was a silence then he leaned forward, his linked fingers resting on the table. 'I need to tell you something else. The truth, Evie. My truth.' He studied his hands a moment, turning them over and back, brushing off a minute piece of flaked skin. When she raised her brows, he continued. 'There might be letters to the editor in the Ballarat and Bendigo newspapers from people defending the police and maybe, also, articles in retaliation.' He stopped a moment. 'So I want you to be … prepared if certain things about me come to light.'

'Worse than the things Edwin has accused me?' Evie asked. She took a sip of tea, still too hot.

Fitz smiled his lovely smile, only now it was a little sheepish. 'Well, yes.' He dropped his voice. 'You remember—of course you do—our many discussions about why we shouldn't marry.'

Evie stared. What on earth did this have to do with anything? Unless he thought Edwin was going to name him as a third party or something ridiculous. So, Edwin's reasons were misguided by jealousy or … *Oh, for heaven's sake.* That wouldn't be it. Or—oh no—*God forbid*, Fitz. Did he *want* to marry her after all? *Oh, good Lord, no.* She had to set him straight.

She whispered furiously. 'Fitz, I do remember, and before you say anything more, if the truth be known, you and I … it didn't feel right to me.' She ploughed on. 'For you, either, if we're both honest. Nothing's changed for me in that regard. I see no point marrying you even though we are really good friends. I'm told it's the best basis for marriage, but not when what we want from our lives isn't at all compatible.' Breathless, she said, 'You have to agree, it's true.' Had she made it plain enough?

He held her gaze for long moments. 'Of course it's true. Absolutely true,' he said. 'I certainly agree.'

Oh, thank heavens.

'But there's more to it,' Fitz said. 'There's a bigger reason it wouldn't have been right.' He took up his cup and swallowed a big drink of tea before checking she was ready to listen. 'Then or now, just to be doubly clear.'

Well, it can only have been one thing. 'You loved someone else.' She couldn't be cross about that; of course not. 'It would've been disastrous to marry if your heart was elsewhere.'

He nodded, bemused, then shook his head slightly. 'But not like you think.' He stopped, was—unusually—struggling to find the words.

'It's quite all right, Fitz.' She knew she was missing something, but for the life of her Evie couldn't grasp what it was.

He took a breath, then reached across to cover her hand with his. 'You see, that particular someone else, well, he left me because of our love.'

His touch was light on her hand, it lay over hers, warm, a comfort. He was her friend …

Wait. Did I just hear him correctly?

'Evie,' he said patiently. 'He was my lover. I loved him with all my heart and I know Augustus loved me.' Fitz inhaled deeply. 'But he turned away, the family pressure was too much, and he married. A woman,' he clarified unnecessarily. 'By my nature, I love men. Not women, not like that. Only men.'

Her friend, Fitzmorgan O'Shea, had loved another man. *I love men. Not women.* Evie wasn't so naïve that she didn't know of it, only … She glanced at their clasped hands then at Fitz's handsome face; his solemn gaze was intent on her, expectant.

'Oh, Fitz. I'm—' Confused, stunned. She wondered why he'd ever talked of marrying her. Turning her hand under his, she tentatively gripped his fingers. 'I'm sorry I'm thick,' she whispered. 'I wouldn't have ever— I didn't know.'

'Augie was before your time, a while ago now.' He gave a little laugh. 'We have to hide who we are to the outside world, you know.' She gave a short nod and he sat back. 'So when he left me, I thought about what he'd done by marrying and why. I wondered if I could do the same. I met you and thought you'd be the perfect foil for me.'

Perfect foil. Her friend had just said that.

He held her stare. 'But in the end, I couldn't see myself living a lie, Evie. I couldn't do it to you either.' Squeezing her hand, he said, 'I can only imagine the agony Augie's living. At first, I thought he'd be able to carry it off, but I don't think that now. I couldn't have.' Fitz's grip tightened a little more. 'Even knowing there's the threat of death by a mob, or worse, imprisonment, and being attacked in there if I'd continued on my merry way, I still couldn't go ahead and marry. You see, my father—' He cut off, patted her hand as she sniffed, bit her lip. 'Now, stop that. Don't you dare snivel. I'll find somewhere that suits me. I'll find my people.'

My people. But who were she and Raff— *Oh.* 'And … Raff?'

Fitz burst a laugh. 'God, Evie, your face.' He tapped their hands on the table. 'Never, ever Raff. *Ever.* He's my friend, only that, and the big lug is a ladies' man through and through. You must know that.'

Of course she did. Relief swept through her. Other thoughts whirled but she couldn't catch them all at once. Tugging gently out of Fitz's hand, she lifted the teacup and carefully took a few sips, trying to steady her racing mind. The first thought to slow down and form was that Mrs Kingsley had cut off the rest of Edwin's letter to the editor. He must have alluded to something.

Groping in her little bag, she withdrew the newspaper clipping and handed it to Fitz. 'This was sent to me.'

Reading a few lines, he closed his eyes and exhaled loudly. 'So, there you are. Cooper has found something and it's already started. I wonder what the rest of the letter said.' He rubbed his eyes. 'Christ,' he muttered then blinked at her. 'Sorry, Evie. I just hope the police don't take any notice of it. I'll have to be on the move, more than ever now.'

'I was hoping you'd be at my hearing,' she said. 'I've been summonsed to appear on the tenth of next month.'

'Maybe. If I can. But I should move along, stay out of the way.'

'Where will you go?' Evie cried. 'Why not wait for Raff? What if—'

'I'll go wherever I end up. As for Raff, he could be ages returning, though I strongly suspect not.' He gave her a grin, raised his eyebrows. 'I see how he looks at you. All that smouldering masculinity, all that fire in his blood just for you. Good thing I like 'em lean, not big and muscly.' Evie's face bloomed. 'Oh, stop it,' he said, a gleam in his eye. 'Raff is just itching to snatch you up and … gobble.'

She blurted a laugh despite a suspicion he was being … lewd somehow. Was he? Oh, she had no idea.

'That's better,' Fitz said. 'And it's as clear as it's always been. He wants you, Evie. He's carried a blazing torch for you for years.'

'I didn't—'

'Of course you didn't. You were in love with me—'

'I was *not.*'

'—and the noble sod thought you were pining for me ever thereafter.' His eyes lit up, then at her frown he held up his hands in protest. He sobered then. 'So, I have more to confess. I still haven't told Raff that I'd—we'd—absolutely finished talk of marrying.'

'What?' Evie was catching that other thread of thought that had skimmed by her moments ago. 'But that was nearly two years ago.'

'You were the perfect shield for me. I told no one otherwise. Who knows, I might yet have come around to the idea of marrying you.' He smiled at her. 'You are the nicest woman I know, a friend, a woman with a pleasant disposition who is gracious and smart, independent.'

Pleasant disposition. Evie sucked in a breath. 'I'd have had some say in the matter.' She was becoming a little tetchy.

He ducked from her glare. 'I know you would. I had to finally let the idea go, and I realise the wrong I've done you. And to Raff, the honourable bugger.'

'You've *realised*?' she cried, seething. 'Did you and Raff, your friend, never speak about it? Fitz, that's downright—' What words were the right ones? At least he looked uncomfortable. 'Selfish, to say the very least.'

Bristling then, he shrugged. 'Don't put all the blame on me, you said all along that marrying me wouldn't be right,' he said.

'Don't dismiss this,' she said, her voice low. 'You knew Raff would never declare for me if he believed you and I—'

'Then why didn't you tell Raff?' he asked baldly.

Her mouth dropped open.

Fitz held up a hand. 'You're right, I was selfish. Sorry.' He didn't sound remorseful. 'He's his own man, though. I didn't need to give him permission.'

'You should have said—'

'Truth be known, he went back to Ballarat to his business—as he would've done anyway—without asking me a thing, and I didn't offer a word either. Then I took off. So, *status quo*. We both dodged Bendigo afterwards for the same reason: you were there. Me, to avoid your disappointment—'

'No, not that,' she said, yielding only a little with the squeeze of her hand again on his.

'—and Raff to avoid unrequited love.'

'Did he say that?'

'Never. I just knew.'

'You should have told him,' Evie stormed between her teeth.

'I wasn't going to risk losing my chance at a so-called acceptable life until I was sure it wasn't for me. And if the big lug couldn't work out to carry you off for himself, who was I to tell him? He still hasn't done anything about it, has he?'

'Fitz.' A chide.

'Don't go all school-marmy on me. A clever woman like you should have figured out how to show him you were keen.'

'Don't turn it around. You're not off the hook here, Fitzmorgan O'Shea.'

He shrugged again, not the least concerned. 'Neither are you. I know you noticed how he looked at you.'

'I thought there was a *you and me* at the time,' she huffed, and withdrew her hand, unsure now what she'd been thinking way back then. 'And, if I had taken any notice of Raff, we both would have been betraying you.'

'Oh, come on, Evie. A little dramatic,' he admonished, sitting back.

Were her reasons for letting Raff slip by her wispy and weak? She'd been seen with Fitz with whom she'd talked marriage, had enjoyed long walks and afternoon teas and dinners out in the public eye. Come to think of that, Raff was there for a lot of those times. Then, when it ended with Fitz, there was the gossip. That was hard enough to live down, but there'd have been more gossip if she'd taken up with someone else too soon, especially Fitz's best friend. Not that she'd thought it was an option at the time: Raff had left town.

The distance from her home in Bendigo to Raff's home in Ballarat was two days—*oh, that excuse is so lame now*—and she'd had no chaperone if she were to have visited. Besides, Raff certainly hadn't given her any reason, any indication to think … She'd buried herself in her work with Mrs Downing, trying to pull the measly threads of her life together. Her sister gone to the river, her mother passed away. Then Edwin Cooper. *Oh, damn Edwin Cooper.*

'Your silence is surprisingly unusual,' Fitz said. 'Are you thinking again?'

'Very funny, Fitzmorgan. I'm angry at you.'

'You're angry at yourself.'

'At you,' she confirmed, testy and on edge.

His tone changed, softened. 'About who I am?'

She slumped at that, but it wasn't difficult to answer truthfully. 'Who you are is the person I've always thought you to be: my friend,' she said and stared at her hands in her lap. 'What I can't understand is that as *my* friend you didn't—' She fixed her gaze on him. 'My life married to you would have been a bewildering, unhappy one.'

'But we didn't get there, Evie. Desperation drove me after Augie, survival shifted my focus for a while. In the end, I couldn't go through with it. It was my father who really changed my mind. I clearly recall how resentful my mother was of him.'

'Your father. How?'

'My strong opinion is that I'm very much like him. Not meant to marry a woman.'

'Oh, but they had your brothers and you—' She stopped.

'A biological urge I have to assume, the type of which I've never experienced.'

So damned naïve, Evie. She didn't know where to look.

'Are you horrified about who I prefer to live with?' he asked. He wasn't sparing her.

Taking a breath, she said, 'I'm not … I don't …' She floundered. How does a man love—live—with another man *that* way? Then she blushed, a heatwave on her cheeks.

Oh.

A little laugh escaped him. 'So, we won't talk of that,' he said. 'Not for a lady's ears, is it, and hardly a convivial subject at the dining table.'

'I'm … out of my depth, Fitz.'

'Polite.'

She hesitated, fiddled with her serviette. 'Should you even be telling me these things?'

He leaned back, swiped a crumb from the table, eyes downcast. When he looked at her, eyes bright, he said, 'You're my friend, are you not, Evie? I need my friends.'

Awkward and disconcerted, she was caught short, couldn't articulate, not yet. Talk of relations between men and women were not for a lady's ears—on any occasion, she'd been told. Oh, she knew more about that than some, thanks to her married friends. But not this. It brought another furious blush.

He clearly had no remorse about the fate he might have dealt her. But, no matter, it hadn't happened, thanks to good sense, hers as much as his. He was right; it was as much her responsibility. She would always have listened to the voice inside that said marriage to Fitz would not be right. But he was her much-loved friend, she knew it, her happy, charming, attractive, clever Fitz.

'Just be honest in future,' she said.

'I'll try my best.' After a moment, he gave her a broad smile. 'We should write more now we're not betrothed.'

'That sounds so odd.' She couldn't help allowing her own smile.

He dropped the mirth. 'You are my friend, Evie. I don't want to lose you.'

Beats of silence slipped by before she spoke what she knew to be true. 'You haven't.' She pressed his hand closing over the newspaper clipping. 'And be careful. Whatever he's written, it's so awful of Edwin.'

He read it again briefly, mouth pinched before pocketing it. He sat back and stared into the distance across the dining room.

All this had made her giddy. A silence lengthened. Then she remembered what he'd said at her door. 'You said you had information from Constable Stillard.'

'Seems tame now after our conversation.' Fitz trailed his fingers on the tablecloth as the waitress brought two plates of scrambled eggs with warm bread and butter on the side. She set the dishes in front of them and he tucked in as soon as she left. 'A body has been found on the river, still dressed in police uniform.'

Evie had just taken up her knife and fork. 'McCosker.'

'Apparently.'

'Drowned?'

He shrugged. 'Initial report says his neck was broken before he went into the water.'

'That's not tame.'

He pointed at her plate. 'Eat, Evie.'

'Raff wouldn't—'

'Raff didn't kill McCosker. He could have, and with bare hands, but he wouldn't have. We just have to hope the coroner finds no reason to call foul play.'

Chapter Fifty-three

Raff couldn't be absolutely sure, but he reckoned it was the *Sweet Georgie* steaming downriver. It would be on its way to Cobram, and on to Echuca from there.

He sat atop Bluey, watching. He hadn't been seen, he was too far back. If he was a wanted man he wasn't about to compromise anyone else. He'd try to slip back into Cobram, maybe find the Robinsons, get information, and keep out of sight until he knew he was not blamed for McCosker's death.

Evie had to get on board the little steamer and head for home. *Evie. Jesus Christ.* What was he going to do about her? And Fitz? He'd be fine, he'd blend into the scenery with his pen and inkpot. But what if Evie and Fitz still— Christ, no. Not possible anymore, surely. Even if Fitz would benefit from the cover of a marriage. *Just not to Evie.* No one was going to marry Evie, except him, for Chrissakes. If she'd have him.

He watched the little paddle-steamer disappear around a bend. Another day and a half's ride to Cobram but on the water … He had to get to Evie, soon. Had to let her know how he felt once and for all. Maybe she'd still choose Fitz or … someone else. But at least it wouldn't be that bloody arsewipe Cooper. Not when—

Bluey stomped his hooves.

'Sorry, old mate. Getting myself worked up.' Raff slapped the horse's neck affectionately. Blucy wasn't having any of it. He tossed his head, chewed at the bit, snorted. 'All right if you say so.' No doubt the horse was smarter than he was. Raff stared down-river. *Evie*. 'Let's flag down that paddle-steamer, boy.' He gave a tap with his heels and Bluey took off.

Chapter Fifty-four

Cobram

Laughing, Evie stood on the veranda of the hotel and watched Fitz leave. He'd only turned once to wave, and it had descended into a frenzy; a bee or a wasp must have settled on him. Patto swaggered proudly, calmly walking out of view, his hand-flapping master on his back. And then they were gone.

Earlier, Evie had accompanied Fitz to the cemetery, and just like she hadn't needed to visit Meryl's gravesite, Fitz didn't seem too keen to linger at John's. Damp-eyed, all he said as he gingerly sat his hat on his head, was, 'A waste of brothers. We could have done better, the three of us. I should try to find Lawrence, our older brother, and tell him about John. But I don't know where to start looking.'

Fitz had said it was best if he left today. So why didn't it feel that way? She was alone in Cobram. Fitz was gone; horse and rider no longer visible. Raff nowhere in sight. The Robinson's hadn't come back to town and Evie was in no mind to seek them out at their property for another goodbye. She would write her thanks once she got home.

Home. Where was that, exactly? A place where she could work her magic over sumptuous fabrics, wire frames, and lush feathers and ribbons. A place where her thimble-hardened fingers were deft and creative. That was home, the refuge in her craft. She could work anywhere, but there wasn't anything for her here. So what point was there to wait? None.

The little wharf had no shade, and her petite hat was no defence against the sun so she sat under a tree a little further away where she had a good view along the river. The steamers and barges came down on water flowing from the snowy reaches much further up, towards the mountains. Would the stream be thin there? Cold and icy clear? How wonderful one day to trek to its beginnings, to its headwaters. Its source might be a spring, or a mushy pond somewhere. She'd heard of the great confluence of the Darling and the Murray downriver from here. That would also be a magical place to visit one day, especially if the drought broke and the rivers ran. The mighty rivers.

A steamer came into her sight. *Too big.* She could try and buy passage on another boat, but being with another woman, having Mrs MacHenry on board, afforded better security. Although eager to get to Echuca and to the train station, safety came first. Too much had happened to make a mistake that would cost her unnecessarily. She settled back against the tree; she'd wait until the very last, until dusk and then, if still no *Sweet Georgie*, she'd have to go back to the hotel for another night.

The heat built steadily as the morning lengthened. Dozing, lulled by a light breeze, her head bobbed and she jerked awake. There was the small white-hulled craft heading steadily downriver towards the wharf. Clambering to her feet, she grabbed her bag, and with the other hand on her hat, she marched down to the little landing and waited for Joe to tie up to a stanchion.

Chapter Fifty-five

Murray River

'Nah, mate, the *Sweet Georgie* is a day ahead of us, yer missed her,' the deckhand yelled over the water to Raff, his hands cupped around his mouth. 'I reckon she'd be downriver from Cobram by now. We can take ye and ye horse on board though.'

Raff had waved them on. Evie would have boarded the *Sweet Georgie*. She *would* have. No point Raff trying to make Cobram in a tearing hurry now.

And what of Fitz, the bloody so-and-so? Where would he go? Unless Evie and Fitz … *Forget that. It wouldn't have happened.*

He took it easy on Bluey after that. He'd make Bendigo in reasonable time without breaking his horse's back. When he learned that Evie was safe from the idiot Cooper, Raff would head on home to Ballarat and his wheelwright shop, pick up where he left off, let things settle down. He'd wait to hear from Evie, if she was going to write. Then visit her—if that's what she wanted. He'd hear from Fitz somewhere along the line, maybe Raff would read a newspaper article penned by him. He wasn't worried about Fitz's whereabouts, the fella seemed to have nine lives as it was. They'd meet up again soon, somewhere.

That is, unless Fitz and Evie had— *Not gonna happen.*

Raff was still a day out of Cobram so he looked for a place to make an early camp. He'd start the next morning before dawn. The river was on his right; he wouldn't doss down by the water, but maybe high on a bank somewhere that gave him easy access.

A yell. Ahead, a rider was waving him down.

Jesus. What were the goddamned chances? *Fitz.*

Scraping out a deep pit, and bordering it with a ring of motley rocks, they started a fire. They had kicked away leaf litter and kept the flames low, well clear of overhead branches. Bully beef was heating in the can.

Fitz pointed at the scar on his head. 'Get these out, would you?' he asked. He sat cross-legged on the dirt.

Raff used his knife to nick the stitches and tug the threads away. He swabbed the healing scar with rum and stood back, chucked the swabs into the coals. 'Job well done. It's nice and clean. Waste of rum, though.'

'Start telling me the story,' Fitz said, rubbing his scalp. 'Better I hear it straight from you than anyone else.'

Squatting by the fire, wolfing down his share of bread and the bully beef, between mouthfuls, Raff said, 'Not much to tell. I chased McCosker hard. He took a detour, heading away, before coming back to the river. Was easy in the end.'

Fitz, still on his backside, looked up sharply. 'What was?'

'I didn't kill him. He fell when his horse stumbled.'

'They said his neck had been broken.'

'He was thrown down a steep drop, landed face first in the water. Did my job for me.'

'Wasn't your *job*,' Fitz growled.

'He was gonna kill you, Fitz. He threatened Evie.' In the silence, Raff drew in a deep breath, dunked the bread into the mushed beef, took a bite. 'You left her in Cobram, did you?'

'The paddle-steamer was due in, the one she said you both arrived on, so she was going to board that.' Fitz's smile was thin-lipped. 'Our little tempest will be all right.'

'You didn't want to go with her, or take her with you?'

Fitz snorted. 'Got news for you, Raff, haven't you heard?' He reached over for another tin of beef, pierced the lid and threw it onto the fire.

'Not from you, I haven't,' Raff said, his voice edged. 'You two had talked before about marrying. I don't know whether—'

'Not the case anymore, and not for a long time. All right? You happy? Marrying's not for me, never will be. You know it, Evie knows it too now, and why.'

Raff stared at him.

'Yes, Evie knows,' Fitz grated. 'For Chrissakes, she was never interested in marrying me.'

'Fooled me then,' Raff said, cranky and winding up. 'She must have been at one point, the way you two kept on about it.'

'Maybe I was the only candidate.' Fitz laughed at him. 'You weren't stepping up, were you, mate? *You* never made a move, never said anything to her.'

'She wasn't free,' Raff ground out. 'My best friend was with her.'

Fitz spread his hands. 'She's free now, and have you done anything about it?' A beat. 'Didn't think so.'

'Took your bloody time letting her go. You knew I wasn't going to move unless you said. That doesn't seem to mean anything to you.'

Fitz only gave him a glance. In the dimming light, his eyes glinted. 'I just— You know I can't live my life out in the open like you can.'

'You can't hide behind a woman's skirts either,' Raff muttered, holding his temper.

'I know that,' Fitz fired back. 'And I also know you can't be riding in to save me from my fate every time.'

'For Chrissakes, save yourself. Don't head for the clubs, don't go into the bottom of a bottle.'

'I don't anymore. I hardly drink. I'll damned well find my own people, don't worry.'

Raff stood, kicked the empty beef tin into the flames. 'You should have said about Evie.'

'You're not stupid,' Fitz said sourly, and hurled a stick into the firepit. 'One word from you at the time and she'd have leaped across a table into your bloody lap. She'd have been yours just like that.' He snapped his fingers. 'You never gave it a good crack, Raff. So don't keep blaming me for all your dithering about.'

'And where would that have our bloody friendship?' Raff tossed at him, unable to hold back. The thread of heat barrelled up his throat.

Fitz waited another beat. 'You're right; I took my time, but I wouldn't have married her in the end. I couldn't do it to myself.'

Raff snorted. 'Big of you, you selfish bastard. You—'

'I couldn't do it to *her* either,' Fitz cut in. Chucking a stone, he ducked his chin. 'She's a good friend to me.'

Uneasy silence hummed between them.

'And I couldn't do it to you.' Fitz scratched in the dirt and hurled rocks into the fire, stone after stone. 'But it's not my bloody issue that you were too busy being an honourable fella.' He relented at the look on Raff's face, dusted off his hands. 'I know I took advantage of that. I'm sorry. I said as much to Evie. I've seen how she looks at you.'

'Oh, how's that?' Raff's chest thundered. 'Last time we were all together you were out like a light after a tap to your noggin and a nap in the sunshine.'

Leaning forward, Fitz used a piece of tree limb to snag the last unopened tin of bully beef from the coals. 'She must be getting on,' he said, conversationally, stirring Raff. 'Near thirty, I reckon, if not there already, so if you want to make an honest woman of her, mate, and get some babies in her, you better hurry up. She'll be wanting a nice little home, and a great big breadwinner. She needs a man to come home to her every night, no mistaking it.' The tin rolled towards him.

'Evie doesn't need anything, Fitz.' Raff heard his voice harden. 'She didn't want to be married. I heard her telling you loud and clear she wasn't going to traipse all over the countryside behind a husband.'

'She does want to be married, mate, she just doesn't want to be a slave to it. She'll get her business up and running, mark my words, and damn me, if she won't be proud as punch of herself. You'll be pushing it uphill if you leave it any later getting your next generation out.' Fitz pulled a face. 'You know, I thought for a time back then that, if I could convince you both, I'd marry Evie, and you could be the one to sleep with her, get those babies.'

'*What?*'

'She loves you; she loves me.' Fitz's shoulders rocked side to side.

'She doesn't love you like that,' Raff exploded.

'Never mind that now. It could've worked, though. We were all friends.'

Raff could've smacked Fitz into next week. 'You're twisted. Evie would never have … And we're not some damn bohemian—' Raff stared at him. 'How did you even think of something like that?'

'We were all friends,' Fitz repeated as if it needed clarity. 'Was worth a shot.' He gave a wry smile. 'I was plucking at straws, you know, hadn't fully accepted who I was.'

Christ. Raff stood there, swiping a hand through his hair. Bugs dived on him and then into the flames, crackling, popping, sizzling. The bully beef tin groaned.

'I was scared, Raff, after Augie, after the threats his family aimed at him, and me. I couldn't work out what I was gonna do.' He lifted his shoulders again. 'I've kept my head down since Augie; the world's not a great place for my kind.'

'Augie? Why don't I know who that is?'

Fitz stared at Raff a moment. 'Long time ago now. Augustus Pine. Someone I loved for years. Someone who chose another life.' He looked at his hands. 'Took me years to come back from that. I had to hide. Still do, but I want a companion.' He looked up, fervent, ragged. 'I just don't want to get myself killed for it.'

'I know that,' Raff said. His temper dropped away, and he stared into the night sky. Took a couple of deep, deep breaths. Stars were bright, here and there. Clouds scudded in patches. The moon was rising. 'I don't want that happening either. You're like a brother.'

Fitz ignored the platitude. 'You don't have to worry about ever being hauled off to gaol for how you wanna live,' he said. 'Yet here you are, still lagging with Evie for some reason.'

'First, I thought she was marrying you, then I thought she was marrying that idiot—' Raff lost his air then. The thought of either of them touching Evie …

Fitz held up his hands again. 'I know our little tempest wants you, no one else, it's written all over her. Better hurry up. You were too bloody slow on the uptake before.'

Raff glared across the crackling fire. 'There was a reason for that, *mate*.'

'Ah, yes, the other excuse, that Cooper fella.' Deflecting and unabashed, Fitz got to his feet and headed to his saddlebags on the ground by his swag. 'Speaking of him.'

Raff's temper bounced hot in his chest. 'What about him?'

'I show you this, I don't want you to get your damn bowels in a knot.' Fitz handed him the scrap Evie had given him from the newspaper. 'Read it by the fire and don't get it all burned. I'll need that copy to write my article.'

Angling it towards the firelight and reading, Raff's jaw set. *Shit. Shit.*

'Piece of work, isn't he?' Fitz snatched it back before Raff could ball it up.

Moths sizzled. A mosquito buzzed. Raff wiped his face with both hands. 'Do you know if Evie received a summons from the Bendigo court?'

'She did, has to appear the tenth of next month,' Fitz said, folding the sheet and tucking it back into the saddlebags. 'I'll go back there for Evie's case, if only to write it up for the paper, then I'll leave town and that suits me. Even though McCosker's dead, I won't live in Bendigo or Ballarat again after this letter.'

Raff dropped his chin, shook his head. 'Christ,' he muttered.

'You need to get Cooper, Raff. He's the one you have to stop now. He'll keep after her,' he said. 'As it is, she'll be tarred with this, her association with me.' Fitz tapped his bags again, meaning the message within the clipping. 'Even family will turn their back,' he said, remembering his past. 'You don't want that, either of you.' Then he settled by the fire and reached for the cooled tin of beef. Using his kerchief to hold the tin, he cranked it open with his knife, and cut half the contents from it into Raff's bowl. Fitz started straight from the tin, scooping out the mush with the knife and slurping.

Raff let his temper leach and sat in the dirt. Fitz's brother John hadn't turned his back; he just hadn't understood him. Now John was dead. Fitz would be hurting, deep down. No time left to make things good between them. There was only one other brother, he recalled.

He ate, thinking. 'So, what happened about that Haines fella?'

'In the lock-up, still denying John's murder. Once my article is published in the local rag, and others, he'll have less of a leg to stand on. I know it was him who bashed me with a rock but my say-so won't be enough.'

'You got proof he did anything else illegal?'

Fitz shook his head. 'But there'll be people come forward. I reckon the Robinsons will head up a willing group of folk. Someone will know something, suspect something, and bullies don't last forever, they're cowards. I'm guessing there's plenty who don't believe Roy Bayley just up and left of his own accord.'

'Another murder?'

'I'd say so.'

Raff finished his meal. 'Where will you go now?'

The glow of the fire rippled over Fitz's face. 'John's widow lives about directly south of here, couple of days at most. I'll tell her, face to face, what happened to him. I know they weren't on speaking terms, but she has to know. Then after Evie's trial I'll move on, maybe try and find my other brother.'

'Disappear into the night, you mean.'

'Yep.'

At dawn, the sun not risen yet over the trees, the horses had been saddled, the fire well doused, and all traces of their camp scattered.

'Write up a good story, Fitz,' Raff said.

'Have no doubt. Not sure if it'll be by Mr Fossey or an anonymous correspondent, but it will make fine reading.'

Raff reached over and grabbed Fitz in a sort of a hug, sort of a headlock, just as they'd done as kids, then as young men. 'See you, Fitz.'

'Goodbye for now, my friend. I'll see you in Bendigo for our little tempest's tilt at justice,' Fitz said and planted a hard kiss on Raff's cheek.

Raff snorted a laugh. 'Get off,' he said and shoved him away.

Fitz grinned, climbed into the saddle, turned Patto. With a touch of fingers to his hat, he rode away.

Watching him, Raff's chest filled. *Good luck out there, old mate.*

Chapter Fifty-six

Bendigo
Wednesday 5 October

Evie waved the MacHenrys goodbye from the wharf. It had been a reserved journey back to Echuca. Though she couldn't tell them what awaited her in Bendigo, not to people who barely knew her, who knew nothing of what it all meant to her, she relayed the Cobram tale of her sister having died, the crooked policemen, the trouble, the deaths … The MacHenrys had most probably wondered what sort of person they'd stumbled upon.

Then Mr MacHenry had related some of their tale. Of murder, family secrets and crooked dealings. Evie had been wide-eyed listening to all that. How had they ever survived their story?

'Seems trouble finds folk no matter which way they turn, Miss Emerson,' Dane concluded after a fond and lingering glance at his wife. 'But we were very fortunate.'

Evie didn't wait at the busy Echuca wharf to see the *Sweet Georgie* leave. The place was bustling, and the earlier she made it to the railway station for the journey to Bendigo, the better. God only knew what awaited her there.

Back in Bendigo, the railway station was as busy as Echuca wharf had been. Clutching her little bag, Evie headed for the concourse, hoping to hire a cab, and head for her home.

Waiting outside the terminal, she became aware of chatter and laughter behind her, female voices. She whirled, only to be met with gloved hands over mouths, and women staring at her, nodding and pointing, no doubt recognising her. *Oh dear.*

A searing glance at them and they turned their backs on her, the milliner, the subject of the letter written by Edwin Cooper. In that instant, if Edwin had come within coo-ee of her, she'd have chased him with a big stick and cracked him a couple of beauties—and felt sorry for the stick.

When she finally flagged a cab, she climbed up and huffily directed the driver to Mr Campbell's office. Better to do that than go straight home not knowing what was going on. Even if Mr Campbell couldn't see her right then, Miss Juno would be able to relate whatever had transpired in Evie's absence.

'Are you quite all right, Miss Emerson?' Miss Juno had directed her to a seat in a spare office and had given her a cup of tea.

Perhaps she looked a sight; breathless and a bit nervy, her hair not properly tended under a dowdy hat, and her dress creased and dusty from travel. All the same, Evie nodded. 'Quite all right. I had to come straight away. You see, Mrs Downing—Mrs Kingsley she is now—sent me the newspaper clipping of what Edwin Cooper had published.'

'Oh, yes, I see. Well, Mr Campbell has a client with him who should be out directly. There is a little time before the next appointment, so I'll find out what is happening if he gives me permission to tell you.'

Miss Juno was impeccable, as usual. Her dark hair, parted in the middle and drawn back into a somewhat old-fashioned bun, was neat, not a strand out of place. The dark-blue dress she wore was plain, nipped at the waist, sleeves buttoned at her wrists. Her hands were slim, nails and fingertips a little ink-stained, markers of her trade.

Evie at once felt a kinship. 'Do you enjoy working here, Miss Juno?'

'Yes, I do,' she said, her eyes lighting. 'And the longer I'm indentured, the more exciting it becomes. Of course the trouble is, with that, I get to see a much darker side of humanity than I'd like. Over the years, one begins to wonder if people ever really change.' She tilted her head. 'And you enjoy your work, Miss Emerson, I can tell. I really must come to your studio to purchase one of your creations.'

'I do enjoy it. This little dear isn't one of mine, thankfully.' She patted the navy cap and cleared her throat. 'Mrs Kingsley is a fine employer. But now she's remarried, I'm not sure what will become of the studio. So, I want to start my own business.'

Miss Juno had no time to comment on that. A gentleman, hat in his hand and a grim look on his face, emerged from the inner sanctum. He nodded at the two women, addressed the clerk.

'Miss Juno, I'm to expect Mr Campbell's invoice directly.'

'Yes, Mr Caldwell. It'll be in the earliest mail.' Miss Juno gave Evie a small smile and disappeared into Mr Campbell's office. She returned a few minutes later, closing the door behind her. 'Well, to your case, Miss Emerson. You know that the summons has arrived?'

Evie knew it, but her teacup rattled on the saucer anyway.

Miss Juno went on. 'It must seem daunting, but you're fortunate to have the Kingsleys on your side. And Mr Barrett has done some wonderful detective work. Mr Campbell is very happy with the results.' She leaned forward and lowered her voice. 'That's about all there is to tell you … of that side of things.'

'Oh?'

'As Mr Barrett was having a spot of difficulty with the ladies who've been in this situation before you with Mr Cooper, we suggested something to help with the problem.' She paused and lowered her voice even further. 'I was sent to interview them and had them sign statements attesting to Mr Cooper's treachery.' Miss Juno sat back. 'They *all* have. It's most exciting.'

Evie's mouth dropped open. 'How many ladies?'

'Three.' Miss Juno was very pleased with herself. 'They are all here in the district. One had to be enticed from her parents' country home, but we were able to secure her statement attesting to Mr Cooper's vile character.'

'That's wonderful.' Evie set her cup and saucer on the desk. 'But can all of that be put to the magistrate?'

'I don't know.' Miss Juno lifted her shoulders. 'I presume so. It is relevant and it does mean that Mr Campbell has something to fight with.'

'Will the ladies have to speak to the magistrate?'

The clerk shrugged again. 'You know how it goes, Miss Emerson, we women can be our own worst enemy. Not only are we at times complicit in denigrating our sisters, but we are also reticent to come forward when needs must.' She took in a deep breath. 'I'm hopeful these ladies will be courageous for a while longer.'

Evie's hopes deflated. 'Why would they help me?'

'Because nobody helped them, not at the time they needed help, or beyond. That's what I put to them. Seems it was convincing. I said that perhaps if we win against Mr Cooper, their lives will be better for it.'

They heard the front door open and Miss Juno excused herself to meet the next client. Evie could hear the rumble of a male voice, and Miss Juno sounded delighted in her responses.

Next thing, she was back in the room. 'Mr Barrett is here, Miss Emerson.'

Miss Juno stepped aside for a man whose warm greeting was polite, his smile reassuring. The white streak in his hair was startling. He dipped slightly towards Evie.

'Miss Emerson. So pleased to meet you.'

Mr Campbell received Mr Barrett, whose appointment had been the next one, so Miss Juno and Evie were also invited to attend. Evie related everything about meeting with Raff and Fitz, and her learning of Meryl's death. Then the horrible altercation with those crooked police and Mr Haines.

Almost an hour later, her head spinning, Evie flagged down another cab, longing for home. But first she should try to see Mrs Kingsley and find out whether she still had a job.

She needn't have worried. Alighting at Mrs Kingsley's new residence, even before she'd turned and paid the driver, the front door was flung open and out the lady sailed, in a dark-blue gown, not the black she usually wore.

'My dear. My *dear* girl. Oh, I'm so happy you're back. Come in, come in. I'm sure you have as much to tell as I do.' Mrs Kingsley led her back inside. 'And look who's here, how timely. Just visiting, mind you, catching up.'

Evie could have cried. Ann and Posie stood, and the three women folded in a tight embrace.

'We've been so worried for you,' Ann said, planting a kiss on Evie's cheek.

'Doing all that, and going all the way there—it was so brave of you, Evie.' Posie held her at arm's length, smiling, tears glistening.

Mrs Kingsley waved everyone to the seats. 'We'll have to squeeze in a little, but we want to hear everything.'

Evie's news of Meryl and the little boy, of Constable O'Shea and the awful McCosker, crushed Mrs Kingsley. She had to take her fan and flap it about as perspiration popped onto her forehead.

'How awful for you, Evie,' Posie said, a hand at her throat.

'Simply dreadful for you, darling girl,' Ann said, and reached over to pat Evie's hands. 'I'm so sorry.'

'And to have to come back to this horror with Mr Cooper. The man is reprehensible.' Mrs Kingsley's fan was still flapping madly.

'Yes, we curse the day we introduced you to Edwin Cooper,' Posie said. Ann agreed with a vigorous few nods.

Evie gave a little laugh then changed the subject. There wasn't much more she could cope with; she'd be a mess in no time. 'But to good news. Your news, Mrs Kingsley. Married life again. My congratulations.' She began to take off her hat.

'Dearie me, let's put that little horror into the fire as soon as we can,' Mrs K said and took it from Evie, dumping it into the bin at her feet. That cheered Evie no end. Still fanning, Mrs Kingsley gave Evie a big smile. 'Yes, it's lovely being married to dear David, and of *course*, I'll keep my studio open.'

'That's wonderful.'

'Goodness me, yes. So you still have your job, couldn't do without the best milliner in the colony.'

'I agree wholeheartedly,' Ann said. 'The best milliner and our best friend.'

Evie nodded, happy for the show of confidence. 'Thank you.' Now was not the time to tell Mrs K, or her other friends, of her plans. Besides, things were still so topsy-turvy, there wasn't much to mention yet.

Mrs Kingsley took a breath then launched again. 'I have to tell you that we visited your house and Mr Cooper had been there, so we had the locks changed again on your behalf. I have the key here for you. Mr Campbell and Mr Barrett have been very active.

It seems perhaps they'll get their teeth well and truly into the awful man. Not to mention the wonderful work Mr Campbell's clerk is doing.'

'I've just come from there. Mr Campbell was kind enough to see me straight away.'

'Oh, that's very good.'

Ann got to her feet. 'We'll leave you to discuss that business at Mr Campbell's office. We were only dropping in on Mrs Kingsley to see if she'd heard from you, and what a bonus to have caught you the day you returned. Posie, shall we arrange to meet up at the tearooms sometime soon with Evie?'

'Let's. I'll call on both of you in the next days to let you know when. All right?' Posie's warm brown eyes were brimming when she looked at Evie. 'We missed you. So worrying.' She reached for Evie's hands. 'You're back now. All will be well.'

The women waved as they headed away from Mrs Kingsley's house.

Closing the door behind them, Mrs K shooed Evie back to her seat. 'Lovely that you have such delightful friends in those two. Such decent women.'

'And their husbands,' Evie said. 'They've been very good to me in all of this.'

'And certainly Mr Campbell *and* Mr Barrett will make sure the rest of it will be very good too.'

Evie dragged in a breath as she sat. Not only would she have the expense of her lawyer involved, but the private detective too. 'This is going to cost me quite a bit, isn't it? And not just my reputation.' Thoughts of financing a studio dimmed a little.

'You're not to worry. Mr Kingsley is taking care of Mr Barrett's services.'

'What? He can't. He shouldn't. I need to repay him.' She stared at Mrs Kingsley. 'I will.'

'Of course, but it's done for now, my dear.' Mrs K peered at her. 'There are more important matters to think about at the minute.' Then she gulped air and fanned madly. 'Oh blast.'

'What is it? Should I open a window?'

'Oh, this is an inconvenience most of us women eventually have to suffer, I'm afraid.' She took a handkerchief from her pocket to wipe her throat. 'Seems it never stops for women. First our accursed monthlies and having to manage that, then the children come along and we still have our courses afterwards until a certain age when it all stops.' She took a breath, which Evie was grateful for. 'Yes, stops. You'd think there'd be some relief, but oh no. Then this—more accursed changes. Change of life, dear, it's called.' Mrs K blew out a breath and the flapping slowed down.

Evie had heard whispers, but had no idea what this change was likely all about.

'As if we didn't know that life changes, we need a constant blasted reminder,' Mrs Kingsley wept. 'Oh, don't mind me getting upset. But I tell you what: it'd be a better lesson for men; they can hardly bear change at all.'

Startled, Evie waited.

Mrs K sat quietly for a moment, blew out a relieved breath. 'Well, that one's passed, at least. Furious things. Comes on me at all times, a terrible whooshing heat from within.' She patted her neck. 'Dear Mr Kingsley is very accommodating about it all. Fancy being just married and your new wife suddenly drowning in the sweats all day and night, having to leap out of bed to dry off.' She wiped her throat again, mopped her face and waved a hand at a startled Evie. 'But then I think that would prove that I am quite mad, so I just have to hope Mr Kingsley doesn't see fit to put me in an asylum and throw away the key.'

Evie's mouth dropped open. 'Asylum?'

'Oh no, dear, I'm sure Mr Kingsley wouldn't. Never mind. It's not like I'm the first with it, won't be the last. If you live long enough, dear, you'll experience much the same.'

Evie gaped a little. *Quite mad. An asylum.* Dear God, if that's what's still to come, everything loomed an uphill battle.

'And don't you worry about that nasty letter in the paper either, the one mentioning Mr O'Shea.'

Evie's battle didn't seem quite so uphill when compared to Fitz's. But it wasn't Fitz who had leaped into Evie's thoughts at that moment. It was Raff. Where was he?

Mr Kingsley came home from his debt-collecting adventures then insisted they accompany Evie to her house to ensure all was well. Effusive with her thanks for their care and for Mr Kingsley's financial assistance—he waved it off with a smile—Evie felt quite breathless again. Standing at her front door and using the new key, she opened it and stepped into the hallway. Although tidy, and nothing being in any disarray, she realised with a jolt that she would be alone.

Mrs Kingsley understood. 'Perhaps, dear Evie, you could stay with friends for a little while until this business is cleared up.'

But to stay with Ann and Ross Benton, or Posie and Ian Chalmers, surely would present a problem for them too, if Edwin were to make trouble.

'Yes, of course. That's the solution,' Evie said, not really knowing what to do. Going to stay in a hotel might be the best thing of all.

'We'll leave you to it. I'll expect you bright and chirpy tomorrow to continue our work,' Mrs Kingsley said.

Evie waved them goodbye. Closing the door and locking it, she went straight to the kitchen to light the cooker. Next, she'd take a brisk walk to the grocery shop, the baker and the butcher. Then she'd take a quiet moment for herself, contemplating her nerves and the day set for her hearing with the magistrate. Five days from now. *Five.*

She couldn't afford to fall into a heap just yet. Too much to do. She should be alert, sharp. Not everyone need know that she was back just yet. Her heart sank. It wouldn't take long for it to get around once she'd visited the stores. Anyway, there'd been those women at the railway station who'd clearly known who she was.

It would already be all over town.

Chapter Fifty-seven

Cobram

Raff had arrived in Cobram. Needing food, he headed first for the general store, got himself a loaf of bread and some ham. Needing a bath, he checked into the hotel. Needing a drink after that, he headed for the bar.

It wasn't as crowded as he expected it would be late in the afternoon. Few men were in. Amid the sweet stale odour of spilled beer, and the fumes of rum, the mouth-watering scent of lamb cooking somewhere out the back tantalised, had his stomach groaning. The aroma of potatoes roasting in lard … An evening meal would tide him over until he left in the morning to make his way home.

By way of Bendigo. He wouldn't bypass it, not with Evie likely to be in some trouble.

At the bar, he nursed a rum the big barman had poured for him. Moody, going over and over his interactions with Evie since her finding him at the Echuca railway station, the more nervous about seeing her he became. One thing was for sure: if she was in trouble in the courts, he would, he would … *What?* Run her off to his wheelwright shop, protect her behind the anvil and the forge, maybe his timber lathe? Have her live over the shop without so much as her own kitchen, or a copper for laundry? Right. And when was the last time he washed his bedsheets—

Whoa, man. You're putting the cart before the horse.

'Mate, reckon you need company. Save you talking to yourself.'

'Robbo.' Raff laughed a moment. 'Was I making sense?'

'Just a mumble.' Robbo nodded at the barman, who took the coins he slid across the counter and handed him back a beer. 'You hear about McCosker?'

Raff nodded. *I sure have.*

'Haines and the other trooper, they're gonna be hauled off to Melbourne,' Robbo said. 'In fact, they could already be gone, under escort. Constable Stillard weren't too happy to have 'em here.'

'I bet.'

'That, uh, Mr Morgan. I mean Fitz, the other O'Shea. He get away all right?'

'Gone to visit his brother's widow, deliver the sad news.'

Robbo shook his head. 'Aye. All this sorta business is hard on the women, the kids. Left to fend for themselves, and some their little kids dyin'—' He waved a hand. 'Bah. Gotta stop talking about that stuff, the doc says. Gotta stay off the hard liquor, too. I am allowed to have this.' He held up the beer. 'Where are you headed?'

'Home is Ballarat. I'll leave tomorrow morning.'

'A fair few days' ride.'

'I'll cut down to Rochester, maybe Elmore, hitch a lift on the train from there.' He'd be well knackered by then anyway. He was knackered now. 'How's Mrs Robinson?'

'Good. Matter-of-fact, she talked of askin' the powers-what-be how we go about buying up the Bayley place. Acquire it, or apply for it, whatever we need to do. I'm good for workin' at it. We'd sell ours, freehold an' all that.'

For a time, that same idea had appealed to Raff. He shook it off. Not right to be thinking about it now.

Robbo was nodding at nothing in particular; the idea was a good one, it appeared. 'Our two lads are in the cemetery in town here, not on our place, so, nothin' to keep us there, really.' He wrapped both hands around his pot of beer. 'Might be good for Miss Emerson to know she can visit her sister's resting place whenever she feels like it.' He studied his hands, sniffed loudly. 'Bugger it, here I go again.' He wiped his nose with a sleeve.

Raff clapped him on the shoulder. 'I know how you feel, mate.'

They sat at the bar, side by side, silent, and the rest of the world drifted by.

Chapter Fifty-eight

Bendigo
Saturday 8 October

Evie knew her worries were written all over her face when Mrs Kingsley opened the door.

'You do not look rested, Evie,' Mrs K chided. 'What have you been doing?'

For the last three nights since being home, Evie had been sitting in her parlour, or the kitchen, trying desperately not to nod off. She'd bought as many candles as she could afford and sat hour after hour keeping the little wicks alight, her couple of lanterns lit and fuelled, trying to read, to sew a little, to finish some projects started before she'd left on her trek. Her eyes were scratchy and hurt when she blinked.

'You, my dear girl, cannot afford to let your eyesight suffer. You look like you've been working all night. What would you do if you couldn't work any longer?' Mrs Kingsley ushered her into the studio, now crowded, happily, with the tools of their trade. Her husband had ordered another bench built that would hold rolls of fabric upright, just like at the drapery. 'A genius move if I do say so myself,' he'd said and Mrs Kingsley had raised her eyebrows when relating it to Evie, as if to say, 'wonder where that idea had come from?'

'What is it?' Mrs Kingsley asked her now. 'Have you had trouble?'

'No trouble. I just expect it,' Evie said. Every little noise, every creak of her house, every whisper of a breeze shaking the window in its pane had her heart thumping, ears straining. To her knowledge, nothing had happened; no one had been lurking outside.

'That's understandable, but I don't think Mr Cooper will risk any shenanigans now things are coming to a head. The court date is only a few days away. Keep your chin up, dear.'

Mrs K had stopped insisting that Evie come to stay with them, and Evie now wished she'd accepted the offer. Perhaps it wasn't only the threat of Edwin Cooper that worried her, perhaps it was all the whispers and giggles that followed her wherever she went.

Ann and Posie visited and, turnabout, ate an evening meal with her that they brought from their kitchens to save her going out. She wasn't ready to brave the tearooms, she'd told them, not until all this was over. Her two friends had only exchanged a glance at that, and let it be.

'For the moment,' Ann had said, with a look in her eye.

Evie had stopped doing a daily shop, which had been her habit, and only bought goods as she needed them. That way at least, while the gossip about her was still plain as the day, she wasn't subjected to the sniggers as often.

'Lead a man on, she did, or men, I should say.'

'Got rid of one quick enough to take up with Mr Cooper.'

'Fast, that's what she is.'

'Pity she's the best milliner here in town. Where will we go now?'

'The magistrate will sort her out.'

'She won't be around for long with a reputation like that.'

The last was the comment that had her wondering whether she could continue living in Bendigo. She could hear Edwin's sister's ringing voice in the vitriol, and although she never saw

Jane, she was sure the woman was whispering poisonously in the ear of anyone willing to listen, or unable to get away. To clear her name was Evie's hope, and even if that occurred, she knew how mud stuck, how rumours never died. Even if her name was cleared, even if from all the efforts by Mr Campbell, Miss Juno and Mr Barrett, she didn't have to pay Edwin Cooper for the breach of contract, she would have to leave town. She wouldn't be able to stand it here a moment longer.

Leaving Mrs Kingsley would be difficult, but with a little money saved and perhaps a tenant in the house, she'd be able to start again somewhere else. Right now, it seemed all too hard. Her mind was woolly, her thoughts tangled.

There wasn't long to go now, but fronting the magistrate was still two nights away, and she was so very tired. Oh, dear God, she was no good at this.

Chapter Fifty-nine

Bendigo
Sunday 9 October

The train ride from Elmore was welcome; the hard days' riding beforehand had sapped man and beast. As they rattled towards Bendigo, Raff had nodded off, snoring and stinking, sure it was a good deterrent if anyone thought to take a seat in his compartment.

Once arrived in Bendigo, the first thing he did was get to the Bartletts' boarding house. Mrs Bartlett welcomed him back and, when he enquired, she agreed to wash his clothes. Cost him three shillings. Next, he had Bluey take up the comfortable stall at the back of the place he'd enjoyed on his previous stay.

It was mid afternoon before Raff could draw a bath for himself. By the time he sank into the tub the water was lukewarm, but it had never felt so good soaking his saddle-weary bones. He lathered, scrubbed off dirt, dust and dead insects. The dirty water cooled off rapidly and he stood to pour clean water from the pitcher over himself, rinsing. Towelled dry, he dressed in clean clothes from his saddlebags.

From the mirror, a gaunt, shadowed face with hollowed eyes stared back at him. The dense dark beard stubble made him look even more haunted, but—too bad. A shave would have to wait; he couldn't be bothered. Snatching the latest newspapers from the pile nearby, he tucked them under an arm. Barefoot, he left the bathroom, carrying his boots back to the room.

No sooner had he stretched out on the bed, in the same room he'd occupied before, he was asleep, a newspaper draped over his chest. Last thing he remembered, his smile widening, were Evie's knees, the dimple in her left one, as she tried to cover them with her dress after shooting at McCosker.

Evie. Eyes instantly open, he blinked. It was nearing dark outside; the only window in his room was without a curtain and stars had begun to scatter across the night sky.

Dammit, I meant to have a nap, not go unconscious for hours.

Evie. A dream, or thoughts of her had woken him. He swung his legs off the bed and groped for the matches and the candle. No idea of the time. He stood, padded to the window. No moon yet, but it was rising; there was a glow over the end of the street. A few houses dotted here and there had lights glowing. Maybe it was around eight in the evening.

He splashed his face with water from a bowl on the dresser, and rubbed vigorously, drying his hands through his hair. A plan had formed. Part of a plan. Evie's friend Mrs Benton lived nearby and he'd intended knocking on her door to see if, by chance, Evie was staying with her. Now, he'd bypass Mrs Benton's and go straight to Evie's—just to check the place, not disturb her. Even a good friend wouldn't visit a lady unannounced at night, much less a lone male friend … unless it was an emergency. *There's no emergency, Dolan.* If there were lights, she'd be home, that's all he needed to ascertain. If no lights, he'd track back and knock on the Bentons' door. He figured Mr Benton would be home to speak to.

That would do him until morning. By his reckoning, he was half an hour from Evie's house, if that.

He found a vantage point on her street that allowed him a clear view of the front of the house. Her little candles flickered, their light tiny beacons glowing through the thin curtains in the front room. So she was all right. She was safely home. He sighed in relief. He would return in the morning.

Shit, what's that? A shadow. A figure moving stealthily from around the side of the house, stopping to swing slowly left to right, checking the surrounds.

Raff squinted. *So, the bastard has made a move.*

He pushed away from the wall he'd been leaning on, and made his way to the house.

Chapter Sixty

Raff growled low in the man's ear. He squeezed the collar on his shirt, his chokehold tight. 'I said, what the *fuck* do you think you're doing?'

'I heard you,' the man rasped, his hand a steely grip over Raff's on his collar. 'Allow me to introduce myself. Quietly.'

The man's unruffled response was a surprise. Raff gave him a hard shake anyway and didn't loosen his grip. He kept his voice down. 'Go ahead.'

'Bendigo Barrett, Private Investigator.' The man could breathe, but it would have been difficult.

It took a few moments, then Raff pulled him into a better light. There it was, a streak of white hair. That's what Evie had described when they were on the boat. Raff pushed him off, waited until Barrett had caught his breath.

Eyeing him, Barrett took his time before speaking. 'If you have no business with me,' he said between his teeth, 'I need to get on with my work.'

'*My* business is there,' Raff rasped, stabbing a finger at Evie's house. 'And you're the second bloke I've found spying on it.'

Barrett still had a finger inside his collar. 'And you're not?'

Raff was taken aback. 'No. And whose bloody business—'

'Get down,' Barrett ordered, ducking to the ground. 'Look there.'

Raff dropped by his side and followed Barrett's finger which was pointed at Evie's house. Someone was stealing around the place, a man, and when he reached up to bang on one of the windows, Raff took to his feet.

Barrett grabbed him by the arm, hauled him down, his hands now in Raff's shirt collar. 'Whoever *you* are,' he snarled in guttural whisper, '*I'm* here to see that that man is clearly identified as intent on trouble. So unless you're a police officer, I suggest you get the hell out of my way.'

Fury exploded and Raff grappled with the steely grip. Not too many had ever bested him, but Barrett was determined, and strong as an ox. 'Let me at him, you bastard. He's a bloody peeping tom, and worse—'

Barrett shook him hard, his face close. 'If it's who I think it is, he goes before a magistrate tomorrow accusing a young woman of breach of contract—'

'Cooper,' Raff spat. 'And she's Evie Emerson.'

Abruptly, Barrett let him go, shoved him away. 'Who are you?'

The fight went out of him. 'Rafferty Dolan.'

'Ah, Dolan. You were with her in Cobram.' Barrett watched the man still on the move around the house, taking his time, heading for the front veranda.

'I gotta get down there.'

'You go nowhere, not now, and not until this is over.' Barrett grabbed Raff's shirt again. 'If anyone goes, it'll be me. If he sees you, he'll accuse you of God knows what. You've encountered him before, am I right?' At Raff's nod, he went on. 'So he knows you. *I* have to identify him, for Miss Emerson's sake. *I* have to clearly see his face, confront him. Take him to the police station. You understand me? No one else interferes.'

'But—'

'Listen, Dolan. I've been tasked with this, it's on record, and

Mr Campbell, her lawyer, can verify that to a magistrate. If someone else gets to him, roughs him up, he'll blame Miss Emerson for it. That's how he works—he'll put all the blame back onto her, make out he's the innocent party, that she had a bloke with her, therefore she must be a liar and a trollop, that you beat him up on her say so.' He eyed Raff. 'All right?'

Raff gritted his teeth. 'I still don't like it.'

'You don't have to like it, but believe me,' Barrett said, 'it'll damage her further and harm her defence.' He jerked his head. 'Now out of my way. And if you care for her, don't *you* fuck it up. Don't bloody go near that house, you hear me?' He pushed past Raff. For a man not much shy of Raff's own build, he moved fluidly, easily.

I care for her, all right. So I'm not going to be a damned spectator, mate. Raff loped after Barrett, keeping his eye on the form sneaking around Evie's house. He could see Cooper rattling the windows. *The bastard's terrorising her.*

Barrett was nowhere to be seen. Cooper was creeping across the veranda frontage. The idiot; anyone passing by would be able to see him.

Where's Barrett, for Chrissakes?

Then the front door popped open and with the light from the hallway behind her, Evie charged outside waving what looked to be the fire poker. One thump across Cooper's chest, then as he turned, trying to scoot away, she swung again and landed another thump on the man's back. He stumbled, found his footing and took off, scrambling over the low fence.

Barrett rounded the corner of the house from the back and sped after him.

Raff watched Evie let out a mighty yell—frustration, fear—into the silent night, her fists clenched around the poker. She stamped her feet and stomped back inside, slamming the door shut. In the still of night, Raff heard the key turn in the lock. He wanted to go to her.

Don't bloody go near that house.

Stranded by indecision, he waited, heart in his throat. Heeding the detective's warning was all right for a time, but he wouldn't last for much longer.

Thank Christ. Barrett was jogging back towards him. 'And?' Raff asked when he came alongside, puffing.

'I didn't get a good enough look, couldn't grab him. Maybe Miss Emerson saw him clearly.' He looked at his boots a moment. 'She handles a poker well,' he said, hands on his knees, and gave a quiet laugh. 'He should have a couple of tell-tale bruises come tomorrow.'

'I should let her know—'

'No,' Barrett said sharply. 'I followed him to a house, so I have an address to report. A woman opened the door to him, and I believe it was his mother. So that's good enough for now.' He took a breath, still puffing. 'But if he comes back spying, and he could, trust me, it'll be worse for Miss Emerson if you're here.'

'I could grab him. We could haul him off—'

'Look, Dolan,' Barrett shook his head, impatient. 'I've had run-ins before with men like this bloke. They're nasty cowards, and they're cunning. They get around the law, wriggle out of what's due to them, so I'm all about getting the job done right.' He took a ragged breath. 'You will play right into his game if he sees you here. I'm telling you, he'll make it part of the case that another man was hanging around her. Go back to your lodgings.'

Raff waited a few moments. 'I'll stay here.'

'Right where I can see you, then.'

'Two sets of eyes are better than one,' Raff said.

Barrett gave him a look, saw straight through him. 'I get it, I do. You'll be close to her here if anything does happen.'

Raff nodded again, eyeing Evie's house. *But not close enough.*

Chapter Sixty-one

Bendigo

Lucille had to get up from their bed at some wee dark hour and go into the parlour. She carried a damp cloth, a bowl of water and was in a clean and dry nightdress. The sweats had been horrendous; her nightdress wringing, and the sheets would have to be changed.

Good gracious. How awful that this should come upon me just as I get married.

Luckily, David was sleeping soundly, oblivious to her night's discomfort.

She set the water down on a side table and slumped on the settee, wiping her face and neck with the cloth. Ah, sweet relief. But although the infernal *internal* heat had subsided, her feet were cold. How on earth could that be? One end like a furnace, the other like an icebox.

One of her clients, Mrs Dublin, had experienced a burst of heat while having a hat fitting one day not so long ago. No amount of fanning could cool her down, and the poor woman had asked to have help loosening her gown. *Dreadful.* Then she'd waved an elegant hand and simply said that it would soon pass, that it had been going on for years.

Really, no one seemed to know how long this change of life business would continue. There had to be some authority who knew something; the papers always carried advertisements for all manner of things to fix it or alleviate the symptoms, mostly absurd, so it wasn't as if no one talked about it. But where are real solutions—do we women just have to smile and abide as usual?

Lucille knew one woman whose doctor had prescribed her opium. *Good heavens.* When she'd next seen the woman, she was suffering more than just rushes of heat. In fact, she was completely out of herself, vague, dishevelled and as if gone slightly mad. Could hardly blame her, really; the cure was probably as bad as the ailment.

Oh, dear me no, don't mention 'mad', Lucille. That leads to 'asylum'.

There were many so-called treatments she'd learned of over the last year or so. Some ladies in her millinery studio offered up snippets of their suffering and their medicines. One had told her that she was taking a powder made from cow's ovaries.

Good Lord, drinking cow's *milk* was bad enough. Lucille never even took milk in her tea. Not for her, that 'cure'.

One treatment she'd heard about bemused her far more than others. Apparently, some doctors, perhaps not those in the colonies, thank the Lord, believed that the physical manipulation of a woman's private parts brought some relief—quite heady relief, it was whispered, even pleasurable. And the ladies would return to further exhaust the doctors, whose poor wrists and hands had suffered dreadfully. *Outrageous.* How could that be deemed medical? No one was going to paw at her privates in the name of science. A doctor, for goodness' sake, spending time gliding his fingers over a woman's …

She suddenly focused instead on David. Her nethers had become quite tingly, all that manipulation and fingers gliding … Perhaps one's new husband could be trained to achieve this … relief for his wife. *Interesting.* She reached for the cool cloth once more.

'My dear, what are you doing?'

Startled, Lucille sat bolt upright. Her husband had shuffled in carrying a candle, its little glow flickering. She was so very glad he couldn't see the lascivious thoughts written all over her face.

'Oh, David, I'm sorry if I disturbed you. I got a bit hot, you see, and threw off the covers. I came out here to cool down so I wouldn't wake you.'

'That wouldn't have bothered me. I must say though, tomorrow—or perhaps it's already today—Miss Emerson having to front the magistrate has quite got me in a knot. I'm restless myself.' He waved a hand a little. 'Move over a bit.' He set the candle down next to the water bowl.

He was in his nightgown too, and shuffling over to make space for him, she felt him land beside her, his thigh solid. She slid her hand onto it. *Oh.*

'I know Mr Barrett is on the lookout for her,' Lucille said, trying to focus. 'But I do worry that the plan to entrap Mr Cooper has put our Evie at risk.'

'Mr Barrett will not let anything happen to her, be assured.' He patted her hand that now rested on his leg. 'Cooper won't be able to resist a woman alone in her house, especially Evie. He'll have to try something. We know that from the other ladies who've reported to us. Mr Barrett will identify him and drag him off to the police, I'm sure of it.'

David's thigh was warm. He'd leaned into her while he was speaking, and she found she had a strong urge to run her hand up and find the bulge between his legs. Her neck grew hot. *Please God, don't let me break into a sweat when I'm trying to seduce my husband.* Her hand settled higher on his thigh. She pressed gently and waited.

'Once Evie is before the magistrate, if Mr Barrett has caught Cooper at it, Mr Campbell will attest that—'

Lucille slid her hand further up.

'—the detective had been engaged to seek out—'

Her fingertips lightly skimmed his upper thigh, and she brushed the fold of his belly.

'—other ladies who have come unstuck once involved with Cooper, the low scoundrel—'

Lucille turned a little to face him, her eyes searching his, her fingers resting on the thin fabric of his nightgown over his pubic hair.

'—through no fault of their own, and who are now—'

She lowered her hand between his legs, covering the hardening length there.

'—willing to provide written testimony of the same—'

Tightening her grip, she slid her hand lower until his legs parted.

'—and are quite ready, once again, if requested, to speak to the magistrate and stand against Cooper.' He took a breath. 'Lucille, I daresay I might have to press my mouth against your breast, suckle a little, then lift the hem of your gown and have my way with you.'

Smiling, she reached between his legs, now open, and squeezed. 'Oh, I think it is I who must have my way with you, dear husband,' she said, and took his hand to slip it under the soft fabric of her nightgown.

Chapter Sixty-two

Bendigo
Monday 10 October

Miss Juno was at Evie's front door early in the morning. 'Mr Campbell thought you might like some company while you get ready,' she explained. 'The magistrate will see us at ten.' Her grooming was meticulous, as usual, even at this hour. She stepped past Evie and into the hallway. 'Let's start with a cup of tea. Down this way?' she asked, removing her gloves. 'Are you all right?'

Evie nodded. 'A bit shaken, to be honest.'

Miss Juno pressed her arm. 'We heard that you might have had a bit of bother last night. Mr Campbell wants to reassure you that all went as well as can be expected. Mr Barrett has done a fine job.'

Evie followed Miss Juno into the kitchen. She didn't have the energy to explain about all the candles sitting around, burned down to stubs. 'Mr Campbell already knows I had a "bit of bother"?'

'Mr Barrett was surveilling, you see, and followed a certain nuisance of a man from here to a woman's place, the man's mother we believe. Mr Barrett reported quite early this morning at Mr Campbell's home. Very diligent.'

Evie groped for a chair and slumped into it. 'The nuisance rattled my windows and the door handles.' She rubbed her eyes with the heels of her hands. 'I'd much rather he'd been apprehended. I'm exhausted and tetchy.'

Miss Juno had filled the kettle and was stoking the cooker. 'Nearly over. Today is the day.'

'I'm worried the magistrate will find against me.'

'My dear Miss Emerson. Mr Campbell is your lawyer, and he and Mr Barrett are your champions. Clearly also, Mr and Mrs Kingsley. Now, you must assist by being quite calm, well dressed, your face washed and complexion clear. After our tea, we will use the tea leaves in a pouch of muslin over your eyes to give them a rest.' Miss Juno sat at the kitchen table.

'Is this your usual advice, Miss Juno?'

The woman smiled, and her plain, sometimes sombre features bloomed, transforming her. 'We will give these dastardly Cooper creatures a run for their money. For once, we have managed to convince a number of women to write statements regarding the truth of their matters with Mr Cooper. If the magistrate looks at even a couple of those, he will see a pattern emerging.' Her smile broadened. 'I always find it exhilarating when women band together to fight a common enemy.'

Evie was tired. 'Men? Surely not all of them.'

Miss Juno reached over and pressed her hand. 'Oh, of course not. Now come along. By mid afternoon this will all be behind you, and you can begin life anew.'

Evie dragged in a big sigh. 'I don't feel I have the energy.'

'You have more than you know. I do realise, however, that you might have spent a great deal of it whacking Mr Cooper with the poker.' Her eyes were merry.

Evie gave a burst of laughter. 'Oh, there's certainly more where that came from, Miss Juno.'

'I'm sure. In self-defence, of course.'

'Could he state that I attacked him?'

'He could, but we have a witness who saw what he was up to, so his argument would fail.' Miss Juno reverted to her serious self. 'You were defending yourself and your property. Soon, he won't be a problem for you.'

'Edwin Cooper is wily and manipulating,' Evie cried. 'Will anything really stop him, win or lose?'

'We will stop him bothering you, Miss Emerson. Whether it stops him from doing it to someone else in the future, well … Mr Campbell has long come across this type of behaviour in people, mainly men, I'm afraid.' Miss Juno's disapproval showed in a frown. 'It does prove to be almost intractable. Conviction and gaol is best, preferably for a long time. But a conviction is not always a sure thing, and is very hard to come by.' She took a breath and added, almost apologetically, 'And even if the law does do something about them, sometimes they can't be stopped. There's a scientific medical thread, in England and on the continent, which theorises that the behaviour has something to do with Narcissus, if you read Greek mythology, exploring the behaviour as a mental condition. Apparently, it's thought to be imbedded in the personality, and not curable.'

Oh dear. That did not bode well at all.

'How on earth do you know—'

'My father's brother is a physician in England, very much interested in the criminal mind,' Miss Juno said, smiling. 'Our letters are quite interesting. The papers on the subject are indeed illuminating.'

Oh.

The courthouse, the building, had never appealed to Evie. Perhaps it was knowing what went on inside; all that law business, where people's emotions were set aside while wrongdoings were dealt with coldly and without favour. *Supposedly.*

She must be overtired; of course the courts dealt fairly. *Really, Evie? Ask any woman if the courts deal fairly.* Frustrated and foggy after her few terrible nights, she tut-tutted. *Oh, for goodness' sake, fair or not, what will be will be.*

Relatively new, the court building had risen slowly from dirt and rubble and into the great ugly nub it had now become, the work continuing. Evie had watched its progress along with everyone else, but never in her wildest dreams had she expected that she would have to attend a session here herself, in front of a magistrate. Hopefully with Mr Campbell's help the situation would not be as daunting as she feared.

Directed down a corridor towards the courtroom and accompanied by Miss Juno, Evie had passed a small room in which had sat Edwin Cooper, his mother and his sister. Haughty glares had met her gaze as she passed them. She'd begun to shake, desperately glad she hadn't been told to sit in there with them. Miss Juno had just given her a pat on the back, as if to say, 'Come along.'

The first thing that hit her as she entered the courtroom was the scent of oily furniture polish on new timber, and the smell of recently applied paint. There were no windows, just vents high up on the wall. A sudden weight dropped on her chest. *No way out of here except behind me.*

Mr Campbell was already in situ at a table facing the magistrate's bench. He stood as she approached and, towering over her, he bent a little. 'Miss Emerson. How are you?'

'I truly don't know, Mr Campbell.'

Miss Juno indicated that she should sit on the chair between Mr Campbell's and the one she would take. She removed a writing pad and pencil from her bag and sat back, her hands clasped primly on her lap. The room was empty of other people. Adjacent were another table and three chairs. That must be for the Coopers.

'Now, this is not a court with a jury, Miss Emerson. We are only before the magistrate, a Mr Rudge, but he will rule. He's a decent fellow, a family man, has a second family now, after his first wife died. He's well used to shenanigans and has had many cases before him. I must warn you, though. At times he can be cranky and somewhat eccentric. He might appear sometimes as if he's asleep—'

Evie's few hopes sank.

'—but I can assure you, he will not be.'

Daring only to look behind her the once, she saw a number of people filing inside and taking up the seats in the courtroom. Mr and Mrs Kingsley each gave her a quick smile, Mr Barrett was there, Ann and Posie had come in arm in arm, each giving her a little wave as they shuffled towards their seats. She turned back, aware that others were still filing in, the chatter subdued. She hoped they were 'her' people, but didn't turn around again to check in case her glance accidentally met with the Coopers'.

Raff. If only Raff were here.

Her mouth was dry. She knew a journalist from the newspaper would be here, but would they treat her fairly?

Oh heavens, Fitz should be here, too.

And then it began.

Evie held her breath. Everyone stood as the magistrate came through a door behind the bench and settled in his chair. Indicating with a wave of his hand that they should sit, he looked about the room and the people seated at the back. His gaze alighted on the plaintiff and defendant, and their supports, as if studying their characters. She felt a hot rush of blood to her face and neck as he assessed her.

He swung to the Cooper's table. 'Mr Cooper. No lawyer for you?'

Edwin stood. 'I have no need of one, sir. My charge will stand on its own merit.' Evie could just imagine the smug glance Edwin slid at her.

'Is that so?' Mr Rudge peered at Edwin. 'Well, you first. Off you go.'

'Me? He's the lawyer.' Edwin pointed at Mr Campbell.

The magistrate rolled his eyes. '*Cooper v Emerson*, Mr Cooper. The plaintiff, that's you, goes first.' When Edwin stuttered, Mr Rudge overrode him. 'Mr Cooper, the documents before me say you are charging Miss Emerson with breach of marriage contract.'

'I am, sir.'

Arrogant, self-righteous, haughty ratbag. Evie didn't glance sideways at him.

'Who have you there, the two ladies with you?'

'My mother Mrs Cooper, and my sister, Miss Jane Cooper.'

'I see.' Mr Rudge took a good look at them, scowling for some moments, squinting, then tucked in his chin appearing to read further. 'You seem unlucky in the marriage stakes, sir. There are quite a few of these cases mentioned here in the papers before me.'

Mr Campbell started. 'Your—'

'Is there?' Edwin asked, rattled.

'Well, Mr Cooper?' the magistrate asked.

Edwin recovered. 'It's true, of course. I am unfortunate. My nature is to take the high emotions expressed to me on face value, and I believe them to be true, and honourable. I fear perhaps my naivety in these matters works against me.'

Evie heard the outright lie with her mouth open. She stared at the magistrate, who had his head bent still perusing the documents in front of him. Had he even heard the despicable liar? Was he awake, or had he dropped off, despite what Mr Campbell had said?

Then the magistrate's head bobbed up. 'Really? And what high emotions were expressed to you by the defendant?'

Evie's colour rose again. The room was silent except for Mr Campbell's large fingers tapping a pencil rhythmically, softly on the table.

'That Miss Evie Emerson, the woman sitting right there bold as brass, agreed to become my wife.'

She only heard her own intake of breath, felt her heart hammer. *Liar.*

The magistrate regarded Edwin head to toe. 'Was there swooning, or smelling salts needed to rouse her from the effects of her over-excitement at the undoubted happy prospect? Did she make a great show of spreading the titillating news that she was to be married to … you, to all her friends?' At Edwin's bemused shake of his head, Rudge went on. 'There was hardly high emotion on her part then,' he said dismissively. 'But I grant you, the news might have evoked emotion in some folk. Amusement, perhaps.'

There was a snicker of laughter.

'Despite her reputation,' Edwin continued, unabashed and righteous, 'I offered her the sanctuary of my name.'

What? Evie glanced in horror at Mr Campbell, who merely raised his eyebrows in the direction of the magistrate.

'Your Honour,' he said tiredly.

Mr Rudge nodded at him, but waved at Edwin. 'Do please continue.'

'She admitted to me,' Edwin said, encouraged, 'that she had allowed another to dally with her—'

Evie's breath stopped. There was a sudden kerfuffle in the gallery behind her but she didn't dare look.

'—but because she was enamoured of me, had regretted her sin, and begged me to accept her. Which, of course, I did.'

The magistrate's eyes disappeared into slits. 'Did you say "sin", Mr Cooper?' His button nose had folded into wrinkles, shortening it.

Edwin faltered. 'I did.'

'Pompous of you, isn't it?' Mr Rudge glowered. '"Who among you is without sin, cast the first stone", eh?'

Bewildered, Evie stole a glance at Mr Campbell, who appeared not to be following either. His usually bland and kindly face was lined with consternation.

Edwin hesitated again. 'Well, I—'

'And you offered your proposal, even aware of such a "sin"?'

'I am a good man, Your Honour.'

'Lord save us,' the magistrate muttered. He lifted his chin. 'Well, Mr Campbell? What say you about your defendant?'

After his initial assessing of her, Evie was sure the magistrate hadn't so much as noticed she was still sitting there. What hope did she have if he wouldn't even try to gauge the honest person she was?

Mr Campbell stood. 'Your Honour, I have been engaged to defend the spurious charge of breach of contract.'

'Quite.' Mr Rudge was nodding. 'Mr Campbell, what do you make of Mr Cooper's … whatever you want to call it?'

'A fabrication, sir.'

'What part?'

Evie burned at that.

'All of it, including his very last utterance,' Mr Campbell said, decisively. 'You have the documents we prepared to back our case.' He sat.

'Mmh. So, back to you, Mr Cooper,' the magistrate said, his eyes wide. 'You offered your … sanctuary, only to have it rejected. I'd have thought, man, that if the lady had "sinned", her rejection would have let you off the hook.'

'It was the promise of a happy marriage, a loving home. An obedient wife. And … a man needs his comfort.'

Gorge rose in Evie's throat, and her mouth twisted. The gallery had gone quiet.

'Yes, yes. So, you say Miss Emerson accepted you and that you fully believed, like the rest of us about to marry, that all those wonderful things would come your way?'

Low laughter issued. Mr Rudge's gaze lifted to the people at the back.

'I … I did, sir.'

'Clearly, man, you've not been married before. Some might congratulate you for that.' His squinty, piercing glare glowered at those whose laughter had once more bubbled forth. He returned to Edwin. 'Sit down, Mr Cooper. And you lot,' he said pointing to the gallery, 'be quiet.' At the immediate hush, he pointed at Mr Campbell. 'Your turn.'

On his feet again, Mr Campbell wasted no time. 'Your Honour, Miss Emerson agreed only to *consider* a proposal of marriage, and within two days had declined the offer, perhaps mistakenly in person.'

Evie stared down at her hands.

'It seems that Mr Cooper here took advantage of this and has attempted extortion and intimidation thereafter,' Mr Campbell stated.

Edwin leaped to his feet, a protest at the ready.

'Sit down, you,' the magistrate barked, and he waved to the bailiffs who started forward until Edwin dropped back to his chair.

'Not only has he attempted to physically coerce Miss Emerson—' Mr Campbell paused as a guttural sound emitted and a short scuffle ensued from somewhere behind, '—but he also attempted to damage the reputation of her employer, Mrs Kingsley, a well-known milliner in town. Mrs Kingsley was nearly served with an eviction notice from someone known to be an associate of Mr Cooper, and Mr Kingsley himself was assaulted by—'

'Not relevant here, Mr Campbell, and you know it.'

'Attesting to character, Your Honour,' Mr Campbell said, without falter. 'Then there were the two notices in the newspaper, which no doubt Your Honour has seen, that are malicious. Libellous.'

'Hmm. We might speak to libel another day.' He seared a glance at the Cooper table. 'But I agree, the notices are not at all gentlemanly, to say the least.' Mr Rudge addressed Edwin. 'But you're not here because you're a gentleman, are you, Mr Cooper? Not against the law for you to be a sewer rat, is it?'

'I—'

Evie turned to look. A tic had begun over Edwin's left eye.

'Quiet. Don't need you to answer to that.' Mr Rudge huffed. 'What else have you got, Mr Campbell?'

Miss Juno handed Mr Campbell a sheaf of papers. 'These here, Your Honour,' he said, 'are statements written by some previous victims of this family's activities. Those activities include what appears to be blackmail and, shall we say, hush money or, in some cases, hush jewellery handed over by the victims in order to have Mr Cooper remove himself from their lives forever.' He took another few sheets from Miss Juno. 'As you're aware, we have Miss Emerson's report to police, and this paperwork is a report from Mr Bendigo Barrett, Private Investigator—'

'Disgusting.' Mrs Cooper voiced her opinion.

'Not a word out of you,' the magistrate snapped, and only let his glare move once the woman sank into her ruffled feathers.

Mr Campbell continued. 'Mr Barrett who, only last night, reported seeing this individual'—a long arm and pointed finger was aimed at Edwin—'lurking about and peeping into Miss Emerson's house in the dead of night.'

Gasps rose from the crowd behind Evie.

'Lies.' Mrs Cooper again.

'I said, not a word. Another outburst and I'll have you thrown out on your bustle, madam.' The magistrate, ignoring the indignant huffs of the Cooper ladies, turned to the lawyer. 'Really, Mr Campbell, a private investigator?'

'Whose work has been invaluable in securing such statements, and who has been assisting my clerk, Miss Juno.'

'Mmh.' Mr Rudge considered that. 'All right, his reputation is supported by the worthy Miss Juno.' He nodded, unsmiling, at Miss Juno then peered at Edwin again. 'What say you, Mr Cooper? Were you lurking?'

'I was not.'

'Miss Emerson has previously made a report that speaks to that very activity, and we have another witness who says that yes, you were lurking, and peeping as well.'

There was a familiar grunt of anger from behind her, but Evie dared not turn around to see. *Raff?* It had to be.

'Wasn't me,' Cooper said, his voice firm. 'They're lying. She's mistaken. I professed love for her and she made promises.'

Evie sat forward, hands flat on the table. Miss Juno laid a hand on her arm and whispered, '*He said, she said.* Don't bother getting upset. It's preliminary.'

'Your Honour,' Mr Campbell began, 'my client vehemently denies any breach of contract because there was no contract. A completely false declaration of an engagement from Mr Cooper by way of an advertisement in the *Bendigo Advertiser* is *no* contract. Furthermore, nor was an engagement ring ever presented.'

'She sold it,' Edwin cried, leaping with gusto onto another lie. His mother was on her feet beside him.

Evie's mouth dropped open. Now accused of theft. How low will he stoop?

'Is that right?' Mr Rudge leaned forward, his jaw jutting. 'Mr Cooper, do you have a bill of sale for such a ring?'

Evie turned finally to glare at Edwin, who was still on his feet, and gaping like a fish.

'No? Interesting. If there is no ring, that would be lying to the court.' Mr Rudge dropped his chin again, held up a finger that silenced Edwin's sputtering. He shuffled the papers one-handed, his finger still in the air. 'Then there was the following letter to the editor, Mr Cooper, the one where you are warning other unsuspecting gentlemen of Miss Emerson's so-called dubious character, and that of a former suitor of hers.'

Evie was mortified. Did the magistrate need to enunciate quite so clearly?

Edwin tugged at his lapels. 'Only right and proper.'

'Except it isn't, Mr Cooper. It's more libel on your part, which might need addressing if someone wished to bring it before me,' Mr Rudge emphasised. 'And close your mouth. You, too, madam, I won't hear a word from you,' he said to Mrs Cooper. 'Sit down, both of you. Mr Campbell, please continue.'

Mrs Cooper aimed a vicious glare at Evie, as did Jane.

'Your Honour, this matter should never go further than here,' Mr Campbell said. 'Not only do we have statements from other victims of this racket, but also other newspaper reports over the years from surrounding districts' local papers in which the Cooper family's dark deeds shine.'

'Newspaper reports?'

'Yes. Due to the nature of the issue, we hadn't time to interview as many women as we'd hoped, so with the help of a journalist, we were able to secure these.' He waved articles cut from newsprint.

Evie let out a breath. *Fitz—it would have been him.*

'Not exactly evidence, Mr Campbell.'

'And notes recorded at a few other court sessions that certainly attest to the characters of those sitting at the plaintiff's table today.'

Edwin shot to his feet. 'Notes and … and newspaper articles,' he thundered, outraged. 'Do I need to say something about that, Your Honour?'

'No, Mr Cooper, you need not. I can see quite plainly they are newspaper articles, thank you very much.' Titters sounded from the crowd behind. The magistrate beckoned with his fingers. 'If you will, Mr Campbell.'

Mr Campbell nodded at Miss Juno who delivered the clutch of papers to the bench. Mr Rudge took his time perusing them and, once again, Evie felt sure he had nodded off, his chin disappearing in folds of florid skin at his collar.

Then he popped out his chin and after shuffling to find a certain page, said, 'I see here on your application, Mr Cooper, that you are suing Miss Emerson for two thousand pounds. Pray tell how you arrived at that paltry sum for the enormous loss of your future comforts.'

Sniggers rose again. Mrs Cooper pushed out of her chair and marched out of the courtroom. Evie was mortified all over again. Her breath had become short and she hung her head. Miss Juno tapped Evie's arm for attention and patted under her own chin. *Chin up*, Miss Juno encouraged.

'Do you believe that Miss Emerson has such funds to offer, Mr Cooper?' the magistrate asked.

Oh my God. It's Mama's bequest to me and Meryl. The house and the money.

Edwin tried to maintain his composure. 'I was led to believe that our life together would be comfortable and in a secure home—'

'That *you* were not providing. Is that right?'

Evie sat up straight and turned to scowl at Edwin, her mouth firmly closed.

'She … threw a heavy decanter at me,' Edwin sputtered.

'I shouldn't wonder,' Mr Rudge said. 'But what's that got to do with anything? Did it break over you, Mr Cooper?'

'No, it—'

'Ah, then she can't charge you for damages. A pity.'

Mr Campbell coughed. A giggle erupted from somewhere. Edwin's face bloomed as if with a morbid rash.

'Though I see in Miss Emerson's statement,' Mr Rudge went on, 'that someone broke into her home and did indeed smash a heavy decanter, an antique I'm told, by taking a hammer to it. Then left the guilty instrument for all to see. This vindictive, small-minded creature had also ruined a number of specially crafted ladies' hats. Was that you, Mr Cooper, stomping all over hats like some wayward child? Don't lie to me again.'

Edwin was trying to think of an answer.

'No matter,' the magistrate announced. 'As to Mr Barrett, the, ah, private investigator, his report states that he saw you outside Miss Emerson's place just last night, late, attempting to make an unlawful nuisance of yourself—'

'I did no such thing. It's outrageous to suggest that a man of such a low profession should have his word considered over mine—'

'A peeping tom, you are, sir,' the magistrate snapped. The court fell eerily silent. 'And Mr Barrett hardly needed to intervene, because it says here that Miss Emerson leaped to her defence on the veranda of her home and struck you with a fire poker, not once, but twice.' He took a deep breath and checked another paper. 'Once on the chest, then once on the back, as you were running away, no doubt your tail between your legs.'

A guffaw erupted collectively from the back of the room. Evie was on her feet, horrified that her frustration and terror of last night, resulting in her attack on Edwin, was now the subject of amusement. Miss Juno's fingers clutched her sleeve, encouraging her back to her seat. She collapsed into the chair, Miss Juno's arm on hers.

'Mr Cooper,' Mr Rudge said, pointing a finger, 'remove your jacket and shirt and present yourself.'

'I will not.'

'Very well.' He looked around the courtroom. 'I find that Miss Emerson has no breach of contract case to answer. I rule for the defendant, and that the plaintiff will pay court costs, plus a sum of two thousand pounds damages to the defendant. That figure must sound familiar. Am I clear, Mr Cooper?'

'But that's not—'

'It's that or a gaol term, which, to be honest, considering there are a number of statements from other ladies, I would much prefer for you.'

'I'm not on—'

'Not on trial here yet, Mr Cooper, and consider yourself lucky. I know there is only one other way to stop men like you if a gaol term is not imposed, so be very careful out there from now on.'

Mr Campbell's eyes widened and he began to stand.

Edwin's jaw shook, his chin puckered. 'What a load of rot,' he muttered between his teeth.

'What did you say?' Rudge snarled at him.

The bailiffs had straightened and Edwin dropped his glare.

'In fact,' Mr Rudge frowned as he considered his next words, 'if I find you back in my courtroom for the smallest misdemeanour, I will make sure you are charged for everything on these pages.' He slapped a hand over the paperwork in front of him. 'And I will lock you up for the term of your natural life.'

'You can't do that,' Edwin shouted.

'Starting with contempt of court,' the magistrate shouted in return.

The bailiff stepped up to take a stunned Edwin by the elbow. Jane Cooper thrust out of her chair and marched towards Evie. Miss Juno sprang to her feet, blocking the woman. Everyone stood, chairs scraped, voices hushed as Mr Rudge tugged his gown and straightened.

His voice rang out. 'As for you, Miss Jane Cooper.'

Jane spun to face him, mid Valkyrie charge.

'I believe you've recently made my stepson's acquaintance, Mr Alistair Worsfold.' He waited as Jane blinked at him, the shock evident on her face. 'As of today, remove your poisonous self from his company or you might very well land here in my court as well.'

Jane sucked in her cheeks, her blush starting at her nose and flaring over her wide forehead. She pushed her way out of the room. Edwin had already disappeared with the bailiff.

Miss Juno pressed her lips together, eyes merry.

Mr Rudge waved a hand at the clerk.

'All rise,' the clerk of court intoned. 'Session is over.'

Mr Campbell approached the bench, calling Mr Rudge back before he closed the door on his chambers. 'Your Honour, ah …'

The public filed out, gossip a blur in the air. Evie remained where she was, still stunned.

Miss Juno began to pack up the papers and nodded surreptitiously towards the bench. 'Wait with me so you can hear, Miss Emerson,' she said, her voice a whisper.

Mr Rudge stood at his door waiting for the lawyer to reach him. 'Mr Campbell, I know what you're going to say, but I am sick to death of philanderers, wastrels and timewasters. Mr Cooper is all of that, and worse, I have no doubt. Also his family.'

'My concern, Mr Rudge—'

'It was hard to resist, all that theatrical thunder of mine.' The magistrate made no effort to drop his voice. 'Think I damn bamboozled the fellow. Don't look so glum. Maybe some of my colleagues might have dealt with him differently, less harshly, and allowed blame to fall on the innocent woman, but allay your fears, if that's what your frown indicates.'

'Your Honour, I'm certainly not questioning you'—which he was—'but Cooper might believe he has cause now to try again in the court, perhaps might think he has been dealt with unfairly.'

'His prerogative.' Impatient with that, Mr Rudge waved a hand. 'My judgement was fair, justice was served and dispensed. Dear God, man, I'm nearing the end of my illustrious and practically useless career, and it's about time justice and the law came together for once, don't you think? Besides, who's going to challenge me—Cooper? I don't believe he has the funds,' he said, 'or the bollocks, sir, hence his deplorable, cowardly activities.' Mr Rudge nodded to where people had been seated at the back of the courtroom. 'I saw there was a journalist present. Today's session will go far and wide thanks to the article he'll write. I'll go out on a blaze of glory, and justice will be the hero. Good day to you.' He closed the door behind him.

Mr Campbell returned to the table, where Evie was helping Miss Juno slide the last of his documents into a large satchel. He looked at both women. 'I've never, in all my days …' he said, shaking his head.

Mr Campbell left the courtroom moments after Evie had thanked him.

'A very good outcome, Miss Emerson,' Miss Juno told her on the steps outside, smiling, and then she followed her boss into a cab and it drove away.

Mr and Mrs Kingsley came up the steps for her.

'Edwin is under orders to pay within the month, or a custodial sentence will be placed on him,' Evie said to them.

'Rightly so, the beggar,' Mr Kingsley said.

'I doubt he has any money, though,' Evie said.

'Can't be disappointed, dear. He's certainly a low type of man, and this is at least his comeuppance.' Mrs Kingsley patted Evie's arm. 'I do believe there's a journalist of note here,' she said, a look in her eye.

Evie craned her neck around the people milling outside, and saw Fitz with notepad and pencil, grinning at her. She covered her mouth before her shout of glee could escape. Then someone else caught her eye. Raff stopped alongside Fitz, frowning darkly. He tipped his hat, nodded at her. Delighted, happy as a lark, her smile wide, she started towards him, but he held up a hand to say 'stop'.

Confused, she halted. It didn't matter. Her poor heart raced cheerfully. *He's here.* Evie tried to keep Raff in sight, but the bright light of day was eye-watering and she was momentarily blinded by the sharp sunlight. Suddenly, Mrs Kingsley yelped as she was bumped aside, and Mr Kingsley grunted an 'Oi,' in protest at the clumsy pedestrian.

Then Edwin had his finger thrust under Evie's nose. 'I'll get you. I'll come for you in the dead of night and you'll be damaged goods for sure after that,' he snarled, his voice low. 'You'll pay me to go away, and even then, don't count your chances I'll stay away.'

Mr Kingsley jostled him and yelled for help. Jane was trying desperately to drag her brother away when the court bailiffs rushed out to clear the footpath. The Coopers stormed off, pushing their way out of the crowd.

Evie's hand was on her throat, the hard thump of her pulse giddying. She was shaking. Had anyone else heard? The Kingsleys, worried and angry, herded her into their cab.

Raff was nowhere in sight.

Chapter Sixty-three

Early the next day, sitting in the studio, Mrs Kingsley had Evie's hand in hers. She had insisted Evie stay at their house last night.

'I'm just so very glad it's over,' Evie said, despite Edwin's threat still rolling around in her head.

'The man is abominable,' Mrs Kingsley said. 'I'm quite sure his threat was an empty one. Those sorts are all bluster.'

Evie wasn't as sure.

'And just bear in mind,' Mrs Kingsley said, 'that no matter what article appears in the paper detailing the outcome, people will still gossip about all this for quite some time.'

'I don't think I'll ever live this down,' Evie said, her tone sour, her mouth grim.

'Rage is futile against the nature of vicious gossip, my dear, which sticks rather more than the truth, despite proof and a magistrate's ruling.' Mrs Kingsley squeezed her hand. 'I know you feel your reputation is at stake.'

'It's had a stake through its heart already, Mrs K,' Evie said.

'Now you're despairing. We know you better than the gossips. Give them nothing but a proud lift of your chin.'

Rueful, Evie considered the hats and the fabrics, the messy table with the huge shears, the pin cushions, and boxes of feathers and trinkets. Millinery was her life, working with gorgeous bits and pieces to make equally gorgeous creations. Her mind would be swept into a cool and calm place with a needle and thread in her fingers, and a picture in her head of a beautiful work of art to adorn a lady's head.

'Do you believe that Craig, Williamson will agree to exhibit after all?'

'The store had better change its tune,' Mrs Kingsley said, but her smile was weary. Then her eyes rounded and a sheen of perspiration covered her face. 'Oh, for goodness' sake.' She dropped Evie's hands to reach for a cloth draped over a bowl of water. 'Honestly,' she said, wringing out the cloth and patting her face and neck. 'This is hardly bearable.'

Evie chewed her lip. 'Anything I can do?'

'Well, apart from mixing a potion of newt's tongue and essence of mole, I don't think so. I'm not about to try opium, or powder of cow's ovaries, or something derived from the testicles of Lord-only-knows what creatures.'

Evie gulped down a bark of amused surprise.

'I could go ahead and keep myself drunk as a monkey; some say that's supposed to help. Help what, exactly?' Mrs Kingsley was in fine fettle as she blotted her face and decolletage. Taking a breath, she felt around on the bench under pieces of velvet and lace to find a bigger fan. 'I'm so glad of these little beauties; they help. I have them all over the house. Probably better than waving hocus-pocus over me.'

'I'm so sorry it's happening, Mrs Kingsley.' That sounded lame in the face of all this. Evie was well out of her depth. 'I hope when this change of life afflicts me, I'll have your sense of humour.'

'You'll need it.' Then Mrs Kingsley tut-tutted, and the fan was retired to the bench. 'Oh, I've gone on and on again, haven't I?'

'It's all right, Mrs K. I suppose we women should all learn these things, but it seems to be …'

'Taboo,' Mrs Kingsley supplied and huffed. 'How ridiculous. Happens to all of us. I hope your mother gave you some instruction on your bodily functions. You didn't have to wonder if you were bleeding to death when you were twelve or thirteen, did you?'

'No, thankfully. She did give me some information about certain things. But not about this.'

'Was she very old when she died?'

'Fifty-two.'

'Ah. Perhaps she didn't realise what was happening to her—that's if anything was happening.' Mrs Kingsley sighed. 'My two daughters are in Melbourne. I have yet to speak to them of these things. Perhaps when next they visit.' She was quiet a moment then, shrugging, she reached for the fan again. 'It's not something we women chat about in groups at afternoon teas, or during the rallies for voting rights and such, but here, one on one in this little studio, we do talk, as you well know.' The fan flapped open. 'I see a great many women my age swooning from internal combustion, or falling asleep in the chair at eleven in the morning because of sleepless nights, or complaining of headaches, or—another worry—loss of interest in their husbands.' She slid a glance at Evie and smiling then, confided, 'Can't always blame change of life for that one.' Fanning again, she said, 'My mother died at sixty-eight, and she never said a thing to me. Not one whisper that she'd experienced any of this, or that this might occur. I can only presume what horrors she might have gone through. Awful, just awful.'

'What is the good of it?' Evie asked. 'I know I must have my monthly courses if I ever want children, though I don't know why, but what is the reason for this change?' She frowned. 'Although, being older, I shouldn't imagine monthly courses would be welcome. Well,' she said on reflection, 'they're not welcome now.

Why can't the courses plain stop when we're older and we go back to normal, just not being able to have babies?'

'Oh, don't ask me the wisdom of it, if there's any at all,' Mrs Kingsley said, her fan waving. 'Probably nature's way of bumping us old girls off so we're not in competition for young breeding stock.' She harrumphed. 'Not that we'd want babies at this age, for goodness sake. Grandbabies, of course. We can hand them back.'

Evie bit down a smile, didn't know what to say to that.

'I'll tell you this,' Mrs Kingsley said. 'There's one good thing about these ferocious surges. Outside the court yesterday, I had a surge so strong that I could have sallied forth and beaten the daylights out of that despicable Mr Cooper with my bare hands, raging at him, pulling his hair and gnashing my teeth. And the bonus, I wouldn't have cared a hoot about who saw it.' She burst out laughing.

Evie couldn't control her laughter, then. 'Oh, what a sight that would have been,' she said.

'Indeed, and well deserved, the sod.' Mrs Kingsley smiled broadly while wringing out the cloth again. 'That manager at Craig, Williamson better watch out and not give me any more trouble about our exhibition.' Then, taking Evie's hand, she said, 'So you'll be all right at home tonight?'

After the ordeal in the court, Evie had thought hard about going home, then thought of nothing else but Edwin's terrible intimidation. When she'd relayed to Mr Kingsley what Edwin had said, he'd immediately taken her to the police station where she filed another complaint. But as soon as Evie had signed the thing, she knew it would be a worthless piece of paper. The look the trooper had given her was dismissive, derisive, but he had said they'd be visiting Edwin Cooper. She wasn't completely satisfied it would stop him, but at least it might encourage him to cool off. Despite what Mr Rudge had said to him, it was foolhardy to expect he would.

Mr Kingsley poked his head in the door. 'All right in here, my dears? Ready to go when you are, Evie.' Mr Kingsley would drive her home. She'd return the following day to resume work with Mrs Kingsley.

'Are you sure you'll be all right, my dear? You've had a terrible few months.'

'I will. I just have to get on, Mrs Kingsley.'

When they arrived at Evie's place, Mr Kingsley insisted on checking doors and windows and, once satisfied, doffed his hat, climbed back on board his cart and turned for home. Afterwards, Evie headed to the store to purchase stock for her pantry, and once again at the butchers and the baker, she was shunned. Her blood hummed. While the verdict in her favour wouldn't yet have filtered through to the community, it still didn't bode well for her future in Bendigo. That, and the fact that Edwin Cooper might still remain in town and be an ongoing problem.

By the time she'd returned to her house, she was steaming, and thinking drastic thoughts about packing up and finding another town in which to live right that afternoon.

The night was uneventful. Or she assumed as much because she hadn't heard a thing. She'd been so exhausted that not even anger had kept her awake. She'd slept like the dead and nothing had disturbed her.

The next morning, despite scratchy and puffy eyes—she admitted to a fit of tears in the small hours just before dawn—she was determined to put behind her the shock of finding Fitz so hurt, Constable O'Shea's murder, her firing a rifle at someone, the court case and all the adventure of the past month. Meryl's death and her grief was another matter. *And Raff, well, Raff wasn't here.*

Today she would start to work out what to do from now on. She had the house, her mother's inheritance, her craft and her talent. That was portable for the most part, she could take her skills anywhere, order fabric when she needed it. Perhaps she'd rent a new residence somewhere and work out of a room in it.

She would figure something out, if only she could keep the rage that was building inside her from bursting through the dam.

She pulled on her gloves and donned one of her favourite hats. That was sure to cheer her. It was a little toque of soft mauve velvet with a pale teal band and a maroon spray of feathers pinned to it. *Very smart.* It was a perfect contrast to the outfit she wore of the very latest fashion, a tiny black-and-white houndstooth-check day dress. No one else in town was wearing it. In fact, it was hardly in Melbourne. She'd had to order it especially.

Opening the front door, she stepped outside, locked it behind her, pocketed the key, and turned.

Raff Dolan and Bluey were outside the gate. Her heart took a leap. Raff, solid, strong, a light in his eye and his hat in his hands, and great, big, beautiful Bluey freshly groomed—they were a handsome pair. Both were staring at her.

'Raff.' She took the few steps forward and stopped, so pleased to see him that for a long moment, she lost any more words.

'Good morning, Evie. I trust you had a good night's sleep.'

'I did. And you?' She smiled or tried to smile. His horse was all packed up; Raff must be leaving. Goodness, her heart had started to gallop.

He nodded, but wasn't smiling. 'I'll walk with you if you don't mind. Where are you going?'

Chapter Sixty-four

Bendigo
Wednesday 12 October

Christ, if she wasn't the best thing he'd ever seen.

He had to tell her, he had to say something before he left for home; before he lost his nerve. Fitz had insisted he did, but what in Christ's name did *he* have to say about it, his best mate who'd strung them both along. Raff could well remember Evie talking to Fitz when they all thought he was on his deathbed, telling him she loved him.

He and Fitz had had words about it again last night when they'd camped a little way out of the city. They'd roamed Bendigo, keeping out of sight, but the scrub was best in which to lay low, or more to the point, settle an issue.

Fitz had bellowed, 'I was bloody unconscious at the time, you fool, I never heard her say that.' He barely took a breath. 'And she does love me, just not like *that*.' He stabbed Raff in the chest with a forefinger. 'Only as friends. You're using it as an excuse, damn you.'

'You think what you want, O'Shea.'

'I do. I will.' Fitz backed off a little. He held up a hand. 'Hey, I'm not fighting with you about Evie again. She's my friend, so are you. God knows, I need all I have.' He tossed the remains of his tea into the dirt. 'You should've muscled your way in, taken a swing at me. Been a knight in shining armour.'

There'd been no point taking a swing at Fitz. 'You don't do that to friends,' Raff said and poked at the little campfire. 'Friends don't do that to you.'

'Well, not too late is it, for you and Evie? No real harm done, right?'

Jesus.

Silence let tempers cool. Fitz had gone to his saddlebags and reefed out a wad of paper. 'Read the article I've written on the court drama. I'm not only sending this to the Bendigo paper, but Ballarat as well, spreading the net wide. Edwin Cooper and his family won't want to bob up anywhere around the district.'

Raff took the papers, still irritable. 'Good.'

Fitz chewed his lip a moment. 'I hope it goes some way to atone for wasting Evie's time, and what that might have caused.' Fiddling with his shirt sleeve, he added, 'And for you too, over Evie. I told her the same.' He gave a laugh, part apology, part defence.

Raff grunted. 'Big of you.' Didn't make him any less angry about it, but to what end? If he and Evie were meant to be together, they'd work it out themselves. Still, it didn't stop his blood running when he thought of how Fitz had manipulated—

'I was looking for a way to survive. I'm still looking.'

'I know.' Raff dropped his chin. There it was. *Survival.* So he let it go; he had to. Water under the bridge.

'I thought Bendigo Barrett was going to strangle you at the back of the courtroom when Cooper was spruiking.' Fitz gave a laugh. 'Strong bugger.'

Raff had wanted to leap onto Cooper the moment he'd begun uttering his lies. Barrett had clamped Raff in his seat. 'He stopped me looking a fool, more than once.'

'He did.'

After another rum or two by the campfire, they'd bunkered down for the night.

This morning Fitz left on Patto at dawn with few words. 'This is it. Goodbye, Raff.'

It shouldn't have been awkward, but it was. Fitz hadn't wanted to say goodbye to anyone, and nor did he say where he was headed. Just the way he wanted it.

Now Raff walked alongside Evie, tugging Bluey. 'Fitz left early this morning. Couldn't hang around, you understand.'

'I do.'

'After he left Cobram, he got down to see John's wife, and then decided to come back, just to write up your, uh, court thing for the newspapers. He wanted to make sure you got the best.'

Evie gave him a glance. 'Where's he going? I couldn't find either of you on Monday afterwards to ask.'

'I don't know. He'll keep roving, I reckon.'

'Oh.'

He glanced her way.

'Something wrong, Raff?' She sounded clipped. 'He'll be all right, you'll see.'

'I know he'll be all right, the great git.' They walked on in uneasy silence for a bit, Bluey clopping behind them. 'I hope you're all right after the courtroom business, and everything.'

'I think so, all things considered.' She had a set to her mouth, was maybe not happy about the court thing after all. 'Shooting at people. Hitting someone.'

'And those couple of swings you took with the poker looked pretty good.'

Evie stopped, and a whisk of cold air slid over him.

'You saw that?' Her face was stony.

Raff put his hat back on, flapped the collar of his shirt. *Shit.* Now the sun seemed to be warming him up all of a sudden. He nodded. 'I saw someone creeping around your house. It was Barrett watching Cooper creeping around. I got to Barrett, who told me not to go any closer to your place.'

'Why were you even there? I wasn't told that,' she said, sounding tetchy. Frowning, she started to walk again. She was watching her feet. 'What time was this?'

He shrugged. 'Uh, late.'

'You were outside my place, late?'

'I'd got in from the railway station, went to that boarding house.'

She had picked up the pace.

'I took a nap, woke up and just thought I'd—'

'What?' she snapped. 'Just thought you'd what? Come to my place, *late*?'

A little bewildered, he just shook his head. 'To make sure you were all right.' His throat tightened. *What the hell is she mad at?* 'You know, after the McCosker thing. Your sister. All that.'

'You were there, late, and that awful man was terrorising me, and … and you didn't—'

'Barrett's orders. He didn't want anyone seen at your place while he was trying to catch Cooper.'

'You didn't think to come and get me?'

'I did. I did think of that.'

'But you didn't come and—'

'Then you came out with the poker, and Barrett was chasing him.'

'I was out of my mind scared, Raff.' She walked faster.

Jesus, she's mad at me. I should've ignored Barrett, should have blundered in. 'Barrett said he had it in hand. He made it clear I wasn't to be seen in your company, even in your vicinity. He said it would damage your reputation—'

'My reputation was already damaged thanks to Edwin Cooper.'

She speared a glance at him, her eyes flashing with a glitter of tears.

'Evie. Don't let all that worry you. It doesn't mean anything now.'

'It means everything for some stupid, *stupid* reason.' She was nearly skipping, she was walking so fast. 'And means nothing at the same time.'

He didn't understand that. He had to watch for carts and horse riders as they crossed a main road, but she just charged out anyway, head down. He kept up with her. 'I don't care about the court thing. Makes no difference to me you being accused of all that stuff. The magistrate threw it out. It doesn't matter to me what went on before—'

'*Nothing* went on before,' she seethed.

Jesus. He kept saying the wrong thing. 'I meant—'

She stopped and twisted towards him. 'You think my reputation is … that I'm … sullied?' she squeezed out. She hadn't shouted, thank Christ, but she was mad enough, wild.

'What are you talking about?'

'That's what Edwin Cooper intended in there. Didn't you hear him? That accusation will stay with me forever. That's what people will remember, will talk about, will think of me. I know that's why Mr Barrett wasn't going to let you come near me, it was to make sure that evil man didn't have any *more* ammunition. But Edwin won't be stopped, do you understand? He's already threatened me again.'

'*What?*'

She waved him off, clamped her mouth shut a moment. 'Oh, it's just fine that a man doesn't need to be beyond reproach, or to be a virgin, does it, to keep his reputation intact.' She spun. 'Doesn't matter ever. He's *never* sullied. Are you unsullied, Raff? Are you a virgin?'

He held up his hands, temper rising. *Chrissakes, ladies don't* talk *about this stuff.* 'What's that got to do with anything?'

Hands on hips. 'Well, are you, Raff Dolan?'

'Of course not,' he blustered between his teeth. He had to keep his lid on. Early-morning pedestrians had noticed their raised voices. 'What did you mean before, that he's threatened you again?'

She ignored him. 'And do you think anyone cares about *your* reputation? Do you think *I* care about that?' She turned and marched on.

His reputation?

He'd only dug the hole deeper for himself and he couldn't figure out how he'd started digging. Bewildered, he only knew he had to stop talking. He caught up to her. 'I don't want to talk about this now, Evie.'

'Oh, of course you don't. You're not the one with a *bad* reputation. Edwin openly accuses me, not only of being with him, but being with Fitz. But Edwin wasn't prosecuted for vicious libel, was he? Only false accusation about breach of contract.' She stopped walking again, took a big breath then flicked a wrist towards the corner. 'It's this street. Not far. You don't have to come any further.'

'Wait, wait. If your reputation's bad, I *don't care*, I'm not worried about that,' Raff ground out—but he should've shut up. He knew it immediately. For some reason, it had been the wrong bloody thing to say. Again.

'That's just it,' she said, eyes flashing. 'I never *had* the kind of reputation for anyone *to* worry about. And now, you don't care that it's bad.'

He stood there, flummoxed. Had Fitz said 'tempest'?

'I care. I … don't care.'

'For God's sake, it'll never leave me alone. Edwin is still a threat to me, Raff, and because he said—' She stopped abruptly.

'Yes?' Raff's chest thundered. 'Because he said *what*?'

Evie just stood there, shaking with anger in front of him, her eyes wide on his.

'Evie, tell me. Because he said *what*?' He reached out for her.

Stepping back, she said, 'Let Mr Barrett handle it. Goodbye, Raff.' She marched away.

Barrett? Fury remained bottled up inside him. Raff wouldn't follow her. She was too dangerous right now. *But what in God's name just happened?* He had no bloody clue. He and Bluey stood there watching her stride up the pathway to Mrs Kingsley's and head inside without a backward glance.

The horse tugged on the reins and Raff agreed. 'Yeah, old mate, time to head home.'

He stood there a moment longer. *Let Barrett handle what?* She could only mean handling Cooper, and his threat.

'But there's something we need to do first, Bluey.'

Chapter Sixty-five

Ballarat
Saturday 15 October

'Hey, are you up there, big brother?' someone shouted.

It was either Fergal or Red. In the loft above his wheelwright shop, Raff unfolded out of his swag on his great bed. 'What?' he yelled down, eyes sticky, bleary.

'Day's nearly over. Hurry up.'

Redmond. He was always on the tear, filling up every second of daylight hours. Raff cranked an eye open at the cruel streak of sunlight slicing through the gap in the shed's timber walls. It was sometime early morning; late as far as Red was concerned. Raff had only ridden in yesterday, mid afternoon. No need for him to be up early for chores or jobs. Pa had called Raff's younger brothers home the same week he'd departed for Bendigo, and there were hardly any workshop jobs left to be done. Their uncle, Skelly Dolan, had happily let them go, couldn't afford them on his dairy property any longer.

'If I never see another pail of milk, it'll be too soon,' Fergal had grumbled last night. 'When I got home here, I even washed me clothes twice in one week to get the sick stink of spilled milk out.' He let everyone know about it until they piled their laundry onto him too. That had shut him up.

Raff pulled on his trousers and took the ladder to the floor. He headed outside to the privy and, on the way back, saw that his pa had driven in, the old cart and horse he kept at home both still in good working order.

'Good to see you, boy,' his pa said to him. He called each of his sons 'boy', and it didn't matter who answered if he hadn't addressed them by name. He was tying up outside. 'Got the tea on, boy?' he yelled. Red answered.

Paddy ambled into the workshop on bowlegs, hitching one leg as he walked. Something to do with his hip, he said. There was always a great expulsion of breath when he sat, and a groan when he stood. Though in pain, he rarely complained about it. He settled into a chair at a bench, lifted his chin at the pannikins nearby waiting for the brew. 'Tea. Good.' He huffed as he looked around the workshop. 'Looks like ye might be out of a job here, Raff.'

'Might be.'

'Ah, it's good to see all me big brawny lads together again. By hell, look at the three of yer.'

Raff's brothers were the same build as him, if a mite leaner. Redmond named for his blaze of russet-red hair, and Fergal as dark-haired as Raff, but with a mass of long droopy curls that reached just beyond his collar.

There was a merry glint in Paddy's eye. 'Did the boys tell yer I had an officer of the law turn up lookin' for ye? Same one as before ye left, I reckon.'

'What did he want this time?'

'Didn't say once he was told you'd gone orf.'

Red had taken the pannikins and was dunking them into the billy. He slapped them on the bench, the brew slopping. 'Reckon it was over some fella who'd been left on their doorstep all thumped up.'

His father just raised his eyebrows. 'Have to be on yer guard, Raff, lad.'

Raff grabbed a pannikin from Red and pulled it towards him, snatching his fingers from the hot handle. He rolled the cup between the palms of his hands, calluses hardened against the heat.

Paddy nodded at Raff's knuckles, scraped, red and, in spots, scabs forming. 'Looks like you might have delivered another package somewhere lately, son.'

He had, wasn't able to hide it. Raff flexed his hands a little, careful not to split open a large, stubborn scrape. 'Maybe.'

Raff hadn't left Bendigo after seeing Evie storm off. *Vicious libel … he's still a threat.* She'd cut off from saying something else. It had rankled him, and he'd wandered here and there, had a drink at a pub, wandered back, waiting.

Then he'd seen Cooper in Evie's street late in the afternoon. Just after dusk, he followed him and, sure enough, the arsewipe was causing trouble for Evie again. Barrett's warning, and Evie ordering him to leave it, still rang loud in Raff's ears, but he had to act, had to do *something*, and without detection.

'Some fella get in your way, brother?' Fergal asked him.

Edwin Cooper's chin cracking.

'A nuisance,' Raff said.

Cooper's cheek taking a blow that would've knocked Bluey over.

'How'd he pull up, this nuisance?' Red was eyeing the rough knuckles.

'Won't be a nuisance again, I reckon.'

'Good job. Break any bones?'

Nose smashed, split eyebrow, a broken tooth maybe. A rib gave way, possibly two.

'None of mine.'

'Sounds like he came off second best then.'

Edwin Cooper won't be attracting any ladies for a while.

'Yep.'

On the ground, messy, dazed, there hadn't been any sound except the first squeal as Cooper tried to run, the bloody coward. Picked him up by the collar. 'Arsefly, you so much as look in Evie's direction again, I'll track you down, and it won't be a couple of lily-livered taps next time.'

'Did you leave the package at a police station again?' Fergal was grinning at him.

'I did.' Raff had thought to leave Cooper on the path outside Evie's place, but decided it was best to remove him. So he hauled him over Bluey's back and dumped him at the station. He stuffed a note of instructions, written in pencil, inside Cooper's jacket pocket. Then he wiped down the saddle and headed out on the road, riding for Ballarat, two days away.

'Goin' back to Bendigo any time soon, son, to have another crack?' Paddy asked, a shrewd gleam in his eye.

Fergal slurped from his tea. 'At what?'

Raff aimed a flicker of a glance at his father. 'Don't reckon.'

'*Oi*, brother,' Red said to Raff, eyes bright. 'You got something to tell us, have ye?' His freckles stood out through the sparse russet stubble of his beard.

'You lot,' Paddy said to his younger sons. 'Get. Don't come back till I tell ye.'

'Pa, there's no—'

'Get yer arses out there in the yard and tidy up.'

Red jerked his head at Fergal. Taking their tea, they headed outside.

Paddy watched them go and leaned back in the chair to study Raff. 'But did yer talk to her at least, boy?'

Raff shook his head. 'I was about to, but I got … I didn't understand what she was saying *at* me.' He frowned. 'I let it go, let her walk away. It was safest.'

'Safest?' Paddy regarded Raff from head to toe. 'Aye, I could see you'd be in danger from a slip of a lassie.'

'I got tongue-tied, Pa. I dunno, missed my chance.' Raff took a swallow of tea, cool enough to take a gulp.

'And ye're not happy about that?'

Raff gave a short shake of his head. 'Too bad. Got this place to look after.'

'Ye're the eldest of me sons, boy, and I know ye think ye got a job to do with lookin' out fer us, but it's time to start thinking of yeself.' He waved away the look Raff gave him. 'Those youngster brothers of yours have come into their own, they don't need you or me, just look around.' He waved a hand. 'They've proved it recent like.'

'You're right enough there.'

Paddy went on. 'Ye're well over thirty, Raff. She's been on yer mind for years now. Tell me this,' he said and reached over to tap Raff's knee, 'can you go on livin' and never tellin' her you love her, and waste yer chance to find out what's on her mind?'

Raff couldn't remember all the last conversation with Evie, not word for word, anyway. There'd been too many words. He sat forward, cupped the pannikin in his hands. 'I told her I didn't care about any of the past, and that was somehow wrong. I don't understand her.'

'Ye'll learn to understand her, boy, if ye listen. Ye'll be sure to do it if you love her.'

Raff scoffed, thinking. Or not thinking, only hearing his father making sense, hoping it would sink into his thick head.

'I know how ye feel about the woman,' Paddy said.

Red and Fergal made snorting noises from the doorway, both lifting their pannikins high in salute. 'Ahh, a woman. Rafferty Dolan's got a woman.'

Red strode in and punched Raff lightly in the arm. 'Lad,' he said, approving.

Fergal followed and rubbed a dusty hand hard through Raff's hair. 'Lad,' he echoed Red.

Raff swiped away Fergal's hand. 'Get off.'

'Surely you left her a message, or somethin'?' his father said, exasperated.

'Yeah, Pa,' Raff said. 'I left her something, a message of sorts.'

His knuckles stung only a little as he remembered whacking Edwin Cooper to the ground.

Chapter Sixty-six

Bendigo
Monday 17 October

'Dear Miss Emerson,' Evie read aloud. 'We met on the train station at Elmore and you gave me your card. I'm wondering if you are returning and visiting Echuca, which is where I live. If so, please do bring a range of your beautiful hats. I have mentioned your lovely straw boater to a number of ladies here. Please contact me care of the Post Office, Echuca. Yours faithfully, Mrs Thomas Leane (Eunice).'

'Well, that's wonderful, dear,' Mrs Kingsley said. 'You must have impressed her. By the way, where is that chirpy little boater you were wearing when you left?'

'Fell victim to a toddler, I'm afraid, and is now beyond repair. I can make another.'

'Perhaps the letter from Mrs Leane is a good sign,' Mrs Kingsley said. 'If you really do intend leaving Bendigo, having a few clients before you get to Echuca might be the right idea.' She was fanning again and puffing in frustration. It was a bad day today for the surges, which were coming in rapid succession. 'Of course, I have to say again, I'd miss you terribly.'

In the week since attending court, they had discussed Evie leaving Bendigo. The gossip and innuendo across town hadn't eased, nor had the turning of backs and the finger pointing in a few places Evie had visited. Even Miss Thompson of the Pink had smirked at her. So far, thankfully, nothing of Edwin Cooper had been seen or heard.

The manager at Craig, Williamson store had not contacted Mrs Kingsley again, and nor had she approached them.

'Don't know that I'd agree to display with them now anyway,' Mrs Kingsley had said a little huffily, but sighed. 'However, some of our clients have not yet returned, so we might yet have to re-think that if the opportunity arose.'

Evie folded Mrs Leane's letter and slipped it back in its envelope. It rang a bright note on a dismal day. She would answer it, and plan for a short trip to Echuca. A visit to the printers for some new business cards would be wise, too. She even thought she'd write to Jenny Robinson to ask if she thought the hats might sell in Cobram, although it was a long journey there. Perhaps they could be sent by coach as freight.

Cobram. The lonely graves under sunny skies, a mighty river gliding by, and no one who knew her, or anything of her past. Should she think about making a new life for herself there?

Raff.

She hung her head over a swathe of royal-blue silk she'd picked up to match colours. It came alive in her hands, and had a mind of its own, falling loosely from her fingers.

Raff. He hadn't understood her, and she'd totally misunderstood him. She'd gone off at him, angry, and probably hadn't made sense. She would write, apologising, and leave it at that … except her heartstrings tugged. She wanted to say so much more to him, but it wouldn't be right. Neither of them had declared for the other, hadn't so much as pressed hands. Well, except for that deep embrace in the constable's yard when she'd felt enfolded … in friendship. Was that all it was? It wasn't all there was for her.

Sighing, she rolled the length of silk around her forearm and held it up to the light, this way and that, watching it move. Such an exquisite fabric. Letting it go, it drifted down her arm to land in soft folds on her lap. The silk was cool under her hands, its texture a luxury on her skin, soft, smooth, strong. Durable, yet delicate to the eye.

There had been no understanding that her relationship with Raff might change, and except for that hug of friendship, certainly no other physical contact between them. Evie knew though, given the chance, she'd happily go wherever he was, and stay with him.

Oh, how did you know that? Chiding herself, she shook her head. Foolishness.

Because Fitz had said Raff carried a torch for me. But out of deference to his friend, Raff never made his feelings known to her.

Because he'd chased Edwin out of my front garden and off my property, had chased down that horrible man in Cobram who'd aimed a rifle at me …

Because of how he'd argued his case with me on that last day. The bewildered, tortured look on his face as he was trying to work her out said everything to her.

Because of how he'd looked at me in that split second years ago.

A moment in time she'd never forgotten.

Whenever he was close by, whenever she could see him, she felt happy. She *was* happy.

Oh bother. She tried to bundle the fabric into some order. *Get home, write the letter and be done with it. It'll be up to him whether he answers.*

Then a revelation struck.

Just the other day, she'd been working in the studio and had seen Mr Kingsley arriving home, before his usual time, and almost running up the short path to the house.

'Well, I never,' he'd said, effusive and bright-eyed. He'd smacked a quick peck on his wife's cheek. 'I've just heard over at Mr Campbell's office that the Cooper scoundrel got his comeuppance. Came off rather badly after a big fella got him, was hospitalised for a night or two. Poor sod.' He winked. 'The police came and interviewed Mr Barrett, who of course, and rightly so, knew nothing of it. He had to provide an alibi, they call it, for his whereabouts on that night and also had to present his knuckles for their inspection. Suffice to say, they were clear of any injury. Apparently, Cooper had been given a lesson, driven home by a couple of large fists.'

'Good.' Mrs Kingsley had no compassion for the man. 'Perhaps it was by some dear girl's maddened relative who decided to take matters into their own hands.'

'When did this happen, Mr Kingsley?' Evie had asked.

'The night after the magistrate's ruling. After Cooper had aimed that vile threat at you.'

That had been the same evening handfuls of pebbles had struck her windows intermittently after dark, and blows from a hand had slammed on the weatherboards of her house, up the side and around the back. Evie had tucked herself deep inside again, fire poker in hand, sure she knew who it was, and that was before Edwin's face had appeared pressed against a window. He was resuming his attacks, no heed of the magistrate's warning.

The following morning the Kingsleys had urged her to go to the police once again, but she had not. No point. *No point at all.* She'd then spent night after night on alert again, until finally, she realised that for some reason, Cooper had not come back. She had no idea what had kept him at bay.

Until now.

Raff. It had to have been Raff.

'Oh, look. My dear husband's home early again,' Mrs Kingsley said now, interrupting Evie's train of thought.

She was still wrestling with the fluid cascade of errant blue silk when Mr Kingsley opened the door and waved a newspaper.

'Ladies, good afternoon and you'll never guess what. Allow me.' He threw his hat to one of the benches, turned the paper to the light and read, his voice booming, '"I, Edwin Cooper, unreservedly retract my false, spurious and malicious accusations against Miss Evie Emerson that were printed in untruthful advertisements in previous editions of this newspaper. Miss Emerson and I were never engaged and I humbly apologise to Miss Emerson, and subsequently to her friend, Mr Fitzmorgan O'Shea, for any libel, and beg their forgiveness. Signed, Edwin Cooper."'

Evie's mouth dropped open. Mrs Kingsley's, too. They both stared at Mr Kingsley.

Mrs Kingsley recovered first. 'Beg their forgiveness,' she scoffed.

'And here's the reason why it happened,' he said. He leaned towards the two women and lowered his voice, as if someone outside might possibly hear him. 'One of my friends in the constabulary told me that when Cooper had been dumped at the police station in the dead of night by a big fella—you remember I told you? Well, there'd been a note jammed into the unconscious fellow's coat, citing that he'd been found peeping again. It also gave Mr Cooper a set of instructions that were to be strictly followed: it was to be this exact confession and apology to Miss Emerson in the paper,' he tapped the paper, 'Or …'

'Or what?' Mrs Kingsley breathed.

'Or more of the same for him by this mystery man. No one's identified him, though. Cooper could not.' Mr Kingsley shot a glance at Evie. 'Or would not.'

Mrs Kingsley clapped her hands. 'Oh, a knight in shining

armour. No, not that exactly. A mystery guardian, or perhaps—the Scarlet Pimpernel.' The fan was busy.

'Not exactly the Scarlet Pimpernel either, dear Mrs K,' said Mr Kingsley. 'How about—' His brow creased as he stared at her. 'Are you all right, m'dear?'

Mrs Kingsley was waving her fan madly and mopping her neck once again. Her face was a mottled shade of red. 'Of course,' she cried, and laughed gaily. 'I'm just a little warm. Nothing to worry about.'

Evie rested the silk in her lap, gathering it absently again before it slithered to the floor. *Raff.* It had to be. Where was he? It wasn't as if she'd asked him to stay away. Well, she hadn't asked him to stay close, either. *Oh bother and blast.* Their last discussion—argument—had been heated.

'Evie, whatever's the matter? That scoundrel got his comeuppance.' Mrs Kingsley had stopped fanning and was peering at her. 'The retraction should make you jump for joy.'

'It does, of course,' Evie said, her voice drifting, her shoulders drooping.

'Mr Kingsley, would you be a dear and put on the kettle?'

After taking a look at Evie, he headed out the back. 'Shall do.'

Mrs Kingsley watched him go before leaning in closer. 'What is it?'

'I argued with Rafferty Dolan, over my … reputation. He said he didn't care that it was bad.'

There was a pause from Mrs Kingsley. 'This is Mr O'Shea's friend, that lovely man with the dark hair?' She had met Fitz and Raff years earlier.

Evie nodded.

'Tell me exactly what was said.'

Mrs Kingsley listened intently, poking in a question here and there. She sat back.

'My dear Evie. *He* didn't say it was bad. I think he was saying that he didn't care what others thought, that he knows you well enough. Couldn't that be it? Am I making sense for you?'

Evie nodded again. *Oh, for goodness' sake. Write him that letter and eat humble pie.*

Chapter Sixty-seven

Ballarat

Paddy Dolan had given Raff a hard thump on his thigh. 'We don't need ye here. Take yeself off and get rid of them doldrums. Fergal and Red have got this place covered. Just don't drink yeself into a stupor.'

'And when have I ever done that?'

'Just don't. Get the hell back to Bendigo. Knock down her door if you have to.'

'That would go down a treat, Pa.'

'Man can't leave things unsaid, ye daft bugger. None o' this thick-headed, silent stuff. Man's gotta take action.' Paddy left the stables, his gait hitching as he headed back to the workshop.

A man's gotta be careful with Evie Emerson. She'd been through the mill, and not only had Raff let her down—albeit on Mr Barrett's orders—but Fitz, too. Would she ever speak to either of them once all the kerfuffle had blown over and the facts were plain to see?

Raff sat on the rail in Bluey's stall, one of two in the stables out the back of the shop. Three weeks he'd been home, and Pa was right; his younger brothers had the shop in hand. The place was working well for all of them. Fergal had been working the forge in Uncle Skelly's dairy, so he'd put himself up for the blacksmithing side of things, more common with wheelwrights these days. Despite Pa's previous grumbling, Raff had already brought in pre-manufactured hubs and other parts made with iron and rubber. And Red had decided that there was more work to be had if every week one of them visited outlying properties in their dray and brought repairs back to the shed. Word had got around, and the place was filling with repairs and not only that: with orders for building new carts, or new wagons, far more than just wheelwright jobs.

Raff had to admit he wasn't needed and now his pa had told him too, though for a different reason. Maybe his old man had a point. One way or the other, if he went to see Evie, Raff would know for sure, face to face. And if that blew up, he'd go onto Cobram, to check if he still liked the area. He quietly hoped Robbo hadn't bought the Bayley place. And if that was no good, well, maybe he'd roam a little, like Fitz.

But he'd miss Evie if he did that. Miss seeing her face. Miss the chance to see that dimple in her knee again. When she'd wrapped her arms around him, only that one time, he had to admit he loved her, deep, deep down, and had done for years.

So why was he so goddamned slow on the uptake?

His cleaned, rolled swag hung on the back wall and his saddle shone after a good rub of dubbin. His saddlebags were plump with camp vittles and his water bottles were filled with fresh water. He was all set.

A man's gotta take action.

Chapter Sixty-eight

Bendigo

Evie had only sent the letter to Raff three days ago, so there was no point worrying any time soon. *Just forget about it.* She hadn't exactly poured her heart out, but she had apologised for her outburst and let him know that she believed there was more for them to discuss … if he had a mind for it. She'd invited him to reply … if he pleased. No point beating around the bush. Cutting straight to the bone was the only way. At least with the stretch of some weeks since the day of the trial, she'd had time for clarity. She didn't scold herself too much for waiting so long to write to him.

Apart from driving down to Ballarat and throwing herself at him, she'd done all she could. He'd either reply or he wouldn't. At the clunk in her chest, she turned her thoughts away and put herself to practical use in Mrs Kingsley's little studio. She packed boxes with an assortment of hats—most of them had been destined for the display window at Craig, Williamson—and prepared for her temporary move to Echuca. If it worked out there (another clunk), she would find permanent accommodation in the town and start her life again.

'I'll miss you and the studio,' Evie had said to Mrs Kingsley earlier in the week.

'So you think you will make a long-term move?'

'It's looking likely.'

'I understand, I do. I'll miss you too, and so will our customers. The charitable ones, that is. Well, even the not-so-charitable ones,' Mrs K said. 'Somewhere else will gain from your marvellous expertise. Promise me you'll send a few things our way for sale if you can.'

'I will, Mrs K, I promise.' Evie took her hands.

'And Mr Kingsley and I would visit wherever that is, of course.'

'You'd be very welcome.'

And so it was considered done. Evie had already let her house. The thought of staying in it one more night had given her the shakes, so she was happy for the circumstances to propel her into action. She'd rented it to a young couple who were expecting their first child. They'd move in today, after she departed on the train. It had given her a pang when she met them. Such hope in young people. *Oh, for heaven's sake, I'm not that old* … It was just that she might have missed her chance. With Raff.

But this was no time to be a shirker in the event of life. *Her* life.

The evening before, Evie had been rattling around her tidied house, eager to move. Ann, resigned to her leaving, was supportive and had held her tightly in a hug. Posie had been ambivalent, worried on one hand, happy for new opportunities on the other. Both would write, both would visit. 'We certainly will,' they'd said.

Perhaps one day they might, Evie thought, but they too had lives to lead. Perhaps children in their futures.

Mrs Kingsley sailed into the room. 'I think that's the lot for now. Oh my, two big trunks. Well, ladies do need hats.' She glided a hand over Evie's large hat box. 'And this is the ivory gauze and the beautiful peony shades, isn't it? A spectacular creation. Do look after it. You'll have to have an event to show it off. Thank goodness the depression is just about done and dusted. Perhaps some visiting clients from the city will be able to purchase it.'

Evie smiled at that. She wouldn't be selling it; it would be her signature piece, and on show for her events.

Mrs Kingsley held a finger in the air. 'Now, you make sure to pay a lad to get those big trunks from the station to your boarding house, won't you? Mr Kingsley and I will help you load up this end, make sure everything's all right.'

Everything had been all right for some time; clearly whoever had given Edwin his 'lesson' had ensured it was a good one. Ann Benton had told Evie only last week that she'd heard the Cooper trio, Edwin, his mother and his sister were packing up and leaving town.

'You could stay,' she'd cried.

Evie had shaken her head. Every time she thought of staying, Edwin's awful menace had her shaking in her boots, looking for shadows where there were none. Things were better now; she would take deep breaths and push the fear of him aside.

Ann's news had mobilised Mr Kingsley who checked with Mr Campbell. Edwin hadn't yet paid his due. *Ah well.* Evie hadn't had that money to begin with, so she wasn't missing it, but she could have used it to repay Mr Kingsley's generosity. Edwin would find himself in hot water if he didn't pay it, though—and that didn't bother her in the slightest.

'I just hope I don't accidentally bump into him somewhere, Mr Kingsley.'

'I'm sure you won't, my dear. I suspect it will be some time before he recovers any mettle.' His eyes lit up at that.

Mrs Kingsley waved a fan over her brave smile. She seemed to have fared a little better lately, but the fans were still within easy reach wherever she went. Thanking her lucky stars the surges had dropped away somewhat, she'd reported to Evie that she'd still been experiencing some sleepless nights, and some foggy days. For now at least, the rabid flushes of heat and night sweats had eased.

'And thank goodness for that. Poor Mr Kingsley, but he's been such a rock. Encouraged me again to visit the doctor,' Mrs K said. 'Couldn't see old Dr Philips, so I got some young fellow. Not sure I liked him. All business, no empathy. He dismissed my symptoms simply as hysteria, *things common to women of my age*, is what he said. Supercilious upstart. Can't tell you how low that made me feel, as if I'm ready for the rubbish heap. It's not like it's our fault, is it?' She waved the fan in the air. '"I'll give you *hysteria*", is what I said—to myself. I could have picked him up and thrown him out the window. Thank goodness *he* didn't prescribe that new treatment some—' She stopped.

Another heat surge no doubt, Evie thought. Mrs K had gone a bright red.

'A new treatment, Mrs K? Some hope after all?' she asked.

'Not … tried and true, dear,' Mrs K said. The fan opened and flapped with the energy of previous days. 'Suffer it, was what I got. I don't think he could even say "menopause". That's what it's called, you know.' She leaned towards Evie. 'Clearly, they don't know a thing about it.'

'The doctors?' Evie was appalled that this might also be her fate, and shocked that so little was known about this common event, still on the horizon for her.

'Yes, the doctors, or anyone, come to think of it. It's just put up and shut up, really.' Mrs K's mouth turned down.

'I've read that there are a few women entering university now, studying medicine.' Evie slipped that in as Mrs Kingsley took a breath. 'A woman in Sydney, for one, was the first in about 1885, I believe. Then there is Doctor Constance Stone and her sisters in Melbourne who—'

'Yes, yes and the others enrolling not soon enough.' Mrs Kingsley looked at her. 'You know a little bit about these women, do you?'

'Only what I've read in the papers. The sisters established a hospital for treating women and children just a couple of years ago, but they might not be interested in this *menopause* either.'

Mrs Kingsley harrumphed. 'They will be when they arrive at it themselves.' She smoothed her beautiful pale silvery blonde hair into place. 'In the meantime, I'll make it clear to all and sundry that we women are not frivolous over this change of life thing, or any other blasted change month by month.' Then she added quickly, 'Nor are we going mad, although I can understand some believing it of themselves. I've felt quite demented at times.' She pressed Evie's hand. 'Not that I'd say that aloud,' she said, then laughed. 'Not too often, anyway.'

Evie hadn't wanted to think about it. Her monthly courses were uncomfortable enough without putting her mind to the next awful phase of her female biology. Or for going mad. Besides, change of life was years off. Years and years. Surely there'd be better help by the time she needed it. Of course there would be … wouldn't there?

'Promise me you'll be careful, my dear Evie,' Mrs Kingsley continued. 'Because … well, I can't always be there to look after you.' She laughed again, a little self-conscious as tears popped. 'When I can't reach my daughters so easily, I … you …'

Oh. Today's conversation was about more than biology.

'I promise,' Evie said and laid a hand on Mrs Kingsley's arm. 'And I promise I will always stay in contact.' The woman had been a staunch ally, a mother figure since Evie's mother had died.

'Good, good.' For a moment, Mrs K blotted her eyes.

Evie squeezed her arm. 'Your friendship, Mrs Kingsley, your mentoring, has been a gift that's meant the world to me.'

'Oh, oh,' Mrs K said, dabbing with her hanky again. 'Damn perspiration.'

The subject changed smartly when Mr Kingsley arrived with the cart. It was, with some relief, time to depart the house for the railway station.

There, that awful Miss Thompson of the Pink, fully decked out in frothy, frilly glory had thrown her a cheeky wave. Evie boarded the train without giving her a second glance, waved madly to Mr and Mrs Kingsley, found her seat and settled in.

The train rattled and chugged its way out of Bendigo and in a few short hours, she'd alight at Echuca and find her way to the boarding house she'd contacted. For now, her previous train journey was front and centre of her mind, the time she'd found Raff's hat, then him as she'd disembarked, how she had travelled with him, bickered with him … fired a rifle. Worried for him. Missed him.

Another dull clunk hit her chest. The future stretched out before her, with no Raff in sight.

Chapter Sixty-nine

Bendigo

Lucille took the reins after David pulled to the curb. 'I'll just get a newspaper,' he said, and lifted a hand to attract the paperboy. 'Then we can go home and settle in by the fire.' The late afternoon had grown cool, and the light breeze had freshened. Flipping a penny to the boy, David leaned out and grabbed the paper. He handed it to Lucille and took the reins again.

She checked the front page as they drove on. A couple of advertisements caught her eye. Dorman's Chemist was touting 'Pennyroyal Mixture for all female irregularities'. She tut-tutted, was way past believing the so-called benefits of Pennyroyal. *What rubbish; it's a nasty thing. Charlatans, all who dispense it.* A Professor Garfield from Collins Street in Melbourne offered 'LADIES' his 'triple power Female Pills' to restore 'regularity instantly'. She harrumphed, didn't believe that the 'regularity' it purported had anything to do with one's bowels. More likely it was supposed to *restore* a woman's 'regular' monthlies. She felt sure young girls in trouble, or older ladies not wanting another child would flock to that 'cure'. Most probably it was that damnable Pennyroyal cleverly disguised. Galbraith Chemist offered Nerve and Brain tonic—well, that might be worth a chance, if it didn't involve imbibing an opium derivative, which it probably did.

Craig, Williamson Propriety Limited also had a huge space, drawing attention to its stock and merchandise. She sighed. This week it should have been her hats—Evie's hats—occupying that advertisement space. Well, too bad for them and the ladies of Bendigo; those hats were off to Echuca and some very appreciative ladies there, no doubt.

Evie, I miss you already.

Turning the page and folding it over as their cart pushed against the breeze, the headline of a story on page four caught her eye. 'Oh, Mr Kingsley,' she said. 'I think our journalist, Mr Fossey, has submitted an article.' The paper jigging in her hand as their buggy rolled along, she smiled as she read aloud. '"Death of Fugitive, the Notorious and Fallen Ballarat Police Sergeant".' Skimming a little further, she gave a cry of surprise. 'And the next story he's written: "Sharp Acquittal by Magistrate". Oh, I can't wait to read that one.'

'Good Lord, I hope they're both juicy. Shall we read together at home over a cup of tea?'

'Good idea,' Lucille said, although she could barely drag her gaze from the lively words, and desperately wanted to read it aloud to him as they drove along. She couldn't help it. After skimming a few lines, she said, 'Mr Kingsley, I think you're really going to enjoy this.'

Chapter Seventy

Bendigo

Raff and Bluey had been ambling along in the afternoon sun. They'd already camped a night after a long day on the road from Ballarat, so Raff was keen to find another site to rest their weary bones.

There was a party coming towards him from Bendigo and they met at the crossroads at Newstead. Furniture and belongings were stacked haphazardly in a cart and two women sat in the front seat, one of whom, the driver herself, had a very large, floppy hat. Raff recognised them.

He tugged on the reins and pulled Bluey to one side of the road. As the cart drew abreast, he peered into the back of it. Sure enough, Edwin Cooper was propped up on all manner of bags and blankets, and dozing, mouth open.

Head in the air, fearful, her eyes darting, Miss Jane Cooper did not look at him. Raff nudged Bluey closer.

Edwin opened his eyes. 'Why are we slow— You,' he sputtered and pushed himself further back amid the bags. One eyebrow had gauze over it, and when his mouth dropped open, there was a gap where a tooth had been. His nose was at an interesting angle, and still swollen.

'Mr Cooper, it looks like you and the ladies might be going to Ballarat.' Raff crossed his wrists, draping the reins in his hands as he sat in the saddle. 'I suggest you don't.'

Edwin, his colour already pale, blanched to grey.

'And who are you, young man, to intimidate a stranger on a public road, in broad daylight?' Mrs Cooper queried, imperiously. 'Taking advantage of innocent travellers, I presume.'

'You and your family are hardly innocent, Mrs Cooper.'

Startled, the older woman squinted at Raff.

Jane aimed an elbow at her and grated, 'Shut up, Mother.'

Raff leaned forward. 'I don't suppose you're used to being on the receiving end.' He peered at Edwin, who couldn't scramble further back in the cart. 'You usually work under cover of darkness, or behind the skirts of others. Paid your dues yet, Edwin?' He pushed back his hat, not worried that he would be recognised. 'Miss Cooper, my strong advice is that you take a right turn here'—he waved at the road in front of them—'away from Ballarat and head towards Maryborough.' He thought for a moment. 'Make sure you pass through the town and keep going. If I hear you've taken up there, I might come looking for you.' He nodded, satisfied that they remained dumbstruck. Tipping his hat, he continued his ambling ride towards Bendigo.

Not too far down, he turned in the saddle to look back. The cart had made a right turn and was trundling towards Maryborough. Only for an instant did he feel remorse for sending the Coopers towards the good folk in that town.

Once more, Raff would take a bath at Bartletts' boarding house. By the time he'd got into town it had been too late to risk visiting Evie. He might just get the door slammed in his face. At least he'd have happy news to impart; the Coopers had left Bendigo.

Stripping down, he stepped into the warm water. The stern colourless sign *No Smoking Cigars* was still in his line of sight. Reading would blot that out. He reached for the latest newspaper on top a stack nearby, folding it open on page four. He snorted to himself. Fitz had sent in his 'Mr Fossey' article, and the report of McCosker's demise was under an eye-catching headline. It was full of colourful descriptions and the heroic deeds of an unnamed pair of men. Two intrepid ladies had been 'instrumental' in chasing away the desperate criminal and were singlehandedly the heroines of the day with the swift capture of Constable Porter, ex Sergeant McCosker's henchman. McCosker had bungled his ambush of innocent settlers and had escaped along the river at Cobram.

Fitz had it sounding like he'd witnessed the whole adventure.

'According to the coroner, McCosker met Death with a broken neck,' Fitz had crowed. 'His body was found on the riverbank, thereby ending the reign of terror this corrupt police officer had inflicted not only on the hard-working gold merchants of Ballarat and their families, but also the unsuspecting citizens of the Murray River town of Cobram.'

Fitz lamented the death of 'trusted police officer, Constable John O'Shea from gunshot, his loss sorely felt by those who knew him. The criminal who had murdered him, Ernest Haines, well known in the area, was apprehended and at present awaiting trial, enjoying the hospitality delights of good Queen Victoria's Pentridge Prison.'

Immediately below was Fitz's report on Evie's appearance in court, under the headline, 'Dubious Character Leaves Town'. The article was scathing of 'the unscrupulous, farcical Cooper family and their contemptible deeds'.

Good thing Fitz had used a pseudonym for the pieces. The McCosker story was one thing, but Fitz's story on the Coopers was borderline. He'd left out nothing, added his praise for an intrepid and honourable private investigator, Mr Bendigo Barrett, and had lively descriptions of the guilty parties: 'Edwin Cooper, amusing in his foppish pomposity', 'Mrs Beryl Cooper and the inflated sense of her standing in society …' and 'Miss Jane Cooper seemingly unaware that her hat appeared to have been retrieved from the ragbag'. He also cited partial statements made by other victims. How Fitz had come into those, Raff didn't want to know.

But the last lines were more than memorable. 'It is this journalist's humble opinion, after observing a mighty magistrate in fine fettle dispensing his particular brand of justice, that a more deserving woman by name of Miss Evie Emerson could not be found. Magistrate Rudge exonerated this most worthy person and dismissed outright the scurrilous claims against her. To those who have slandered and disrespected this woman on the flimsy but defamatory workings of the Cooper family, I say to you, shame! Your day will come,' Fitz thundered.

It was signed, Your Roving Reporter, Mr Fossey.

Raff leaned back and laughed. *Good on you, Fitz.*

Raff approached Evie's house. She should've been just about on her way to work. *You've waited too long already, you fool. Hurry it up.* He tied Bluey to the gate, took three steps past the little garden, which had sprung back to its former glory, and knocked on the door. This time, he wouldn't go until he'd said his piece, leaving Evie with no doubt about how he felt, and what he wanted. The nervous thud of his heart ignored his determination.

A stranger answered, a cheery-faced, dark-haired woman who was big with child. 'Good morning.' Her smile was bright and happy, as if all was well in her world.

At a loss for a moment, Raff simply stood there, hat in his hands. Then, 'Good morning. I'm looking for Miss Emerson.'

'Oh, she's gone,' said the woman. 'My husband and I have rented the place from her.'

'Gone,' he repeated. He hadn't thought she would leave. She'd gone before he could tell her—

'Yes,' the young woman said, with a beaming smile, 'we've been here two weeks now.'

His disappointment sharp, his gut hollowed for an instant. Thanking her, turning away, he stared at Bluey. *Left, and gone where?* He looked back to ask, and before he could, the woman called out.

'I believe she's gone to Echuca for a while if that helps.' She laughed when he grinned broadly at her. 'You're welcome.'

Chapter Seventy-one

Echuca

It hadn't taken long to settle in. Evie had found the Echuca boarding house easily, and Mr and Mrs Gibson, who operated it, were a decent couple. She could relax a little. Thankfully, when sinking into her comfortable bed at night, the shakes no longer infuriated her, and her dreams were not filled with disturbing images that woke her with trepidation. From time to time through daylight hours, she caught her breath at a sound or a fleeting glimpse of a shadow, but lately she'd felt her fears dissipating. That was good, a relief, because she refused to have someone with Edwin Cooper's odious character in control of her feelings.

Mrs Gibson had instantly become a client and had avidly set about writing invitations for appointments for fittings in the parlour. The house had at one time been something of a grand place, so there was plenty of room for Evie to work from there. The downturn in the economy had given the Gibsons an opportunity to purchase the house and open it up to boarders.

Evie was preparing to go down to breakfast with the only other guests, an older couple visiting relatives who had no room to house them. Her appointments didn't start until after lunch, so her time was her own. If only the weight in her chest would ease so she could enjoy it. Perhaps she'd been too hasty believing she wouldn't miss Raff, that she could get on with things and start all over again. She'd waited every day for a letter from him.

Maybe one wouldn't be coming.

Oh dear. That felt worse. She sniffed, shook her head to dislodge the thought.

Dressed, she carried a straw boater made from good old cabbage-palm fibre. Her much-loved black-and-white houndstooth fabric made an elegant band. A tight black bow was stitched at the front, and ribbons fell at the back. Her day dress was white, the bodice nipped in at the waist, overlaid with broderie lace, and wearing her black boots she thought the whole look said 'Fashionable Businesswoman'.

Ready for the day.

Sort of. She had to talk herself into it every morning.

Heading along the hallway, she hesitated at the dining room. The light streaming in from the windows at the front door was too tempting; a sunny day had dawned, beckoning her. She positioned her hat on her head, poked in a pin and kept walking outside.

At the bank of the river, observing the bustle on the water, the paddle-steamers jostling for position at the wharf a little further downstream, she stopped, a dusty patch at her feet. Ants scurried to and fro. She was glad of her hat; the sun had risen higher and was beating a gentle throb on her head.

Glancing upriver in the direction of Cobram, she wondered how Jenny and Mr Robinson were faring. Meryl, and the sadness of all that time came to mind, and the gunshots, the fear … *Take a deep breath, Evie.* Even so, Cobram was on a pretty part of this mighty river. The sandy stretches were engaging, the people friendly. What would it hurt to try to get there before she lost all confidence in her new self, and—

'I knew it was you.'

She spun.

Raff. And Bluey, who blurted at her, tossing his head.

Raff grabbed at his hat, her feather still in it, and swiped his wavy black hair back behind his ears. Beard stubble shadowed his cheeks and chin.

Oh, what a sight he is.

'Can't miss me,' she said, with a nervy laugh, her heart pounding. Her breath whisked away for a moment. Goodness, how she loved this man, how she loved just looking at him.

'That's true,' he said. 'I'd know you anywhere.' That green-eyed stare of his was gentle on her. 'I reckon I might even recognise your hats.' He scuffed a boot, his smile lopsided.

'A wheelwright who knows ladies' hats.'

He lifted a shoulder. 'Excellence when I see it.'

That warmed her. Smiling in return, she nodded towards his hat. 'I should make you a new one. That one has certainly been around the traps awhile.'

'This? It's all right, but if you do, I'd have to keep the feather and have it stitched in tight, like I did with this one.'

Her heart leaped. His gaze roamed her face, warmed her cheeks. Then the ear-splitting blast of a whistle cracked the air around them. Evie winced, laughed again, holding her hands over her ears.

'Come sit with me somewhere. We'll find a shady tree.' He landed his hat back on his head and just like that, he took her hand, tucked her at his side.

They walked along as if—as if they were stepping out together, taking a promenade. Bluey nickered. *With horse in tow.* No one was forgetting Bluey.

'I wrote to you, Raff,' she began, and cleared her throat, 'to apologise … to say that I'd been a little sharp last time we spoke. That was the content mostly. You hadn't received it?'

He shook his head.

She hurried on, now or never. 'Also to say that I … hoped we would see each other again.'

His eyebrows rose. 'I was coming to find you anyway, letter or not.' The dark glance he aimed at her was weighty.

'Oh.'

'And when I found you, nothing was going to stop me saying my piece, Evie. I went to your house in Bendigo first,' he said, 'in broad daylight, I might add.' She ducked her chin at the look he gave her. 'The lady there told me you'd come here. Why Echuca?'

He wasn't looking at her now but staring ahead. His hand, its rough calluses, strong fingers, was still closed over hers. Rafferty Dolan had hold of her hand and every part of her sang.

'Mrs Kingsley and I are overstocked,' she said as they walked. 'So I'm selling hats here. Once Edwin Cooper had spread his rumours, the manager of the Bendigo store with whom we'd had an arrangement, declined to honour it.'

'Their loss,' Raff said.

'Anyway, I didn't want to stay in Bendigo. I've sort of moved here.' She didn't know how he'd take that; it was so far from where he lived.

'Sort of?' He indicated a eucalypt on higher ground a few feet away. At its base was a rough-hewn timber plank on two cut stumps, a makeshift bench seat. 'Looks as good a place as any.' When she sat, he reached into his pocket, withdrew a torn piece of newsprint and handed it to her. 'This might go some way to help fix a few problems in Bendigo.' He slung Bluey's reins loosely over a low branch.

She read Fitz's reporting. 'Mr Fossey speaks his mind,' she said after a while. 'He's made my situation clear.'

'He does good work, that's for sure.' Raff took a seat beside her. 'Though Mr Fossey also has a lot to answer for.' At her glance, he added, 'Between friends.'

The colour rose in her cheeks, she could feel it. Fitz's half-baked apology at breakfast that day came back to her. 'I know what you mean.'

'I believed for a long time that you and Fitz would … you know, have married,' Raff said.

'And Fitz did not disavow you of that opinion at any point.'

'My fault. I didn't outright ask him and he wasn't going to say *unless* I asked. The wily bugger knew how I felt, but he was intent on serving his own purpose.'

Knew how I felt. In the silence, Evie turned over his words. Then she said, 'I can't begrudge him, not really.'

Raff lifted his shoulders. 'Maybe not.'

'I wasn't about to marry him, you know. He wouldn't have talked me around,' Evie said softly. 'I didn't feel right about it. Neither did he, despite thinking he could've carried it off. He remained true to himself in the end.' She slipped her hand back into his and gave a little laugh. 'I'm eternally grateful for that. It would have been a disaster.'

'For all of us,' Raff said, looking down at their hands. 'I—'

Evie waited, her breath short. When no more was forthcoming, she said, 'And those years ago, when Fitz left Bendigo, you did too. You went back to Ballarat. I didn't write to you then because nothing had been said between you and me so I didn't think … And you were his best friend.' She sighed, shrugged. 'I would never have come between you.'

'Damn him,' Raff muttered with a laugh. 'For a year and a half, more, I thought you two—' He rubbed his forehead. 'Then when I saw Cooper's advertisement I realised you couldn't have been with Fitz, but once again it looked like I was too late.'

Paddle-steamers manoeuvred around one another in some river-polite way. The *Hero* was reversing into position not far from where they sat. A whistle shrieked, men shouted.

'We've forgiven Fitz, haven't we?' she asked.

'We have.'

'He knew we would. He knew because we're friends.'

'You're right. We're his friends and he's our friend.'

Holding hands, so naturally, sitting with Raff by this river. How would the next few minutes pass, much less the next days, or years? A magpie warbled close by, his mate joined in, full throated, joyous. *Beautiful.* A whiff of eucalyptus floated by, and the damp scent of river mud rose lazily on the light breeze.

Raff was staring at their hands. He shifted his gaze to the boat edging its way closer to a mooring. 'Thought I might like to live in Cobram.'

'I've thought about living there, too.' Evie glanced at him as she said so. 'I'd be able to work there, and I'm sure the Robinsons would become … our good friends.'

He turned to her, eyes fervent, smile hesitant. 'I'd make sure you'd always have a home, and be safe, wherever we are, if you'll have me.'

'I'll have you.' Smiling, she placed her hand on his chest and felt the faithful thud of his heart against her palm. 'Home and safe is here.'

'We have to make up for lost time,' he said, holding her hand against his chest.

'It's not lost, Raff.'

He stared out across the water than back at her, those green eyes bright. 'I have loved you since the first day I laid eyes on you. That day when Fitz was spinning you a yarn in the tearooms about Porky Trotter. Do you remember?'

'The poor man, you two chortling about him like that.'

Raff laughed. 'It was a real pig, Evie.'

'Oh.' She laughed with him. 'Well, it was certainly a memorable first meeting then.'

He snatched off his hat, touched the feather. 'What I remember most about that first day was the look in your eyes when you handed this to me.'

Evie remembered those unguarded few seconds.

He squeezed her hands. 'I remember your laugh, and that your happy face lit up my day. I love your sad face too, even when it gets all screwed up. I love the way you are about your hats, that you're brave, and how loyal you are to your friends.' Tucking in his chin, he hid a smile. 'Even the way you handle a rifle, and a fire poker.'

'New skills for living out here in the country.'

The green eyes glinted. 'I love this dimple here,' he said, a light finger on her chin, 'but my favourite is the dimple over your left knee. I make no apology for gawping when you were defending us all against McCosker.'

'Ah.' Other events had been more worrying than her knee being on show. 'Well, although a lady should never mention such things, there is a dimple over the other knee as well,' she said, and added, 'you'll find.'

The gleam leaped and his grip tightened on her hand. 'So that sounds like we're going to give us a good go of it then.'

Pushing back her hat, she cupped his face. 'Let's give it a good go—if you'll have me, that is. I'm told I might go mad at some point.'

'Mad, sad, happy, bad. I'll have all of you.'

She pressed her lips to his.

'You're smart, too,' he said. 'I won't be going anywhere if you keep doing that.'

Still holding his face, Evie said, 'That's the whole idea, Rafferty Dolan.'

Author note

I began writing this story in July 2020. Once accepted by my publisher, and after the year it takes to whip it into shape for you wonderful readers, it was due for release in 2022. But *The Forthright Woman* (2022) herself pushed ahead of it, so here we are, in 2023.

The River Murray itself is one of the reasons I keep bringing my stories back to the river system: we mustn't lose sight of its crucial importance. Water management was a contentious issue in the drafting of our Constitution pre-Federation. One comment made in the day was if the issue 'had not been settled, there could have been no Constitution and no Federation.' (JA La Nauze, *The Making of the Australian Constitution*, Melbourne University Press, 1972, 208.) You can read more about the issue of water management and the constitution in 'The Constitution and the Management of Water in Australia's Rivers' by Paul Kildea and George Williams (*Sydney Law Review*, Vol. 32, No. 3, pp. 595-616, UNSW, 2011).

My maternal grandmother, Lena was a milliner in Melbourne in the 1920s and continued her craft when she became a single mother of three in the 1930s. She died in 1970, aged 67, then recently divorced by her only husband. She so loved a good hat.

Menopause in the nineteenth century, or any time, would not have been for the faint-hearted (still isn't), was much misunderstood then and not much better understood today. At least in the twenty-first century there is some relief from symptoms although there is still very little acknowledgement of it needing to be treated. Half the population will eventually experience it. When I began to research the subject for the story, there was a light-hearted discovery: in the nineteenth century there was an interesting theory for treatment, the one Mrs Kingsley had heard about and decided to try for herself. Then I learned about the film, *Hysteria*, 2011, directed by Tanya Wexler, produced by

Tracey Becker, Judy Cairo and Sarah Curtis. A fun watch, based on the true story of Dr Mortimer Granville in 1880.

Depression and post-natal depression are represented in the story, and again, not much was understood by the medical profession of the day, although both conditions had been recognised over the ages but the real causes were unknown.

Also in the story, Dr Kennedy, a historic figure in Cobram, treats a sunstroke sufferer by advising he gets a good soaking with cool water. While rivermen would have been aware of this treatment, it wasn't accepted medical practice for some time after this particular period and in some areas of medicine, it is, apparently, still in contention. However, with the river handy, the practice worked for my story.

One of my characters is gay. His story reflects family, social and legal attitudes of the day. His desperate attempts to try being someone he is not, and conform in order to survive, created havoc for him and his fellow characters. His demise could, in reality, have been much worse. Brave and courageous, finally honest with himself, he is simply a (fictional) human being, navigating his way through life.

Breach of Contract was a legal avenue for slighted parties to take after a courtship break-up if they so wished. I had a lot of fun learning some of the complaints. I also had fun with Magistrate Rudge in the story who was totally fed up with the criminals and fools who've come before him. His handling of a plaintiff, who displayed what might be called 'narcissistic tendencies', was all his own doing. However, a person with narcissistic tendencies such as the plaintiff's is not to be taken lightly. A diagnosis of narcissistic personality traits as a mental disorder emerged in the modern age, in 1898, when British essayist and physician Havelock Ellis identified it as such. The condition has been recognised for centuries. In the story, apprentice lawyer, Miss Juno's relatives in England were aware of Havelock's theory. In 1980 it was officially recognised as Narcissistic Personality Disorder and criteria was established for its diagnosis. It is a most insidious disorder.

Breach of Contract of Marriage was a real issue for some, and while it was often treated with hilarity or derision—by journalists and the general public, it clearly meant a great deal emotionally to those who were involved. When researching, I found the articles written on some of the proceedings which illuminated the courts' exasperation with the entanglements and subsequent disentangling—before people tied the knot. I used this old law (with regard to marriage) to showcase the very much alive narcissism and 'gaslighting' (the term came much later in the twentieth century) even then, and how it was dealt with by those involved. That our perpetrator in the story got his comeuppance is a source of great comfort to me!

Characters riverboat captain Dane MacHenry and his wife Georgina MacHenry have their own story in the first of my books for HarperCollins: *Daughter of the Murray.* The families' saga continues in *Where the Murray River Runs* and *The Good Woman of Renmark.* Whenever I revisit the River Murray in my stories, you'll find mention of Dane and Georgina somewhere.

Many of you know I've visited Cobram in the recent past, and of course gazed on the mighty Murray once more. In the 1960s, my uncle, a police officer, was stationed there, and it was here that I was given my first glimpse of the river for a month. Onwards from there to Swan Hill. The enigma that is the river, and its magic, has never left me.

Acknowledgements

This story was written some time ago, just before the pandemic, and thankfully this year, it has been refined by editors Lauren Finger (and her exhaustive wrangling of the timeline into shape), and Laurie Ormond, and the ever supportive team at HQ, HarperCollins Australia. While all of my books have a relationship between the lead characters, I wanted this one to have even more of a focus. I hope I've hit the mark with Evie and Raff.

My humble thanks to all my readers who are first and foremost in my mind. Thank goodness for each of you—I get to live my dream.

Big thanks again to Susan Parslow, my beta reader, and to all friends and family who encourage and support me while I happily (mostly) skip along living my dream. There are as many ups as downs.

Thanks to Tee Fraser for her History of Colour knowledge, of tones and shades of colour. The production of colour dyes is a fascinating science, closely connected to fashion and its history.

Thanks to booksellers everywhere! To the Kangaroo Island community for all its support over the years, and early on, to Alison Hewitt in Cobram for a little insight.

Good journalists in the day were well respected, and much the same as it is today, the great ones were targeted for saying too much, speaking out against the wrongs of the day, against the political powers and the corruption that is often associated with tyrants of any level. A few scribes would have roamed the countryside following stories and writing them where they were found. The marvellous National Library of Australia's Trove has digitised countless of their articles from newspapers, and a Google search brings up their biographies.

As always, I am indebted to Trove, and to the wonderful resources that abound around the country in libraries and with historians. Without them, our history, even some tiny snippets of day-to-day living, would not be preserved.